THIRTY-ONE
BONES

THIRTY-ONE
BONES

A NOVEL

MORGAN CRY

An Arcade CrimeWise Book

First North American Edition 2021

This is a work of fiction. Names, places, characters, and incidents are either the products of the author's imagination or are used fictitiously.

Arcade Publishing books may be purchased in bulk at special discounts for sales promotion, corporate gifts, fund-raising, or educational purposes. Special editions can also be created to specifications. For details, contact the Special Sales Department, Arcade Publishing, 307 West 36th Street, 11th Floor, New York, NY 10018 or arcade@skyhorsepublishing.com.

Arcade Publishing® and CrimeWise® are registered trademarks of Skyhorse Publishing, Inc.®, a Delaware corporation.

Visit our website at www.arcadepub.com.
Visit the author's website at gordonjbrown.com.

10 9 8 7 6 5 4 3 2 1

Library of Congress Cataloging-in-Publication Data is available on file.
Library of Congress Control Number: 2021931848

Cover design: headdesign.co.uk, courtesy of Birlinn Limited
Cover photography: Shutterstock, courtesy of Birlinn Limited

ISBN: 978-1-951627-66-9
Ebook ISBN: 978-1-951627-91-1

Printed in the United States of America

To Dad—a proud police officer, no longer with us.
I still miss you.

THIRTY-ONE
BONES

I

Skinning the Cat

'It's the mother lode,' says Effie Coulstoun to the young investor. 'For just a small deposit you get ten per cent of the game and even our worst projections will make you a very rich man.'

Effie looks around Se Busca, her pub; a practised, surreptitious action designed to suggest to the investor that the information she is imparting is not for other ears. Given the bar is closed and empty, the look is just part of the game. Counting to ten in her head she turns back to the young man.

'In fact, Paul,' she whispers, 'you would be a millionaire.'

Paul's eyes flicker in the half-light. His straggly hair and third-hand clothes speak of his financial plight. He lifts both hands from the table and slowly rubs them together. And Effie knows she has him. Right *here*, right *now*, she has him. Another chunk of cash in the pot.

God, but I feel good this morning. Radiant. Sod the eighth decade I'm in—I feel twenty. Those bloody pills are a marvel. Illegal but bloody wonderful. God thank friends with access to such things. Just the job to give me a bit more energy.

'Let me freshen up that beer,' Effie says, rising. She crosses to the bar and stretches across wood that has a lifetime of drink, sweat and tears rubbed into it, and, with practised ease, fills a pint mug with a perfectly poured measure containing 450 ml of beer and a half-inch head. Advertised as a UK pint—it's from the glasses she keeps for the odd tourist who unwittingly stumbles into her pub.

Effie gazes around her domain as the beer settles in the glass, and takes in the dark, low-slung ceiling, underpowered bulbs and shadows that outweigh light ten to one—a deliberate choice in illumination. Cuts down on the need for any redecoration. With no window to the outside world the bar is a spaceship. Go anywhere, be anywhere. To her left, one wall is a shrine to gigs of yesteryear. Torn, faded posters of festivals, concerts, shows. None newer than the late eighties. Some of the paperwork on that wall would be worth serious money, if its condition was better. In the far corner a dirty white pinboard advertises local events and bands. The latest some two years back. Effie doesn't hold with advertising other people's stuff. Not any more. Her notorious tightness with money has deepened with time. Fuck 'em, is her late-age motto. She glances at the ceiling. Banknotes plaster every available inch. At last count there were more than 160 countries represented up there. Total value, 206 euros, at today's exchange rates. Effie had costed it all up a month ago after someone told her that a few of the older notes might have some serious antique value. The someone had been talking piss, but Effie had found the exercise of calculating the notes' true worth oddly satisfying.

At right angles to the bar sits a pool table that can be wheeled away to provide room to play darts on an ageing dartboard. In older days it also allowed a band or a DJ to set up. Not any more. The rest of the pub's furniture is a job lot of chairs and tables that Effie picked up when the Carnes Frías restaurant in the old town had gone tits up. It was the first replacement furniture the bar had seen in twenty years. The regulars had been stunned into silence. Not so much by the surprise of the change. More by the lurid pink colour that both the tables and chairs were painted in. The colour scheme choice of the owner of Carnes Frías going some way to shortening the restaurant's lifespan. Effie reckoned the colour added some brightness to her place. The regulars thought it looked like shit, but still came in for drink.

Beneath her feet the wooden floor, a decade out from its last polish, is seven parts wood and three parts alcohol. The air conditioning is the same ratio on the working to not working axis.

To her right she looks on a row of booths, the last one occupied by the young investor. She returns to the booth, dropping the beer glass on the table before heaving her bulk into the chair opposite Paul. She eyes him up. If he chooses to reject her offer to invest he will pay for the two beers and the packet of cheese and onion crisps she's already given him. But she doesn't expect him to have to pay.

'How was the apartment?' Effie asks.

'Stunning,' Paul replies.

'The new ones will be even better.'

Paul sweeps at the long hair cascading over his face. Effie thinks the shoulder-length mane, scruffy goatee and flea-bitten Afghan coat a crock of crap. It marks Paul out as a prick. But a prick with twenty grand in his account. Twenty grand earmarked for Effie's bank.

'When do you break ground?' Paul says.

Effie smiles.

The dick is trying to use building-developer terminology. Good luck with that. I'm right in the mood for this.

'We need full planning first,' she says, winding up the well-practised pitch. 'But that's not proving to be straightforward.'

'Oh?'

'Nothing to worry about,' she replies. 'It's just, since the Gürtel scandal, in Spain the local authorities are a lot warier over approving developments.'

'I read something about that,' Paul says. 'A massive issue here. Bribery, wasn't it?'

'And the rest,' says Effie. 'And it'll rumble on for years. It's changed the whole political landscape in Spain. It's why we have to show the Ayuntamiento that half of our investors are not connected to us.'

As if.

'They want to ensure we don't have any controlling interest. Especially when we are talking a couple of million per property. It's a pity because we'd love to put all the cash in ourselves. It's such a sweet deal—but rules are rules.'

Paul rubs his nose, 'I have to say I couldn't find anything about any fifty per cent rule.'

That's because it doesn't exist, dickwad. Let's get this done soon. I'm up for another pill.

'It's new,' Effie says. 'George Laidlaw can explain it. He's the legal beagle on this. But it's good news from your end. You only have to front up twenty k as a deposit. The rest would normally be payable when we complete—but, by then, we'll have sold out, be a lot richer and you won't have had to fork out the balance. Twenty k for a million plus—how can that not be the deal of the century? This is better than a lottery win for you.'

Like hell it is.

Paul scrubs at his forehead. 'Why so little cash up front? Seems too good to be true.'

Effie smiles, a crooked beast at best. 'The new rule requires us to deposit a hundredth of the estimated final sale price with the Ayuntamiento on application. We're not allowed to take any more than twenty thousand per investor until planning is approved, at which time, before any more money is needed, we will sell it on to a bigger developer.'

Take it easy, Effie, take it easy. Now for the tricky part.

'Are you interested?' she asks.

'I'd be a fool not to be.'

'You've got that nailed but if you want to go ahead I need you to sign an NDA.'

The lack of understanding on his face is good news for Effie. He isn't an experienced investor. A few have been and they were busted flushes.

'A Non-Disclosure Agreement,' she explains.

'Oh.'

'It's necessary,' she points out. 'You see, if word gets out about this then we'd be cut out in a second by one of the large property developers. This is way too profitable for them not to try to fuck us over.'

Paul's eyes flare.

No swearing, Effie. No fucking swearing. Just keep it calm. But it's so hard to keep it calm. I feel good. Those pills . . .

'Sorry about the language,' she apologises. 'It's just that, although we own the land, the big boys know the system inside out. We need to surprise them. Give them no chance to stop us lodging planning. We did them over once before with the flats you saw today.' Then she adds, 'Beautiful, aren't they?'

Paul nods.

'Well, the big builders were mad as hell about that and won't miss us a second time. This is all about stealth. Playing the game. Catching them cold. If we can do that we're home free. So, we need complete secrecy. That's why I insisted we meet here. If new people turn up at our offices then someone will talk. This town has a gossip vine like no other I've ever seen.'

Offices. That's a laugh.

Paul stares at her. Hanging on every word.

Cat-skinning time. It's cat-skinning time.

'So, if you are in, it's simple,' Effie says. 'As one of a small number of hand-picked investors you put in twenty k, we put in the rest. When we sell for, our best guess, ten million—that's a lowball estimate—that'll give you a million for your share.'

'How do the buyers of the land still make money when we make so much?'

I like the 'we' in that sentence.

'Easy,' Effie lies. 'The whole thing is worth twenty million. We take ten. Their build costs are about five, that leaves them five million profit, maybe more if the market moves up.'

'You've got all this worked out.'

Oh yes, we do, Paul. Oh yes, we do. We, we do, we do—we soooooo do.

'Sweet, isn't it?' Effie says.

She sits back, conscious that the space between her and the table is all stomach. But at her age who really gives a shit? At her age all she wants is out of this place and Paul is probably the last step in that plan towards the goodnight cash mountain she has been working towards. Her 'time to check out' money. North of a million euros already. Not enough for all of the team involved to fuck off but more than enough for a seventy-eight-year-old woman who is sick of sloshing booze down ingrates' throats. And she holds all the cash. Possession being nine tenths and all that.

Paul sips at his beer and Effie slides a couple of sheets of paper across the table.

'These are the bank details, account number and NDA,' she explains. 'But you need to be quick. All the others have paid and we submit planning soon.'

As if.

Paul examines the papers.

'If your money isn't in by close of banking tonight,' Effie adds. 'Then we'll assume you are out. I've more people in reserve that will drop the cash with us first thing tomorrow and then the deal is closed to anyone else.'

'How long will it take before it all pays out?' Paul asks.

Not in a million years, now just get on board.

'Wheels move slowly in El Descaro,' Effie replies. 'Could be a few months, but once we get our submission in, and it's in the public domain, we're home free. The big boys might shout and scream but they can't stop us.'

'And after planning is submitted they can't kill it?'

'It's much harder for them to do that after we lodge and, anyway, our betting is that one of them will buy us out instead.'

'Betting?'

'We don't know quite which one will bite, but one will. As I said, this is sweet. You've seen the land. Front-line sea view. The last virgin plot of its kind in the town. The words prime real estate were created for it. And you saw the quality we are aiming for. Top dollar property.'

The apartment Paul had seen that afternoon had been sorted out by George Laidlaw. He knew the building's management company and at this time of year all the apartments were locked up tight. Paul had been led to believe that they were Effie's previous consortium's build. The clincher as it were. Very high-end finish. Very expensive.

'So, are you in?' Effie asks.

Paul rotates his beer glass, dragging his finger across the condensation ring on the table.

'Maybe a million and a half,' Effie states. 'If the wind blows the right way. But the clock's ticking.'

Hands rubbing. Eyes flicking. Breathing rapid.

Cat skinned.

'I think so,' he says. 'I'm just nervous. It's my university money that I'm risking.'

'Of course you're nervous but think of what you can do with 1.5 million—you could go to any university in the world—or just bug out.'

Paul stares at the table and whispers, 'I'm in.'

'Great,' Effie reaches across the table. 'Welcome on board.'

Fan-bloody-tastic.

Paul takes her hand and they shake. When Effie withdraws the shake, she has to wipe the sweat from her palm on her dress.

At that moment the pub door slams open.

The door had once graced a printing business in the old town. When the business had closed down, to be converted into studio apartments, the door was surplus to requirements. Effie had been sipping a *café con leche* in a nearby café when she had seen the door being removed. A hundred euros to the boss man and the workers had dropped it off at her bar. A free night on the booze had paid for a local chippie to size and fit it. It was a brute of an item. Solid oak. Worth twenty times what Effie had paid. It was also a monster of a thing to open. And that's why she had bought it. A recent break-in informing her that her pub, a building that she thought an almost impregnable, windowless concrete shell, was not quite so inviolate.

Hence the surprise when the door slams back on its hinges with what appears to be consummate ease. The inside door handle punching a hole in the cheap plasterboard wall. Sunlight streams in, briefly framing a figure flying into the pub.

Effie and Paul turn at the noise.

'I want my fucking money back.'

The new arrival screams the words.

Effie sighs.

The weightlifter. The bloody weightlifter. I should have listened to my gut. I thought him too sneaky to pull the wool with such an obvious scam. But he'd been keen. Very keen. For good reason and keenness had led to blindness. But now ...

'Did you hear what I fucking said?' the new arrival says. 'I . . . want . . . my . . . fucking . . . money . . . back . . .'

Effie squeezes her bulk from the booth and rises, with a grunt.

'Simon,' she says as she approaches the man.

'You're a fucking con artist,' is the reply.

As the door swings closed, the man's outline transforms into that of a five-feet-four-tall individual with the chest of Popeye. Wrapped in a tight white T-shirt and beach shorts, his massive upper arms and thighs give him an almost comical appearance, out of proportion to his height—compensation for his shortness writ large in the hours of pumping iron and steroid abuse. Effie is an inch taller and, with her excess fat broadening her physique, the two face each other across the pub floor like some revolting gone-wrong Munchkin–Mexican stand-off.

'Simon,' she repeats.

'Money . . . now . . .' he replies.

'Simon.'

'Fucking . . . now . . .'

'I—'

'No excuses, you thieving cow,' he says. 'That land is contaminated.'

'Simon, we know this, calm down.'

'And you don't even own it.'

'We do own it—'

'The fucking rear. You own the fucking rear. Not the front. No one knows who owns that. And that's the only access to your fucking site.'

'We do know who owns it.'

'Who then?'

How the fuck do you know all this?

'A local,' she replies.

'Bollocks. The council thinks it's some guy in Moscow who owns it. But the address they have is wrong. They can't trace the owner. The Russian bought it ten years ago.'

'It was sold to us.'

'You are just fucking lying,' the weightlifter spits. 'There's no

8

record of any sale in a decade and the bit of land you own is worth fifty grand. Max. The clean-up will cost a minimum of half a million and even then, you still won't have any access to the site.'

'Simon, if you would just sit down I'll explain.'

Paul stands up, circles Effie and Simon without a word, and leaves. Effie watches him with a sigh.

Shit. That's that one gone.

'Look, Simon, please take a seat and I'll get you a beer,' Effie offers.

'Just give me my twenty grand back.'

Effie moves to the bar, grateful that the usual suspects are still half an hour from frequenting her establishment. An empty pub means that this might still be rescued.

'Simon,' she says. 'Let me get George down here and he can explain it all. It's not like it looks.'

'I don't want to talk to Laidlaw. He's in this up to his neck. I'm going to the police,' Simon says.

Effie changes tack at the mention of the authorities. She knows she has no time to dick around. With an effortlessness born of years on the grey side of life Effie reframes the conversation in a moment.

'If you do that your fucking twenty k will never surface,' she says.

Simon's face creases.

'Then it's *fucking* true,' he says. 'This is all a big con.'

It is, and I need another pill.

Effie turns back to the bar and repeats the art of pouring beer from the wrong side, dropping a couple of fingers of liquid into a small glass. She reaches into her pocket and quickly throws two white pills into her mouth and washes them down with a slug of beer. She pushes the glass aside.

Better.

'I'll tell you something, Simon,' she says, turning back to him. 'Go to the authorities and you'll never see your money.'

'I want it back.'

'It doesn't matter what you want,' she says. 'It only matters what I'll give you. That's how it works within these walls.'

Simon's anger tips off the boil as confusion races in. He hadn't figured much past screaming for his money. He'd come here and not to the authorities, when he'd found out the truth, because he really needed his money back. And needed it now. The gym he'd opened down near the beach had tanked big time. By catering for muscle builders like himself he had miscalculated. The area wanted for health palaces for the young and retired female brigade. What the muscle-heads wanted was the nasty, but very cheap, hole that nestled in the rear of a car workshop, buried in the back end of the old town. Simon's twenty-grand punt on Effie's building scam was a last desperate attempt to save his skin. He'd been ill advised on who to borrow from for his venture.

'It's my money,' Simon says.

'And do you think bursting in here, screaming like a loon is going to get it back?'

'It's all a con.'

Effie shrugs and pours him a beer. Simon might have arms and legs like telegraph poles but his gut speaks of a beer sponge. He takes the alcohol.

Feeling real good now, Effie my girl. Loving those pills.

'So you've said,' points out Effie. 'But the question is—have you told anyone else about this? Because if you have then you can say goodbye to your twenty k. And from what I hear, that will place you as the hot favourite to take a dive off Acclana Cliffs with ten stone of anchor chain wrapped around your balls. The Charles brothers can be a little bit touchy when people don't pay back their dues.'

The last of Simon's anger flows to the floor at the mention of the brothers. He'd known their reputation when he'd borrowed the cash but they had been deceptively nice when laying out the terms. Full of reassurances that it was in their interest to see local businesses thrive. They'd even offered to take out a couple of memberships for themselves.

'How do you know about them?' he asks.

'Simon, this town is hard-wired to spread news. Especially bad news. Fuck your high-speed broadband or 5G or any other tech on this planet, El Descaro's got it all beat. It's bloody telepathic.'

'You won't get away with this,' Simon says. 'When people find out you'll be fucked.'

Effie laughs. 'What are you talking about, Simon? We've already got away with it. The money is in the bank. And if you breathe a single word three things are going to happen.'

Feeling fine, my dear, real fine.

Effie moves her considerable backside a few inches, nestling the stool into her arse crack. She glances at her watch. Still twenty minutes to doors open.

'Firstly,' she says. 'Your money will never return. Secondly, I'll give the Charles brothers a little call. Explain that I've heard you've stumbled on a bit of bad luck. That a small bird told me you had pissed their money up against a wall. That you are now claiming to have invested in our little venture. A claim I'll refute. A claim that has no backing. After all, you have no paperwork.'

'I've a bloody bank transfer to your account for twenty grand.'

'My account? I don't think so. I don't know who you gave the money to but it certainly wasn't me.'

'People will come after you.'

She laughs again. 'Do you think we didn't think of that? Really?'

Shit. I feel . . .

'I need that money,' he says.

'And thirdly,' Effie stutters as she speaks. 'I'll call Pat Ratte.'

Simon freezes. Every muscle locking. His eyes fixed on Effie. 'You wouldn't.'

Whoa. I really don't feel right.

'Simon, I've been in this game for a ton of years. You don't stay on top without staying on top. Do you get my meaning? Information is king. You cut Ratte in for fifty per cent of the new gym. Which as we all know is fifty per cent of fuck all now and if the Charles brothers are a vile force to be reckoned with, they are nothing in comparison to Ratte.'

What in the hell is wrong with me? I feel terrible.

Effie had only found out about Ratte's involvement a few days back when a drunken conversation between Pete Richmond and Eddie Alderley in the bar had morphed into a pissing contest on who knew the hardest bastard. Ratte had been the trump card for Eddie and during the exchange Eddie had let slip that Ratte was in for fifty per cent of Simon's gym. Info that Effie had gratefully tucked away.

'So, Simon, stop being a dick and sit down.'

Fuck, I feel bad.

Sails becalmed, Simon looks around the pub.

'Ain't anyone here to help you, Simon. And if you want a little bit of advice, I'd think of leaving the pub soon. It's the darts league tonight and Mikey Charles is our team captain. He'll be in here soon for a bit of practice.'

I can't breathe.

'My money,' Simon whispers.

'Simon, I need to sit down for a second . . .'

Effie's last words on this earth settle on the pub atmosphere like a dark cowl. Her face twists as someone presses a two-ton lead weight on to her diaphragm and sends an electric shock up her left arm. Sweat erupts on her forehead.

Simon watches as Effie throws her right hand to her chest. A grunt and she drops. A lift going down. Cables sliced. Brakes shot. Gravity king. She face-plants the floor, no attempt to break the fall.

The doctor will say that Effie was dead seconds after hitting the wood. The autopsy will reveal a massive heart attack brought on by arteries so blocked they would be shown to a visiting set of medical students as an example of what chronic overeating does.

Simon stands for a few seconds, unsure exactly what to do. His first thought is not to drop to his haunches and help Effie. His first thought is that he has just watched his twenty grand die in front of him. Eventually, when his brain clears a little, he moves forward.

'Are you okay?' he utters, looking down on Effie.

The words sound dumb as soon as they are out.

Behind him a voice sounds.

'Effie,' the newcomer shouts and rushes forward.

As the newcomer bends down he asks Simon, 'What happened? Did you do this?'

The accusation stuns Simon. 'No, George. She just dropped.'

'Effie?' says George Laidlaw, reaching for her hand before shouting at Simon, 'Call an ambulance, man.'

Simon reaches into his shorts for his phone. And hesitates. He stares at the phone.

'112, man. Call 112,' says George. 'Oh God, Effie.'

Simon calls the number and in broken Spanish says, '*Necesito una ambulancia.*'

He gives the operator the pub's name as George tries to find Effie's pulse. George doesn't know CPR but tries anyway. After a couple of minutes he gives up, slumping back.

'They will be here as soon as they can,' says Simon as he kills the call. 'What do we do?'

'Do?' says George, standing up. 'What can we do? Effie isn't going anywhere except the mortuary. So, if you ask me, we pour ourselves a drink and wait on the ambulance. That's what I'm going to do.'

DATE: Jueves 14 de Noviembre de 2019
Esta es una copia de la traducción al inglés de la entrevista con la persona o personas nombradas.
(The following is a copy of the English translation of the interview with the subject or subjects.)
PRESENT: Capitán Lozano, Teniente Perez and Daniella Coulstoun with her legal representative Jose Cholbi

TRANSCRIPT AS FOLLOWS:

SPANISH POLICE OFFICER CAPITÁN LOZANO (CAPITÁN L): Señorita Coulstoun, my name is Capitán Lozano. Do you require an interpreter?

DANIELLA COULSTOUN (DC): No. My lawyer will help out.

Note: all questions put to Miss Coulstoun were translated by her lawyer, as were Miss Coulstoun's answers.

CAPITÁN L: *Muy bien.* Can we start by you telling me your full name?

DC: Daniella Euphemia Coulstoun.

CAPITÁN L: And can you please state, for the benefit of the tape, where you live?

DC: 32 Ryder Avenue, Clarkston, Glasgow in the UK.

CAPITÁN L: And how long have you lived there?

DC: A little over twelve years.

CAPITÁN L: And what is your occupation?

DC: I'm a call centre operative with an insurance firm.

CAPITÁN L: And when did you arrive in Spain?

DC: On November the sixth.

CAPITÁN L: And why are you visiting El Descaro?

DC: My mother died.

CAPITÁN L: Euphemia Coulstoun?

DC: Yes.

CAPITÁN L: A heart attack?

DC: Yes.

CAPITÁN L: And you were in the UK when she died?

DC: Yes.

CAPITÁN L: Where exactly?

DC: When I heard or when she died?

CAPITÁN L: Both?

DC: I was at work when she died and at home when I was contacted by George Laidlaw.

CAPITÁN L: And you flew out to make the necessary arrangements?

DC: No, those were done by George.

CAPITÁN L: Señor Laidlaw made the arrangements?

DC: Yes.

CAPITÁN L: You were not involved?

DC: Other than saying a few words at the crematorium, no.

CAPITÁN L: And did you know if your mother had health problems?

DC: Not that I know of. But she was seventy-eight. Can I ask, is it usual for the police to ask questions about a heart attack?

CAPITÁN L: The death was sudden, Señorita Coulstoun. All sudden deaths are investigated.

DC: Even heart attacks?

CAPITÁN L: When I think we should, yes. When did you last talk to your mother?

DC: Last Christmas.

CAPITÁN L: And when did you last see your mother?

DC: About two years ago.

CAPITÁN L: You haven't seen your mother in two years?

DC: That's correct.

CAPITÁN L: Can I ask why?

DC: It's complicated.

2

Touch Down

The plane touches down to a smattering of applause. Why are they clapping? Relief? Appreciation of the pilot's skills? Sarcasm? Celebration? All four. A cheesy tune tells me that ninety-something per cent of flights land on time. I'm happy for them. I look out the window. ALICANTE ELCHE is the branding above the terminal. Early November and the mid-morning temperature is already sixty degrees, sunny with a light northerly wind. This information was imparted to me by the overweight man sitting in the middle seat next to me. A man who has oozed fat into my space for the entire flight.

The passengers around me rise to don coats and retrieve bags. I'm happy in my seat. Fast as the turnarounds are nowadays it'll still be a good ten minutes before enough people have exited to make it worth my while standing. And it's not that I'm in any hurry. Funerals are not something that I seek out as a rule. I'm anti-death. Live forever. No grim reaper for me. The exception. Immortal.

I stare out the window at the tarmac, conscious that the fat man next to me is rooting around at my feet.

'Sorry,' he says. 'I dropped my pen.'

I smile at him but don't offer to help. There's not enough room for two of us down there. He grunts and groans as his hot and sweaty thigh presses mine into the fuselage. He's sporting grey sweat patches the size of footballs under each arm. The fetid stink of his unwashed pits has been my companion for three hours. The woman on the aisle seat had sprayed perfume so often during the flight, to cover the smell, I'd swear she was crop dusting. But I didn't complain about that. The sweet aroma had provided temporary relief from the man's stench and I'd joined in with my own perfume as needed. To compound matters, an hour into the flight, the man (a sales rep taking a few days to soak up the sun and the beer) continued the nasal assault on me by starting to pass wind on a regular basis. A smell that provoked coughing as far as four rows down. Sitting next to it, I could taste it.

Then again, what do you expect for fifty quid each way, Glasgow to Alicante?

The man stands, relieving the pressure on my leg. He turns and smiles at me. It takes real self-control not to vent forth on bodily cleanliness and his diet. I make do with a grimace that I hope conveys disdain and disapproval in equal measure.

As he fumbles for his bag in the overhead bin I sigh at the situation I find myself in and sigh again as the man releases some more gas. I plant my face in the window and breathe through my mouth. A hoodie behind me swears and mouths off about someone on the plane having colon cancer. Patrick is clearly well used to such abuse and blanks it easily. Fair call. Walk in someone else's shoes and all that.

As the air-side crew manoeuvre the stairs across the tarmac to the front of the plane, I wonder if it's possible to sneak into the toilets, hide and fly back home. Assuming, of course, that this plane isn't heading for other climes first—although even that thought has appeal. More or less anything has appeal when it's your mother's funeral you're heading for and you feel like an interloper rather than the sole grieving daughter. Mum doesn't deserve my disdain or my childish attitude. It's simply a matter of guilt stacking on guilt.

I sit it out until the last passenger is exiting the plane, rise, grab my bag and trudge to the door. The air crew are already checking the seats for detritus left behind. I slope down the stairs to the tarmac and meander towards the terminal. I'm in no hurry. The closer I can arrive to the time due at the crematorium, the better.

Passport control is a scrum of people trying to judge which of the electric dog traps has the quickest moving queue. I'm the only one looking for the slowest. Too soon I'm presented with a gate; requiring the help of a young man to figure which way up my passport needs to be inserted into the scanner. I draw no complaints from waiting passengers for my ignorance as I'm the last through.

As I stand on the escalator, going down, I pull my mobile free from my pocket and fire it up. A few seconds later, as I pass into the baggage hall, my provider texts me to tell me how much they are going to rob me for using my phone. I've a down-at-heel, pay-as-you-go, ancient iPhone with no international roaming deal. I could easily tip my bank account into the red with just a few texts or ten seconds on the web.

I follow the signs saying *Salida* and await the incoming text from George Laidlaw. He'd volunteered to pick me up and said he'd text and meet me on the other side of the baggage hall exit doors.

I exit the baggage hall to discover a barrier separating the waiting hoards from the arriving passengers. A smattering of crudely drawn cardboard signs dot the crowd, most displaying a misspelling of a name. The high-tech amongst the pick-up mob have iPads flashing their welcomes.

George steps from the crowd. One of Mum's oldest friends, he's a heavy-set man with a whale of a stomach and a neatly trimmed grey beard. He's wearing light-coloured chinos and a collared shirt. His shoes are classic loafers. He oozes legal from every pore.

'Daniella,' he says, extending his hand.

I take it and I'm subjected to a fierce handshake. No doubt honed over the years to impart confidence and exert control over his clients.

'George,' I reply. 'Thanks for coming to pick me up.'

'There wasn't much option,' he says, his tone in reprimand mode. 'You don't drive, you said you were skint, the taxi to El Descaro costs over a hundred euros, and the first bus available would arrive there twenty minutes after your mother's funeral starts. So here I am.'

Not a word of condolence to be had.

'I got here as quickly as I could,' I say. 'Why is the funeral so soon?'

'This is Spain. Twenty-four hours to forty-eight hours is the norm. Not that you would know anything about that.'

I decide not to respond, choosing to fall in behind him as he marches through the terminal with a determined stride. It's clear he's none too happy with me.

When we arrive in the car park I discover that George drives a Jaguar S-Type. The leather interior has seen far better days and it reeks of stale cigar smoke. The beige roof lining was probably Arctic White when the car rolled from the production line. George urges me to get in. He navigates us out of the car park and up on to a round-about before plunging down to a dual carriageway. All without uttering a single word. He presses his foot to the floor and we surge forward, soon picking up signs for Valencia. He grunts something about it taking 'time' to get to El Descaro.

Twenty minutes later, when we hit some toll gates, he stops to take a ticket and turns to me. 'Have you prepared what you are going to say at the crematorium?'

'I'm expected to speak?' I ask.

'Of course you are,' he spits back. 'Someone has to. Effie wasn't religious so the priest is only there for protocol. You're her daughter.'

'What am I supposed to say?'

'Whatever you want, but it would be nice if you talked about her life.'

Tricky. I've been a bit part for twenty years.

'George, wouldn't it be better if you did that?'

'Would it fuck.'

That's that then.

A text pings in on my phone. It's George telling me he's at the meeting point in the airport. You've got to love latency in technology.

George slams his foot back down and we race forward on to the motorway. I settle for staring at the scenery and forty minutes later we skip by an ocean of high-rise blocks.

'Where's that?' I ask.

'Benidorm,' George replies.

'Bloody hell, it's huge.'

Mountains rise ahead of us like a scene from *Game of Thrones*. Spectacular. We zip into a tunnel with signs telling us to switch on our lights and drop our speed. George does neither.

'What time do we have to be at the crematorium?' I enquire.

'In just over an hour. It'll be tight. We both need to change.'

I look down at my black blouse, black denims and black Vans. Change? I'd been hoping to put my dark grey jacket on and be good to go. I don't have an alternative range of funereal clothes in my bag. I had considered buying a dress, but having only ever owned one, now too small round the waist and frayed at the edges to be seriously considered for a funeral, I'd decided against it. Mum was not one for fancy dresses and I'm strictly a T-shirt and jeans girl. So, it's not disrespect that drives my choice of attire. More a desire to be true to what Mum and I had. Which wasn't much. But what it was, wasn't bullshit. And a posh dress is bullshit in my eyes.

As we exit the tunnel I think on my flight back in three days. I would have flown back tomorrow but I have an appointment to see a local lawyer in the morning to look over Mum's will. George had been cold as a penguin's foot when I'd called and told him about the lawyer. George felt he should run with the will but I wanted someone who hadn't been done for fraud to look after Mum's affairs. And that ruled George out. He'd been struck off the UK lawyer's roll many years back for, amongst other things, siphoning off clients' funds. The details were cloudy but his presence in Spain coincided with the Law Society's announcement of his demise. The same day, I'd heard. Maybe even the day before.

'George,' I say, hoping for a little thaw in the car. 'You knew Mum well. How was she . . . at the end?'

George flicks the steering wheel to slipstream a truck. 'She was Effie. What else do you need to know?'

No thaw yet.

'I mean how did she seem?'

'What do you want me to say? That she was ready for a heart attack? Had it writ large across her forehead. You know the sort of thing. Here comes the big one. Blood Vessel Blockage are in the house playing their biggest hit—Acute Myocardial Infarction. Last time *ever*.'

What in the hell?

'George, I'm just asking.'

'Well, fucking don't. Later. Not now.'

I thought we were cruising close to the top speed of the car but George manages to coax another ten miles an hour out of the engine. We bullet through the sun-bleached hills in silence. Me wondering where in the hell George's anger is really coming from. Him leaning forward, crouching over the steering wheel, flecks of red speckling his face, knuckles sheet white. I settle back, burying the questions, wondering why a man I hardly know would launch off like an Exocet to a daughter on the way to her mother's funeral.

We exit the motorway via another toll gate, George inserting his credit card to pay. He pushes it into the slot as if trying to slice through a cheap steak with a blunt knife. The road sign beyond the gate signals eighty kilometres an hour as the upper limit. We're passed that speed ten seconds onto the road; a two-way ribbon lined with commercial property and the odd café.

We soon slip towards the coast and roar into El Descaro. George zigzags through classic Spanish back streets and heaves his foot on the brake outside a white three-storey building with a small sign in the garden reading *Hotel Pequeño*.

I get out, grabbing my bag off the back seat.

'I'll be back in fifteen minutes. Be ready.' George says this into a tyre-smoking slipstream as he flees the scene.

I'm left standing on the pavement. A little shocked.

The garden that guards the hotel is neat. I push open a metal gate and approach the front door. A small buzzer serves to alert the hotel staff to people's presence. After a couple of minutes of pressing, knocking, scouting and a scanning, I'm thinking no one is home. Then, with sloth-like speed, the door opens and an old lady appears, hair tied tightly in a bun, her body wrapped in a bright white apron covering a black ankle-length dress.

'*Buenos días*,' she says.

'*Buenos días*.' I'm now stretching my Spanish. 'Coulstoun?'

'*Perdón*.'

'I am Señorita Coulstoun,' I say. 'I have a room booked.'

At least I hope I do. George has arranged this.

'Coolstone,' she repeats. '*No tengo a Señorita Coolstone*.'

'Me,' I say, pointing to my chest. 'I am staying here.' I point to the hotel. 'Eh . . . *dormir aquí*?'

She looks at me with that blank look reserved for those with an idiot on their doorstep.

I try something else. 'Señor Laidlaw?'

'*Ah, sí*, Señor Laidlaw,' she replies with a smile. '*Éll reservó una habitación para usted. Vale*.'

She opens the door and I'm allowed to enter. The hallway is tight, barely enough room for one person to pass along at a time. A cross with Jesus hangs on one wall and a small mirror, ringed in black metalwork, sits opposite. The floor is laid with bright terracotta patterned tiles and, in the midday sunlight, motes of dust float. I've stepped into a quieter part of the planet.

The hotel owner climbs the stairs at the end of the hall, encouraging me to follow. At the top an even smaller hallway reveals two doors. The hotel owner pushes the second one open and walks in. I trundle after her, banging my bag off the wall.

The room continues the tiny theme. A lone single bed and a foldaway table the only furniture. No wardrobe in sight. The owner smiles and waves at the room. I smile back. I can't see any sign of a toilet.

'The bathroom?' I ask.

'*Como*?'

I mimic washing my hands.

'Ah, *el baño*,' she says.

She retreats to the hall and points up another set of stairs. '*Es el primero a la izquierda*.'

She waves with her left hand and I'm guessing she means the toilet is up the stairs and on the left.

'*Gracias*,' I say as she scuttles along the hall and vanishes down the stairs.

I re-enter the bedroom and remove my toiletries, spreading my jacket on the bed. The jacket's wrinkled but with no place to hang it up, it will have to do. I'd planned a shower but if George is right about being back in fifteen minutes I'm stuffed. I've had five of those minutes already.

I grab my toiletries bag and climb to the bathroom. Bleach-clean, it continues the miniscule thing. Sitting on the toilet means placing my feet in the shower and the wash-hand basin wouldn't hold enough water to wet a postage stamp. I do my best to clean off the travel dirt and resort to the old trick of overdosing on perfume and deodorant. I brush my hair but to little avail. It doesn't behave. Then again it never has. I descend to my bedroom just as the buzzer on the front door sounds. I check my mobile. Fifteen minutes since George sped off. I close the door to the bedroom as I leave, slinging my jacket on.

The hotel owner is nowhere to be seen when I reach the front door and the Jag is waiting, purring gently. George, window down, is waving frantically at me to get in.

He examines my clothes.

'No dress?'

'I don't own one.'

'They don't have clothes shops in the UK?'

I ignore that.

We roar away and, less than ten minutes later, we wheel through the gates of the crematorium. The car park is busy and people are pouring in through the front door.

3

A Fixer

I'm standing at the front of the *tanatorio*. Everyone's eyes are fixed on me. Mum's coffin behind, lid open. I can almost feel her eyes on my back. Rows of brown plastic chairs, sporting shining metal legs, range in front of me, all sat on top of highly polished marble. Every chair is full, maybe eighty or ninety people in the room. A few are standing at the back. To my left there is a wall of glass with a set of double doors leading to a gravel surround outside. Beyond the gravel small, gnarled trees dot a bare landscape. The priest, standing behind a white linen-covered table, signals for me to start. I let an uncomfortable silence build.

What do I say? What is expected of me? Back to my childhood? Platitudes? Make up shit?

When my gran passed away it was my mum that took centre stage for the eulogy. I was six at the time and too young to take it all in. My memory of the day is a vague cloud of tall strangers, whispers and the smell of bleach and whisky. But I have a clear recollection of what Mum said through a shaky VHS video that one of my uncles shot; an odd deed to undertake at a funeral but one that has afforded me a memory of something solid at an age when most memories are tinged in vagueness and lies.

In the video Mum is standing at the foot of the pulpit, looking sad and uncomfortable. She is wearing a midnight-black prison sack-cloth dress. Her mum's death and her lack of religious conviction are scribed in her tear-streaked face. The voluminous dress stays still when she moves, making it look like she is speaking from inside a small, funereal circus tent. Her hair, usually a wild bush of flying ends is scooped high on her head, held in place by a ring of black tape. She holds a single sheet of paper in her left hand but never looks at it once as she speaks. We were often forced to watch this video. A macabre ritual, at indeterminate intervals, that involved shortbread, whisky and a pot of tea—my gran's favourite trilogy. I haven't watched the video in two or more decades but Mum was secretly proud of her words that day and I'd occasionally find myself reciting the opening lines when I'd heard that someone had died. I'd do so alone, under my breath. A silent prayer to the departed. With nothing else springing to mind I break the uncomfortable hush that is blanketing the room with Mum's words.

'When the living depart this world,' I say, 'we look upon it as the last full stop at the end of a book. That the person is gone. That they have no more role to play in our lives. That it's time to type those two words, "The End".'

The silence in the room is, if anything, deeper but a little less awkward.

'Yet this is not true,' I continue. 'The dead live on. Their memory an everlasting presence in the heads of friends and of family. Sadness and grief giving focus to what they were and what they did. But, more importantly, what they have left behind. Their legacy. And when, in time, those memories fade, the strongest ones will survive. The real essence of Mum. And it is those memories we should think on here.'

I let the words settle, wondering, not for the first time, did Mum write those words or did she find them somewhere. With eyes on me I leave Mum's speech and set out on a trail of my own.

'Mum,' I continue, 'was never what you would call conventional.'

A burble of laughter.

'I was born later in her life than I think she wanted.'

I laugh this time and add, 'I don't think that. I *know* that. When most kids were being escorted to primary school by young mums fresh out of their teens, I was sent on my own. Mum focusing on work and bringing in cash. Focusing on cleaning the engineering factory she worked in for over twenty-five years. I swear that if it had been possible I'd have been born on that factory floor, put to one side and only taken to the doctor to be checked over once the factory siren had blown.'

There are another couple of small laughs.

'But if Mum instilled one thing in me it was that, in life, you get a job, put your head down and work. Until she quit, I really thought she'd be at that factory till she retired. Then she surprised me, and her friends, by buying the pub out here on the day I turned sixteen. A day that she upped sticks and moved to Spain. No reason given. At least none was given to me and I was left to move in with my aunt till I finished school.'

I pause. Not sure where this track is taking me.

'As you might know,' I continue, 'or maybe you don't, Mum also never told me who my father was. Not even a hint. I asked, many times, but she didn't even try to lie. She just told me it was better I didn't know.'

An awkward shuffling creeps across the room. Feet moving, hands crossing and uncrossing, bums rubbing on seats. Some eyes looking away.

'If I'm honest'—I plough on—'and today seems as good a time as any to lay cards on the table . . . many of you knew my mother far better than I did. Our relationship was, at best, distant. I reached out a few times, but, for whatever reason, Mum was cool towards me.'

For cool read ice-cold.

'But that didn't stop her being my mother. That didn't stop her being the one that brought me into this world. A woman who worked to put bread on the table and shoes on my feet. She may not have been the first to reach for the hankie when I cried or there when I needed a shoulder. That's because she didn't give much truck to emotional outbursts. She was too practical for that. She saw herself as a fixer. That was her role in life. At least it used to be. Maybe she changed after she got here. But Effie, as you knew her, was a fixer to me in every sense of the word. A fight at school. Effie fixed it. The day I was caught shoplifting. Effie fixed it. The morning I caught our next-door neighbour, pants around his ankles, playing with himself outside Mum's window. Effie fixed it.'

The shuffling reaches a new level but I'm now on a bright shiny path that's opening up in front of me.

'And that's how I'd like to remember her. A seventy-eight-year-old woman with a solid reputation for trying to fix the world. A fixer that made her, in my eyes, a force of nature. That maybe, when things are a little tough, it would be useful to say to yourself: *what would Effie do?* At least, in some way, she would still be here, and that seems about as good a thought to finish on as any for Mum.'

I stop, stepping away from the front and return to my seat. George glares at me and whispers as I sit down, 'Is that the best you could do? A *fixer?*'

As the first tears I've shed for Mum well up in my eyes I look at him.

'What was wrong with that?' I burble as the priest stands up to dismiss everyone.

'You have to ask?' George replies.

I do have to ask. My words may have been unplanned but they were from the heart. I feel anger rising. A desire to lash out. I bend down and, loud enough for everyone to hear, I say, 'My Mum's dead, George. So, for a few minutes, just for a few minutes, get off my *fucking* case.'

That really takes the wind out of the building.

MINESTERIO DEL INTERIOR
GUARDIA CIVIL
PUESTO DE EL DESCARO

DATE: Jueves 14 de Noviembre de 2019

Esta es una copia de la traducción al inglés de la entrevista con la persona o personas nombradas.

(The following is a copy of the English translation of the interview with the subject or subjects.)

PRESENT: Capitán Lozano, Teniente Perez and George Lorne Laidlaw

TRANSCRIPT AS FOLLOWS:

SPANISH POLICE OFFICER CAPITÁN LOZANO (CAPITÁN L): Señor Laidlaw, my name is Capitán Lozano. Do you require an interpreter?

GEORGE LORNE LAIDLAW (GL): No. My Spanish is fine.

CAPITÁN L: *Muy bien*. Can we start by you telling me your full name?

GL: George Lorne Laidlaw.

CAPITÁN L: And can you tell me your age?

GL: Sixty-seven.

CAPITÁN L: And where do you live?

GL: Carrer Del Mar de Azure, Apartmento 5, in El Descaro.

CAPITÁN L: Señor Laidlaw, can you tell me how you knew the deceased?

GL: Why do you want to know that?

CAPITÁN L: It is just a question. I have to ask. After all, Señora Coulstoun died suddenly.

GL: Doesn't everybody?

CAPITÁN L: They do, but some more suddenly than others.

GL: Are you saying Effie didn't die of a heart attack?

CAPITÁN L: No. It was certainly a heart attack.

GL: Then why the questions?

CAPITÁN L: Because, Señor Laidlaw, that is my job. Do you wish to cooperate?

GL: Do I have to?

CAPITÁN L: Well, you came here of you own free will. I thought that meant you would answer my questions.

GL: Free will? Really? I think not.

CAPITÁN L: You can leave any time you want.

GL: Again, why the questions?

CAPITÁN L: Señor Laidlaw. We treat all sudden deaths in this manner. Will you help?

GL: Really? Effie's death is hardly suspicious. She died of a heart attack. Effie was vastly overweight, did no exercise and had a diet that was mainly fat and sugar. I'd say she died in exactly the way she should have. So I ask again. Why the questions?

CAPITÁN L: Señor Laidlaw, acting this way does not help either us or Señora Coulstoun.

GL: Nothing will help Señora Coulstoun. She's dead.

CAPITÁN L: Señor Laidlaw, is it right that you helped Señora Coulstoun soon after she arrived in Spain?

GL: It's a long time ago, but yes. I helped her acquire her pub, if that's what you are referring to.

CAPITÁN L: Señor Laidlaw you are not a registered lawyer in Spain.

GL: No, I'm not.

CAPITÁN L: So why would she ask you to help her?

GL: What in the hell has that to do with anything?

CAPITÁN L: Señor Laidlaw, I am just trying to ascertain your relationship to the deceased.

GL: Okay, I'm not a registered lawyer here in Spain but I know enough local law to offer my services as an advisor. It's not illegal and I can point to no end of satisfied clients if you really want to know how good I am.

CAPITÁN L: Señor Laidlaw, I believe you left the UK under what could be called a cloud.

GL: I wanted a change of life.

CAPITÁN L: You were struck off as a lawyer in the UK.

GL: A travesty.

CAPITÁN L: One you did not challenge?

GL: I think I'm going to end this interview. I see no relevance to Effie's death in what did or did not happen twenty years ago.

CAPITÁN L: Señor Laidlaw, who benefits most from Señora Coulstoun's death?

GL: Pardon?

CAPITÁN L: Is it not correct that you advised Señora Coulstoun on her will?

GL: That was also a long time ago.

CAPITÁN L: And, Señor Laidlaw, who benefits most from Señora Coulstoun's death?

GL: Daniella.

CAPITÁN L: Señorita Daniella Coulstoun?

GL: Yes.

CAPITÁN L: And, Señor Laidlaw, once again, where were you before you found Señora Coulstoun in Se Busca?

GL: I'm not sure that I want to answer that.

CAPITÁN L: Why not?

GL: It's complicated.

4

Look at Me

The only change in the pub since I was last here are the lurid pink tables and chairs. Every one of them is currently occupied. The pub is full. Standing room only. When we arrived back from the *tanatoria* George had guided me, in silence, to a spot at the end of the bar, and here I stand, looking out on the sea of humanity. I recognise a couple of faces but other than George I can't put a name to any. I have a coffee in front of me. Everyone else is on alcohol. I deeply wish to be anywhere but here. After shouting at George, a sadness had welled up in me that I hadn't expected. I'd convinced myself that my mother's death was just another bump in my road. Something to be ridden over and put behind. Mum and I had so little contact in the last twenty years that I'd compartmentalised my life into BM and AM, Before Mum and After Mum. Almost as if, twenty years ago, she had passed on already. Only Christmas cards, birthday cards and the odd visit breaking the illusion that she was gone. Other than that, it was life without her.

It was that stupid speech at the crematorium that had broken the dam. Using her words. *Mum's* words. Words I've seen played out on the TV a hundred times. Words that I had grown to detest because, after we had watched the video, Mum would descend into a blackness of soul that haunted everyone around her. She would transmute, for a few hours, from the fixer to the aggressor. Lashing out at even the slightest misdemeanour. Then with no word of apology the fixer would re-emerge and things would settle down to the norm, until the video was pulled out again.

I'd vanished into the toilets after shouting at George and if I was supposed to thank those that attended, I'd avoided it by sitting on an ice-cold pan for half an hour, crying. Eventually George had come and found me. The car park was empty when we'd emerged into the sunlight. I'd thought about blanking the funeral tea in the bar but that would have been an insult to Mum.

Now, standing amongst a lake of strangers, it's taking deep self-control not to wade through them and leave.

I notice a man pushing through the crowd. I have a vague recollection of him. He's Asian. Indian maybe? I struggle to recall his name when I realise that he's heading right for me. Dressed in skin-tight black jeans with shiny winkle-pickers, he cuts a cool figure. His hair is well styled and his skin has a healthy sheen. Good moisturising regime, or just bloody good genes? Any way up, he looks good. He reaches me and flashes a smile of precision-whitened teeth. He holds out his hand. He's the first person to try to communicate with me since I arrived.

'Hi,' he says. 'I'm Zia MacFarlane. We met last time you were here. When was that? Two years ago?'

'Something like that,' I reply. 'Hi.'

'How are you doing, Daniella?'

I step back, and move partly behind the bar, and he follows into the gap, giving us a little space. Close up his age shows. At a distance I'd have said late thirties–early forties but under a microscope I'd guess he's in his fifties.

'Okay, I suppose,' I reply.

The chat around us covers our conversation.

'Nice speech,' he says. His accent is vaguely Scottish but has hints of all sorts. A Bassett, as my friend 'Trine used to say. He's also soft spoken, the odd word getting a little lost in the background buzz.

'You think?' I say. 'I'm not sure it went down well.'

'It's a hard thing to do. Speaking at your own mother's funeral. When my mother goes I think she's planning to do the speech herself. Pre-record it. Air a few home truths, knowing there's no comeback. But you did just fine.'

'Thanks,' I say. 'I hadn't a clue what to say.'

'The opening was deep,' he says, moving in a little closer. 'Although the rest could have done without the reference to the man with his trousers around his ankles outside Effie's window. Did that really happen?'

'It did.' I smile. 'He had a thing for Mum and I don't think it was his first time either.'

I'm glad to be talking to someone. Just glad to be talking.

'What happened?' Zia asks

I smile again. 'You'll not believe it. I'd been out in the lane behind the house. I was maybe eight years old. I'd been up at the park with my best friend and had drifted back home because she had to go to the dentist. I think that's why Mr Golding, that's the neighbour, had sneaked in. I went up the park a lot in the summer. And he'd see me go. Waved at me. So when I left with 'Trine he saw his main chance.'

'And?' Zia asks.

'When 'Trine left, I'd kicked around the back lane for a while and decided I wanted a glass of juice so I pushed open the back gate and there he was.'

'What was he up to?'

'He had his chin resting on the windowsill, and his trousers at his ankles. I couldn't see *exactly* what he was up to. But I could see Mum doing the ironing through the window. It wasn't as if she was in her bra and pants or anything. Just a run-of-the-mill summer dress. But it was spider silk thin and you could see right through it if she stood in the light of the window. Obviously, it did something for Mr Golding. So I quietly closed the gate and ran around to the front of the house and in the front door, keeping real quiet. I beckoned to Mum and when she came into the hall I whispered what was going on. I told Mum I thought he was having a crap but Mum knew exactly what he was up to. Mum grabbed our camera—she always kept it on the hall table to photograph strangers at the door and managed to photograph him in the act.'

'You're kidding,' Zia says.

'Mr Golding was way too slow in recognising he'd been made. And that's not the half of it. Mum got the pictures processed.

Twenty copies. Given what was in them she got a friend to process them. I think Boots would have called the police. Then she stuck each photo to a piece of A4 paper and wrote underneath—'Have you seen this man?' She did nineteen of those. Then she posted them all over the scheme. Just as if she was posting up lost dog posters. Mrs Golding had a real bad time on the back of that.'

Zia laughs, then grabs his mouth as if embarrassed by having a bit of fun at a funeral. 'God, that's so Effie.'

'Was it?' I say.

'Was it what?'

'Was that the Effie that lived out here?'

He thinks on that.

'A fixer, you said at the funeral,' he says. 'That's what you called her.'

'Yes.'

'I'd say she was. And some. She was certainly the go-to girl if you had a problem. So why haven't you been out more often?'

The change of direction catches me.

'You're a bit direct,' I say.

'Am I?'

'Weren't you something famous,' I say, dragging a faint memory from my last visit.

'You don't remember?'

'Sorry.'

He flashes his white smile.

'Zia,' he says. '*Look at Me*.'

I have all sorts of confusion written across my face.

'It got to number thirty-eight in the charts,' he says.

'What did?'

'"Look At Me" did. My song was called "Look At Me".'

More confusion on my part.

He steps back a little, places one hand above his head and sings.

Why are you looking at him?

Why do you want him?

Why don't you want me?

Why don't you want me?

Don't look at him, please don't look at him.

Look at me.

No one seems to notice the outburst as he finishes.

'Sorry,' I say. 'It's not ringing any bells.'

He doesn't look too happy at my response. 'I had an album as well.'

'Really?'

'It was also called *Look At Me.*'

'Were you ever on *Top of the Pops*?'

This brings out a much bigger smile.

'Was I ever,' he says. 'Nineteenth of January 1984. Billy Joel, Joe Fagin, Snowy White, Roland Rat, Shakin' Stevens, Bonnie Tyler, Howard Jones, The Icicle Works and Paul McCartney. And to end the show there was me. All introduced by Steve Wright and Mike Read.'

This is something he's obviously said a lot.

'And are you still singing?' I ask.

'I'm working on an album right now.'

George appears at his shoulder. 'Zia, would you mind giving a hand at the bar? It's getting a bit swamped. I knew free drink was a mistake.'

'Sure,' says Zia. 'Is Saucy still standing?'

'Last I saw he'd had a bottle of whisky for his own personal consumption and was sitting under the dartboard with Skid and the Twins.'

'He'll be out of it soon,' Zia says.

'I'd bet he makes a second bottle first but if he does pass out, then all the better.'

Their conversation, dotted with odd names, runs with the familiarity of friends. A smooth acceptance of the unusual in their words. Saucy, Skid, the Twins. Inside names that exclude me from the dialogue.

Zia turns to me. 'Duty calls.'

He rubs a hip on me as he squeezes past me, whispering, 'Time for people to *look at me.*'

I'm not sure what to say to that.

'George,' I start when Zia has gone.

'Say nothing, Daniella. You made me look like a tit in the crematorium.'

'And you were riding my backside on the day of my mother's funeral.'

'As if this is a big deal to you,' he says.

The noise around me drops as George becomes the centre of my universe.

'You really want to do this?' I say. 'You really want to get into this, right here, right now?'

George shrugs. 'Up to you. Your mother was never one for putting off what could be said today.'

'Okay,' I say. 'Give. What the fuck is eating you?'

'You need to ask?'

'I do. I really need to ask. Because I may not have been the daughter of the century but I'm not alone in that. Many daughters don't live in their septuagenarian mother's pocket. So it isn't my absence that's winding up your mechanism.'

'You've got that right.'

'Okay, let me try this on for size, George. Me being here is spiking your guns. Fucking up your day. Pissing on your wall. Kicking you in the bollocks. Spitting on your grave. Ruining your fucking life.'

His face creases at my words. Sometimes I can run my mouth a little too much.

'Am I close, George? Do you think I should just have stayed at home?' I grunt. 'I'm the fly in your ointment and a million other clichés that place me where you don't want me. Well, I'm sorry if my presence here is an inconvenience, hard lines on that one, George. It's my mother that's dead. *My mother.* This is the day of her funeral and I am here. What part of that is wrong?'

He picks at his beard before rubbing a spot on his cheek. 'None of that.'

'Then what? What is it that's eating you?'

'I went to the bank yesterday afternoon.'

He stops talking. Standing there. As if going to the bank was some deep dark revelation that was supposed to shake me to the core.

'And?' I say.

'The bank, Daniella. The fucking bank.'

'I know what a bank is, George. What in the hell are you talking about?'

'As if you don't know.'

He leans in, uncomfortably close. He whispers, right into my ear, spit and all, 'Where's the fucking money, Daniella?'

DATE: Jueves 14 de Noviembre de 2019

Esta es una copia de la traducción al inglés de la entrevista con la persona o personas nombradas.

(The following is a copy of the English translation of the interview with the subject or subjects.)

PRESENT: Capitán Lozano, Teniente Perez and Zia MacFarlane

TRANSCRIPT AS FOLLOWS:

SPANISH POLICE OFFICER CAPITÁN LOZANO (CAPITÁN L): Señor MacFarlane, my name is Capitán Lozano. Do you require an interpreter?

ZIA MACFARLANE (ZM): No.

CAPITÁN LOZANO: *Muy bien.* Can we start by you telling me your full name?

ZM: Zia MacFarlane.

CAPITÁN L: And can you tell me your age?

ZM: Why?

CAPITÁN L: For the record?

ZM: Fifty-five.

CAPITÁN L: And where do you live?

ZM: El Descaro.

CAPITÁN L: What is your full address?

ZM: Why?

CAPITÁN L: Again, it is for the record.

ZM: I don't have a house at the moment.

CAPITÁN L: So where are you living?

ZM: With a friend.

CAPITÁN L: Where does this friend live?

ZM: On Calle Rojo.

CAPITÁN L: Ah. *Vale.* Could you tell me how you knew Señora Coulstoun?

ZM: We've been friends for years.

CAPITÁN L: How did you meet?

ZM: I was singing at a club down on the beach, the old Far Cry club, and Effie was on a night out with some of her friends and we got talking. We hit it off.

CAPITÁN L: You are a singer?

ZM: Yes.

CAPITÁN L: A professional?

ZM: Yes. I had a chart single and an album back in the UK.

CAPITÁN L: Interesting. And where were you when Señora Coulstoun died?

ZM: At my friend's place. Why do you ask?

CAPITÁN L: It is my job.

ZM: Is there something I should know about Effie's death?

CAPITÁN L: Is there?

ZM: I'm confused.

CAPITÁN L: I am simply asking where were you when Señora Coulstoun died.

ZM: I'm staying with a friend. I was at their's that morning.

CAPITÁN L: You live with this friend?

ZM: Live with is a bit strong. I'm in between houses at the moment.

CAPITÁN L: And this friend, they can vouch for your whereabouts?

ZM: Of course. Why?

CAPITÁN L: This friend, who is it?

ZM: Peter Solo.

CAPITÁN L: The racing driver?

ZM: Yes.

CAPITÁN L: And your relationship to Señor Solo is?

ZM: It's complicated.

5

Spanish Law

The next morning, I wake to shit and sunshine. My head is pounding and my mouth is dry but the weather is great. After George had asked about the money—*Where's the fucking money, Daniella?*—things had weirded out a little as the night unfolded. I'd swapped coffee for brandy and was suddenly embraced by the crowds. People took it in turns to offer their condolences and enter into bouts of inane and awkward chat. More brandy had been the only way to deal with the onslaught. And I'm bad with brandy. But it was as if George's cryptic accusation had opened a floodgate of compunction. Each conversation followed the same trajectory—sympathy, regret, reminiscing and finally local absurdity. I was subjected to a litany of stories about my mother's domineering actions. Sometimes the same story, most often a new one. Each with Mum as the god of fixing, my half-arsed speech at the crematorium being bequeathed a vague backhanded compliment by the masses. Then, after each individual had told me their 'Effie Story' they would dive into a pool of local weird dullness. I'd nodded at this till my neck muscles weakened. Mind-numbing account after mind-numbing account of El Descaro's intimate dare-dos were spread before me and that had led to more brandy.

At some point I'd stopped listening, more intent on drowning my grief with the liquor than engaging with the stories. By late afternoon, the attendees had begun to thin out, the hard core set-tling in for the rest of the day, the others figuring they'd spent the requisite time paying respects.

George had descended into a bottle of whisky and eyed me on a regular, but increasingly bleary, basis. Saying little after the money accusation.

At one point I'd stepped outside for air, surprised to find the sun still in the sky. I'd asked someone where the Hotel Pequeño lay in relation to the bar and was informed it was a fifteen-minute walk.

I chose the walk rather than to re-enter the bar, reached the hotel, washed, lay down and woke up fifteen hours later.

I climb the stairs to the toilet and check my mobile to find I'd switched it off at some point last night. I power it up and it bursts into life with a series of texts from George, all timed late yesterday evening, after I'd left the pub, all asking where I'd got to. The last was just before eleven o'clock last night. There's also half a dozen missed calls, again all from George, but no messages have been left on the answer machine.

My appointment with the lawyer is at ten and I shower before venturing out to seek some food. A small café sits on the corner of the next street. It has a few chairs and tables on the pavement. I slump into one of the chairs, bathing in the morning light. I order a coffee and some toast. I show the waiter the lawyer's address on my phone and he points up the hill, indicating with his fingers that it's a ten-minute walk.

The coffee is good and I double down on it. With half an hour to the appointment I ask for a bottle of water to go, pay my bill and leave. I wander in the direction the waiter pointed and I'm soon lost in a maze of pretty, almost identical, back streets. Traditional Spanish shuttered windows and doors litter every building, some are picture postcard perfect. Not knowing exactly where I'm heading I use the age-old tourist technique of pulling up the address on my phone, buttonholing a stranger, pointing at the address and shrugging. This results in me finding my destination with five minutes to spare.

The lawyer's office lies at the top of a four-storey building painted bright white. There's no lift. The stairs smell of lemon bleach. Each landing has a single door sprinkled with an array of small signs advertising the businesses within. On the top floor I push through the door and find myself in a small reception area with an unmanned desk. Four more doors run across the far wall. Four doors. Four businesses. The one I want is the last on the left. I knock and enter.

A small bald man dressed in an open-collared shirt is sitting behind a wooden table. He's studying a laptop and looks up as I enter. His face is pockmarked with long-dead acne and he's wearing a tiny gold stud in one ear. The merest hint of rebellion maybe.

'Señorita Coulstoun?' he says, rising to meet me. His accent is heavy, his pronunciation clipped.

'Yes,' I reply. 'Señor Cholbi?'

He shakes my hand. Firm. I note the manicured nails and the well-polished shoes.

'*Sí. Soy yo.* Please take a seat, Señorita Coulstoun. I will be with you in one minute.'

He returns to his computer.

There are two soft armchairs in the corner of the office. A small coffee table sits between them. I sit down and take in the office. The premises are a shrine to neat and tidy. None of the mess that I've encountered over the years in my infrequent dealings with the legal world. An impressive wall of books dominates two walls. Row upon row of what I take to be Spanish legal hardbacks. Behind Señor Cholbi's desk a window looks out on to another office building. Above my head a watercolour picture of a sailing boat, skipping across some sun-kissed water, sits next to a framed certificate. The only word I recognise on the certificate is *abogado*. Lawyer.

'Señorita Coulstoun,' says Señor Cholbi, standing up from the desk again. 'Would you care for a coffee?'

'Please.'

He worries the coffee machine and fills two miniscule cups, placing them on the table.

'Milk or sugar?'

'Neither.'

'*Muy bien.*'

He sits down opposite me.

'So, Señorita Coulstoun,' he says. 'How can I be of assistance?'

His English is good but the Spanish accent infuses an almost superior ring to his words. But there is something reassuring in the tone. A warmth that speaks of trust and intelligence.

'I'm here about my mother,' I reply.

'Ah, Señora Coulstoun. I was so sorry to hear about her passing. You have my deepest sympathies, Señorita Coulstoun. Your mother was a fine woman.'

'You knew Mum?'

'I would not say that I knew her, Señorita Coulstoun. But I certainly knew *of* her. It is hard to live and work in El Descaro and not be aware of Señora Coulstoun. She will be missed.' Then he adds, 'More by some than others.'

My face shows surprise at the qualification. He reads me.

'Oh, do not take my words the wrong way, Señorita Coulstoun. I did not mean to imply that your mother is not fondly remembered by all. It's just that she had a very tight group of friends from what I understand. It is they that will miss her most. So how can I help you?'

'I need to get my mother's affairs in order.'

'And you wish me to represent you on this?'

His voice rises on the last word.

'That was my plan,' I say. 'Why, is that a problem?'

'Certainly not, Señorita Coulstoun,' he replies. 'But your mother used the services of Señor Laidlaw on legal matters.'

'She may well have done but George is not, as a far as I know, a registered lawyer in Spain.'

'That is true.'

'And I'd rather employ the services of someone who has the proper credentials.'

'And Señor Laidlaw recommended myself for this job?'

'No. I found your details on a local website and checked out your LinkedIn profile. You seem to have a great deal of recommendations. That's why I chose you.'

'Ah, and Señor Laidlaw is happy with you talking to me?'

'I don't really care what Señor Laidlaw is happy or not happy with,' I say. 'You seem a little wary of George.'

He sips at his coffee, briefly glancing at the picture of the yacht.

'I am naturally concerned about such things,' he says. 'This is a small town and reputation is everything, Señorita Coulstoun. There are protocols that need to be adhered to and one of them is not to, how do you say, stand on another man's patch. Is that how you say it? Anyway, Señor Laidlaw may not be a registered lawyer but he is an advisor to many people and passes much work to many of my colleagues when he needs local legal help.'

'Including you?'

'No, I do not accept work from Señor Laidlaw.'

'Why not?'

He uses the coffee to punctuate his conversation.

'I have not been approached by Señor Laidlaw in a long time. He did offer me some work many years ago, and I refused. He has not been in touch since. But this is not relevant if you have decided to use my services. As I said earlier, how can I help?'

His obvious disdain of George reinforces my thoughts on the man. The whispered words on missing money combined with his ice-cold shoulder are now being thrown under a brighter spotlight by Señor Cholbi.

'I'm clueless on what to do in these circumstances,' I say. 'I spent some time on the web trying to make sense of what needs to be done in relation to my mum's death and decided I need professional help.'

'Quite right. Did Señora Coulstoun leave a will?'

I reach into my jacket pocket and extract a sheaf of papers. 'As far as I know, this is her will.'

He takes it from me and reads the front.

'This is a British will.'

'Is that a problem?'

'In itself, no. But it is usual for someone that has any assets in Spain to draft a Spanish will as well. If for no other reason than to make sure this will,' he shakes it, 'takes precedence. Without a Spanish will stating that the British will has precedent then your mother's estate will be subject to Spanish law.'

'I don't know if she has a Spanish will.'

'If she did not, then we need to proceed under Spanish law.'

'And that's a problem?'

'No. Not necessarily. But that very much depends on your mother's assets and whether you have any other brothers or sisters.'

'I'm an only child.'

'That is good.'

His accent makes that statement sound like me being an only child is good for my life.

He smiles, 'I did not mean that the way it sounded. It is just that under Spanish law the eldest male child would automatically receive one quarter of any estate. Since you have no brother that is not a problem. Can I assume that this will leaves everything to you?'

'It does.'

'May I read it?'

'Of course.'

He stands up and walks back to his table with Mum's will, explaining, 'My eyesight is not the best. Even in daylight I need a little artificial light to read by.'

He sits at his chair and switches on the small lamp that stands next to his laptop. He extracts a yellow-paged notepad and a fountain pen from a small cabinet beneath the desk. As he reads and makes notes, I stand up and look at the bookshelves. I was correct. They all look like legal tomes. The exception lies at the end of one shelf. There is a small clutch of paperbacks. All are by Clive Cussler. A dozen of his novels, well worn, covers ripped. I pull one out. It's a Spanish translation. The book is called *Alta Marea*. I put it back and return to my seat.

Ten minutes later Señor Cholbi crosses to sit with me again.

'Okay, Señorita Coulstoun,' he says. 'If this is Señora Coulstoun's last will then it is fairly straightforward. There are a few small codicils relating to some minor items she wishes to bequest to various individuals, but the rest would come to you.'

'What does that mean in terms of next steps?'

'Well, if you wish to engage my services I can begin the processes required. But we must ascertain if she has another will. This one is some twenty years old.'

'She left it with my aunt when she moved to Spain.'

'Who drafted this one? The witness looks like your aunt but there is no indication of the lawyer.'

'I have no idea.'

'I am sorry to say this, Señorita Coulstoun,' he says. 'But I would fully expect your mother to have written a new will in the intervening decades.'

'How would I find out?'

'Señor Laidlaw would know.'

I sigh. 'Would there be a way of finding out without involving George?'

'Of course. If a new will has been properly done in Spain, it will be registered in Madrid. But why would you not want to ask Señor Laidlaw?'

I don't have a ready answer for that one. Call it my gut. Call it a reaction to the question about money from George last night. Call it wariness at the way he's treated me so far.

'Is there no other way for you to find out about a will?' I ask.

'Only the formal mehod via Madrid and that will take time. Maybe your mother may have a newer will in her personal possessions. Have you looked?'

I haven't been to Mum's flat yet. I'd wanted to talk to the lawyer first.

'No,' I say. 'But I'm going to Mum's place this afternoon. Will you take me on anyway, Señor Cholbi?'

'Of course. We need to do some paperwork but we could do that after you check out your mother's home for any sign of a will first.'

'No, let's do the paperwork now. Whether she has another will or not I wish to retain your services.'

'At the risk of upsetting you, that will not please Señor Laidlaw.'

'As if I care.'

He stands up, stretching out a kink in his back and wanders over to the window. 'Join me at the window, Señorita Coulstoun.'

I stand up, wondering what's coming. I move next to him and look down on the street. The entrance I came in is beneath me.

'Can you see that man down there?' he says. 'The one in the black and white striped shirt.'

A man with heavily slicked-back hair is leaning against the wall. His top is a dead ringer for a Newcastle United strip. He's wearing loafers and flared jeans.

'Yes,' I say.

'That, Señorita Coulstoun, is Señor Peter Solo.'

The name has a faint ring of recognition about it.

'He is also known by the name Skid,' says Señor Cholbi.

'Skid Solo?'

'Correct. He is, or rather was, a racing driver and is a part of the small group of people who your mother fostered.'

'Really,' I say. Fostered—an interesting word.

'Before you arrived this morning I saw him standing down there. I saw you walk up the hill and that's when he vanished, only to come back once you had entered this building. He has been there for over an hour now.'

'Odd.'

'He knows Señor Laidlaw well and is—how do you say?—a bit of a sidekick for Señor Laidlaw. Is that the right phrase?'

'I remember George talking about a Skid and some twins last night. But why does the name Skid Solo seem so familiar?'

'I'm told, Señorita Coulstoun, that there was a character in a British comic called Skid Solo, a fictional Formula 1 driver.'

'That's it.'

'Well, Señorita Coulstoun, Señor Laidlaw is not someone to cross. I just want you to be sure of what you are getting into. After all, Señorita Coulstoun, you are being spied on.'

MINESTERIO DEL INTERIOR
GUARDIA CIVIL
PUESTO DE EL DESCARO

DATE: Jueves 14 de Noviembre de 2019
Esta es una copia de la traducción al inglés de la entrevista con la persona o personas nombradas.
(The following is a copy of the English translation of the interview with the subject or subjects.)
PRESENT: Capitán Lozano, Teniente Perez and Peter Solo

TRANSCRIPT AS FOLLOWS:

SPANISH POLICE OFFICER CAPITÁN LOZANO (CAPITÁN L): Señor Solo, my name is Capitán Lozano. Do you require an interpreter?

PETER SOLO (PS): I can get by.

CAPITÁN L: *Muy bien.* Can we start by you telling me your full name?

PS: Peter Solo, but everyone calls me Skid.

CAPITÁN L: And can you tell me your age?

PS: Thirty-three.

CAPITÁN L: Really, Señor Solo. It says on your passport that you are forty-four. Is the passport incorrect?

PS: Eh, not exactly.

CAPITÁN L: And what does that mean?

PS: I prefer to consider myself thirty-three. There's no law against that, is there?

CAPITÁN L: It is an offence to give false evidence.

PS: I thought this was just a friendly chat.

CAPITÁN L: That is so, Señor Solo. But a chat where we are honest with each other would be good. So, are you forty-four?

PS: If that's what my passport says, then yes, but I do not recognise that as my age.

CAPITÁN L: Let's move on. Where do you live?

PS: Calle Rojo in El Descaro.

CAPITÁN L: With Señor MacFarlane?

PS: Who told you that?

CAPITÁN L: Señor MacFarlane told me. Is that incorrect?

PS: It is a temporary thing. He needs a bed for a short while.

CAPITÁN L: And can you tell me how you met Señora Coulstoun?

PS: Effie and I met a few years back. She sponsored my racing car.

CAPITÁN L: I was led to believe that you stopped racing when you arrived in Spain. Did you not have your racing licence suspended?

PS: That was a misunderstanding.

CAPITÁN L: And where were you when Señora Coulstoun died?

CAPITÁN L: In my flat.

PS: With Señor MacFarlane?

PS: What is that supposed to mean?

CAPITÁN L: It means that Señor MacFarlane told me that he was with you in your home on the morning Señora Coulstoun died and that you are confirming this. Are you and Señor MacFarlane in a relationship?

PS: Did he say we were? And why does it matter?

CAPITÁN L: I do not know if it matters. Señor MacFarlane told me it was complicated. I do not know what that means.

PS: It's complicated.

6

Thief

I step out of Señor Cholbi's building and bask in the mid-morning sun. The warmth is welcome. After I'd signed the required papers for Señor Cholbi he had photocopied my mother's will, keeping the original and handing me a copy, which I'd stuffed into my jacket pocket. I'd looked out his window before I left. Skid had still been standing on the same corner. He's gone now.

I'm not a coffee fiend but could do with another. I head away from Señor Cholbi's building and away from my hotel, burrowing deeper into the old town. I turn a corner and enter a large square. A few cafés line one side, with chairs in the sun. The other three sides of the square are surrounded by commercial buildings and a tree dotted park area. I choose the nearest café. As I walk towards it, I turn and catch a flash of black and white in the corner of the square. I stop, waiting, and a few seconds later, Skid pops his head out. I ignore him and sit at the café, ordering up a *café con leche*.

When it arrives, I consider my next move. My original plan had been to fly home the day after tomorrow but Señor Cholbi has informed me that it will take far longer than that to sort things out. I'd suggested that I fly home and come back when required but he'd said that it might be prudent to consider delaying my return to the UK until we establish if my mother has another will.

More black and white appears as Skid does a bad impression of a private dick. This time he appears on the other side of the square, dipping back when I lay eyes on him. Leaving my bag on the chair

I get up and cross to the spot where he just appeared. I stand against a wall and when he reappears I step out.

'Peter?' I say.

The look of surprise on his face can't be real. He can't possibly think he hasn't been spotted.

'I'm sorry,' he says. 'Who are you?'

Maybe he really is that dumb.

'You know fine well, who I am. Why are you following me?'

'I don't know what you're talking about.'

'Does the rest of this conversation go on like this? You pretending you don't know me, that you're not spying on me, that you don't know George Laidlaw, that you haven't heard of my mother, that you weren't once a racing driver?'

He stops me. 'Once?'

'Oh, for fuck's sake,' I say. 'Were you told to act this stupid?'

'I—'

'Look, if you want to find out what I'm doing today, just join me for a coffee. I've no state secrets to hide. But do me a favour and drop the innocent crap.'

His tan is heavy and looks odd, artificial, maybe even topped off with some make-up. He has a small paunch that he rubs as he speaks. A few wrinkles around his eyes place him as older than he dresses. A tiny flake of powder rests in the fold of one wrinkle. Definitely make-up. His teeth are neon white. A man fighting his age? Vanity? Pride in his looks?

'You know where I'm sitting,' I say when he doesn't respond. 'Feel free to come over.'

I wheel away and return to my cooling coffee, wondering if Skid had been in a brain-damaging car crash that might explain his conduct.

He surprises me by following me over and sitting down. He orders up a glass of water.

'So,' I say. 'Shall we start again? I'm Daniella Coulstoun. And you are?'

'Skid Solo.'

'As in the comic-book hero?'

'As in the world-renowned Formula 1 ace.'

Really?

'You were at my mother's funeral?'

'I was.'

'And at the bar, after?'

'Yes.'

'And you knew my mother well?'

'Yes.'

'And yet you never came to say hello.'

'You never said hello to me.'

There's something about the way he speaks that really suggests he's a wheel short of a full set.

'And why are you following me now?' I ask.

'Am I?'

I drain my coffee and push my cup away.

'You were at the lawyer's office this morning—before, during and after my visit—and you've just trailed me to here.'

'Coincidence.'

'That's rubbish.'

'I live here. I can go where I want.'

'And George didn't put you up to this?'

'Why would he?'

Teeth pulling.

'Because,' I say, 'he's pissed off I'm using another lawyer and not him. Could that be it? Or, maybe, he just wants to give you a little exercise and work off that excess fat.'

He can't help himself and rubs at his stomach.

The waiter arrives with the water and Skid busies himself drinking it. Staring into the liquid for some inspiration.

'Look, Peter.'

'Skid.'

'Okay, Skid it is,' I say. 'Skid, I'm in no mood for games. I'm happy to chat, listen to what you might know of my mother. Maybe the odd story. A little colour where I have none. Or we can sit in the sun and chill. Either is good. I plan to kill an hour or so. It may as well be here as anywhere.'

A gaggle of young mothers, prams out front, infants in tow, roll into the square. The kids sprint into the space, soaking up the world, screaming and shouting as they throw their arms out wide, embracing the freedom. The mothers, ranked in pairs, are heading our way and a few seconds later the café has become a crèche. They surround us and it's clear they'd be happier if we swapped our seats with ones inside, to let them circle their wagons. Skid watches them arrive through the bottom of his glass.

'I need to use the bathroom,' I say. 'I've changed my mind about sitting here. I'm going for a walk. And, to save you the trouble of following me, I'm simply going for a wander. Then, after a quick bite of lunch, I'm going to my mother's place. I'll be there by one-ish. Feel free to say hi.'

I get up and one of the mothers eyes my chair.

The toilet is buried deep in the back of the café. Once inside I sit for a few minutes, letting my head roll. When I exit, there are a couple of mothers waiting in a line outside the toilet. I smile at them both and they smile back.

When I re-enter the café, I order the bill in the universally recognised pretending to write on the palm gesture.

By the time I get back to my chair, Skid is gone.

The bill arrives and I go to pay it and notice that my jacket has been moved. I check the pockets. There's no sign of the copy of my mother's will. I think back. Señor Cholbi had definitely handed me a copy of the will just before I left, telling me he had made a couple of copies. I'd placed it in the inside pocket of my jacket. I scan the ground around my seat in case it has fallen out, check my bag, check my jeans' pockets and look back over the square the way I'd come. Nothing. I pay the bill thinking to myself that Skid Solo has just stolen the copy of my mum's will.

7

Home?

It has been nearly twenty years since I was last in Mum's apartment. Less than half a mile from the pub, her flat lies just off the main road leading into the old town. It resides in a seven-storey block of brutalist apartments that were built in the sixties. The lift isn't working, which might go some way to explaining the industrial freezer that dominates the living room, full to the lid with microwavable meals—and could also make sense of the overstocked drinks cabinet.

A layer of dust coats everything around me and the carpet that lies atop the wooden floor is rippled and moves underfoot. The feeling of a time warp lies in the lack of change since I was last here. Mum bought this place on day one of her move to Spain. My memory is hazy but the furniture looks the same. It had come with the place and was on its last legs back then. The two sofas that sit either side of the freezer are roller coasters of lumps and bumps. Once deep red in colour, they've both faded to a sick pink. The only concession to modernity is the massive LCD telly mounted on one wall. Seventy inches, maybe bigger.

The coffee table, lying opposite the freezer, has two working legs. The other two corners are supported by ragged piles of paperbacks. The out of place freezer blocks access to two plastic chairs sitting in a glassed-in balcony. I walk through the rest of the apartment. There are two bedrooms; Mum's and the spare. Mum's has a super-king-sized bed with a crater in the centre that suggests the underside of the mattress must be close to touching the floor. Two heavyweight wardrobes line one wall and the room's only window is blanked by a thick curtain. No rail. Simply nailed to the frame. Beyond the curtain lies a compact balcony that looks down on the street. The carpet in here is even thicker with dust.

The spare room is a Tetris-orientated shrine to a hoarder. There's just enough space to open the door before you hit a wall of nonsense. The room is packed to the ceiling with boxes and a ridiculously wide range of items, amongst which are old vacuum cleaners (three that I can see from where I stand), a motorbike, a cooker, half a dozen car tyres, a tent and a length of what looks like the type of rope for tying up a ship. I close the door to try to banish the smell of oil and rot.

I expect the small kitchen to be a train wreck. It isn't. Neat, clean, bright—all surfaces shiny and units polished. This is not as it was when I was last here. An oversized Aga rules this space. There are two microwaves, side by side, and a US-style fridge freezer. A small kitchen table lies under a window, a colossal steel chair in attendance. The coffee machine wouldn't be out of place in Starbucks. The contrast to the decay of the rest of the flat is marked. But Mum loved her food and drink. Her coffin had been a mile from regulation in size.

The bathroom continues the fresh and bright theme, the bath taking up most of the available floor space. The energy required to heat the water to fill it would break my piggy bank.

At some point I'll need to clear this place out. I had been of a mind to get someone to do it for me and now I'm certain I'm not doing it myself. If I can dig out her personal effects the rest can be dumped.

I return to the living room and scan it, wondering where Mum might keep a will. There's nowhere obvious. No sideboard, cupboards, cabinets. No drawers. Her bedroom doesn't hold any more promise. I check under the bed and discover I was wrong about the mattress; the underside isn't nearly touching the floor. It *is* touching the floor. The wardrobes are stuffed with clothes and nothing else. The kitchen is a blank as is the bathroom. I return to the spare bedroom. The wall of debris looks untouched in years. I poke at it with little vigour and return to the living room.

I wonder what happened here. Mum used to be a signed-up member of the ultra-house-proud association, the local president, and now it feels like she's fallen off the cleanaholic wagon.

Sitting on the arm of one of the chairs I rescan the living room. Maybe Mum kept her personal papers at the pub. I know there's an office back of house. Then I have a CSI moment. From where I'm sitting, staring at the drinks cabinet, an open-fronted affair with no obvious cubbyholes, I spot, to the left, low down, between the cabinet and the wall, a small space a couple of feet square. I stand up and walk over to it. The low-level light of the room doesn't aid my investigation and I have to bend down to get a clearer view. There's an indent in the carpet. Something sat here, and not long ago. Square, sharp edged, it's left a neat dust-free depression. The wall behind it reveals a stain-free rectangle about three feet high. Whatever sat here was a three-feet by two-by-two box of some kind. The lack of dirt in the carpet's hollow signals that it's been recently removed. By whom?

My head doesn't have to wander far to come up with a suspect.

Where's the fucking money, Daniella?

Hidden in the missing piece of furniture, George? Is that what you thought?

I circle the flat one more time. Probing for hidden panels, false walls, loose floor tiles, fake roof timbers—anything that would act as a sanctuary for Mum's vital documents. There's nothing. I return to the shape in the carpet, running my finger around the shape. Safe? Filing cabinet? Heavy, whatever way you stack it, the indent is deep. This time I notice that the wall to the right of the drinks cabinet has a fresh chip out of the plaster. The impression of a corner of something dug deep into the wall. Probably made when removing the box.

I stand up to figure my next move and decide to text Señor Cholbi. *No sign of a will at my mother's. Will try the pub. If that's a blank then it's over to you.*

A text comes back quickly. *Muy bien.*

Before I leave the apartment, I fly by the kitchen for a drink. The fridge freezer has an eight-litre bottle of water resting at the bottom of the fridge section. It's open but I can't bring myself to pour from it. Dead people's food and drink are unpalatable. I close the fridge door and clip the freezer door with my fingers and have a thought. A few months ago I'd read that the freezer was a popular place for criminals to hide cash, drugs and documents. So obvious that the police were often surprised at its continued use. With that thought in mind I open up the freezer and find it rammed with more microwave meals. It would explain the pristine nature of the Aga. It was probably unused. I root around for a bit and come up blank.

I wander back to the living room once more and lift the lid of the chest freezer. I extract a few layers of meals. I'm down to layer four when I notice that an extra-large Chicken Tikka Masala seems much more bashed and worn than the others. I pull out the packet and tip it over to extract the innards from the outer sleeve. Something drops to the floor with a thump. A plastic freezer bag lies at my feet. I bend down to pick it up and let out a small gasp. Even through the frosted material it's obvious that it's full of cash. Before I open it, I check the rest of the freezer and find nothing else of note, other than my mum's obsession with frozen curry.

I close the freezer lid and rest my backside on the arm of one of the sofas. The cardboard outer in my hand is already defrosting. I place it on the freezer lid and turn my attention to the plastic bag. Unzipping it, I drop the contents next to the outer sleeve. Eight tightly packed rolls of frozen 500-euro notes tumble out and another, smaller, bundle of 100-euro notes. I'll need to let the bundles defrost to calculate how much there is. But, at a guess, we are in the tens of thousands.

George's *missing* money?

Mum's money?

A little walking cash for me?

I sure could do with it.

I'd spotted a carton stuffed with plastic shopping bags in the spare room and I fetch a bag back and drop the money in it. I lift the bag, feeling the weight. I know that the 500-euro note is a favourite of the criminal class on the continent. I'd heard that they'd considered banning it to make it harder to move large quantities of cash.

I leave the flat, locking the door behind me. When I emerge into the sunlight I'm acutely aware of the cash clutched in my hand. I'm fairly certain I'm not going to declare it to the masses. My finances are as tight as a snare drum. Mum might just have solved my liquidity crisis, although if it's the money George was talking about, I need to hide it until I can figure what is what. I've no idea where would be safe to stash it, if anywhere. Not at the hotel. I have the feeling that the little old lady owner is well connected with George and is probably, at this moment, giving my limited luggage the once-over. I can't hide the cash in Se Busca. That would be too risky.

I head in the direction of the pub anyway. It lies between the old town and the port; a lone concrete hut built on a piece of wasteland. I'm aiming for the port beyond as it might throw up some inspiration for hiding the money. I pass the pub and note that someone is outside smoking. The front door swings and someone else comes out to join them. I recognise the person smoking from last night but not the other. Unless they are cleaners, someone has opened up Se Busca for the day. No one had said to me. My mum is the sole owner of the pub. Lock, stock and beer barrel. She bought the place sight unseen from an English punter who was on the verge of bankruptcy. As far as I know she has no other partners in the business. So, technically, the business is now mine, if her will is legitimate. But, regardless, someone has seen fit to open the doors for the day and not consult the new owner. I decide I'll front up to that later, once I've found a haven for the bundles of euros.

I keep walking past the pub and enter the built-up area surrounding the port. I vanish into a dark labyrinth of high-rise alleys before emerging at the seafront. A glorious promenade stretches out before me, harbour to the left, beach to the right. A row of cafés, restaurants and shops fronts the beach and another clutch of bars runs out towards the harbour. The promenade is dotted with people out for a walk and, although many of the eating and drinking holes are closed at this time of year, those that are open are doing brisk business. To my right a square leads back into the residential area and on the nearest corner there is a shop renting security boxes called Safety Deposit +.

Just the sort of place to deposit some thawing cash.

I hesitate to enter it for a second. Whoever owns the business is no doubt known to my mum or George, or knows someone who knows my mum or George or knows someone who knows someone who knows my mum or George. I doubt the trail will stretch much further than that. I look down on the plastic bag and wonder what happens when the notes thaw. If I leave them in the bag, will they get soggy and disintegrate? Will the water leak out of the security box and raise questions? Maybe better to let them thaw first, work out their value and then sort out storage.

I sit at one of the beach front cafés, order up a small glass of *vino blanco* and people-watch, keeping a weather eye out for any black-and-white striped tops. If Skid does appear I'm certain he'll deny stealing the will. I'm just grateful that Señor Cholbi held on to the original. Without it, I suspect that Mum's estate would have just become that little bit more complicated.

My wine arrives and I sip it, watching waves break and boats bob. My grief is floating around me, not quite landing full time, but occasionally touching down. My tears at the funeral had surprised me. The feeling of loss deeper than I'd expected. I'm conscious of the things I don't know about my mother and her life here. Words never exchanged. Memories unexplored. The final goodbye an argument at Alicante airport two years ago over a stupid top.

I'd arrived three days before the argument with an olive branch in hand, only to have it broken on the back of my mum's intransigence. Her not wanting to talk about our relationship. Me feeling rejected. I'd seen her only twice. The first time at Se Busca. Both of us drinking too much and screaming blind nonsense. The second time when she'd insisted on joining me on the bus to the airport, where she'd handed me a parcel. In it was a light green-coloured shirt. Functional, not stylish. She'd insisted I put it on. I'd refused.

I didn't feel like stripping off on public transport. By the time we had reached the airport she was yelling about my inability to dress myself. I was shouting about the crap clothes she'd bought me as kid and pointed out that if my dress sense was *warped* she was the one to blame, not me.

Somewhere near the start of the argument she promised she was coming home to sort me out. And then repeated the warning ad nauseam until we reached the airport. She hadn't alighted from the bus to say goodbye, preferring to pay the extra fare to travel ten miles further south, knowing she would just have to return to the airport on the way back to El Descaro.

On this trip I'd packed the top. It lay in my luggage in the hotel. I'm not sure why I brought it with me. It doesn't fit. Maybe I'll pin it to the pub wall. A reminder that you never know when someone will keel over. Last words are rarely planned.

A kid on a hoverboard zips by, his mother, in skin-tight work-out gear, jogs behind him. I adjust the plastic bag with the money, ensuring it lies in the sun, and reach in and squeeze each bundle. They are soft and moist. I work at the edge of one bundle and a note peels free. Leaving my jacket and wine I retire to the café toilet, plastic bag in hand. Once inside the bathroom I sit on the pan. There's a small sink and I tip the notes into it. Working carefully, I peel the cash apart, using the toilet paper to mop moisture from the money, note by note. I stand up, close the pan lid, and use it as a place to stack the dried notes.

Ten minutes later and there's a knock on the door.

'*Perdone?*' comes a woman's voice. '*Necesito el baño.*'

I ignore it.

The knocks become more frequent, then stop. I keep peeling and drying. After twenty minutes I have a stack of money. Counted. Each of the 500-euro bundles holds ten notes. Five thousand euros per bundle. Forty thousand in total with the smaller 100-euro bundle containing ten notes. I dry out the inside of the plastic bag, pocket the 100-euro notes and place the rest inside the dry bag, reusing the elastic bands to tie the cash back into bundles.

When I exit the toilet the woman behind the café's counter glares at me. I shrug and point to my stomach. She shakes her head. I walk to my seat and, clutching the plastic bag, I sit down next to my now warm wine.

Again, I wonder if this is the cash that George was referring to. He was down and dirty angry with me in Se Busca. The implication that I must know where the bank money had gone was clear. It occurs to me that the cash in the plastic bag might be counterfeit. I've no reason to suspect this but I suppose it's possible. I extract a 100-euro note from my pocket, checking to see if anyone is watching, and examine it. With nothing to compare it to I'm unable to tell if it's real or fake. It looks okay to me but that doesn't mean zip. Maybe the hundreds are real and the five hundreds aren't. I need to get a hold of genuine notes and do a little compare and contrast. It'll be hard enough to use such high-denomination notes without getting pulled for passing duds.

It dawns on me that I'm relaxed with the idea of using this cash. Given that I work in the insurance world, I see more than my fair share of fraud. Maybe it's rubbing off on me.

I leave the wine unfinished, place five euros on the table and get up. I spot a hardware store on the square and a few minutes later I emerge onto the street with a small opaque, plastic locking box in my hand. I choose a second café, order up another wine and use their toilet to transfer the loose cash into the small box. Placing the box back in the plastic bag, I leave the wine sitting and cross to the Safety Deposit +.

I push into an air-conditioned world. On my left there is a bank of security boxes stacked floor to ceiling. On my right the wall is full of stationery. A counter lies in front of me, behind which a young woman is attending to a sizeable photocopy machine.

'Hi,' I say.

She looks up and there is a small hesitation before she says, 'Hi, how can I help?'

'I'd like a security box.'

'Sure.'

She pulls out some paper from a drawer and slides it over to me. She's slim with a striking nose that gets in the way of her looks. It draws your eye, to her detriment. Her hair is a wild mop that's current fashion-mag trendy.

'I need a passport and your current address,' she says without taking her eyes off me. There's something vaguely familiar about her. I just can't place it.

It takes me a few minutes to complete the paperwork and pay. The young lady looks at my passport for a few seconds too long and then walks to the stack of security boxes.

'This is yours,' she says showing me a box and handing me a key.

While she returns to her photocopying I deposit the plastic box and leave.

Returning to the café and my wine, I people watch again.

I can see the Safety Deposit + from where I sit and the front door swings on a regular basis. A young man steps out. He too looks familiar. I didn't see him enter so he must have been in the back office. His hair is a sweeping mess, fluffed up, à la Donald Trump. I've seen many a balding man and this guy is losing the battle, preferring to rearrange the stuff from the back to cover the gap at the front. He looks in my direction before going back in.

I check my phone. It's just gone two o'clock.

Where's the fucking money, Daniella?

The thought strikes me again. Is there more cash somewhere—or is the forty-one grand it? The freezer cash could just be loose change or maybe it's the works. Mum withdrawing it all from the bank, freezing it and intending to do what? It's a wedge of cash but not a 'get out of Dodge' lump of cash and George feels like the kind of guy where hundreds of thousands is real money, not tens. I see forty-odd grand as serious pocket money—but does he? Did Mum? Is there more?

The door to the Safety Deposit + opens again and the young lady walks out. Behind her the young man trails. Now I know why he looks familiar. Even at this distance I recognise the dramatic similarity between them. Twins.

They both stare in my direction. A deliberate look. One that lingers on me. I glare back and they seem unfazed.

The Twins.

George had been talking to Zia about the Twins before he'd asked Zia to help out serving behind the bar at the funeral tea. The Twins, he'd said, as if they were a single unit. At some point in my increasingly alcoholic state I think I remember clocking the girl. Along with the names Saucy and Skid, are the Twins part of George and my mum's inner circle? If so, they, like Skid, hadn't said hi last night. And when I'd entered the shop the woman hadn't even cracked a light that she knew me, although she did hesitate before saying hi and she'd lingered on my passport. But why say nothing?

It dawns on me with the weight of a lead cosh that if the Twins are friends with George, I've just deposited forty grand right into George's lap.

DATE: Jueves 14 de Noviembre de 2019
Esta es una copia de la traducción al inglés de la entrevista con la persona o personas nombradas.
(The following is a copy of the English translation of the interview with the subject or subjects.)
PRESENT: Capitán Lozano, Teniente Perez, Jordan Norman and Sheryl Norman

TRANSCRIPT AS FOLLOWS:

SPANISH POLICE OFFICER CAPITÁN LOZANO (CAPITÁN L): Señorita Jordan and Señor Jordan, my name is Capitán Lozano. Do you require an interpreter?

JORDAN NORMAN (JN): No.

SHERYL NORMAN (SN): No.

CAPITÁN L: *Muy bien.* Can you both start by telling me your full names?

JN: Jordan Warren Norman.

SN: Sheryl Tania Norman.

CAPITÁN L: And can you tell me your ages?

BOTH: Thirty-three.

CAPITÁN L: Can you tell me where you live?

JN: We live together on Avenida De Costa Luego in El Descaro.

CAPITÁN L: And you are brother and sister?

BOTH: Yes, we are twins.

CAPITÁN L: Can you tell me when you first met Señora Coulstoun?

SN: She offered to represent us as models.

CAPITÁN L: When was that?

JN: We met her when we were thirteen.

CAPITÁN L: Thirteen?

SN: We did some very big TV ads back then. DressDown.

CAPITÁN L: Sorry?

JN: DressDown. They are—well, were—a huge fashion brand for

kids. Sheryl and I were the face of their campaign for a number of years.

CAPITÁN L: I have never heard of them.

SN: They went bust a few years back.

CAPITÁN L: Ah.

SN: But they were very big at one time.

JN: *Very* big.

CAPITÁN L: And Señora Coulstoun represented you as what? Your agent?

JN: Yes.

SN: She was still representing us when she passed away.

CAPITÁN L: So you are now both working full-time as models?

JN: At the moment we are in between assignments. We run the Safety Deposit +, in the port.

CAPITÁN L: That would seem like a full-time job to me. But you still find time to model?

BOTH: Of course.

CAPITÁN L: Out of curiosity what have you been modelling lately?

JN: Various things.

CAPITÁN L: Like what?

SN: We did a job for Ali Mann recently.

CAPITÁN L: The astrologer?

SN: Yes.

CAPITÁN L: Wasn't he just sent to prison? I seem to remember that he was running some lottery racket. Something about guaranteeing to predict the numbers.

SN: That was the ad campaign we did for him.

CAPITÁN L: If I remember correctly he also went broke, did he not? Declared bankrupt?

BOTH: Yes.

CAPITÁN L: Can you tell me where you were when Señora Coulstoun died?

SN: It was tragic.

JN: Tragic.

SN: The worst.

JN: Worst.

SN: Poor Effie.

JN: Poor Effie.

CAPITÁN L: And where were you both?

SN: When she died?

CAPITÁN L: Yes.

JN: Where were *we* both?

CAPITÁN L: Where were you both?

SN: It was terrible.

JN: Awful.

SN: Poor Effie.

JN: Effie.

CAPITÁN L: Could you just answer the question?

SN: About where we were when poor Effie died?

CAPITÁN L: Please.

JN: Both of us?

CAPITÁN L: Yes, can you tell me where you both were when Señora Coulstoun died?

SN: Well, that may be a little difficult.

CAPITÁN L: Why would it be difficult to remember where you were?

JN: My sister is right; that might be a little difficult.

CAPITÁN L: Look, this is very straightforward. Please tell me where you both were when Señora Coulstoun died.

JN: It's complicated.

SN: Yes, it's *very* complicated.

8

Clyde the Student

Se Busca is busy. I'm not sure if this is the norm for a Thursday evening or if my mum's death might have had some unintended promotional impact. The largest TV is showing the build-up to a football game and a huddle of people in front of it are sipping at drinks, waiting on the match to kick off. I'm sitting at the end of the bar, a Coke in hand, back where I'd sat at the funeral tea. There's no sign of George, Zia, the Twins or Skid. The barman is a good-looking young man with a cutting-edge take on fashion. He's called Clyde and has told me he's sorry about my mum's death six times so far.

'Clyde,' I ask him when he next approaches. 'How long have you been working here?'

'About a year and I'm so sorry about your mum.'

'Thanks, but you don't need to keep saying it.'

'But it was such a shock.'

'Do you work here full time?' I ask.

'No, I'm studying at university in Valencia. I work here nights and weekends. I need the cash.'

'Doesn't everyone,' I reply. 'How did you get this job?'

'My dad knew Effie. I mean he knew your mother.'

'Effie is fine. She seemed to know everyone around here.'

'Isn't that the unvarnished truth?'

An old phrase from a young mouth.

'What are you studying at uni?'

'I'm doing a degree in the history of art.'

'And what lies at the end of that?'

One of the TV watchers rolls up for another beer and Clyde pours it.

'Not sure,' he says handing the drink over and taking the cash. The customer knocks the top three inches off the glass before he reaches the table. Drinking is a serious game in this place.

'Dad's an art nut,' Clyde continues. 'He paints when he's not running his estate agency. Oils. I just fell into the course on the back of his enthusiasm.'

'Is he good?'

'He sells the odd one but he won't be giving in the day job any time soon.'

'And are you enjoying the course?'

'Honestly?'

'As honest as you want to be.'

'Dead boring. I mean real down dead boring. The course is fine, the lecturers are good but I've no interest in the subject. Then again I've only a year left and I can't let my dad down.'

'So what will you do when you graduate?'

His face lights up, 'Travel. Travel a lot. And, after that, who knows? Probably more travel.'

'Sounds like a plan to me.'

Three more people enter the pub. An older man and two younger women. They are lost in chat as they walk in. The man guides the women to the pub's last free table, pulls the chairs out to let the women sit and approaches the bar.

'Hi, Clyde,' he says. 'The usual.'

'Sure, Mr Naz.'

Clyde gets to work and a few seconds later two vodka and Cokes and a large brandy are sitting on the bar.

'Clyde,' I say as he whips a few dead glasses from the bar, 'is it mostly regulars in here?'

'Almost all. We get the odd stray tourist during the summer but you've seen outside. It's not the most welcoming of vistas.'

Another old word. Maybe it's the historical element of the art course shaping his language.

'Although we can sometimes get really busy with outsiders when the right football game is on,' he adds. 'But even then, it's still mainly local expats. The local El Descarons tend to avoid this place. A few call it *Los No Deseados*.'

'And that means?'

'The unwanted.'

'Because Se Busca means "wanted"?'

'Exactly.'

I finish my Coke, 'Is the expat v. locals a thing around this town?'

'Not so much, but we have hardliners on both sides. Expats who have little time for the locals and locals who resent the expats. The rest get on. This town is well off because of the balance of locals and expats from around the world. But you can't keep everyone happy. There are always the angry.'

'Could I have a small wine?' I ask.

'Sure.'

'And do any of the hardliner expats frequent here?'

'Some.'

'Who?'

'A soupçon of them, shall we say.'

'You mean the real hard core.'

'I mean the ones with a chip the size of a jumbo jet on their shoulders.'

'George Laidlaw. Is he one?'

As Clyde pours my drink his head is bowed, uncomfortable with this line of questioning.

'Just asking, Clyde,' I point out. 'I'm the stranger around here.'

'And this bar is now yours.'

'Seems that way. Look. I'd like to check the back office if that's okay.'

'Your gaff, your rules,' is the reply.

I grab my wine and squeeze behind the bar and through the door into the cellar. Dodging kegs and crates I make for the tiny office at the rear. I try the door. Locked. I look around for a key but there's nothing obvious. Returning to the bar Clyde tells me he doesn't know who has the key, but it certainly isn't him.

I spend a few minutes digging around behind the bar and back in the cellar but there's no key. I try the door again. Fair enough. It's probably usual to lock it. After all, I seem to remember it had a safe for petty cash and other valuables.

'Is George due in tonight?' I ask Clyde, sliding back on to the stool at the end of the bar.

Clyde shrugs. 'He's usually in most nights.'

From under the dartboard a voice sings out, croaky, broken, but with volume, 'Effie's girl's a thieving cow.'

It's more than loud enough to silence the crowd. The lone voice of Richard Keys on the telly, handing over to the commentator for the big game, is the only one that ignores the outburst. A chair clatters and a table scrapes the floor, as a figure rises. The man's about five feet six inches tall and dressed in a worn green two-piece suit, blue tie on a grey shirt. Strands of his hair are plastered onto a liver-spotted pate. He grasps the table and pulls himself upright.

'You all heard me,' he says, staring at the customers. 'Effie's girl is a thieving cow.'

I'm not sure if he can see me from where he is. Is this a direct attack or just a statement for the masses?

I drop from the stool and step into the body of the kirk.

'There she stands,' the man says, swaying. 'The thieving cow.'

He needs both hands to hold himself upright and this lasts only a few seconds before he stumbles back and collapses on to the chair. Everyone's eyes are on me and I'm unsure how to react. The guy is as pissed as a newt soaked in ethanol. I've also a suspicion that I'm encountering another of George's inner sanctum. Saucy? The man who Zia had asked if he was still standing?

Is that the full set? Saucy? The Twins? Skid? George? Zia? Mum?

'Thieving cow,' the man shouts. 'Thieving cow.'

Saucy might be down but he's not out. Everyone's eyes are on the prize and I'm it.

In for a penny . . .

I navigate my way towards the man. He's folded almost double in the chair, an empty tumbler in front of him. He looks up as I approach.

'A drink,' he says. 'You owe me at least a fucking drink.'

The words are heavily slurred.

'Hi,' I say, feeling the weight of vision on my neck as others keep tuned into developments. 'I'm Daniella, Effie's daughter. You know, the thieving cow.'

'Yes, the thieving cow,' he says in a south London accent. 'The thieving cow.'

'And you are?'

'None of your business.'

'Is that right.'

'Fucking A, it is. Now get me a drink. Thief.'

I turn around. 'Clyde, could you come here a moment?'

Clyde obliges and, even though the football has kicked off, I have the full attention of the pub.

'Clyde, can you tell me this person's name?'

'Saucy's what everyone calls him,' he replies. 'Arthur Heinz is his real name. He was your mother's accountant.'

'Could you do me a favour and escort Mr Heinz off the premises? Call a taxi for him if you have to and I'll pay but, until I say so, Mr Heinz is barred from Se Busca.'

'The fuck,' says Saucy. 'Barred? You can't bar me. I've known your mother for twenty years. Drank here for twenty years.'

I bend over but keep the volume switch on high for the benefit of the rubber-neckers.

'Mr Heinz, this is now my pub. And regardless of your relationship with my mother, or how much you've spent here, no one calls me a thieving cow. Now leave.'

'I'm not going anywhere you little bitch. You fucking waltz in and act all Lady Muck. You've no idea what is fucking what around here. Thief.'

'Clyde,' I say. 'Can you call the police?'

Clyde's eyes widen. 'Are you sure, Miss Coulstoun? It's not good form for Se Busca to call them in. Your mum always said that we sort our own problems.'

'It's Daniella, Clyde, call me Daniella,' I say. 'And as long as Mr Heinz leaves then we don't need to involve the police. If he doesn't I'll make the call.'

Saucy tries to stand again. The drink beats him and he collapses back into the seat.

'I'm not going fucking anywhere,' he says, face inches from the chair seat.

'Oh, but you are,' I state.

'Fucking touch me and I'll sue.'

'Have it your way,' I say. 'Clyde, what's the local police number? Do they speak English?'

'I'll do it,' he offers, reluctantly.

'Thanks, Clyde.'

Saucy pushes his head up. 'George will chew you a new arsehole, Clyde, if you call the police.'

Clyde walks away and I go with him.

'Clyde, I'll make sure George doesn't blame you if this becomes an issue.'

'No need, Miss Coulstoun. But can I make an alternative suggestion?'

'Daniella, Clyde, please call me Daniella. Miss Coulstoun makes me sound like a school teacher. What's your suggestion?'

'Saucy's been on the pop all day. He usually passes out at some point. We're used to pouring him into a taxi. If you give him another large drink he'll keel over and we can get rid of him. You can still bar him but it would save bringing the police in.'

'Give him more drink?'

'A very large one.'

'And I'll look like I'm backing down.'

'No. I'll give him it. You go to the toilet and I'll also call the taxi.'

The approach has its merits.

'And if he doesn't pass out?'

'I have something in mind that will help him on his way.'

He points to the top shelf behind the bar. 'See that bottle, the one with the bright orange label.'

I nod.

'It's distilled just up the road. It's sixty-two per cent alcohol by volume. It's called *Muerte Naranja*.'

'Which means?'

'Orange Death.'

'You'll kill him?'

'Saucy?' Clyde laughs. 'God no. But it'll knock him out.'

'Are you sure this is safe?'

Clyde nods. 'Honestly, Miss . . . Daniella, you don't want to bring in the jurisdiction if you can avoid it.'

'Thieving cow,' shouts Saucy and seals his fate.

'Make it so, Clyde,' I say as I head for the toilet.

I spend a good ten minutes washing my hands, emerging to find Saucy flat out on the chair. Snoring. Clyde beckons me over.

'He's out. The taxi will be here in a couple of minutes. Can you give me a hand?'

Saucy is skin and bones. We lift him with ease and convey his carcass into the car park. Clyde drops him next to the pub wall, propping him up.

'I've phoned the usual taxi,' says Clyde. 'A guy called Héctor. His car has vinyl rear seats and a rubber floor.'

'Sick-proof.'

'*El Vómito*, as it's known around here. Sick bags and wet wipes included.'

'A niche offering.'

Clyde smiles. 'And profitable. Héctor is time and a half as standard. Double time during *dias festivos*.'

A white taxi wheels in and a tall man dressed in a white coverall gets out. He looks more like a forensic officer than a taxi driver.

'Tyvek,' explains Clyde. 'Héctor's wearing a Tyvek suit. He has a stack in the boot. Saucy is a regular. He's been known to do an *Exorcist* now and again.'

'Nice. Will Héctor need a hand at the other end?'

'No. Saucy lives in a bungalow. Héctor can reverse right up to the front door and drop him off. Saucy's wife will give him a hand in.'

We place Saucy in the back of the taxi and Clyde says thanks to Héctor, slipping him some money.

'I'll make sure you get the cash back,' I say.

'Saucy's wife will square me tomorrow,' Clyde replies. 'She always does and she adds in a tip.'

We watch the car leave, a chill in the wind nipping through both of us. The sky is bright with stars, the moon on the wane, a small clutch of clouds hover over the nearby hill; a slope dotted with house lights.

'Will barring Saucy cause an issue?' I ask after the taxi has left.

'He's been barred before but not for a while. He's usually a quiet drunk.' Clyde shrugs. 'I need to get back in.'

'Sure, on you go.'

I decide to swallow some more air. There was malice in Saucy's drunken attack. Admittedly he'd waited until he was full of booze before braving up but the 'Daniella Fan Club' is increasingly low on members around here.

And what's with the thieving cow thing? The money that George talked about? Is that it?

I wonder if Mum has poisoned them against me over the years. Me, the errant daughter. Uncaring. Uncommunicative. Leaving her poor mother to eke out a living in the sun. Only to appear when she died. Out here for the will. Out for the goodies. To accept the pay-off. It wouldn't take much to see it that way. And it would explain some of the stuff that's gone down. George being ice cold. Skid stealing my mum's will from me. Saucy handing out abuse. The cold eye I got from the Twins. Only Zia has shown any warmth.

I re-enter the pub thinking two things.

What was in the box that was removed from Mum's flat and where is the key to the back office?

MINESTERIO DEL INTERIOR
GUARDIA CIVIL
PUESTO DE EL DESCARO

DATE: Jueves 14 de Noviembre de 2019
Esta es una copia de la traducción al inglés de la entrevista con la persona o personas nombradas.
(The following is a copy of the English translation of the interview with the subject or subjects.)
PRESENT: Capitán Lozano, Teniente Perez and Arthur Heinz

TRANSCRIPT AS FOLLOWS:

SPANISH POLICE OFFICER CAPITÁN LOZANO (CAPITÁN L): Señor Heinz, my name is Capitán Lozano. Do you require an interpreter?

ARTHUR HEINZ (AH): Why would I need one?

CAPITÁN L: I only ask as I want to make sure we understand each other.

AH: I can understand you fine, son. Now what is this about?

CAPITÁN L: Can you start by telling me your full name?

AH: No.

CAPITÁN L: Sorry?

AH: I said no. I'm here because I was asked to come but I don't have to answer any questions.

CAPITÁN L: You don't want to cooperate?

AH: I didn't say that, son. I said I don't have to answer any questions. I didn't say I wouldn't answer any questions. Tell me why I'm here and I'll consider my position.

CAPITÁN L: I'm looking into matters surrounding Señora Coulstoun's death.

AH: Who had a heart attack.

CAPITÁN L: That is what the report says.

AH: And you don't believe that?

CAPITÁN L: Señor Heinz, I am a police officer. I know some things and other things I don't. The more I know, the better I can do my job. Belief is for the church pews. So will you cooperate?

AH: Arthur James Heinz.

CAPITÁN L: And your age?

AH: Sixty-five. Although why the hell that is of any interest to you is beyond me. Does my age matter? Does anyone's age matter? Can you even ask my age? Isn't that against the rules?

CAPITÁN L: Rules?

AH: Interview rules.

CAPITÁN L: This is hardly a job interview.

AH: Pity. I could do with some work. Any jobs going in the station? As Yosser Hughes used to say: 'I can do that.'

CAPITÁN L: Who said what?

AH: *Boys from the Black Stuff*. Wonderful show.

CAPITÁN L: Señor Heinz, have you been drinking?

AH: Is that against the rules?

CAPITÁN L: No, but it is early.

AH: For you, maybe. For me it's just fine. I met up with the boys going off to work this morning. The brandy, coffee and *cerveza* brigade. You know them? Workers getting ready for the heavy shift in construction.

CAPITÁN L: Señor Heinz, I know of many men who have a small drink first thing before work. I would suggest that yours was not small by any measure.

AH: I don't have to work today.

CAPITÁN L: And exactly what do you do for a living, Señor Heinz?

AH: I don't do anything for a living.

CAPITÁN L: You are retired?

AH: No.

CAPITÁN L: Unemployed?

AH: No.

CAPITÁN L: In between jobs, maybe?

AH: No.

CAPITÁN L: Then what?

AH: I am an accountant.

CAPITÁN L: You just said you do not do anything for a living.

AH: I don't call that a living.

CAPITÁN L: What would you call it?

AH: Waiting for death.

CAPITÁN L: Is that why you drink?

AH: Isn't that why everyone drinks?

CAPITÁN L: That is a dark view on life, Señor Heinz.

AH: I'm not interested in the light side.

CAPITÁN L: Señor Heinz, where were you when Señora Coulstoun died?

AH: How would I know?

CAPITÁN L: Well, who would know, if not you?

AH: All the days are the same to me, except the ones that aren't.

CAPITÁN L: Señor Heinz, please just tell me where you were when Señora Coulstoun died

AH: I was drinking.

CAPITÁN L: Where?

AH: To be honest, I'd rather not say.

CAPITÁN L: Señor Heinz, please just tell me where you were when Señora Coulstoun died. And do not tell me it is complicated. I have had enough of that today.

AH: I was with Pat, George and the Twins.

CAPITÁN L: Really, why?

AH: It's complicated.

9

You're Het

'What time do you close up, Clyde?' I ask.

Clyde slides two more beers to a couple sitting on the bar stools.

'That depends,' he replies.

I'm back on Coke. It's gone midnight and even though it's mid-week there's no sign of the pub's clientele moving on. George hasn't been in and the Saucy incident is a thing of ancient history. The big screen is now showing reruns of *Fawlty Towers* with the sound down. Basil is trying to understand why the door to his dining room has been blocked off.

'Depends on what?' I ask.

'On you.'

'Me?'

'Well, normally it depended on Effie. She would usually send me home about now and she would run the bar until she got bored.'

'I've never run a bar before.'

'Well, I'd suggest that you learn. I've uni in the morning and I'm up early to get the bus. I need some sleep.'

It's dawning on me that life is going to be a little complicated from now on in. I hadn't counted on running a pub.

I'd been hoping that George would show and I could front him up about the money thing. There has been a steady trickle of visitors asking for George, all looking disappointed when Clyde told them he hadn't been in. I get the impression George is dodging people. About eleven o'clock I'd texted him and received nothing back. I'd called twice since and both times it had tripped to answer machine.

'Clyde, let's give it another half hour and we'll shut up shop.'

'Sure.'

'Should we announce it?'

'It would help. Otherwise they'll keep ordering.'

'Can you do the honours?'

'Okay.'

He steps out from behind the bar, 'Okay, folks, we're closing a little early tonight. Another half an hour and that's it. So if you want one more drink, now's the time.'

There's moaning, shuffling, scraping and, en masse, the clientele head for the bar. They all order at least two drinks each.

Clyde smiles, a grim one as he serves the thirsty crowd. Half an hour might be a touch ambitious in terms of closing this place down.

I leave Clyde to it and circle the cellar once more. Still searching for the key for the office. But it's a no from the jury. I notice a pinboard with a sheet of graph paper on it. I study the paper and remove it.

'Clyde, what's this?' I say, handing him the sheet.

'The roster for the shifts here.'

'My mum's name is on it.'

'Sure. Her, me, Tara and Colin. That's everyone that works here. I'm off to uni tomorrow and not back till late. Tara's on tomorrow—but only on the day shift. Then it was supposed to be Effie.'

'Who'll cover for her?'

'There isn't anyone,' Clyde says. 'Tara's kid is in the school play tomorrow night, I'm staying at Valencia for the night and Colin's up seeing his brother in Barcelona till next week. It'll be you on duty or we are closed.'

'There's no one else? Someone else I could ask?'

'No. There used to be Saucy but you can't trust him behind the bar any more. George has done the odd shift but he hates it.'

'What about Zia? He did it yesterday at Mum's funeral tea.'

'I'd forgotten about him. He does it once in a blue moon. Never on his own and he might not be free—he sings down at Bar Fidelity on Friday nights.'

I study the roster. My mum is down for a fair slug of the shifts in the next few weeks.

'What if I shut down the pub instead?' I ask.

'You'll piss off the regulars and make the Dog's Bollocks very happy.'

'The what?'

'There's a bar out towards the beach called DB's. We call it the Dog's Bollocks. When we've been closed they get our business. But your mum hated that. A guy called Davie Brost owns it and your mum didn't get on with him. And,' Clyde continues, 'there's the pub ordering to be done.'

'Ordering.'

'From the wholesaler. We're running short on lager and some other drinks. Today is order day. We need stuff for the weekend.'

'Anything else?'

'The bank. There's cash in the till and down the slot.'

'Slot?'

'Here,' he says, pointing to a small slit in the back bar. 'Every hundred and fifty euros we stick the cash in one of these tins.'

He lifts a slim tin the size of a small cigar case from a pile next to the till.

'We put the cash in a tin and slip it in the slot. It falls into the cupboard below. Your mum had the key. That way we don't have too much cash in the till at any one time.'

'And I take it there will be other stuff needing done around here.'

'Lots,' he says. 'Bills to be paid I expect, reps to be seen, there's a couple of functions coming up that need organised. The darts league is tomorrow night. It's a biggie. They'll want sandwiches. It's also a big footie weekend ahead. El Classico on Saturday night and three big Premier League derbies. I think Rangers also play Celtic on Sunday, that will pack this place out.'

'Bloody hell. Anything else?'

'Look up www.eldescarorocks.com.'

'What for?'

'If it's going on it's on that bloody website. Everyone reads it around here. The forum is wild.'

'Wild?'

'People go off on one all the time on it. But if you want to know what the hell is happening around here go on the website. Our calendar is on there.'

I'd no intention of getting embroiled in any of this. I'd not even considered that I might have to be involved in the bar.

'Clyde, do you have Zia's number?'

'Yes.'

'Can you give it to me?'

'Sure.'

I give him my mobile number and a few seconds later he pings me Zia's.

'Clyde, could you do me another favour?'

'What?'

'Can you write down all the stuff you know about the pub? Opening routine, closing routine, wholesalers' details—anything and any numbers, contacts . . . you know the sort of thing. By the way, how are you paid?'

'Cash.'

'When?'

'Usually each night.'

'Okay, take it out the till tonight and add twenty euros for doing the list.'

I'm wondering if it's too late to call Zia when a voice rumbles in my ear.

'Daniella Coulstoun?'

I look up. Someone has let a whale into the pub. A mountain of a man is standing over me. His face has the lived-in look that movie directors pay bucks for. His breath is overpowering. Garlic on garlic with an extra dash of garlic. Yellow teeth sit under pale lips and his eyes are pinholes in a wave of loose flesh that passes for a face. He's blocking out the light from the pub, and probably most of El Descaro, in a suit that's three sizes too small for a man half his bulk. The bright orange trainers aren't helping his style points.

'Pat says you're het for the big one,' he growls.

'I'm what?' I reply.

'Het for it. Day is 'morrow at the latest. Folding the usual. No outsies.'

I have to turn my head away from the smell coming from his mouth.

'Have you got that on your radar, Miss Coulstoun?' he adds.

I look at Clyde who has backed away and is pretending to clean glassware. I can't see if anyone else is watching. This man is an eclipse in action.

'So, will I mouth to Pat we're eetsy peetsy?' he says.

It's clearly a question; I'm just not sure what language it's in.

'I'm sorry,' I say. 'Do you speak English?'

The whale doesn't crack a smile. He simply lowers his growl.

'Think you're up on stage with a trip on, do you?' he says.

It *is* English. Just a version I've not encountered before.

'Look,' I say. 'I've no idea what you're talking about. Who's Pat?'

He lays a monumental hand on my shoulder.

'Pat.' Right in my ear. 'Is the man.'

'That's not really helping,' I reply, my back pressed hard into the bar. 'You see, I'm new around here.'

'I know. You've got the pub gig from the big one. So you are in her shoes as far as Pat is concerned.'

I'm clueless.

'Can you do me a favour?' I ask.

'What?'

'Assume I know nothing about nothing. That I don't know who Pat is. What I'm het for and so on and run it all by me one more time.'

'Are you thick?'

'It would appear so.'

'Pat Ratte has an arrangement with your mother. Cash for services rendered. Security. It's due. Got it?'

'Ah, got it now.'

He turns away and every eye in the house is on us. The whale exits through the door with some effort, leaving the pub a fart of garlic as a parting gift.

'Clyde,' I say.

He walks over.

'Clyde, who, or what in the hell was that?'

'Calls himself Jeep. He's Pat Ratte's minder.'

'Jeep?'

'He drives around in a World War II Jeep.'

'And this guy called rat?'

'It's spelt R.A.T.T.E. He lives up the hill. Big house. He's supposed to be an ex-gangster from the UK. Jeep works for him.'

'Ex-gangster?'

'So they say.'

'None of that seemed very *ex*, if you ask me.'

He shrugs.

'And the money I've been told I owe?' I say.

'Pat runs a security business called RatTrap. Your mum was a customer.'

'By customer, you mean she was part of his protection racket.'

'Your mum thought it was money well spent. She's had Pat sort a few things out for her, over the years.'

I thought I knew a little about my mother but now she's slowly morphing into someone that I really didn't know at all.

'You wouldn't happen to know what the price tag is for this protection?' I ask.

'No, but George will.'

'Of course he will.'

I look at the pub clientele as I slip off my stool. No one seems fazed at the conversation they have just heard.

I say, 'Sorry, ladies and gentlemen but we are closing. Please drink up. As you might expect I'm a little tired and I'd appreciate your cooperation.'

There's no obvious reaction from anyone. I look at Clyde. He jumps on to the bar.

'What Miss Coulstoun is trying to say,' he shouts, 'is that you've spent all your money, now ejaculate the premises.'

This gets a laugh.

'One of your mum's favourite phrases,' Clyde says, as he drops back to the ground. 'When she said it, they knew she meant business. Although I'm not sure they see me as quite the same threat.'

But it works. In a few minutes the bulk of the punters begin to deposit glasses on the bar and nod their goodbyes.

'Clyde, who cleans up?' I ask as the last of the customers leaves.

'Geraldine McLarty will come in tomorrow morning. She has keys. She knows what to do. She'll also set up.'

'Can you add her number to your list?'

'Sure.'

'And, Clyde, how is Geraldine paid?'

We both say 'cash' at the same time.

Half an hour later and Clyde has shown me how to shut down and lock up.

'I'll write all the close-up and open-up stuff on the list,' he says as he turns the key in the front door.

'I have a feeling that list is going to be a godsend,' I grunt.

'Your mum had it all written down in a little black diary in the office.'

'Does Geraldine have a key for the office?'

'Yip.'

'What time does she start?'

'She's an early bird. She'll be in by seven and away by eight thirty at the latest. She has another job up at the old town *mercat* as a waitress during the day.'

We walk out of the car park together.

'I'm this way,' I say, pointing to the port.

With money in the security box, assuming it's not been stolen, I'd decided to find another hotel down at the port and had checked myself in earlier. I'd tried to explain to the old lady who ran the Hotel Pequeño that I was leaving but gave in. She'd watched me leave and must have got the message. I'd wanted out of there. I was sure my bag had been moved by her. Pushed under the bed. She could have been cleaning, but the way things are panning out I'm not up for taking that chance. My new hotel might well be run by another friend of George's and I'd considered moving into Mum's flat, but the thought of the cleaning required and sleeping on the disaster that she called a bed, pushed that idea to the bottom of the pile.

'I'm up the hill,' Clyde replies.

I shake his hand. 'Clyde you're a good person. Thanks for tonight.'

'For what?'

'For being there.'

'No problem. Look, I'll type up that list on the bus tomorrow morning on my phone and send it to you.'

'Thanks.'

We part and I stroll towards the hotel.

What in the hell else is there to find out around here?

(Posted, on a flash drive, to the El Descaro police station on 23 December. No note attached.)

LOCATION: Unknown (likely El Descaro, maybe the Se Busca bar)
DATE OF RECORDING: November 2019—Wednesday 6 November.
INDIVIDUALS IDENTIFIED AS PRESENT: George Laidlaw (George), Arthur Heinz (Arthur), Jordan Norman (Jordan), Sheryl Norman (Sheryl), Peter Solo (Peter), Zia MacFarlane (Zia)

ARTHUR: We're fucked.

PETER: You've got that right, Saucy. Where in the hell is the money, George?

GEORGE: I don't know.

ARTHUR: We're fucked.

JORDAN: It can't just have vanished. How much was there?

GEORGE: I reckon we had close to 1.3 million euros in total in the bank.

SHERYL: And it's all gone? Where?

ARTHUR: We're fucked.

GEORGE: Fuck's sake, Saucy, stop saying that.

ARTHUR: Why? We're fucked. As fucked as fucked can get.

GEORGE: Saying it over and over won't help.

ARTHUR: Fuck all will help.

ZIA: Effie must have put the money somewhere. She was looking after it.

GEORGE: You all know how it worked. We had the bank account with Overseas & Overland. And remember that took some arranging. We had to give two and a half per cent of the take to the manager to play ball. And even that was hard but he's in the shit with his divorce and needed the cash.

SHERYL: And all the money went to that account?

GEORGE: Every time someone signed up for a share in the property scam they transferred the cash to that account.

SHERYL: And there's no money in it?

GEORGE: Not a blind farthing.

PETER: So where in the hell did it all go?

GEORGE: Effie screwed us. She offered the bloody manager five per cent to move it all to another bank.

ARTHUR: We're fucked, and your mate, the bank manager, is what, seventy-five thousand euros to the good?

SHERYL: So where is this other account?

GEORGE: A private bank down in Benidorm. And before you ask, I checked it. That account is empty as well.

PETER: So why don't we get your bank manager to hand us the cash back?

GEORGE: What?

PETER: We tell the manager that we'll grass him up unless he gets our money back?

GEORGE: Skid, are you on drugs? First of all, he doesn't have 1.3 million euros.

PETER: His bank does.

GEORGE: And how does that work?

PETER: He's in charge. He can order the money to be sent to us.

GEORGE: Skid, it isn't his money. It's the bank's money. He can't just use it any way he wants.

PETER: Really?

GEORGE: Really. For fuck's sake.

ZIA: Well, he can hand back his seventy-five thousand.

GEORGE: He could. Except it's gone.

ZIA: Already?

GEORGE: A yacht.

SHERYL: It went on a yacht?

GEORGE: He's an arsehole and it won't be long before he's under investigation. I hear that he's been playing with other people's cash as well.

ARTHUR: We are so fucked.

JORDAN: What do we do? The investors will soon know we haven't applied for planning permission. We were supposed to be out of town soon. They'll look for us.

GEORGE: They already are.

JORDAN: If Effie was planning to screw us over she'd have had to put the money somewhere safe.

GEORGE: Brilliant, Jordan. In case you hadn't noticed she died and she didn't feel predisposed towards leaving a note telling us where she hid it.

ZIA: Did you check her flat?

GEORGE: Yes. Arthur and I took her lock box away but it was empty. We've also been into the pub safe. The same. But she has to have put the cash somewhere.

SHERYL: It's not just been transferred to a third bank?

GEORGE: She took it all out in cash. I threatened my bank manager with violence unless he helped. He contacted the private bank in Benidorm and discovered that Effie was making regular runs to the bank and withdrawing large sums.

SHERYL: So we think Effie had 1.3 million euros in cash somewhere?

GEORGE: It's my guess. And I've no idea where. It could be anywhere. And with her dead it's probably sitting, just waiting to be found.

SHERYL: George, the money has to be somewhere she could gain access to easily. She must have been going to run for it. What about the daughter? Daniella. She's back this morning. She might know something. In fact she could be here for the money.

GEORGE: Effie had no time for her. Hardly spoke to her or saw her.

SHERYL: Blood's thicker than water, George. Effie might have told her what she was up to.

ARTHUR: Fucking A, Sheryl. I think that daughter might know something. That's why she's here. Not for the funeral but for the cash.

Silence.

ZIA: I'm going to say this and say it once: George, are you or any of you in on this with Effie?

Silence.

GEORGE: I'm not, and if we all want to look to each other and start the suspicion game, feel free. But it will get us nowhere and we've got no fucking time on this. But maybe you're right, Saucy. Maybe we do need words with the daughter. What if Effie fessed up to her? That would make a lot of sense if Effie was about to bug out. Maybe the whole estranged thing with them is a cover.

ARTHUR: So what do we do?

GEORGE: Leave that to me. I'll work something out. We need words with the daughter and meanwhile I'd strongly suggest that everyone thinks about their plan B.

PETER: We have a plan B? What's plan B?

GEORGE: Skid, plan B is simple. Everybody for themselves.

IO

The Ex-Patriots

I'm back at the El Descaro seafront, coffee in one hand, phone in the other, wave-watching. It's a little before eight o'clock on Friday morning and I'm hovering my finger over Zia's mobile number. I'd given some more thought on closing the pub for a few days when I'd left Clyde last night, but it's a going concern and I'm now responsible. If there really is no other will lying about, then the pub is part of my inheritance and I don't want to hand the local competition a free pass. Mum clearly worked hard to build it up. If I can find a way to keep things running then I need to. I feel I *have* to. I might not have talked to Mum much over the years but it's not right that I just let her legacy die. I've also Pat Ratte and Jeep to contend with. Would they still want their money if I closed the pub? Probably. And I also need to front up to George about his accusations over the missing bank money, but he's still blanking my calls. I made two more to him this morning.

The *tostada y tomate* is delicious and the coffee is helping lift my mood. When Clyde had chatted through the to-do list for the pub I'd dropped into a mild panic. I am, after all, a woman who likes things organised for her. My call centre screen back home is menu-driven. The caller speaks, I enter their question and my computer tells me what to say.

I call Zia.

'Hi,' I say, when he answers. 'It's Daniella Coulstoun. Sorry to call so early.'

'Hi, Daniella.'

'Look, I'll not bugger about, I need some assistance with the pub and thought you might be able to help me.'

'Me? How?'

'Would you have ten minutes for a coffee this morning?'

'I could do, but tell me what you want first.'

'I'm a bit stuck with the roster at the pub. Mum was down for a fair number of shifts, including tonight, and I believe there are a number of events coming up. I chatted to Clyde last night on it and your name came up as someone that might be able to step in to help.'

'What about Tara or Colin?'

'Both are unavailable for tonight.'

'Isn't Tara in this afternoon?'

'I think so.'

'Then she can teach you. It's not hard.'

'It's a big night according to Clyde. I just need someone there tonight for a wee while. Otherwise I'm on my own.'

'Yes, it's the darts final. It'll be busy. Okay, I can meet you. But I can't promise anything. I can be at the café next to Hotel Pequeño in half an hour and we can chat then.'

'I've to nip into the pub to see the cleaner soon. Could we meet there instead?'

'In half an hour?'

'Can you make it an hour?'

'Okay, see you then.'

I check the time. If I'm quick I'll catch Geraldine McLarty before she finishes cleaning. I pay the bill and stride up the road and out of the port, coffee sloshing in my stomach, sun on my back. It's glorious to have sun at this time of year. The endless rain and wind of the west of Scotland seems a million miles away. At some point I'll have to call my workplace and tell them I'm not returning; that is if I decide to stay on for a bit. I'm on a zero hours contract so they won't be too fussed, but if I extend the time away too much, they'll can me.

As the pub heaves into sight I see a lone car parked near the front door—a dented, off-white Fiat Panda. There's a small lady just leaving the pub and she looks like she's locking up.

I jog into the car park, shouting, 'Mrs McLarty?'

The lady turns. Wearing tight blue jeans and a white blouse hidden beneath an apron, she's younger than I thought at a distance. Her hair is a close-cropped blonde crew cut. Her arms are covered in tattoos. She looks at me warily.

'Sorry, is it *Miss* McLarty?' I ask.

'Neither. Just call me Dine, everyone calls me Dine.'

She pronounces it 'Deen'.

'You'll be Effie's girl,' she says.

'I am.'

'I'm sorry about your mum. She was one of life's characters.'

'So everyone tells me. Is that you finished cleaning?'

'Yes. Why? Do you want to check my work?'

I shake my head. 'Certainly not. I just need the keys to the office. I couldn't find them last night.'

She roots in her apron pocket and pulls out a key ring with a large black metal circle hanging from it. It's branded Guinness.

'This is the only set I have. I need them back.'

'Where can I drop them?'

'Do you know the *mercat* in the old town?'

'I think I passed it yesterday.'

'I work in there until two o'clock at the tapas bar near the west entrance. Can you get them to me by then?'

'Sure.'

She opens her car door and then turns back to me.

'Miss Coulstoun?'

'Daniella,' I say.

'Daniella, can I give you a word of warning?'

'Certainly.'

She leans on the car door.

'Don't take this the wrong way,' she says. 'But this needs to be said. And it's better said now than later.'

'What is best said?'

'In simple language, you're not from around here.'

'Sorry.'

'Take that observation any way you want but you aren't one of *them*.'

'One of who?'

'Effie's mob.'

'I'm family.'

'No, you're not,' she says sternly.

'I'm Effie's daughter,' I state.

'I'm not stupid. I know that, but around here you're not even close to being *real* family. Don't go thinking that being Effie's girl will buy you anything in this neck of the woods. Se Busca isn't normal. Trust me. It's its own world. And, if you don't mind me saying, not a nice world. Your mother was right in the middle. Queen Bee, shall we say. Se Busca spun on her axis and the occupants with it. With Effie gone there's a vacuum and if there's one thing that's certain, it's that nature hates a vacuum. And if you think you're the heir apparent, you're not. There's way too much self-interest around here for an outsider to get in that easily.'

I'm not quite sure how to respond. I go to open my mouth but she puts her hand up to silence me.

'I'm not quite finished,' she says. 'Things have been more tense than usual around here. Something is going on and it involves the Ex-Patriots.'

'The who?'

'The Ex-Patriots?'

'Who are they?'

She studies me. I feel like I'm being assessed for a job I never applied for and have been found wanting.

'George, Jordan, Sheryl, Skid, Saucy, Zia and your mum. The Ex-Patriots.'

'The Ex-Patriots?'

'A play on expatriates,' she explains. 'They are the real power-house around here and your mum was their leader. I'd love to say they were a force for good but I'd be lying. They are out to feather their own nests. And they were up to something of late. I've no idea what, but they'd become even more secretive recently. Very early-morning meets in the back of the pub, like on the day of your mum's funeral, that sort of thing.'

'And my mum was the *leader*?'

'Effie was up front, out front, lots of front. That was your mum. I don't mean to speak ill of Effie but you should know the truth. She was in with a bad lot. And whatever they were up to, her death may have blown it wide open. If I were you I'd watch my step and maybe even think about locking a few doors behind you.'

'You're kidding?'

'Daniella, around here kidding isn't something that gets much of an airing. I'm serious.'

With that she leaps in the car, leaving me standing.

On my own.

11

The To-Do List

The scent of bleach hangs in the air as I push into the pub. Mixed with furniture polish it almost, but not quite, overcomes the deeply embedded stench of booze. I take Dine's advice and lock the door behind me. It makes me feel more secure but only a little. I nip behind the bar and into the cellar. Dine has tidied it up, neat, well organised. I fumble through the keys on the fob until I find the one for the office and open it up.

The room is small, barely fifty feet square. A squat table supports an ageing PC with an oversized armchair sitting behind it. A gun metal grey filing cabinet lurks in one corner and an Ikea bookshelf in another. The bookshelf is full of crime novels. On the floor, next to the filing cabinet, is a black safe. The door is open and the inside is empty. I try the filing cabinet and notice that the lock is broken, forced open at some point. The bottom two drawers contain glasses, a small plastic ice bucket and three bottles of rum. The top two drawers contain files. I flick through them. Everything from the events schedule to ancient advertising fliers and beyond, all neatly lined up and indexed. But, at some point, a large file has been extracted, leaving a hole. There's no obvious sign of any will.

The desk has one drawer and it too has a busted lock. It's full of pens, pencils and various other ragtags of stationery. I scan the bookshelf and flick open a few novels but there's no sign of any hidden paperwork. I double check the filing cabinet and come up blank. With another look round the room I realise there's nowhere else obvious to hide anything. So I look for the less obvious.

The floor is covered in a rug that, in its day, would have been a riot of colour but is now a tranquil sea of muted browns and greys. I lift up the corner to reveal floorboards. I look for any loose boards. Nothing. I check the walls and the ceiling and conclude that the game's a bogie.

I kneel down to examine the safe more thoroughly. It has been jimmied open, shining scars around the lock suggesting that it was quite recent. I examine the lock on the filing cabinet and the one on the desk drawer. I'm no forensic expert but the damage to all three looks fresh.

Someone has been in here recently, searching.

And one gets you fifty I know who it is.

I take out my phone and text Señor Cholbi. *Definitely no sign of any will. Can you kick off the process?*

The reply is swift. *What does Señor Laidlaw say?*

I reply. *I cannot get a hold of him. He's not returning my calls or texts. I need to start sorting this out. Can you please just start the process?*

A reply pings back. *I can, but I need some money on account. Say 500 euros.*

Okay. I'll drop it in this morning.

I exit the office and lock the door behind me. Back in the pub I look at the coffee machine. I wish I knew how to operate the thing. I settle for a Coke and plonk myself on the stool I've now adopted as my own.

I pick up a nearby notepad and scribble on it.

TO DO
- Drop keys with Dine.
- Drop 500 euros with Cholbi.
- Track down George.
- Meet/find/suss out Pat. Pay Pat?
- Read/action list from Clyde, when it arrives.
- Darts league, weekend football etc—ask Zia?
- Clear Mum's flat.
- Let my work know I'll not be in.
- A million other things.

I smile at the last line and text my employer that I need a week off. The reply is curt.

May not be a job when you get back. My company is clueless on the HR front.

And I'm clueless on what is really going on around here. I don't know any of the people who seem to be circling my life at the moment. There's Dine's cryptic warning about the Ex-Patriots. George asking me about the missing money. Saucy having a pop at me about being a thief. Skid stealing the will. All of it stacks like a pile of paving slabs about to fall over and crush my legs.

I pour myself another Coke and look around the bar. It's well stocked but mostly with brands I don't know. High up on the gantry are a few upmarket whisky brands. All look like they've been sitting there since the Stone Age. The glass washer is open and empty, glassware neatly stacked and racked under the bar. The till is open and empty and I wonder where the cash is. Then I remember the tins that Clyde talked about. The cupboard below is locked and I try to open it but none of the keys on the key ring I have fit it.

I'm flicking the white ball around the pool table, thinking, when there's a knock on the door. I hesitate to open it. Just for a second. Dine's warning in my head. I shake the thought loose and unlock the door.

Zia is standing there.

'Hi,' I say, stepping back to let him enter. 'Thanks for coming.'

'No problem,' he replies.

He looks good in black jeans, a white T-shirt and black trainers.

'I'd offer you a coffee,' I say as I walk to the bar, 'but I think you need a degree in astrophysics to operate the machine.'

'I think I know how to work it but a water will be fine.'

'Tap?'

'Bottled, please.'

It takes me a few seconds to track down the water. It lies in a chest chiller beneath the lager font.

I pass the water over to him with a glass.

'Ice?' I ask.

'No thanks.'

I drop on to my bar stool and Zia sits next to me.

'Look,' I say, 'I'm sorry to bother you on this. I know we don't know each other but given what's happened I need a little help with the pub.'

'I don't like to run the bar on my own.'

'I get that but if you can just help out tonight I'll figure something for the next few days.'

'The darts teams will want fed. Sandwiches and lots of them.'

'Did Mum make the sandwiches?'

'Effie,' he laughs. 'God no. Effie knew how to programme a microwave and that was as far as her culinary skills stretched. If you call Vicente at El Pan in the port he'll know what to do and when to drop stuff off.'

'El Pan?'

'A *panaderia*—you know, a baker's?'

'Oh. When do I call?'

'You should have called yesterday. I tell you what, *I'll* do it on my way back home. We are a good customer I'll see if he can turn it around for us.'

'Thanks.'

'Se Busca goes on,' he says.

'Sorry.'

'It's the sort of unofficial motto of the pub. It means that come hell or high water, life goes on around here.'

'Sounds a bit cold.'

He nods. Zia has a warmth about him that seems at odds with his Ex-Patriot friends. The fact that he came along to see me at such short notice just adds to the impression of open-heartedness.

'I agree, but it's what it is within these walls,' he replies.

'What about the football at the weekend? Will that be hard to handle?'

'I wouldn't sweat that. As long as the telly is on and the drink is flowing then it'll be fine. But you'll probably need help at the bar.'

'Are you free?'

'I'm not sure. Let's do tonight and we'll see how it goes.'

I relax a little. 'So you'll come tonight?'

'Only if you shadow Tara this afternoon. Then I'll help. At least you'll know the basics before we have to work together.'

'Clyde said you usually sing somewhere on Friday nights?'

'No tonight. Night off.'

I stretch out a foot and catch Zia staring at me.

'What?' I ask.

'You know, you don't look anything like Effie. Has anyone ever told you that?'

'Except the hair.'

He laughs, a gentle sound. 'True, you have your mum's wild hair but not her weight or her features.'

'When I was younger Mum told me I took after my father.'

'Effie didn't talk about him to me.'

'She didn't talk to me about him either. I've no idea who he is or if he's still alive.'

'That must be tough.'

'I get by, but it would have been nice to know who he was.'

He leans in a little and a light whiff of sandalwood scent comes with him.

'You didn't talk to your mum much?' he says.

'No, I didn't. We fell out last time I was here.'

'And you've not heard from her since then.'

'Cards and a thirty-second call at Christmas.'

'Nothing else?'

'Like what?'

He backs off. 'Oh, nothing. Just asking.'

It sounded like more than that. Like we were just about to get into a Q and A.

'Look, Daniella, I need to be going,' he announces.

'Already?'

'Why, is there anything else we need to talk about?'

'A lot and not a lot. I'm doing the fish out of water bit here.'

'Did Effie leave you the pub in her will?'

The question is from left field and catches me cold.

'Eh . . .'

'I only ask as it seems you are taking on the place.'

'It would be mine anyway. Mum owned it.'

'Maybe.'

'What does that mean?'

'Effie was thinking of selling. In fact, she might even have done something about it. I'd check it out if I was you. It would be a bit awkward if she'd sold it and the new owner arrives.'

There's another knock on the door. A hard, incessant knocking that goes on longer than is polite. I look at Zia.

'Who would that be?' I ask.

'I've no idea,' Zia says.

I cross to the door and open it. A small, barrel-chested man with arms and legs the size of tree trunks rolls in.

'Are you Effie's daughter?' he says as he reaches over a vast belly to shovel an enormous T-shirt, soaked in sweat, into his shorts.

'I am,' I reply.

'Where's my fucking money?'

Zia appears beside me. 'Simon, this has nothing to do with Daniella.'

'What doesn't?' I ask.

'Twenty grand,' Simon says. 'I need it back now.'

'Who owes you twenty thousand euros?' I ask.

'Effie, your mother,' he shouts, continuing to stuff his T-shirt away. 'She took twenty thousand for a fucking scam and I want my money back or I'm going to the police.'

Zia takes point, standing in front of me. 'Simon, this isn't the time or the place. George is the one you need to talk to.'

'He's blanking me. I'm sick of calling him.'

'He will get back to you. He knows what's what with Effie. I don't and Daniella certainly doesn't.'

'Fuck off,' he spits. 'Zia MacFarlane, it's you and the fucking Ex-Patriots who are all in this together. I'm not stupid.'

'And I'm telling you,' Zia says, 'that George is the person you need to talk to. There's nothing for you here.'

Simon looks unsure of what to do next. He stares at me and back to Zia.

'I'm not leaving,' he splutters, 'till I see my money. I've people on my back. This morning a brick came through my window. So I'm not going anywhere.'

'Yes, you are,' comes a voice from the door.

Simon spins and George steps from the light into the dark.

'Laidlaw, why have you been blanking me?' Simon says. 'Where's my fucking cash? I need it now.'

'I've been blanking you Simon, because I don't take kindly to be sworn at on my answer machine. I don't know what you've heard or think you've heard but nothing has changed with Effie dying.'

George glances at me when he says this.

'Now, Simon,' he says. 'Please leave and I'll catch up with you at Karen's place for a coffee at noon. Then we'll see what is what. You were here when Effie died so a bit of decorum with her daughter wouldn't go amiss.'

'You were here when Mum died?' I stutter.

He ignores me.

'Sure, George,' Simon shouts, 'and what are you going to do at Karen's place? Make up some bloody fantastic story about how everything is okay, the land is fine, the access is fine, the money is cool. Eh?'

'I'll tell you what I will say if you don't leave,' George replies. 'I'm seeing the Charles brothers at lunch time. I'll tell them that you were in here screaming for money. They'll love that because that sounds a whole lot like you don't have a pot to piss in and you are in far too deep with them for that. They won't take well to the news you are broke. A brick through the window will be the least of your worries. So leave now and I'll see you at twelve. Or stay and I'll make the call.'

Simon doesn't move at first. His face is scarlet, eyes wild. He says nothing but, after a few seconds, turns and walks out the door. George follows behind and turns the key to lock the door.

George stands, looking at the door, flicking the key ring with his finger. He speaks without turning. 'Zia, you can stay or you can go.'

Zia walks up to George. 'If it's all the same I'd rather stay.'

George turns around. 'A threesome it is,' he says. 'Zia, can you work that coffee machine?'

'At a push.'

'Can you see if it will push out a coffee or two?'

'I'll try.'

'Okay, Daniella,' George says, sitting at a nearby table. 'You and I have some serious fucking business to talk about.'

12

George

'Daniella, do you know why I'm here?' George says as Zia tries to coax the espresso machine into life.

'Something to do with money?' I venture.

'Daniella, everything is to do with money. Tell me something that isn't. I mean do you know why I'm here, in El Descaro?'

'No.'

'Your mother, that's why.'

'How so?'

'I helped her buy this place. Did the legals and much more.'

'More?'

'There's a lot you don't know, Daniella.'

His tone is teeth setting. Smug with a coating of arrogance.

'I know that you were struck off back home,' I retort. 'And I hear you slip locals the real work out here that you can no longer do. So, what exactly *did* you do for Mum?'

It's a cheap shot but the man has been riding me since I got into town.

'Don't be so naive, Daniella. What are you trying to do? Offend me? The real work around here *is* the up-front shit. Not the crossing the Ts and dotting the fucking legal Is that the pen-pushers do. That's the easy bit. I've got credibility around here. Not that you'd know.'

Nerve. Hit.

'Is there a point in there?' I ask. 'Other than blowing your own trumpet?'

'There is and it's to do with my relationship with your mother and the small matter of some missing cash.'

'What, the twenty k that the midget bodybuilder was just on about?'

The smell of the coffee being brewed cracks the atmosphere. Zia is humming. It sounds like the song that he told me had charted for him.

'Twenty thousand?' says George. 'Twenty grand is sod all in the scheme of things.'

So, the money I've stashed in the Safety Deposit + isn't all of it, or maybe even any of it.

'It's a lot of money to that guy Simon,' I say. 'And I wouldn't say no to twenty grand if you have it lying around spare.'

'Black or *con leche*?' shouts Zia from behind the bar. 'I think I have this thing on the run.'

'Black for me,' says George.

'Can I have milk?' I say.

We wait until Zia comes over with three coffees. He places them on the table and sits next to George, opposite me. Two v. one is the way it's going to be.

'Okay, George,' I say. 'Let's get this done. Say whatever it is you need to say. After all, you're the one trying to lead this little choir now Mum's gone.'

Zia throws him a sideways glance when I say this.

'How do you figure that?' he asks.

'Well, let's see,' I say ' You've not returned a single call or a text from me. A stream of people came in last night looking for you and you were AWOL. Simon there has been hunting you down and only just found you. I reckon you've been working on the money problem, whatever the problem is, trying to figure it out. Which places you as the lead on this, unless all the others are buzzing away trying to fix whatever it is you're trying to fix.'

Zia smiles. 'She's not stupid, George. You've been taking on Effie's role right enough.'

'Someone has to,' George says.

'And,' I add, 'I'd guess you've failed to find the money and you suspect I know where it is, so now you need me in on the loop. And that's why you're here.'

'Not stupid at all,' says Zia.

George grimaces, 'Aye, not stupid and not much of a daughter.'

I let that one ride. He's trying to put me on the back foot. Rile me. I may not be of his world but I'm well used to dealing with the irate, the irrational and the devious. Every working day of my life I grace the telephone line of JustYou Insurance. I'm on the front line of the claims side of business. Handling people is all part of the job and there are a few golden rules in my game. Firstly, and it's always first, do not get emotionally wound up by the client and their problems. As my boss says, at least half a dozen times a day, 'Cool is good. Hot is not.' It sounds like something from a fortune cookie but it is his one and only decent piece of advice. Cool always wins.

My own personal way of dealing with hotheads is not to lose sight of what any conversation is *really* about. Punters will try anything to pull the wool. My favourite moment of late was a call from a young man claiming that he'd been decorating his living room and had accidentally spilled a pot of paint on his carpet. The carpet was, of course, expensive. The paint damage, of course, extensive. The request was not for a new carpet, it was, of course, for cash. In an attempt to railroad me, the caller had gone on the offensive from minute one. Always a sign of someone on the con. I'd explained that, much as he'd like a cheque in the post that day, my company had a process and it was highly unlikely we would pay cash anyway. More likely we'd replace the carpet. That didn't go down well. Neither did my request for the original invoice and any photographs of the damage. He got angry. According to him we were shits. He got down and personal claiming he'd paid his premiums for years and now *I* was trying to cheat him. I didn't rise to the bait. When he stated that he was a first-time claimant I'd calmly read the history on the computer scheme and pointed out that this was the third claim from the same address. His wife having unsuccessfully made two earlier demands. I read them to him. A burnt sofa (cigarette burns) and a cooker fire. Both had been rejected. The claimant called me a cheating little fucker and at that point I should have hung up but I didn't. With my computer prompt screen flashing red, beware, I simply stayed on track, with a warning on language. With no photographs and no carpet—it would seem that the carpet had already been disposed of—I explained that we couldn't settle the claim as we required proof of the damage. He told me it happened three days ago and that the carpet was so bad they'd had to sling it out and had only just got around to calling. The carpet was worth at least two thousand pounds, he said. His actual words were *two fucking grand*. Second language warning. Three and you're out. According to the claimant this was more than I earned in a month. Which was true. And that people like me got joy out of ripping off the hard working. Not strictly true—but not as far from the truth as it should be. I stuck to the script. Kept control. No carpet—no claim. Suddenly the caller had an amazing piece of information to impart. The said carpet may have been thrown out but it was still residing in the back garden. Well, I said, here we have an opportunity, I'll despatch an investigator to examine the carpet and if all is right we can settle this. Cue another burst of anger. Why won't a photo now suffice? Because, I said, I need to have such an expensive carpet professionally assessed, I bullshitted. These items can sometimes be saved by a good restorer.

The claimant had two choices. Back off and admit he was at it or let the investigator see the carpet. He chose the latter route.

The report from the investigator was simple. Yes, there was a carpet. Yes, it had plenty of paint on it. And no, we shouldn't settle.

I'd called to impart the news to the claimant. I didn't have to. The report came in when I was going off shift. I could have flung it to a colleague to handle but I didn't want to. I wanted to make the call. And so I rang, and told the claimant we wouldn't be paying. Why?—was the howling cry of anguish on the phone—*why* was I declining a fucking genuine claim? I'd said that there were two simple reasons for declining the claim. Firstly, the carpet in question was worth, at best, one hundred and fifty pounds and with a two-hundred-pound excess on the policy there was no point in settling. He'd screamed at me, claiming the investigator couldn't tell a decent piece of cloth for one you'd wipe your arse with.

'*What is the second reason?*'

'*When did this accident happen?*'

'*Last Monday.*'

'*Six days ago?*'

'*Yes.*'

'*Six days ago, you spilt paint on the carpet.*'

'*Yes.*'

'*Could you tell me why, after a full five days, when our invest-igator got there, that not only was the paint still wet, it was so wet it was dripping from the edges?*'

In my world, everyone is on the con. Full stop. And the key is to stay in control.

I look at George. Insults or not, he's not going to steer this ship.

'George, is that how this goes down?' I say. 'You resorting to personal slights? If so, I'll be off and you can drop me a text with whatever it is you want to say.'

'George, really?' says Zia.

George is not the apologising sort. He just rattles on. 'Okay, let's cut to the chase. Your mother owes us a lot of money.'

He leaves that hanging there, searching my eyes for a reaction. I give little.

'And?' I say.

'And we want it.'

'George, I'm sure you do but, as you may or may not know, I'm not exactly flush with cash.'

I pause, wondering if he knows about the money in the security box down at the port.

'I don't care about your shitty little bank account,' he says. 'I care about the money your mother had.'

'For the sake of clarity, how much are we talking about?' I ask.

'Enough.'

'Enough for what?'

'Enough.'

'You're not going to tell me. Are you?'

'It's enough.'

Control time.

'George, I play this game at work. We call it hold-back.'

'What?' says George.

'What you are doing is known in my game as hold-back. It's an old trick. Probably one you used a lot as a lawyer. You have a vital piece of information that only the guilty party could know. If they reveal they know the info—bang, they are guilty. So you hold it back. That way if the guilty party slips up and mentions it—you have them cold. In this case you are holding back the exact sum of cash you are owed by my mother in the hope that I'll mention a number. If I do you'll know I know more than I'm letting on. Hold-back. Simples.'

Zia can't help but laugh a little, 'She's got your measure, George. I hadn't even thought of that.'

George pounds the table, 'You think you're a smart arse, Daniella?'

'No, I don't,' I say. 'I don't think anything of the sort. But I do get my chain pulled for a living. That I have to live with. But I don't put up with it very well in my private life. And you, George Laidlaw, are yanking that private chain. So, get the fuck on with it. My mum owed you money. So what? You're the legal expert—doesn't the debt die with the person?'

'Not always,' he replies, his volume on an upward trajectory. 'But in this case it doesn't matter. This isn't the sort of debt that plays by any normal rules. This is the kind of debt that gets paid back no matter what the fuck you, Daniella Coulstoun, think or do.'

Zia isn't comfortable with the way this is going. He slides his chair back, unconsciously putting some distance between him and George. I'm more sanguine about it all. I'm guessing the thirty-six grand I found really isn't the 'it' in this. I'm thinking the number is much larger. And clearly George thinks that I can find it. That's why he's here. And if he's been trying to track it down and I'm his best bet, well, George is putting a lot of his future on me knowing something. And I know sod all. But, as they say, that still puts me right in the driving seat—even if I don't have a blind clue where he's going with this.

'George,' I say, 'given you've had a good root around Mum's stuff I must be a bit of a last resort.'

'I've touched nothing of your mother's,' he snarls.

'Sure you haven't,' I say. 'What about the missing box from Mum's flat? Or the busted safe through there,' I point to the back bar. 'Or the busted desk lock and then there's also the broken filing cabinet. All fresh. All you?'

He blanks that. 'Daniella, we will get this money back.'

'I know of no money, George. Okay, to be fair, I've not seen Mum's financial position yet. She could have been loaded. But I doubt it. Her flat is decorated in late last owner. The pub needs more licks of paint than a 1930s freight steamer and last time Mum offered me any cash I was popping acne. Anyway, I've got a lawyer looking into it all.'

'Cholbi?'

'Yes.'

'I could have helped. There was no need to go to him.'

'Funny, George. Real funny. Help me? Given the way you've behaved since I landed, why the hell would I ask for your help on anything? Anyway, there's probably no need to wait on Mum's finances being revealed, you already know there's nothing there. You wouldn't be here otherwise.'

'I've no idea what your mum has in the bank.'

'Give it a rest, George. It's just one lie after the other. In the filling cabinet,' I flick my thumb towards the door in the back bar again, 'there's a file missing. A gap. A file that sat between the tab marked Electricity and the one marked Golf Day. So maybe one starting with the letter F. It was a big file. The gap is large. I'd guess it was called Finance. Stuff like Mum's bank statements. The works. So you know fine where she's at financially. Lying about this shit just makes me want to get up and walk out.'

Zia flushes a little. 'Daniella, you have to understand, we are talking a lot of cash here.'

'So you say. And I'll say it again. I've no idea what you are on about.'

George stands up, cracks his knuckles and crosses to the bar. He pulls a bottle of whisky from the gantry.

'A bit early,' I say to him. 'I thought it was that guy Saucy who had the issue.'

George ignores me, pours a couple of fingers into a glass and drops in a few ice cubes.

'Effie was a good woman,' George says, his voice less on edge as he sips the liquid. 'Not the warmest person I've ever met but she knew how to look after those who looked after her. I thought I knew her well, better than most, and then she goes and does this to me.'

'*You?* Shouldn't there be an *us* in that sentence, George,' I say, looking at Zia.

'Fuck off, Daniella,' he says.

He paces a little.

'Daniella,' he says. 'I'm now going to give you a little lesson on Spanish law. Something for you to chew on. To think about. There's a body out there called the Office for Asset Recovery and Management. It has a Spanish title but the English will do for now. It was set up in response to something called Article 10 of Directive 2014/42/EU of the European Parliament, passed on the third of April, 2014.'

'Riveting,' I say.

'It centres on the freezing and confiscation of instrumentalities and proceeds of crime in the European Union.'

'Wow.'

'Now there's a bunch of Spanish laws that apply here but in essence this organisation is tasked with recovering any assets they can from criminals.'

'You should ask Spielberg to make it into a film.'

George sits on a bar stool and takes another slug of whisky. 'And this bar we are sitting in, along with Effie's flat and the money she has in her bank account are all fair game for this organisation.'

I bite. 'And why would that be?'

'You might not know it but both the flat and this pub are debt free. And, since you are her only daughter and heir, they are also both yours. So, I would ask a simple question—doesn't it worry you that all of this might be taken away?'

'George, I didn't even know they were debt free until you told me.'

'Probably three to four hundred grand in value, all told. This pub might look rough but it turns good money. A nice earner. The flat is a little run-down but prices in the old town have rocketed lately. What do you earn back home, Daniella? Minimum wage?'

I keep my peace.

'You could have a good life here, Daniella. House, business, and it all pays a damn sight more than minimum. Sun *and* money—and I could make it all walk away tomorrow.'

'Can't you say anything straight—or do you have to dance around every subject?'

He drops off the stool and starts to pace the room again. In his mind's eye he's back in court, in his legal heyday, delivering the coup de grâce to some poor soul.

'Okay, I'll be straight,' he says. 'For a start the pub and the house have nothing to do with the money we are owed. But that doesn't mean they are clean. Your mum washed up on this godforsaken shore with barely a penny to her name. Now, I'd like to say that she quietly worked away, building the business and paying off her debts like a good taxpaying resident. Except I can't. Effie wasn't the sort to wait. She short-circuited the earnings process and paid zero to the Spanish tax boys. The pub, the flat, were paid off years ago and well before any legitimate cash could have done so.'

'Ah,' I say. 'Let me take a wild stab. I help find your money or you let leak about the dark and devious ways my mother earned her cash to this Office for Asset Management and they take it all away.'

'Office for Asset Recovery and Management,' he corrects. 'But exactly. Good girl. You help and I say nothing. You blank me and this whole lot goes.'

I rise. More to stop George taking the high ground than a need to stretch.

'What a load of bollocks, George. The pub and flat are no longer Mum's. They are mine. How can this organisation claim anything that's mine?'

'I'll send you the relevant web link if you want,' George says with a quiet smugness. 'But, trust me, go ask Cholbi if you want, they can most certainly chase you down. And they will. It happens all the time.'

Zia is watching the exchange like a punter at a tennis match. Only I notice that when George speaks a darkness passes over his eyes. And when I speak they sparkle a little. Or maybe my imagination is in town for a party.

'You seem to think this is a big threat,' I say, walking over to the bar. 'That I'll bend over backwards to protect my legacy. Well, George, let me point out that two days ago I didn't even know I had a legacy. If you're saying all this might vanish into the coffers of the Spanish judicial system, so what? So what?'

George doesn't respond right away. He moves to a wall adorned with ancient music posters and specifically to a corner with local ads. He pulls a few flyers free, selects one and pins the others back. He drains his glass as he drops a flyer on the bar in front of me. It's for something called 'El Descaro Vibe'. A festival that was held two years ago. It's in Spanish but I can discern enough to figure out a list of bands had played at it over a two-day period. I don't recognise any of the bands.

'What's this?' I enquire.

'It used to run every year,' George says. 'Down on the beach. A music festival and a carnival. Your mum set it up, maybe ten years back. It did quite well. Started small—a single night across a few bars, including Se Busca, broke out into an all-day affair in the car park outside here and finally it moved to the beach and became quite a large event.'

'I've never heard of any of the bands.'

Zia chips in, 'Not back in the UK you wouldn't but here in Spain some of them are household names.'

He points to one called *La Pandilla Mezclada*.

'It means The Mix Gang,' Zia says. 'There were five in the band.'

'Five plus one,' says George. 'Zia sang with them for a few years.'

'We had a record deal,' Zia says. 'But it never quite worked out. Still, the band had a couple of chart hits in Spain before I joined. They could draw a fair crowd. Same for some of the others on this list.'

'Says a lot for your mum, in her late sixties, setting this all up,' George adds. 'Pity it got canned.'

'I suppose there's a point to this little story or are we on another trip round the long way?' I say.

'Only that your mum had a knack for turning a buck.'

'So why did the festival shut down if she was so good?'

'Two years ago she knew she needed some serious licences to get any bigger and also required a large upfront cash injection. As I said, your mum could turn a buck but she also knew when to walk away from something. Everyone told her she should keep going with the festival. It was a real success. But she got chatting to a few people in the festival world. The heads-up was how hard it was to make good money, year in year out. So she quit.'

'Okay, so you say Mum was good at this stuff. But she wasn't that good. Festival aside, she had a bar, a small flat and not enough cash in the bank. Not exactly Bill Gates.'

'Better than most around here,' says George.

'And that's supposed to convince me that her legacy is worth fighting for.'

George pours himself another whisky. A large one. He digs out some more ice. 'Are you sure you don't want a drink, Daniella?'

'I struggle with coffee at this time. Alcohol would lay me out for the day.'

'I hope you don't mind if I do.'

'What choice do I have?'

'Okay, Daniella,' he says, dropping on to the stool next to me. 'You blank us and I'll guarantee that all this goes bye-bye. If you think all the hard work your mum put in is worth pissing away. Feel free.'

'What evidence do you have?'

'About what?'

'That Mum's legacy is illegal.'

'Glad you asked, Daniella,' he says. 'Just recently, I've spent a few hours reminiscing. Noting where your mum's money came from over the years. How little tax was paid. How many cash deals were done. Who she did them with. You know the sort of thing, just the run of the mill criminality. I had most of it tucked away in my head—but the file through there helped.' He points to the cellar. 'So

I wrote it all down. Filed it with a lawyer friend. An "anything happens to me please hand this to the right people" sort of lawyer friend.'

'And you'll be clean in all of this? Your name won't appear in any of these "deals"?'

George rubs the rim of his glass and lifts his finger to his lips.

'Of course my name will appear,' he says, licking his nails. 'But given the shit storm that's about to descend over the money your mother has stolen from us, that will be nothing. I'll happily live with the risk.'

'And that's your threat? I lose the pub and flat. Something I never had.'

'You lose more than that. You're the daughter, Daniella. How much did you know about her dealings out here?'

'Nothing.'

'Are you sure? Did you benefit? Maybe my reminiscing is hazy but I'm sure that Effie mentioned your name a few times. Especially relating to the nastier of her co-conspirators. You know, I'm certain she said that some of the real good money earners were down to you. Isn't that right Zia?'

Zia says nothing, looking anywhere but at me.

'That's crap,' I say. 'Who the hell would believe any of that, whatever that is? I saw Mum three times in twenty years. Talked to her maybe a dozen times. Hardly the buddy-buddy relationship of a criminal duo.'

'So you say, Daniella. But in these days of encrypted WhatsApp, anonymous email accounts, burner phones—who knows what's possible? All I know is that some of the names on my sheet that did deals with your mum are not guys who will take kindly to being dropped in it if I leak what really went on around here. And with your mother out of the picture then you are a nice juicy worm waiting to be squished.'

I push back from the bar.

'I'm out of here.' Then I think on that. 'No, George, *you* are out of here. This is my place. It's bad enough you've treated me like some piece of crap on your shoe since I got here. That you don't even have the common courtesy to return my calls. That you're freeloading on my drink. Forget all that. Now it's some half-arsed blackmail attempt. Piss off, George. You're a fucking failed lawyer in a backwater dump trying to play the big man. A failure of a man who got struck off for dipping his sticky hands in the till. And all you've done, in the last fifteen minutes, is to reinforce what a bent piece of shite you are.'

'Don't you fucking badmouth me, girl,' he grunts.

'Or what, George, or what? Eh? I'm not a *girl*. I'm a woman and not one that's worried about some made up scribblings. So just give it a fucking break and piss off.'

George moves towards me. 'Do you know who—'

I shoot forward, pushing down hard on my heels. 'Do you know who I am? Is that what you were going to say? George, go play with yourself.'

I'm inches from his face, blood boiling. *Cool is good*, cool is gone.

'George, I don't care who you are,' I shout. 'I don't know you and I don't want to get to know you. Right now, you're breathing air that good people need. The sort of people who care about someone else other than themselves. So, do us all a favour and . . . stop . . . fucking . . . breathing . . .'

George slams his hand on the bar and, for a second, I think he's going to hit me.

'Stop it,' Zia shouts. 'Both of you, stop it.'

I storm over to the pool table, pick up the white ball and launch it at the wall. It embeds itself in the plasterboard.

I hear George roar behind me. 'You're an evil fucking witch,' he shouts.

Zia has George by the wrist, pulling him back, shouting, 'George, sit down.'

'My mum must have been blind to you,' I snarl at George. 'You're a piece of piss. Now get out.'

He moves again but Zia has both hands round his left wrist acting as an anchor.

'Just leave. Leave right now,' I say.

He wriggles a little to free himself from Zia.

He shakes his head. 'This isn't over, Daniella. Not by any stretch of the imagination. Your mum stiffed us for a lot of money and I think you know something about that. So, I'm not going to vanish, or lie down, or crawl away. That isn't going to happen.'

He heads for the door.

'Take a last look at your pub,' he says. 'By tomorrow it'll be crawling with police and you'll be up to your neck in explanations that you don't have.'

He slams through the door.

Zia flops into a chair. 'God,' he says. 'I've never seen him like that.'

'He's a nasty piece of work,' I say.

'Never like that,' he repeats. 'Angry, yes. Shouting, yes. But I really thought he was going to hit you.'

'So did I. Maybe you don't know him that well.'

'Twenty years, Daniella. I've known him twenty years. You really got under his skin.'

'Or the missing money has. Money has a way of changing people. Tell me, how much does he think my mother took?'

'A lot.'

'What's a lot?'

He pauses, then slowly says, 'Between the seven of the Ex-Patriots there's supposed to be 1.3 million euros lying around somewhere.'

Shit.

13

The Black Hole

'Zia,' I say as I exit and close the pub door behind me, welcoming both the heat and the air as they take me away from the toxic atmosphere inside. 'Are you going to tell me what in the hell my mother was doing with 1.3 million euros?'

Zia follows me across the car park.

'It's complicated,' he says.

'I'm sure it is. But try me.'

'Let's walk,' he says.

'Good for me. I need to go to the old town anyway,' I say. Partly because I need to cool down from the incident with George. But also because I need to hand the pub keys back to Dine at the *mercat* and pay Señor Cholbi his five hundred euros. I'm not going near the Safety Deposit + for any cash. I've enough from Mum's stash in my pocket. The Twins are part of this Ex-Patriot thing and I don't want them seeing what is in that box. If they find out that it's full of cash that will just telegraph all the wrong things to George.

As Zia and I begin to walk, the air stirs with the buzz of insects and the distant hum of the main road lying a quarter of a mile away. We are the only people on this stretch of pavement. I let Zia get his thoughts in order while mine are still scrambling over what George has got me into.

'Zia,' I eventually say. 'Was what George said about the way Mum earned the money for the pub and flat right? And will he really grass up how she earned her cash?'

I'm not expecting an honest answer. He's one of George's friends. But I have to ask.

'Daniella, you need to understand a little background first.'

'Do I?'

'Yes, you do. You don't know any of us. Saucy, Skid, George, the Twins, me. How could you? You probably think that we're a bunch of failed UK dropouts.'

I don't answer.

'It's what you get out here from some people, especially those that are out on holiday. They think we couldn't cut it back in Blighty and opted for the easy life in the sun. Or they think we're running away from something, or someone. That we're hiding, doing nothing useful and whiling away the hours until we die.'

This is not a new train of thought for him. It sounds well worn. At that moment a sun-mottled car rattles past before saying good-bye to us with a belch of fumes.

'Well,' he continues. 'Unless you've got money in the bank, life ain't that easy here. It's a bit cheaper to live, sure, but jobs are thicker on the ground for the Spanish than the expats. A lot of people work hard out here. Take me. I sing six, sometimes seven nights a week. But you just see a failed eighties pop star with a stupid dream.'

'Zia, I know nothing about you or your career. I have no idea what your dreams are.'

'Daniella, I'm in my fifties and had a hit single nearly forty years ago. Now I'm singing at midnight to a bunch of lushes who would rather drink than listen. I know I'm not going to return to the charts, or anything like that. I know those days are gone but I like perform-ing and I think I still have a future in better places than I'm frequenting now. I really am trying to record an album. But you need some cash to do that. A little butter to pay for some time in a recording studio. A little soap to smooth out the financial bump that comes when you stop working to focus on your dream. And I don't have that cash.'

'And wouldn't that be as true back home as it is here?'

'Sure, but life looks at you in an odd way when you live here. It promises so much more and what it all comes down to is that it's warmer, you can do more outdoors and the rest is still a slog.'

'And you came out here for an easier time and it isn't easier? Is that what you're telling me?'

'Yes,' he says, signalling to cross the road. 'I thought there was a better chance of reviving my singing career here. Effie thought so too. But I was wrong. She was wrong. It's harder.'

'But there's no end of bars and restaurants. Places to perform.'

'There's no end of tourist bars and restaurants looking for cheap acts that can meld into the background or to lead a chorus of ABBA classics. Not exactly the sort of place an ex-pop star can be rediscovered.'

'So why stay here?'

'You can't escape a black hole.'

I step over a dog turd that looks like it was shit by a Clydesdale. 'Black hole?' I say.

'El Descaro's the original black hole. Massive gravity. No way out. You try to leave and it pulls you back in.'

'Come on Zia, anyone can leave.'

'It's harder than you'd think.'

'What is? Leaving the draw of nice weather and cheap booze? Is that it?'

'In part, but it's also admitting you failed. Going back to the UK with no story of success is a sore place to go. I know some that have done it. The conversation is always the same back home. People asking why you left Spain. Why are you back enduring the wind and the rain? And you have no good reason that makes any sense or that anyone believes. Daniella, what would you say if you knew someone that had been out here for two decades and they roll back into your neighbourhood?'

'If they moved back to my scheme, I'd think they were off their head.'

'There you go. And the longer you stay out here the harder it gets. The more years to explain away. Years that slide by so easily. So, you convince yourself that you can still make it and then one day, if you choose to go home, you can do so with your head held up high and a backstory that will make people envious.'

We're entering the old town, buildings rising on either side.

'Okay, I get that.' Although I'm not sure I do. 'But what's the story on Mum and the money?'

'One last thing and I'll tell you about the money. You need to understand that all of us still think we have a shot at the title. Skid on his driving. The Twins in modelling. Saucy was an accountant to some serious hitters and when not on the booze can still give financial advice like no other. Even George has a smart legal brain. But every one of us needs some walking money to escape this place and help realise what dreams we have left. Or at least put them to bed once and for all and retire.'

'And this money that Mum took from you all was the solution.'

'In part.'

'So, 1.3 million euros, split seven ways. What's that? A hundred and eighty-odd grand each.' I figure. 'It's a lot, but that won't last too long and I take it it's not legal?'

He sighs.

'So,' I point out, 'that would mean you would be on the run with a less than a life-changing amount of cash.'

He sighs again. 'I know. We all got carried away. Effie told us it was going to be a bigger haul. Closer to a million each.'

'That much. Then you are well, well short.'

'And I guess that's what convinced your mother that one seventh of 1.3 million isn't life changing either. But 1.3 million is.'

'So she planned to escape with it all?'

'Given what we know—yes.'

'And where did all this money come from?'

He stops walking.

'We all own a bit of land on the seafront,' he says. 'It's contaminated and has no access to it. But around it the prices of apartments have gone ballistic in the last two years. Our land can never be worth anything. It has no access to any roads. But there's another bit of land that would allow us to build a connection, if we owned it. But we don't. It's owned by an absentee Russian who no one has seen or heard of in ten years. So Effie figured out that if we packaged our land right, pretended we had a deal for the other land and sold a good story we could make cash.'

'How?'

'Have you seen *The Producers*?'

'The film, musical?'

'Yip.'

'What about it?'

'Well, in it they figure that if they make a play that is a sure-fire flop, they can sell multiple times fifty per cent of the show to investors. And if they make a sure-fire flop for peanuts, the producers make a fortune because the backers would expect to lose their money. Effie worked out we could do the same for our land. Pull together a prospectus, convince people we were on to a winner and promise them massive returns for a share of the deal. In each case the investor pays twenty grand up front, hoping to multiple that by fifty. A deal so sweet Effie expected hundreds to dive in. All we had to do was collect the cash and run.'

'You're kidding.'

'I'm not, and it wasn't simple. It involved non-disclosure agreements to keep the investors from talking to anyone else. We had to show them apartments that they thought we had built in the past to convince them the quality was going to be top end. Brochures were needed and a ream of other stuff as we tried to string it out long enough to snare as many investors as possible.'

'It sounds nuts. Who the hell would fall for it?'

'You'd be surprised how gullible people are if they see easy money. And your mum knew just where to go to land the investors.'

'Where?'

'The sons and daughters of the expats out here,' he says, looking around. 'A lot of them were born and brought up out here. Many are bored or hate their life in the sun but can't get out. A life in the sun isn't for them. For those guys this is all they have. This is all they know. There is no road back to the UK for them because there is nothing back there. And their life here is going nowhere. Thousands of them are second generation adults feeling that they were conned. Dragged out here so Mum and Dad could sit under the sun and drink. At best they are waiting for Mum and Dad to die. At worse they are scraping by in bars and shops, washing cars, doing odd jobs—anything for cash. But they hate it. Those were the guys Effie went after. Guys who wanted to throw a finger up at their parents by landing a fortune and taking off.'

'Are there enough of those type of people with cash to invest? Twenty thousand euros is a lot of cash.'

'When you think you are going to land a million you'd be amazed how many people found a way to raise the money.'

'And it worked?'

'To the tune of 1.3 million and counting.'

'But you expected more?'

'A lot more.'

'And no one knows where this money is now?'

'No.'

'And the investors are now starting asking questions?'

'Yes.'

'And my mother took this money and put it somewhere.'

'As far as we know. Now you know why George is so mad. We all are. The money is not where it's supposed to be and now Effie is dead we can't find it. Effie was good for me. There for me. Someone to talk to. And then she does this. Takes our money. *My* money. My *escape* cash. My way out of here.'

I lean on the wall of the house we are standing in front of, feeling the radiant heat seep into my bones. Above me a woman is hanging out washing on the line, she looks down on us. On the balcony above her I can hear a baby crying, and above that, music is drifting from inside. Life is stacked on top of each around here.

'And you all think I know where this money is?' I say.

'Maybe. But even if you don't, you are in a far better place than the rest of us to find it.'

'Why is that?'

'You need to tidy up Effie's estate. You can ask the questions we can't. Look for the money by talking to people. Use the estate as cover for probing. And you can do it quickly. Because we need to find the cash yesterday. But none of *us* can ask too many questions. We'll set a hare running and the investors will get wind. And then it'll fall apart. But you can hunt with impunity. Find it. Help us.'

I stand away from the wall. The kid stops crying. The music stops playing. The woman hanging out the washing vanishes indoors and in the silence and peace I smell one big stinking rat.

'Wait a minute,' I say. 'This is a set-up?'

'What?'

There's no surprise in his face. He knows what I mean.

'This conversation,' I say. 'Is this conversation all a set-up? Did George prime you to say all this? Did he? Was this plan B if threatening to blackmail me failed?'

Zia looks back down the road. A woman out with a kid in a pram appears and squeezes past. Zia steps off the pavement to let her pass. When the woman has moved on, Zia lingers on the road.

'Well?' I say.

'I'm just trying to make you see that you can help us.'

'It *is* a bloody set-up. I'm right. George had a go at blackmail and now you're trying to do what? Make me feel sorry for you? Sorry that your little scam didn't pay off? That life out here is tough and that I can help make it better?'

'We need that money, Daniella, and you can help.'

'Well, I just told George to fuck off and I'm saying the same to you. Tell George to stay away from me and that goes for you and that crazy gang you belong to.'

I walk after the lady with the pram, shutting Zia off.

A few minutes later and I'm standing on the pavement outside Señor Cholbi's offices.

I'm so angry.

DATE: Jueves 14 de Noviembre de 2019

Esta es una copia de la traducción al inglés de la entrevista con la persona o personas nombradas.

(The following is a copy of the English translation of the interview with the subject or subjects.)

PRESENT: Capitán Lozano, Teniente Perez and Jose Cholbi

TRANSCRIPT AS FOLLOWS:

SPANISH POLICE OFFICER CAPITÁN LOZANO (CAPITÁN): *Buenas Tardes*, Señor Cholbi.

Jose Cholbi (JC): *Buenas Tardes.*

CAPITÁN L: Can you start by telling me your full name?

JC: Jose Antoine Cholbi.

CAPITÁN L: And where do you live?

JC: Carrer Barbecho in El Descaro.

CAPITÁN L: And you are a lawyer?

JC: Yes.

CAPITÁN L: Do you represent Señorita Daniella Coulstoun?

JC: You know I do.

CAPITÁN L: Can you tell me what you are representing her for?'

JC: I am helping her with the estate of her mother.

CAPITÁN L: And is there anything unusual with this estate?

JC: I am bound by client confidentiality.

CAPITÁN L: I would not ask you to break that but you must understand that there are certain aspects relating to Señora Coulstoun's death that we need to investigate.

JC: Of course.

CAPITÁN L: Can you tell me if Señorita Coulstoun was aware of her mother's activities in Spain?

JC: I cannot.

CAPITÁN L: You cannot because she did not know or because you cannot say?

JC: I cannot say.

CAPITÁN L: So it would be a surprise to Señorita Daniella Coulstoun that her mother's estate may have been obtained by illegal means?

JC: If you are asking if she was aware of her mother's activity in this country, it would not be breaking any confidence to say that, as far as I am aware, she had very little contact with Señora Coulstoun for many years. Does that answer your question?

CAPITÁN L: I do not know. However, I am led to understand that Señora Coulstoun's estate was healthy.

JC: What is healthy, Capitán Lozano? My own mother left less than two thousand euros on her death. She was disappointed she had to leave anything. Her wish was that she spent every penny she had on herself. That is what I would call a healthy estate.

CAPITÁN L: It is one way to look at it. But Señora Coulstoun's bar was a good, going concern.

JC: I would not know.

CAPITÁN L: You said you are representing Señorita Coulstoun on Señora Coulstoun's estate?

JC: As I said earlier, I am. On a few fronts. Why are you so interested in such facts?

CAPITÁN L: Because I am good at my job. You said a few fronts. What else were you helping her with?

JC: It's complicated.

CAPITÁN L: *Sighs.*

14

No Means No

'So, Señor Cholbi, what you are saying is that, if what George Laidlaw implies is true, my mother's bar and her flat are at risk of being seized.'

I'm back in the same chair I'd occupied when I'd first met Señor Cholbi in his offices. He has five hundred euros lying on his desk. He had not squirrelled it away when I'd handed him it. Instead he summoned the receptionist and asked her to provide a receipt for the money.

'Señorita Coulstoun, I do not know what risk there may be as I have no idea what your mother may or may not have done. However, Señor Laidlaw was correct when he told you about the Office for Asset Recovery and Management. It exists and exists for the purposes he outlined. And,' he adds, 'if you are aware of any reason why your mother's assets may be tainted then I would no longer be able to represent you.'

'Why not?'

'Your involvement could be classed as a criminal act. You a co-conspirator. An accessory after the fact as you would say in the UK. So, I will ask you, are you aware of any issues with the bar or apartment or the way they were funded?'

'Señor Cholbi, until less than an hour ago I wasn't even aware that my mother's bar and flat were debt free, never mind where she may or may not have got the money to pay for it all.'

'Then, Señorita Coulstoun, we are good.'

'Did you look into finding another will?'

'I have not, but now we have payment on account I will commence the proper process. But can I make one thing clear? If there are any issues with your mother's estate or even a suggestion there are issues, it will extend the whole process by quite a time and I may well have to step back.'

'How much longer will it extend it?'

'That depends on what, if any, issues arise.'

I look towards the window and wonder if Skid or Zia or George or any of the other Ex-Patriots are out there. I didn't want to react to George's threat of reporting my mum's potential criminal action. In the main because, if my mum's estate, forgetting the complexity that the missing 1.3 million might bring, is worth a few hundred thousand euros and the bar is a going concern—well, a life in the sun has its appeal. I'd thought about that as I'd dropped off the keys for Dine in the *mercat*, a gorgeous building full of specialty fresh food vendors. I'd even thought about it while sneaking in a small glass of wine, perched at one of the tables at Dine's tapas bar.

'What's next?' I ask Señor Cholbi.

'We move to probate.'

'What do we need to do that?'

'For a probate we need the death certificate. This is the most important document. I can get that from the Civil Registry. With that I'll apply to the Last Wills Registry in Madrid for a certificate stating if your mother held a will in Spain at the time of death and in which Notary's office it is being held.'

'Will that take long?'

'In Spain everything takes longer than the British think is reasonable.'

'What else?'

'I'll need to prepare a list of all your mother's assets and obtain the relevant documents to prove the existence and value of all assets. We will require bank certificates for all bank accounts stating the funds held in the accounts at the time of death. We need documents relating to any debts. We require any life insurance policies. You will need to acquire an NIE number in Spain. I will arrange for that in due course and you will need to, later on, accept the inheritance before a Notary Public. Can I also warn you that, in Spain, any death duties are payable within six months of the death? But we will get to that once we know the size of the estate.'

He stands, cracking his knuckles as he does so.

He continues. 'It is also normal to settle all outstanding bills etc prior to gaining any inheritance, although there are ways to make this easier.'

'It all sounds complex,' I say.

'It can be. Or sometimes it is simple. You said you were an only child but does your mother have any other dependents?'

'No.'

'Then it may be easy.'

'Anything else just now?'

He rests his backside on his table. 'Not for the moment, other than to warn you that crossing Señor Laidlaw was not wise.'

I'd told him about my little tête-à-tête with George.

'He was being an arsehole,' I say.

'Everyone needs an arsehole, Señorita Coulstoun.'

I smile at that and wish him well before leaving.

No one is lingering near the building when I leave. I need another coffee and return to the main square and the café I sat in not twenty-fours earlier, working my head over the issues facing me.

If my mother really has over a million euros hidden away then I don't see George or any of the others walking away from me if I'm a possible solution. The scale of the scam will see to that. The sum may not be big enough to let them change their lives but it might be enough to let them leave town for quite a while, especially if they are about to face a hoard of angry investors, not to mention the police.

I think on what George said about the flat and pub. In total, if George's valuation of the business and flat is right and I add in the missing cash—we are talking near 1.7 million euros. I also think on something that Zia said.

I text Señor Cholbi. *Zia MacFarlane said Mum may have sold Se Busca. She may also have sold the flat. Is there a quick way to check this?*

The reply comes back in a few minutes. *It will be part of the process I am undertaking to check such things. But I will put in a call to the land register just now and ask if there has been any activity.*

I'm thinking that if there is no flat, no business and the shit is about to fly on the missing scam money then my flight tomorrow is still booked—and I'm gone.

Quicker than I expect a text pings back from Cholbi. *According to the records your mother still owns both her apartment and Se Busca. She may have agreed to sell them but the transaction has not gone through yet. If she has verbally agreed it would not show. I also checked the online listings with estate agents and nothing appeared. Again, this is not definitive, it may have been a private sale.*

Inconclusive is the word on that one.

I decide that I'll go to Se Busca this afternoon and learn a few of the ropes from Tara anyway. Before that I ask the waiter for the menu and order up *una ración de albondigas y pan y aioli y una copa de vino blanco.*

The square in front of me is alive with people walking and talking. Most are wrapped up in coats, even scarves, despite the warmth. But they are used to a far hotter average temperature than me. Back in Glasgow this would be a taps-aff day—sunbathing on the mind and skipping off work the norm.

The thought of work is far from my mind but it returns as George's words about the bar, the flat and a nice life in the sun float in the lunchtime air. Pushing the scam money to one side the idea that there might be a comfortable life for me out here keeps winging its way to the front of my thoughts. Back home I'm going nowhere. I'm not motivated enough to push for promotion, nor would I want it. Most of my fellow grunts despise the bosses. The managers may get paid a little better than me but, from what I can see, those few extra pennies only bring the promise of fiercer abuse, longer hours and deeper misery. I'm not sure that a bar in Spain would be my choice and I consider the printed bar roster which tells me that although the bar might be profitable it does so because of control of costs. One person on the bar at a time is the norm.

Cash flow is obviously king and keeping costs down the money shot. Who knows, maybe I'd enjoy working a bar. After all, I've always enjoyed the flip side.

I chew on the meatballs; they're delicious and the wine begins to take the edge off this morning's insanity. I wish I had a paperback at hand to truly clean out my mind.

When Jordan and Sheryl, the Twins, appear above me, I sigh.

They sit down at the table.

'Shouldn't you two be minding the store down at the port?' I say.

Both are dressed identically—white jeans, white T-shirts and white trainers. I look at them. I'm not one for the pages of fashion magazines but neither of the twins have what I would call a classic model's face. Noses too big, eyes a little wide set, lips thin and in Jordan's case the Donald Trump haircut is definitely there to hide the male pattern baldness that's creeping in. Both are also a little on the plump side. There are jobs for the larger model but I would have thought that the market for ugly, fat and, in Jordan's case, balding models, was limited.

'We shut for siesta a bit early,' says Jordan.

'Early,' repeats Sheryl.

'It's your business. I suppose you can shut when you want,' I say.

'It's not our business, we just work there,' Jordan points out.

I push the last meatball into my mouth and begin to wipe up the gravy with the bread. I swallow and size both up. 'Did George send you?'

'No,' says Sheryl.

'No,' repeats Jordan.

They're both bad liars.

'Of course, he did. Why else would you be here? George has had a go at me. So has Zia. I assume Saucy is too drunk to be of use and I'm not sure Skid has the mental capacity to try to convince me to help. So here you both are. Your mission, having chosen to accept it, is to convince me to help you all and I'll say what I've said twice already. Eff off.'

'We need that money,' says Sheryl.

'Money,' repeats Jordan.

'So everyone keeps saying, and I keep saying the same thing. I know nothing about it.'

The waiter comes over and the two of them order a glass of *vino tinto* each, large ones.

'You may not know about the money but you can help us all the same,' says Jordan.

'Help,' says Sheryl.

'Do you two do that all the time?' I ask.

'Do what?' says Sheryl.

'What?' says Jordan.

'That,' I say. 'That there. Taking words from each other's sentences and repeating them.'

'Do we do that?' says Sheryl.

'Do we?' says Jordan.

A kick around with a football breaks out with some of the kids in front of us, presumably on their lunch break. One boy is wearing a Barcelona top with Messi picked out on the back, another is sporting a Juventus top with Ronaldo across his shoulder blades. I watch the kids for a few moments and realise the worst two players are Messi and Ronaldo. Adoration doesn't buy you skill.

'Listen to what we have to say,' says Jordan. 'Just listen.'

Before Sheryl can speak I put my hand up. 'I'm not for listening to anything if you are going to pull that *Dumb and Dumber* thing as you both speak.'

'Jordan, let me,' says Sheryl. 'Look, Daniella, I know it didn't go well this morning. George can have a short fuse but if you can just listen to what we have to say then we'll be gone.'

What's to lose?

'Okay, ten minutes, absolute max.'

'Can I tell you a little about us?'

'Is it necessary?'

Jordan leans back and lets Sheryl run.

'Jordan and I owe a lot to your mum. She represented us for years.'

'As models?'

'Yes. We had big success as kids. At thirteen we were the face of DressDown.'

'The kids' fashion retailer.'

'Yes.'

'Didn't they go bust?'

'They did but it was a big deal for us.'

I have the vaguest of recollections of a campaign. 'Something to do with a white horse, wasn't it?' I say.

Both smile. Sheryl's is the widest.

'The horse was called Donna,' Sheryl says. 'We rode her in TV ads for nearly two years.'

'Now I remember. Two kids on one horse riding through a shop. Corny but memorable. *Gall-up to a bargain*?' I say.

Jordan nods. 'That's the one.'

'No wonder they went bust,' I say. 'And what else have you done?'

The smiles both fade.

'Bits and pieces,' says Sheryl. 'We recently did the Ali Mann ads.'

My blank look encourages her to reveal more.

'Ali is a big thing in spiritualist circles.'

'Anything else?'

'We had stuff in the pipeline until your mother sadly passed away.'

It sounds like they had nothing.

'So,' I say, 'to fill in the time you run Safety Deposit +.'

'It's only for a short while,' says Sheryl.

'Until the money from the scam comes through.'

Both of them swivel their heads, checking that no one is listening.

'Keep it quiet,' says Sheryl.

Jordan can't help himself and repeats, 'Quiet.'

'Go on,' I say.

'Well,' says Sheryl, 'if you really don't know anything about the money, you can still help.'

'Go on.'

'You are talking to a lawyer about Effie's estate.'

'That's none of your business.'

'I know, but as part of that process you could ask a few questions in places that we cannot.'

'Zia has already made this pitch. Not an hour ago. What's new?'

'I know he has, but it really would set alarm bells ringing if we started to enquire where your mother might have put the cash. But in your case, you have all the right in the world to ask, as has your lawyer. No one would blink an eye.'

'An eye,' says Jordan.

I glare at him and he shrugs.

'We can also cut you in,' Sheryl whispers.

This is the new news. I laugh, too loud, and a few of the other customers turn to look.

'You lot have to be the worst set of criminals I've encountered, and I've talked to a lot, trust me.'

Both of them screw up their faces.

'Come on,' I say. 'You can't see how stupid this is? You tell me I'm the only one who might be able to help you find this money, if there is any. So you threaten me, then you try to make me feel sorry for you and now you offer me up to be part of this nonsense. Putting me right in the line of fire when your so-called investors come calling. Not to mention the police. And for what? What's the split? What would that be for me, a seventh of the cash?'

'Five per cent,' blurts Jordan. Sheryl throws him a withering look.

'Oh, bloody brilliant.' I laugh again. 'So I find you over a million euros and all I get is a lousy five per cent.'

'Not so loud,' says Sheryl. 'It's our money. We can share it how we like.'

'It's not your money. It's the poor bastards' you conned out of it.'

'It's ours,' says Sheryl. 'It's our money.'

Jordan adds. 'Ours.'

'It isn't,' I say. 'And even it was, you still haven't seen the light on this.'

Nothing registers with either of them.

'Let me make this really simple,' I say. 'If there is money, and I'm not sure there is, but if there is and I find it—tell me this. Why in the hell would I let any of you know I'd found it? I could locate it, bury it and walk away. Come back another day, especially once all six of you are locked up and off I go to live a merry life.'

Neither of the Twins know how to respond to that. It's clear they hadn't given much thought to how this conversation might go. George had primed them and they had delivered. And delivered badly. I'm finding it hard to think that George didn't figure on me going solo on this. Hard to tell a woman that 1.3 million is missing and not expect her to think that maybe she could take the whole action for herself.

'So that's a no,' says Jordan.

'Jordan, Sheryl,' I say, 'there are only so many ways to say no in this world and the easiest is to say no. Please pass this back to George. No, I won't help find whatever dirty money has gone missing. No, I won't be asking anyone anything about the cash. No, I'm not getting involved. No, I don't want any cut. Just no. *No means no.* I'm going to sort out my mother's stuff and then I'll see what's what.'

Sheryl drains her glass. 'Daniella, that money was our way out. Jordan and I were going to take acting classes. We've been told we have promise.'

Given the hash they'd just made of delivering George's lines I don't see promise, I just see false hope.

'*La cuenta,*' I say to the waiter.

He brings the bill and it has Jordan and Sheryl's drinks on it as well. I put enough money on the small silver salver for my food and drink before pushing it over to them.

Sheryl inspects it as if it's infectious.

'I'm not paying for your drink,' I say.

They root around for change and drop a stack of coins, some fluff and a sweetie paper into the bill tray. The waiter picks it all up and returns two minutes later.

'*Falton dos euros,*' he says.

I don't know what that means.

'We're two euros short,' says Jordan.

'Not down to me,' I say. 'I put in exactly what I owed. You guys are short.'

Looks are exchanged.

'We don't have any more cash on us,' says Sheryl.

'So why did you order the drinks?'

I pull out a 5-euro note and hand it to the waiter, indicating that I don't need change.

'You two are a real piece of work,' I say.

I stand up, survey the square and choose a direction.

'A piece of work,' I repeat as I leave.

DATE: Jueves 14 de Noviembre de 2019

Esta es una copia de la traducción al inglés de la entrevista con la persona o personas nombradas.

(The following is a copy of the English translation of the interview with the subject or subjects.)

PRESENT: Capitán Lozano, Teniente Perez and Pat Ratte

TRANSCRIPT AS FOLLOWS:

SPANISH POLICE OFFICER CAPITÁN LOZANO (CAPITÁN L): Señor Ratte, my name is Capitán Lozano. Do you require a translator?

PAT RATTE (PR): What for?

CAPITÁN L: I want to make sure my questions are understood.

PR: I'll let you know if I'm struggling. Does that work for you?

CAPITÁN L: Yes. Can you tell me your full name?

PR: Pat Ratte.

CAPITÁN L: Is that your full name? Not Patrick?

PR: Pat.

CAPITÁN L: And where do you live?

PR: In a house.

CAPITÁN L: Where, Señor Ratte?

PR: Outside El Descaro.

CAPITÁN L: Does it have an address?

PR: Yes.

CAPITÁN L: Which is, Señor Ratte?

PR: Outside El Descaro.

CAPITÁN L: My records show you are living in a villa on the old El Descaro road.

PR: So why are you asking?

CAPITÁN L: I am required to, Señor Ratte.

PR: Well, you've asked.

CAPITÁN L: Am I right in saying that your home is built on the old Castillo de Ayer?

PR: Yes. Yesterday's Castle.

CAPITÁN L: And the old castle is now part of your home?

PR: Yes.

CAPITÁN L: I am impressed, Señor Ratte. Gaining such planning permission to build on such a venerable castle must have been difficult.

PR: Not when it was crumbling to the ground and I rescued it.

CAPITÁN L: Rescued it. Does it not now contain a swimming pool?

PR: Yes.

CAPITÁN L: Hardly a suitable use for such an ancient building.

PR: Am I here to defend my architectural choices?

CAPITÁN L: No, Señor Ratte. I am just interested in such things. My father was a history teacher. And I like history.

PR: My father was a coalman and I hate the stuff.

CAPITÁN L: Señor Ratte, can you tell me where you were when Señora Coulstoun died?

PR: Am I under suspicion of something?

CAPITÁN L: No, Señor Ratte. I am just following up on some matters.

PR: What day did she die?

CAPITÁN L: You do not know? You went to the funeral. She died two days before that.

PR: I was around.

CAPITÁN L: Doing what?

PR: None of your business.

CAPITÁN L: Señor Ratte, how well did you know Señora Coulstoun?

PR: Effie and I go back a bit. Game old bird she was. Bloody tough. Fair but tough.

CAPITÁN L: How did you meet?

PR: We were both drunk.

CAPITÁN L: Explain.

PR: Effie was at a party I attended. We both got drunk and started chatting.

CAPITÁN L: When was this?

PR: Ten years or so ago.

CAPITÁN L: And would you consider her a friend?

PR: Effie didn't do friends. She did acquaintances.

CAPITÁN L: And you were an acquaintance?

PR: Yes.

CAPITÁN L: No more?

PR: And what does that mean?

CAPITÁN L: I hear that you and Señora Coulstoun saw each other on a regular basis.

PR: We did. She was a client of mine.

CAPITÁN L: Of RatTrap Security?

PR: Yes.

CAPITÁN L: And there was no more than business between you?

PR: Not that that makes any odds now.

CAPITÁN L: I don't understand what that means, Señor Ratte.

PR: Nothing.

CAPITÁN L: Let me ask you again. Where were you when Señora Coulstoun died?

PR: I told you. It's none of your business.

CAPITÁN L: Why not?

PR: It's complicated.

15

Five Grand

For a Friday afternoon Se Busca is busy, or maybe it's always like this. I'm beginning to suspect that George's talk of a profitable business is not hot air. I'm tending the bar with Tara, a forty-something-year-old woman with startling eyes and a sharp tongue. Every question I've asked so far has been met with a reply that places me as a complete fool.

'Tara,' I say, 'where do we keep the peanuts?'

Without turning, she says, 'Where else? In the bloody cellar.'

I've already been there but decide to give it a second look before asking her again. I find them, hidden behind rolls of paper towels. An obvious place, really. I refill a few of the small plates that we litter around the bar and serve a couple of customers with lager. Unlike most of the other bars in town, my mother insisted all drinks are paid for once poured. I'd asked Tara why. and she had pointed out, in forthright language, that some of the regulars could sit for hours and when presented with a bill would argue the toss on every drink. My mum had got sick of that and had switched to the Brit method—money on receipt.

Tara and I settle into a routine. Me asking dumb questions, Tara giving curt replies. I'm just beginning to feel like I'm getting my feet under the table when the pub door opens and Saucy walks in. Inwardly I sigh. He's defying the ban. Another small power play, probably initiated by George.

He walks up to me. 'Before you say anything, I know I'm barred. But we need to talk.'

'Barred is barred.'

'And we still need to talk. I'm happy to do it in the car park.'

His voice is strong and his eyes, although streaked with red lines, are steady. I'm thinking he's not been near the bottle today.

'I'm not doing what George wants,' I say up front. 'I'm so finished with that conversation.'

'This isn't at George's behest. Five minutes is all I ask.'

'Fine, five minutes, over there,' I say, pointing to an empty table.

I expect him to ask for a drink but he doesn't.

As I sit, I say, 'Okay, fire on. And be quick.'

'I know you think I'm a drunk.'

I shake my head. 'I don't need your life story. It seems everyone in your crew thinks that telling me their reason for being here will somehow convince me to get mixed up in this nonsense.'

'Daniella, whether you like it or not you *are* mixed up in this. Threatening Jordan and Sheryl that you could find the money and keep it wasn't smart.'

'I didn't say I was going to do that. I said I *could* do that. There's a big difference.'

'Not around here. Nobody in this neck of the woods would turn their nose up at the chance of landing that kind of money.'

'I'm not from this neck of the woods, remember.'

'Neither was I and now look at me. El Descaro hooks you quickly, Daniella. It's already working on you.'

'In what way.'

'Are you going home tomorrow?'

'That's the plan.'

'Then why bother learning how the bar works and arranging with Zia to help you cover tonight. Why not just shut the place, sell it and be gone?'

'You're an accountant. Is it not better to sell a going concern than a dead one?'

'Shutting up for a week or two wouldn't matter. There's a few buyers around here that would snap your hand off for this place. And I think you know that. Forgive me if I don't believe you're getting on a plane tomorrow. I've been in this game too long not to be able to sniff out someone's true motives. I've played with some of the biggest boys in the play park in my day, Daniella. This place gets its claws into you very, very quickly. So I'm going to give you a little free advice and, trust me, I don't do free very often.'

I let him roll.

'Daniella, you're going to help us. And before you get on your high horse, I'll tell you why.'

I wait.

'I'm going to tell you something that isn't well known around here and a true secret is a rare thing in El Descaro so I'm asking you to keep this to yourself.'

'That depends,' I say.

'On what?'

'On what it is you are about to tell me.'

'It's a personal matter about your mum.'

'Go on.'

Tara looks over at us. The bar is getting busier. She can cope but I'm getting the eye anyway.

'Daniella, George and your mother go back a long way.'

'Twenty years. He said he helped her buy this place.'

'Longer than that, Daniella.'

'How much longer?'

'Make it close to thirty years.'

'Mum knew him back in the UK?'

'He came out here about two years before your mum arrived and prior to that they were an item.'

That closes down the noise of the bar. Suddenly it's just me and Saucy.

'An item?' I gasp. 'George and Mum?'

'Yes.'

'That's not possible. I'd have known.'

'You'd have been—what?—fourteen when George came out here. Do you remember much before you were fourteen?'

'I'd remember if Mum had a long-term boyfriend.'

'From what I know they were very discreet. George was married back then.'

'Mum's got thirteen or fourteen years on George.'

'Love has a way of overlooking age.'

'You said they *were* an item. Until when?'

'Maybe ten years back. No big fallout. Your mum just told George one day that it was over.'

'And that was that?'

'Not for George but he learned to live with it. When your mum made up her mind about something there was no changing it.'

'And no one knew about them?'

'No one knew that their relationship was UK born and bred. And certainly not that it had ten years in it before they arrived.'

'She never said a thing to me.'

'And she never would have. But I'm reckoning that with her gone it's only fair you know what you're dealing with out here. George is on your case because he thinks you abandoned Effie. Even hurt her. Zia told me he nearly hit you. George might be a bit of a loose cannon at times but he's not violent. I've never known him lift a finger. It scared Zia and scares me. He needs your help. Let's be straight, *we* need your help. And we need it yesterday. Saying no to George is a knife to him. He's struggling with the idea that Effie rolled him over. And now you're threatening to do the same.'

'I didn't threaten anything.'

'Yes, you did. Look, all of us have cash issues. Once the whole story breaks we'll have no choice but to run and we can't run far on fresh air.'

I let the news about George and Mum sink in a little, allowing the world around me to drift back in. I have no recollection of George, or anyone else for that matter, around Mum when I was kid. At no time was there ever a man involved that I knew of. Of course, if George was married, and they were seeing each other away from the family homes then I'd be none the wiser. Mum liked to take breaks. Sometimes without me.

'If Mum and George were a thing,' I say, 'why did George come out to Spain so long before her?'

'He was to set up a new life for them both. They gave themselves until you were sixteen to get things sorted. It was George that found this town and this bar. It was your mum that made it successful.'

'George says she did so with dodgy dealings.'

Saucy smiles. 'So what. Good money or bad, this place works.'

'And then my mum rolls over on someone she loved and cared for.'

'I don't get that either. We all worked hard to land investors. And she's rolled us as well. Good and proper. And that's hurt us all. She would have known what she was leaving behind. The crap that would land on us all. With no money we're all stuck here to face the music or, at best, face a life scrabbling around the wilds of Spain trying to scrape a living, while avoiding the investors and police.'

'But how could this scam have ever made enough cash for all of you?'

'In early 2019 five people nearly got away with 5 million euros with a property scam out here. We reckoned we'd get even more. We were wrong. At first it was easy to find investors but it got tougher. The 5 million scam in Mallorca put some people around here on red alert so we had to stop targeting locals. We tried for Brits that were looking to move out here and fancied a chance to set themselves up for life. That had limited success.'

'And once you got the cash in the bank you were all going to head for the hills?'

'My guess is that we would have all cut free today or tomorrow at the latest. Word is getting around.'

'Therefore, I'm no use to you anyway. You're out of time.'

'Not quite. We can probably buy a few more days by announcing we are about to lodge for planning and then delay it a little. Your mum's death will also help. People are sympathetic. And if *you* can track the money down by then we could still get away with it.'

I lean back in the chair, thinking.

'I'm struggling with this,' I say. 'It's as if all of you think that me helping is some sort of panacea and one that doesn't consider the impact on my life. As soon as I help you I'll be part of this and when it all goes south, and you all run, I'll be the one waiting on the knock on the door. Why in the hell would I want that?'

'You wouldn't be on the hook for anything. All you need to do is ask the questions that we can't of the people we can't. It'll simply look like you are tidying up Effie's estate. You just keep us in the loop. Then tell us where the cash is.'

'And if I find the money, I just hand it over?'

'Yes.'

'Why?'

'Because George really can sink this bar, the house and then he'll take you down with us.'

'I told George I don't take well to threats.'

'Let me make this clear then,' he says. 'This is no threat from George. It's from all of us. So here's something else to think on. And it's not a threat, it's a straight up promise. Help us and we will all go away. Don't, and you're going to jail with us all.'

I look at him. Taking in the words.

'We'll all say you were part and parcel of it all from the outset,' he says. 'What have we to lose? You, on the other hand have it all to lose.'

'You'd do that?'

'Not if you help.'

'And if I just go home tomorrow.'

'You lose both the bar and the house—and we still implicate you.' He stands up. 'So what's your answer?'

'Fuck off.'

If I expect a reaction I'm disappointed.

'Be serious Daniella,' he says. 'We're not going to fuck off. I think that the money is out there and I'm convinced that you can find it. You might even know where it is and you're not getting away with that. We let Effie roll us but we won't let her daughter do the same. Help us and you could have a nice life out here. Don't and we'll do everything we can to hole you below the waterline. We are giving you until Zia comes on for the shift tonight to think it over. Tell him what your answer is then.'

He stands up and walks out of the front door. I sit for a while.

Thinking. Thinking that this is all sliding to a very bad place and that I'm not in control. And keeping control is my watchword. *Always keep control.*

After ten minutes I get up.

'Tara,' I say. 'What needs done?'

'Are you finished your break?' she snaps. 'Then get the dirty glasses.'

I bar-fly the room, stacking up the glassware. I fill the glass washer and circle back to the tables, wiping them down. All the time I'm trying to figure what to do next. Will the Ex-Patriots really carry out that threat? The more I chew on it the more convinced I am that they will. Things look bad from their end. No money and investors beginning to get wise to what is going down. I don't know enough about buildings and planning to work out if they can stall it all for a bit. Mum's death has probably given them a little breathing space and if they can pretend they're going to submit something to the local council, something that stands up to scrutiny, then, if I was an investor, I might think things were still on track. Because anyone in on this scheme has to be flying on trust in the first place, so a few days' grace might be achievable. Unless Simon the muscleman isn't the only one that's figured the game's up, because once the scam starts to collapse it'll come down like a house of cards in a wind tunnel.

The one thing the Ex-Patriots do have nailed is that I *am* in the ideal position to probe deep into Mum's dealings. There have to be clues as to where the cash is, if she took it. If she was making plans to leave, there has to be a trail. I just need to find it and follow it. That's something I'm good at. Years in the insurance game has given me a nose for what's right and what's wrong, where to look and where to avoid.

I pick up a few more glasses and return them to the bar.

'You'll need to start setting up for the darts league soon,' Tara informs me.

She vanishes into the cellar with these words. She may as well have just told me to decipher Egyptian hieroglyphs wearing a blindfold. The pool table sits where the darts players would throw so, on the assumption they don't chuck their arrows over pool players, I figure I'll move the table. There's a contraption below the table that has wheels and is clearly meant to lift the table up and allow it to be wheeled where required. A friendly customer, sporting an ancient Live Aid T-shirt, sees my confusion and lopes over.

'I know how to do it,' he says.

He plays with the mechanism, lowers the wheels and points to the corner. We push the table and, as if by magic, the customers in our way part, the ones in the corner we are aiming for rising and moving their tables as we approach. We settle the table against the wall and the friendly customer lowers it.

'Thanks,' I say.

'No problem, the table top is over there.'

Having spotted it earlier on I'd wondered what the large piece of hardboard lying against one wall had been for. It neatly covers the baize. An ideal place for the sandwiches that should be on their way.

'It needs the cover,' says Tara, returning from the cellar.

I look blank.

'In the bloody back.'

Of course.

I find a threadbare, daisy-patterned tablecloth under the boxes of nuts, behind the paper towels.

Once I've covered the temporary table I ask Tara, 'What time do the darts start?'

'Seven thirty.'

We're a good few hours out.

'Why set up so early?'

'Bloody practice.'

A couple of customers are already at the board. Each with their own set of darts. The displaced customers have rearranged the tables and chairs into an arc, to get a better view of the board. One table, excess to requirements, has been collapsed and stored. This place is a well-oiled machine, admittedly in need of some TLC, but there's a smooth rhythm to how it all works. A familiarity brought on by years of routine and regulars who consider the place a second home.

'Who is playing who at darts?' I ask Tara.

'It's us v. DB's. Final game of the season. Grudge match. They are one point ahead of us in the league. Whoever wins tonight takes the title. It'll be busy.'

And with Zia not a fan of working the bar and me a novice, busy should be fun.

Zia arrives ten minutes before his shift and by then the pub is properly heaving.

'Did the drink orders turn up today?' he says as he drops his coat in the cellar.

'I've no idea,' I say.

'Tara, did the orders arrive?'

'No. Did you place them?'

'No. Daniella, did you?'

'No,' I reply. 'I wouldn't know where to start.'

Zia grimaces. 'Shit.'

He does a fly round the cellar and emerges, announcing, 'This will be tight. We've half the stock we'd normally have for a night like this.'

'Can we get more?' I ask.

'There's no way the wholesaler will deliver a big order tonight. But call anyway. Just tell them to send what they sent last week and get it here tomorrow. The phone number is on the wall. Ask for Susan. Do not talk to Michael. He's a lazy swine. And ask Susan if she could at least tip a couple of kegs of lager in her car and drop them off tonight.'

I find a sheet of phone numbers next to the roster and identify the number Zia was talking about. I call and after a few minutes Michael reluctantly passes me to Susan. She says they'll get the order to us in the morning and she'll be down about eight o'clock tonight with some lager.

I return to the bar and thank Tara as she packs up to leave. I tell her to take her pay out of the till. I get a grunt in reply.

'Where are the sandwiches?' I say to Zia.

'Bollocks, I don't know,' he replies. 'They should be on their way. Héctor's mobile is on that list of numbers. Call him.'

He's juggling four orders while talking.

'Daniella,' he says, 'once you've made that call go fetch dirty glasses.'

I call Héctor who tells me, in broken English, that he is on his way but since Zia only phoned this morning it is all a rush. I then hit the tables for the glassware as more people roll in, double teaming with Zia to clear the rush once the glasses are in the washer. The pulse of the place settles into a steady stream of people wanting drinks, me collecting and washing glasses and Zia moaning about how low we are on some stock.

Héctor appears half an hour later and, with some skill, navigates a giant board of sandwiches to the pool table. I have to pay him in cash. He waves as he leaves, holding the door open for the arriving DB's darts team, who enter decked out in T-shirts with a photograph of a pair of dog's bollocks emblazoned across their fronts. Underneath the canine testicles, the letters DB's are printed in some arcane sci-fi script. The shirts look offensive to me but no one else seems to be that bothered and the entire DB's team wears them with pride over their beer bellies.

The Se Busca team are dressed in red polo shirts with *Se Busca Darts—We Throw Caution To The Wind* across their backs.

'Which ones are the Charles brothers?' I ask Zia, remembering the discussion between George and Simon the muscleman.

'The two bald ones with tattoos on their necks,' replies Zia.

'Evil-looking bastards is a phrase that comes to mind.'

'Not so loud,' he hisses.

I take the rap on the knuckles and return to feeding the hoards liquid and rescuing empty vessels.

Zia hasn't mentioned the deadline set by Saucy for me to say I'll help. Nor has he mentioned the money. I'm not inclined to encourage him to talk about either. As the darts match gets under way Susan from the wholesaler appears and I help her in with the kegs of lager. She's also brought bar-sized bottles of gin, vodka, rum and pouring whisky along with four cases of bottled beer, explaining that she knew we must be running low, unless I'd decided to use a new supplier. I assure her that I haven't changed anything. Zia thanks Susan for her foresight.

'We might just get through this,' Zia says to Susan. 'But I'll need the proper order in the morning.'

'It'll be here,' she says before turning to me and adding, 'and it's cash on delivery for the kegs and bottles.'

I raid the till and have to empty my purse to pay.

With this she leaves, a roar going up as our team takes the first leg.

Our team. I note my thought.

As I collect more glasses a tall man with a swept-back grey mane of hair, large overcoat and shining teeth appears in my life.

'Daniella,' he says.

'What can I get you?'

'Five grand.'

MINESTERIO DEL INTERIOR
GUARDIA CIVIL
PUESTO DE EL DESCARO

DATE: Jueves 14 de Noviembre de 2019
Esta es una copia de la traducción al inglés de la entrevista con la persona o personas nombradas.
(The following is a copy of the English translation of the interview with the subject or subjects.)
PRESENT: Capitán Lozano, Teniente Perez, Daniella Coulstoun and Señor Cholbi

TRANSCRIPT AS FOLLOWS:
SPANISH POLICE OFFICER CAPITÁN LOZANO (CAPITÁN L):
   Señorita Coulstoun, when did you first meet Señor Pat Ratte?
DC: Two days after the funeral.
CAPITÁN L: Under what circumstances?
DC: He came to the bar.
CAPITÁN L: Se Busca?
DC: Yes.
CAPITÁN L: What for?
DC: What does anyone come to a bar for?
CAPITÁN L: A drink?
DC: Yes.
CAPITÁN L: Anything else?
DC: There was a darts match on?
CAPITÁN L: Señor Ratte came to see a darts match?
DC: Not really. But he certainly interrupted it.
CAPITÁN L: Why was that?
DC: Pat and George got into it.
CAPITÁN L: Got into what, Señorita Coulstoun?
DC: Each other.
CAPITÁN L: A fight?
DC: Yes.
CAPITÁN L: About?
DC: My mother.

CAPITÁN L: An argument about your mother?

DC: Yes.

CAPITÁN L: Then a fight.

DC: Yes.

CAPITÁN L: And this argument about your mother, what were the specifics?

DC: Eh . . .

CAPITÁN L: Don't tell me. It's complicated.

16

Thirty-One Bones

'And you are?' I ask the overcoated man who has just asked me for five thousand pounds.

'Pat Ratte,' is the reply.

The RatTrap man. The protection racket man. Jeep's boss. And I assume the five k is the price tag for his security services. Well, at least I know I've enough money to cover this instalment of protection in the Safety Deposit +. Unless this is a weekly occurrence. I decide to play dumb, an act I'm good at.

Jeep is standing at the door, watching and blocking out the world.

'And this five grand is for what?' I ask.

He pulls me by the arm to the end of the bar, away from prying ears.

'Jeep already explained that.'

'The human whale that has English as his third language.'

'Jeep makes himself understood. He's good at that.'

'And what does this five grand buy me?'

'The same that it did for your mother, peace of mind.'

'Expensive.'

'Cheap,' he replies. 'I'm offering you your mother's deal. Ten grand a year, five every six months, and you get security and highly beneficial pricing on all your stock from your wholesaler. It almost pays for itself.'

'I'm sorry if I don't shake your hand for such a good deal.'

He steps closer. 'I don't do jokes. I don't do light-hearted. I do what I do. Five grand, tomorrow morning.'

Up close his voice carries real threat. He's a man used to this type of work. He taps the bar. 'Anyway, this could be your last payment. This place won't be your problem for long. If you see sense. And while you think on that I'll have a large Balvenie. Top shelf, second bottle from the end. No ice and put it in a Glencairn Glass.'

As I reach up to grab the bottle I scan the glasses. Pat comes around the bar and lifts a tulip-shaped glass from the pile.

'This is the glass I use. The official glass for whisky. No other.'

I pour.

'Zia, how much is Balvenie?' I ask.

'Pat doesn't pay,' he replies.

I'd guessed this but I'm not going to bend to the wind quite as quickly as that.

'Really. Okay, Pat, I'll knock it off your bill.'

He doesn't smile but he does retire to the far side of the bar and muscle a man off a stool.

There are some big men in the bar now. The Charles brothers, Pat, Jeep—one hell of a smell of testosterone is wafting around here.

And talking of testosterone, in walks George.

'Hi, Pat,' George says, squeezing in next to him.

'George,' Pat acknowledges.

'I'll have what Pat is having, Daniella.'

All friendly with me. As if our earlier confrontation hadn't happened. He starts chatting to Pat. Too quiet for me to hear. I take a moment to decide if I'm going to serve him or not. But there's no point in starting another fight here and now. When I drop the drink on the bar next to him the two of them stop talking.

Pat announces he's off for a slash and I'm too slow to get away before George grabs my arm.

'Okay, are you going to help or not?'

'It's not that easy.'

George slaps his hand on the bar. A few people turn.

'Daniella, it is easy. Help or go to jail. That's how simple it is.'

'I can't.'

'You can and you will. Not because you owe your mother for

abandoning her. Although you do. Not that you couldn't have a nice life here rather than the piss one back home. Let me tell you the real reason. See that man?'

George points to Jeep.

'Daniella, I've just acquired his services from Pat. A short-term contract that may or may not have to be carried out. The terms of the contract are simple. If you help us then nothing happens to you. If you don't help us he has strict instructions to break thirty-one bones in your body.'

I didn't hear that right.

'What?' I eventually say.

'There's no reason behind the number thirty-one. And I'm not even sure if it's possible to be that exact. But it sounded like a good number. My birthday. I'll let Jeep worry about the details of how he counts them.'

'This is insane,' I gasp. 'You can't do that.'

George places both hands on the bar. 'That's where you are wrong. I can and I have. I've no more fucking time, Daniella. This needs sorted now. People are circling. I need that money and I need you on the case and motivated to fix it first thing in the morning. So, this is the deal. You start looking tomorrow morning and then, by tomorrow evening at five o'clock, you tell us where the money is.'

'You can't be serious. I've told you I don't know where the cash is.'

'You have a whole day to find it. Say no to this now and Jeep starts breaking bones tonight. Say yes and he holds off on the snapping until tomorrow at five. But if you turn up nothing he starts breaking. If you try to leave he starts breaking. Tell anyone about this and he starts breaking. Do you get this? I really will take away this pub, the apartment, your freedom and *now* your health. There are no ifs, no buts—just fucking do it.'

Pat reappears and sits back down next to George.

I step away, stunned. I stumble into Zia, right behind me. He must have heard what George just said.

'Glasses, Daniella,' Zia says.

I stagger out into the melee and swipe at empty pint pots. My legs are rubber, my head is mince. Jeep is watching me with a grin of anticipation. He curls both hands into fists and bangs them together, thumb to thumb, then snaps both hands down, imitating the breaking of a twig. I drop a glass and it smashes. I get the usual pub round of applause.

Zia throws his hands up. 'Get the brush, Daniella.'

Fetching the brush is done on automatic. I clean up the glass and pile more glasses into the washer. I help Zia get orders done, swap out a keg, clean piss from the toilet floor, mop up three spills, strip the covers from the sandwiches for the half-time food, dig out a case of bottled beer, stick the bottles in the fridge and on and on and on with just one thing on my mind.

Thirty-one bones.

Thirty-one. Who the hell threatens to break thirty-one bones in a woman's body? In *anybody's* body. Zia shouts at me on a regular basis as my mind wanders and I misfill the washer, mishear orders, mispour drinks.

As the climax to the darts game builds, the bar quietens for a few moments. I slump against the back bar, Zia standing in front of me.

'Zia,' I say.

'Yes.'

'Did you hear what George said to me?'

His answer fills my boots with dread.

'We've no choice, Daniella. I'm sorry but this has to be done. I don't agree with George on violence. But we need that cash.'

'Zia, he's going to get that guy Jeep to hurt me. And hurt me bad.'

'Not if you help. Help us and nothing happens.'

I retreat to the cellar and slump on a keg. Head in hands.

So fast. So fast downhill. Mere days and this is a mess. My life back home suddenly looks inviting. I think I should just get on the plane and run. And keep running. As if reading my mind, at that moment, Jeep appears at the cellar door, checking I've not bolted out the back way. He strides over to me and with no preamble slaps me across the back of the head. I tumble to the floor.

'That's for garters, starters. A cookie-wookie taster, let's call it,' he says.

I lie on the floor, unwilling to move. I'm not a flight or fight person when it comes to fear. I'm a curl up in a ball person. Vanishing into myself, seeking safety in mental rather than physical distance.

I place my head on the cool of the stone floor and close my eyes. Jeep leaves. The hubbub in the bar is a distant hum, the hiss of the lager venting through the pipes a gentle wash of sound. After a while I roll on to my back and stare at the ceiling.

Zia comes in. He looks down on me.

'What in the hell are you doing?'

'Wishing I was somewhere else.'

'And I wish you were somewhere else as well,' he says. 'Like out there helping me.'

'Zia, what did I do to deserve this?'

'Deserve what? A pub, a flat, cash in the bank, a chance to change your life?'

'You know that's not what I mean.'

'Jesus, Daniella, you need to grow a pair. No one is asking you to kill anyone. Just find the money. That's all.'

'That's all? That easy, eh? Just find 1.3 million euros.'

'Yes, it is that easy. It's in cash and your mum took it. She's hidden it. And she's not had long to do it. It's hard to hide that much cash. It'll be local, your mother wasn't one for travelling far. She must have been planning to run and would need access to it quickly.'

'She could have sent it to the UK.'

'Would you? Would you trust the post? I'd keep it bloody close if it were me.'

'You know that guy Jeep is going to break my bones if I don't help.'

'Daniella, what bit of *you have no choice* are you missing here? Now get the hell up and give me a hand out there before we have a riot.'

A loud crash from the bar turns both of our heads. Zia exits. He's back a few seconds later.

'George and Pat are squaring up to each other.'

He vanishes. I stand up and follow him into the bar.

The darts match has stopped. A crowd of people circle the dartboard. I push through and find George and Pat facing each other, the crowd forming an arena around them.

'You'll take that back,' says George to Pat.

Pat has handed his coat and jacket to Jeep. Pat is probably in his mid-seventies but he cuts a mean figure. No gut, tight upper arms, wide chest. He could probably bench-press two of me. I'm also guessing that Pat is well used to street fighting. I've no idea if George is but he's showing no fear even though Pat has bulk to spare and George is a good six inches shorter.

'No, I won't,' says Pat.

Someone shouts out, 'Square-go.'

Others take up the chant.

'*Square-go. Square-go. Square-go. Square-go.*'

'Okay,' says George. 'Let's settle this the Se Busca way. A square-go, it is?'

'Fine by me,' replies Pat.

'Who's got a square?' George asks the crowd.

'What are they talking about?' I whisper to Zia as he sidles up to me. 'In Glasgow a square-go is a fight. Are they going to fight?'

'Shit,' he says. 'Yes, they're going to fight. The square in a square-go is a piece of cloth. You'll see.'

One of the Charles brothers steps forward and hands George a white handkerchief about a foot by a foot square. George takes it and lays it on the floor between himself and Pat, a diamond, a corner pointing at each of them.

'Someone toss a coin,' says Pat. 'I'll call heads.'

The crowd holds a respectful distance; some are on chairs to see over those in front. It's like a dog-fighting pit.

'What in the hell are they doing, Zia?' I ask.

'Your mother introduced it as a way to sort out disputes,' he replies quietly. 'She got the idea from some US sailors who came through town years back. It was their way of settling arguments. The two men in dispute place the toes of their shoe on the point of the hankie nearest them. Facing each other. The first to move their foot from the hankie loses.'

'I'm still not getting this.'

'You will.'

One of the Charles brothers tosses a coin and calls out tails. George smiles. Pat's face is a rock.

'No face, no balls,' says Pat to George.

The crowd chant the words in reply. '*No face, no balls. No face, no balls.*'

'That means they can't punch each other in the face or below the belt,' explains Zia.

I'm still not sure what in the hell is happening here.

George shuffles his free foot and pivots, ensuring his other foot stays on the hankie. Pat stares him down, his right foot on the opposite corner of the white material. George clenches his fist and takes a swing at Pat's stomach. Pat rolls a little to the left but George's punch still digs into Pat's gut. Pat grunts. Everyone cheers and a second later they all start shouting, '*Foot on. Foot on. Foot on. Fooooooooooooot on.*'

'That means Pat didn't take his foot off the corner of the hankie,' explains Zia. 'It's now Pat's turn to throw a punch.'

'Is this for real?' I say.

'First one to step off the hankie loses,' he says.

The crowd change the chant and start, in unison, to count down from thirty. '*Thirty, twenty-nine, twenty-eight, twenty-seven . . .*'

'What now?' I ask.

'Pat has to throw a punch before they count to zero. If he doesn't, it's George's turn again.'

'Why the count?'

'If they didn't count, a person could stand there, when it's their turn, for hours. The count ensures a swift conclusion to the fight.'

As the crowd counts down past fifteen, Pat lets fly. He aims his punch at George's kidneys—a real piledriver. George swivels and Pat's fist clips George's stomach instead. Despite it being a half-blow, George still doubles up.

The crowd gasp, there's a pause, then a cheer as they realise that George hasn't staggered off the hankie.

'*Foot on. Foot on. Foot on. Fooooooooooooot on.*'

The count starts again. '*Thirty, twenty-nine, twenty-eight* . . .'

The pub is baying for blood, howling for it.

George takes the count down to ten, using the time to recover from Pat's punch. Pat starts to shift his body left and right. A moving target. George lets loose. The blow crashes into Pat's side, just below his rib cage. Pat staggers. The crowd let out a collective '*Oooooh.*' They all look at his foot and then cheer.

'*Foot on. Foot on. Foot on. Foooooooooooooot on . . . thirty, twenty-nine, twenty-eight . . .*'

Pat grimaces, but triumphantly points at his foot, still resting on the hankie, and balls up his fist for his next shot.

He takes the count all the way to five before driving his fist home. And despite George's attempt to block the blow with his arm, Pat sticks one right in George's solar plexus.

George collapses to the floor and I, like everyone else, lean in to see if his foot is still on the material.

It isn't.

'*Foot off. Foot off. Foot off. Foooooooooooooot off*' is the chant.

Pat stands back and the Charles brothers step in and lift George up. He's clutching his stomach, breath coming in lumps. Pat puts out a hand.

George looks at it for a second and then takes it.

They shake.

Another cheer from the crowd.

What a place this is.

The mob disperses in a mist of bloodlust. The bar looks a far darker and more dangerous place at this moment. As if I've seen its true soul for the first time. A home for the angry, the disenfranchised. The ageing posters and the tacky money hanging from the ceiling no longer looking shabby chic, they are what they are; totems to a bad place. The bare concrete walls oozing violence. And all this tells me one thing.

George is serious about hurting me.

The speed at which the darts match gets up and running again, the customers' swiftness at replacing the furniture, Zia's rapid return to the bar, the throng of people that, in seconds, forms around the bar, waiting to be served—all speak to a familiarity with what has gone down. This bar has rules that I don't understand.

George and Pat slump back on their stools and resume drinking, as if their fight was a quick game of pool and the drinks the afters.

Zia signals me to get back to work.

The rest of the night passes in a flushed haze. After watching the square-go, I'm in no doubt that George will set Jeep on me if I don't find the missing money. The predilection for violence around here suggests that the number thirty-one is just his way of saying that Jeep won't stop until I cooperate.

The only other significant event that night occurs when the Se Busca darts captain, one of the Charles brothers, throws home the winning double. The DB's team don't take this well and I fear a full, non-square-go-orientated fight will break out, but things ease down a notch once the trophy is presented and the DB's team leaves. This precedes a drinking frenzy of shots and beer.

At two o'clock Zia tells me he needs to call it quits, and I try to tell the residual crowd we are closing. They ignore me until Pat stands up and tells everyone to fuck off. This has the desired effect and the pub empties like a burst water balloon.

'Five o'clock tomorrow evening,' says George as he wobbles past me. 'Or snap, snap, snap . . .'

He continues to repeat the word until the pub door closing shuts him off.

I look around. The pool table is back where it should be, the hardboard cover is against the wall. Tables are in their original positions and glasses are stacked on the bar. The stage has been cleared for tomorrow's act.

'What set George and Pat off?' I ask Zia as he pulls on his coat.

'They were arguing over your mother.'

'Mum?'

'Pat was an item with your mother. George blames him for her stopping their relationship.'

'Pat Ratte and my mother?'

'They were close. Right up to the end.'

'He's charging her protection money. How is that close?'

'That's business.'

'Do you know what, Zia? I was half thinking that maybe there was something in coming out here. Running this place. But I don't think I could after tonight. This isn't sane.'

'It is what it is and it needs to be what it is. The people who come here like it that way.'

'The violence? The atmosphere?'

'It has rules. It has order. It has security.'

'God, Zia, there was nothing secure about tonight.'

'Not from where you stand but El Descaro tolerates Se Busca and Se Busca ignores El Descaro. You're standing in an independent state. And that state is a safe haven for the regulars. Now if you don't mind I'm going to take my pay and leave.'

I watch as he extracts cash from the till.

'You'll need to be in mid-morning for the wholesaler,' he adds. 'Tara isn't on till one o'clock.'

'I'm supposed to be looking for the cash.'

'You'll only need to be here at eleven. That's the drop-off time. It'll take fifteen minutes max.'

He leaves.

Once more I'm on my own.

17

If You See Sense

The hotel bed is a place of torture. At any one time it's too hot, too cold, too lumpy, too smooth. A streetlight outside the window is overly bright for the thin curtains. A couple in the room to my left are starting on their third bout of love making. On the other side someone is watching late-night Spanish TV. My toilet has backed up and the smell, despite me stuffing a towel under the door, is ripe, sweet and clawing. The air conditioning is on, the internal fan is whirring and rattling, it's gone five o'clock and my eyes haven't closed since I lay down.

In the depths of the night lies a bleakness that casts a deep shadow on what is going on in your life. Rationality has vanished in this cramped, airless cell. I've convinced myself that there is no money, or if there is, that I will be unable to find it in time and the hospital will be my hotel for the night ahead.

An hour earlier I'd packed my bag, a two-minute job. The taxi rank outside is empty, but a card from reception promises twenty-four service from ED Taxis. My plane is due to leave at eleven o'clock this morning. If I go now and get airside, I'd be out of the reach of George, Pat and the whole crew. Leaving Cholbi to sort out what he can.

Except.

I rise and pull back the curtain. Jeep is sitting on a street bench beneath my window. He had followed me to the hotel. He's there for the night. He sees me looking out and does the twig breaking gesture with a big smile.

I drop back to the bed and sit.

And sit.

Half an hour later I stand up, shower, dress and exit the hotel. The sky is still dark but a stain of grey is creeping in over the horizon. Jeep is surprised to see me. He stretches and yawns as I turn onto the seafront. He follows me.

I'm the only person up and about as far as I can see. No early morning joggers or dog walkers yet. I aim for the harbour, breathing the fresh air, hoping inspiration and saviour lies in the ancient tang of salt-laden oxygen. A few fishing boats are tied up for the night but the bulk of the harbour is given over to leisure craft. I wonder at the cost of a few of the bigger monsters that lie here. Certainly 1.3 million euros might buy a decent yacht but I once watched a programme about a top-end boatbuilder and one figure stuck in my mind. A million pounds a metre. That was the starting point from their end if you wanted a halfway decent floating gin palace. I can't see much mileage in a yacht a little over a meter in length.

At the end of the harbour jetty, I drop onto the concrete and dangle my legs over the edge, staring into the dark water. I could as easily slip into the liquid below. Let the cool embrace me. Head dipping beneath the surface. Exhaling. Dropping to the soiled basin below and, when it's too late to make the surface, inhale.

Kicking my heels against the stonework I pick up a rhythm from earlier.

Foot On. Foot On. Foot On. Foooooooooooooot On.

A simple rhythm. After a while I begin to count, from thirty, backward and, with each count, I shuffle my backside a little closer to the lip of the jetty. At twenty I can feel my weight starting to tip me forward towards the water. I compensate by leaning back while still shuffling forward as I count. I speculate whether Jeep would jump in after me if I fell. Does his remit extend beyond surveillance to rescue? Am I that valuable? Or was his briefing too quick, the deal done without full thought, George omitting the part that I was no use to man nor beast if I was dead?

As I reach fifteen, it's a struggle not to slip from the stone. My hands are stretched out behind me, head flung back, arse all but in space. Another inch and I'm gone.

I stop counting, teetering, feeling the moment, challenging myself to take it just a little further, just another number would do it.

Just one more shove.

One more.

Above me thin clouds glide across the stars.

I feel myself begin to slip and self-preservation takes over. I spin round and throw myself flat on my stomach, hands scraping the jetty's surface. For a second, I think I've left it too late. That the magnetic attraction of the harbour water has won. I kick my legs and slump to safety, rolling onto the stone.

No water.

For the moment.

I look up and Jeep is thirty yards away, his face screwed into a question mark. I flip on to my back and breathe.

I have one question in my head. Where in the hell has my mother hidden 1.3 million euros? Answer that and a lot of this can go away. I stand up, taking one last look at the water and walk towards Jeep. He moves to one side to let me past, raising a beefy hand as he does so. I flinch. His movement is a little too quick. Threatening. As if coiling to attack. But he's simply getting out of my way. Not readying for more violence.

Violence?

Zia had told me that George wasn't prone to violence. That he had a quick temper but not a violent one. Yet there he was tonight, standing in that circle of gore monkeys, slugging it out with Pat. Hardly the actions of someone who doesn't resort to his fists. Why would Zia lie about that? To convince me how serious George was? To imply that if a normally peaceful man was given reason to lash out he must be desperate? Desperate enough to hurt me? Or was he right? Is George usually all mouth and no trousers? But now, with the betrayal by Mum and whatever shit storm is coming his way, he is playing against type. The last resort. Thirty-one bones. Jeep. Desperation.

He was fast to violence last night. He'd hardly sat down with Pat before they were dancing on the floor. Pat had said something about my mother. What? What would give George reason to front up to one dangerous-looking man? An ex-gangster. A *current* gangster. It must have been something bad. Something that wounded. Something deep.

If I'm to find the missing money, and I'm now almost certainly sliding down the only chute in that playground, I conclude that the key to this is understanding my mother. She is the gravity well in all this. Figure her and I can escape this. But understanding her isn't something I'm equipped to do. I don't know her. She isn't the person who left the UK all those years back. Se Busca is prima facie evidence that she is a woman I know nothing about. A stranger tied to me by blood alone. If George and Pat were intimate with her then they are far better placed than me to work out her mind. Figure the way she was planning to abscond. But George is either clueless or blinded in some way, as he is the one turning to me. So that leaves Pat.

Last payment?

Pat's words from last night play out in my head. When Pat had told me about the protection money he charged Mum he'd mentioned something about a last payment.

Anyway, this could be your last payment. This place won't be your problem for long. If you see sense.

Won't be your problem.

If you see sense.

Zia had said that he thought Mum was selling up. Pat was the one who called last orders last night. Pat is the one who doesn't pay for drink. Pat loved being centre stage in the fight. His face showed it clearly and he certainly revelled in the win.

You're standing in an independent state here.

Zia's words. Was Pat moving in, mentally taking ownership, the new king of Se Busca in waiting? And was he part of Mum's plan all along? Does he know about the 1.3 million euros? They were lovers, she wanted out, who better to turn to than your partner?

I walk into the built-up area of the port, apartments rising around me. The street lights are dim, random dots of red at irregular intervals, casting shadows, illuminating nothing.

Given the little I know about Pat, he would make a highly effective safety deposit scheme for 1.3 million euros. Of course, he would take a cut but, in return, Mum would get a way out of town that was safe and secure.

If you see sense.

That's the killer line from Pat. Why would I need to see sense? Unless the deal with the pub wasn't done. Mum dying before any documentation could be signed. Then if Pat wants Se Busca he needs me to sell it to him. Or *give* it to him.

I spin that thought until it goes no further and realise that with Pat I have a start point. Somewhere to bury the first shovel to dig for Mum's gold. I make my way back to the hotel and set the alarm for nine o'clock.

18

The Ratte's Nest

The alarm goes off two minutes after I fall asleep but the phone tells me it has gone off just when I'd set it. I could easily turn over and grab a few hours more but the number thirty-one is a strong motivator for getting vertical and getting this done. I'd like to ask Cholbi to do another check on the sale of Se Busca or the flat but it's Saturday.

I grab a quick coffee and *una tostada* from the hotel restaurant and head for the Safety Deposit +. I need some more cash.

The Twins smile at me as I enter.

'I hear it was fun at the bar last night,' says Jordan.

'A square-go?' says Sheryl.

'Pat won,' says Jordan.

Sheryl repeats the word 'Pat'.

'I've no idea what it was about other than Pat said something to George about my mother,' I say.

'You've no idea?' says Jordan.

'No,' I say. 'Why, what do you know?'

Jordan smiles. 'Tommy Smithcroft said Pat told George that Effie had been using him. That he meant nothing to her. Even back in the day.'

'Who's Tommy Smithcroft?'

Before they can reply I cut them off. 'It doesn't matter. So Pat told George my mum wasn't ever interested in him?'

'I think his language was a bit flowerier,' says Sheryl.

'And that led to a fight?'

'It's not like George to fight,' says Sheryl. 'Especially not someone like Pat Ratte.'

'For someone who doesn't like to fight,' I point out, 'he's doing a good job of giving the opposite impression. And if he's quick to fight he's even quicker to make up. The two of them sat down for drinks right after, as if nothing had happened.'

'Square-go rules,' says Sheryl.

Inevitably Jordan repeats the word 'rules'.

Sheryl explains, 'Loser buys the drinks. It's the Se Busca way.'

'It's a different way,' I say. 'That pub is a law unto itself.'

'It's our world,' says Jordan. 'Are you going to help find the money?'

'I've not got much choice.'

They both say the same thing at the same time. 'No, you don't.'

I take out my key, open the security door and extract my box. There's a small curtain-draped booth next to the boxes. I pull back the curtain to reveal a waist high table.

'Can I use this?' I ask.

'It's what it's for,' says Sheryl. 'Gives people a bit of privacy.'

I enter the booth and remove six thousand euros from the plastic bag full of money. Five for Pat and the rest to cover the wholesaler bill and some walking money. Maybe Pat's protection payment is a blessing in disguise. It gives me good reason to see him again and given he's the best lead I have in searching for the missing cash, that's a plus. There's also another reason to pay Pat a visit. He controls Jeep and Jeep is George's way of cracking my calcium. Maybe I can use Pat against George.

I close up the box, exit the booth and put the box away, crumpling up a sweetie paper from my pocket and pushing it under the box before closing everything up. If the Twins do a nosey they'll move the paper and I'll know. Then again, they could already have been in it and checked it out.

'Where does Pat Ratte live?' I ask.

Sheryl points behind her and up. 'Up the hill. Last house on the left. You can't miss it. Half of it is a castle.'

'A real castle?'

'Oh yes,' says Jordan. 'And the rest of it may as well be. Security like it was Fort Knox.'

'How long to get there?'

'Walking,' says Sheryl, 'it'll take you twenty minutes.'

That gives me enough time to get up there, talk to Pat, if he'll talk, and get back to the pub for the drinks delivery from the wholesaler. I think about skipping the pub delivery but I'd like to take another look at the filing cabinet in the office and I'm also not prepared to throw in the towel with the business just yet.

I leave the shop without saying goodbye. From the square I can see up the hill. Its face is an acne-covered mess of homes. A single road leads up. I drop into a small supermarket and buy a couple of cans of full-fat Coke. It might be winter but a pharmacy's digital display sign is telling me it's already fifteen degrees. It'll get hotter.

I know going to Pat's home is a long shot. Pat may have nothing to do with Mum's actions, but it's all I have and the clock is ticking—snap, snap, snap. Anyway, Jeep is tailing me. My threat bunny. I'm still thinking that paying Pat the money might go some way to enervating the beating George has arranged for Jeep to hand me if I fail to locate the cash.

As I start to walk I look back on Jeep. He yawns. I got a few hours sleep. Not enough, but I'm not sure he got any. No bad thing if it comes to me running and him chasing.

I begin the ascent by cracking the first of my Cokes. The road is steep and, as I climb, the homes get bigger and the pavement soon runs out. People in this rarefied atmosphere don't walk.

The homes around me, many closed up for the winter, are growing arms and legs. Electric gates, high walls, prominent CCTV cameras. Near the top the climb evens out, giving me a hell of a view of the coastline. Houses up here have the best cinema in the land. Twenty-four-seven sea, sky and coast—all in 16K HD. I sit down on a slice of wasteland and open the second Coke. Jeep is a hundred yards behind me and it's clear he's more blunt force trauma than honed athlete. He has one hand on a wall and is drawing deep. I raise the Coke can to him, offering him a sip, he shakes his head. I take in the view for a few more minutes and, conscious of my bone-breaking clock, set off again.

Rounding a corner brings me level with what can only be described as a house built on a castle. Beyond it is clear of property. The house wall, facing the road, is made of massive blocks of stone. I've seen the like in countless castles back home. It presents a forbidding edifice, used by the architect to provide the same level of intimidation it would have done back in the day. An archway has been cut in the wall, or maybe it was always there. An industrial set of black wooden doors fill it. There's a small door in the right one for the poor people to enter and leave. Fixed to the wall, next to the small door, is a golden sign, shining bright in the sun. Engraved and infilled in deep blue, six-inch-high letters it reads

Ratte's Nest.

Classy.

The top of the wall is crenellated. Two feet by two feet saw teeth running the length. Glinting in the sunlight are shards of glass embedded in every surface and I can see three CCTVs, one pointing down on the gate, one angled to catch people coming up the hill and the other staring out to the empty road beyond. A large sign is pinned on one wall stating the name of the security company that protects the place, their website, phone number and the fact they are on call 24/7.

Next to the small door, a buzzer is fixed below the *Ratte's Nest* sign, a camera lens poking out above it. A squawk box sits beneath the buzzer. I look back and Jeep is still climbing, slowly, phone in hand, probably announcing my arrival to Pat. A bit pointless given the multi-camera array above me. It had occurred to me earlier that Pat might not be in but I don't bag him as the early Saturday morning type. He was heaving down the Balvenie until closing last night. I hit the buzzer and wait. Jeep closes in on me.

It takes four more presses on the buzzer and five minutes before the box bursts into life.

'What the hell do you want?'

'Pat?'

'What?'

'I'm here to pay.'

'Oh.' A pause and then, 'Come in then.'

There's a click and the small door springs open. I push in.

The view beyond whips my breath away and I have to grab the wall to stop stumbling forward. In front of me the driveway zips to the right and towards a massive three-door garage attached to the house. The castle wall stretches past the garage and morphs into a glass walled edifice. Beyond that the house emerges seamlessly from the glass wall and waterfalls, as a series of neon white boxes, down the hill. Each box the size of two tennis pitches and roofed in grass.

Some home.

But none of this is the cause of the breath whipping. That's down to the near vertical plunge to my left. A small barrier runs along the driveway to give an indication of where the driveway stops and fresh air begins. I walk to the edge and look down. Maybe a hundred feet. Straight down. The view beyond is a stone-cold killer. The same as the one from the wasteland, only with all the drama of an uninterrupted, hanging-out-in-space, viewing point. I reach down and gingerly touch the small barrier, thinking there is no way that would prevent a car from going over the edge if it was hit. Given the dramatic sweep to the right of the driveway, driving into here must test your nerve every time. One slip of the wheel and there's nothing but a one-way gravity trip straight down.

I walk down the driveway, hand trailing the wall, keeping as far as I can from the edge. I walk past the glass wall but it's too dark to see what lies inside. I reach a double set of ten-feet-high glass doors in the main building. Through them I can see clean into a living room with a massive window looking down over that view. This is not a home for vertigo sufferers.

Pat appears from a door on the right, dressing gown wrapped loosely around him, a pair of slippers on his feet. He pulls at the front door and stands back as an electric motor takes over and opens it for him. I step forward.

'Christ, but you're early,' he says. 'I'm two hours from wanting out of my pit.'

'I need to be at the pub for a delivery and I just wanted to get this all out of the way,' I say.

'Well, I need a bucket of caffeine and a loaf of toast and cheese to kick-start me. I'd way too much whisky last night.'

'I know, you should have seen the bill.'

'Bill?'

'The one you don't get.'

'You kept track?'

I hadn't but this is all about maintaining some sort of control. Handing over five grand to a complete stranger just because he asks for it is up there with the dumbest things I've done.

'I did,' I say.

Pat looks less intimidating in the morning light. Last night he'd cut a mean figure on the fight floor but now he seems more bent, frail. His face is worn in that way those who over-suntanned in their youth suffer from and his eyes have a yellow tinge that suggests things may not be well in his guts. He still cuts a domineering figure but you can't beat ageing and Pat is late in the last few rounds of life.

'Good for you,' he says. 'Can you frame that bill and send it to me? It'll remind an old man that he's never too old to learn.'

Given his statement last night about not doing light-hearted, this is almost flippant.

'Come in and sit down,' he says. 'In the top room.' He points down the corridor to the glass-walled room looking out on the view. 'Coffee?'

'Please.'

He moves away to his right and I walk on. The top room has the same jaw-dropping impact as the view from the gate. The entire view-facing wall is one single sheet of glass. Short of a helicopter I've no idea how they fitted it. There's serious money at play here and all designed to impress. The room is huge. You could fit my entire flat back home in here and still have space for a bouncy castle. An eight-seater couch dominates the middle of the room, facing out towards the view. To the right, a fully stocked bar takes up an entire wall. To the left is another couch, L-shaped and angled to look out on the view but towards a different segment of the coast.

Around me the room's walls are covered with pictures of racing cars—too many pictures to count quickly. A massive Ferrari flag sits above the bar. The front aero wing from a racing car is fixed on the wall next to the L-shaped couch. The floor is dark granite, spotted with rugs. One of the rugs is printed with the Ferrari symbol.

I drop into the eight-seater, soaking up the view.

Pat takes twenty minutes to return. He's changed into shorts, a Ralph Lauren polo shirt and a pair of green Nikes. His hair is wet and he looks like he's shaved. He drops a mug of coffee on the table in front of me.

'Milk? Sugar?' he asks.

'Milk.'

He moves to the bar and opens the fridge.

'Here,' he says handing me a small bottle.

'That's a hell of a bar,' I point out. 'Why frequent a dump like Se Busca when you have this?'

'Atmosphere.'

'Se Busca has a better atmosphere than here? Seriously? My work toilet, back home, has a better atmosphere than that pub.'

'Who are you to diss the place?'

His tone has hardened quickly.

'Me,' I say. 'I'm the new owner. My pub. My comments.'

'Yes, well, we'll see about that.'

'About what?'

'Your mother and I had an agreement about Se Busca. It was to be mine.'

'Is this agreement in writing?'

'Things aren't done in writing around here.'

I sip the coffee. It's good.

'Things aren't done normal, full stop, around here,' I say. 'But that doesn't mean I'm selling.'

'Effie and I had a deal.'

I stare at the scenery and in a low voice say, 'Aye, well, in case you hadn't noticed, Mum's dead.'

as anyone to have relationships but, somehow, I thought of her as a lone creature sunning herself here with her platonic friends.

'It's George's business,' Pat says, 'not mine. As long as he pays the hire bill I'll leave well enough alone. You don't interfere in a client's business.'

I turn away. My eyes drawn, time and time again, to the view.

'Is that an original castle at the back?' I ask.

'Castillo de Ayer—Yesterday's Castle. Built by a Christian knight, it dates back to the twelfth century, maybe older.'

'What's behind the glass wall?'

'A swimming pool. Anyway, you were here to pay me.'

'I don't get this,' I say. 'Why charge someone you're in a relationship with for protection?'

'It's called security, not protection. And, because that's the way it's done. No exceptions. It's business.'

'And you can't go soft on anyone,' I figure. 'Bad for your reputation. Charging my mother is cold but it doesn't half send a message to others.'

'Think what you want. It's a legitimate charge for a legitimate service.'

'So, I'll get an invoice for it? Do you have a contract with the bar? Do you have a list, stipulating the services I receive for this payment?'

He slides from the stool and approaches me. 'I told you last night I don't do funny. So pay up or I'll ask Jeep outside to come in and see how well you can fly.' He points out of the window.

'That would be hard to explain,' I say.

'What? That you slipped while on the driveway? You wouldn't be the first.'

He has a way of modulating his vocal tone from light to hard. From casual to serious. Doing so mid-sentence. A well-practised art that has real impact and conveys deep threat. I don't fancy a flying lesson that has only one ending.

'I heard you and Mum had a relationship.'

'You heard right.'

'Were you still seeing Mum, at the end?'

He shakes his head. 'Not in the way we used to. Effie had grown tired of this place. It can get to you after a while. People leant on her heavily for support over the years. Any problems and you saw Effie. She used to revel in that. Shone. But in the last few years she grew weary of it. Always being the one that had to find a solution. And for what? The odd thanks and the profit from a bunch of drunks. God, but you should have seen her back in the day. If she'd run for mayor in this town she'd have turned it into the biggest draw on the coast. But you'd have known that if you'd been here more often.'

'You as well?'

'Me as well, what?'

'It seems that everyone thinks I'm the bad girl in all this.'

'And aren't you?'

'It takes two, you know. I reached out a few times over the years and Mum blanked me. She had her life and I had mine.'

Pat rests on the bar. 'You and I need a deeper chat at some point.'

'About Mum.'

'You were her only child.'

'I was her faraway child.'

'She was being a mum. She didn't want you out here for good reason. This is no place for the innocent.'

'Are you saying she was deliberately keeping me away?'

'In a way. She knew what this place was. What she had become – and she wasn't so proud of some of it. Se Busca isn't for everyone. You saw that last night.'

He stops and turns away from me. 'Anyway, pay up and be gone. I'm wanting back to my bed.'

'I'd like to hear more about Mum.'

'I'm sure you would but now's not the time.'

'When?'

'Maybe tomorrow, maybe never, now pay up.'

I finger the money. 'How do I even know that five thousand is the correct amount?'

'You don't.'

I pull out the cash, peeling away ten notes from the bundle. I'm amazed at how cool I am with this. But then again it's not my money and like all found money it's far easier to be parted from than earned crust.

I hand it over and he casually drops it on the bar.

'That'll take care of the next six months,' he says.

'Will it protect me against Jeep?'

'No. That's a different deal.'

'What if I pay you to call him off?'

'No can do, Daniella. That would be bad for business. A deal's a deal.'

'You do see the irony in me paying you five thousand in cash knowing the very man you would send to help me out should I need it is also under instructions to break my skeleton into pieces, later today.'

'You call it irony, I call it the security business. It happens every day. Now I want to lie down for a little longer so I'll say my good-byes and show you the door.'

'Can I ask one last question about my mother?'

'What?'

'Did my mother give you anything of hers to hold?'

'Like what?'

'Anything for *me*?'

I heavily emphasise the last word, looking into his eyes. I'm not daft enough to think he's going to fess up to knowing where the 1.3 million is but I'm good at spotting lies.

He shakes his head. 'I have a few presents she gave me over the years but nothing with your name on it. Why? What did you expect?'

'I'm struggling to find some of her documents.'

'Did you try her flat?'

'And the pub.'

'What documents?'

'It doesn't matter,' I say. 'I'll be going.'

I stand up and take one last, long look at the coast below. I can just about pick out the hardy sun worshippers setting up on the beach. For all the world I wish I was one of them right now. No cares. No threats.

'One last thing,' I say, pointing to the wall. 'I should have asked earlier, but is that a real racing car wing?'

'My passion, racing. I used to be good back in the day. Still like to play around now and then. And, yes, it's a real one. A genuine F1 wing.'

'You'll know Skid Solo then?'

'A tosser. And an awful racer. Your mother could have beat him in that clapped out Mini of hers.'

'Mum had a Mini?'

'Sure. Original sixties job. It usually sits in the apartment's car park or at the pub. You didn't know?'

'There's a lot I don't know about my mother's affairs.'

'Look, I'm tired.'

He escorts me to the front door and nearly pushes me out. As I walk up the driveway, consciously hugging the inside line, the small door within a door clicks open in front of me. Pat has dismissed me and Jeep is waiting.

I wave to Jeep and start down the hill.

Wondering about my mum, about Pat, about the money.

19

Mum's Security Box

I reach the pub ten minutes before the wholesaler arrives, who informs me that she needs to be quick as Saturday is her half-day. When the delivery is complete I hand over more cash and I realise that the cupboard below the till must have tins in it and I still don't have the key. I decide to break into it. I can't keep forking out cash, even with the money I found in Mum's freezer, without recording what's going on. This is a business, after all.

Susan from the wholesaler waves goodbye as I look for something to jimmy the cupboard. I find a crowbar in the cellar and it makes light work of the lock. There's half a dozen tins lying inside. I open them and find one hundred and fifty euros in each one. Nine hundred in total. Somehow that feels light. Last night was flying as was the afternoon before and there should be another few days of takings before that. Zia took his pay from the till, as did Clyde and I assume Tara did the same. I check the till. It has five tens, a five and change. I make a mental note to ask Zia, Clyde and Tara how much they took. Maybe they took more than a shift's worth.

With the number thirty-one firmly planted in my head I go through the filing cabinet in the tiny office again, this time with care. Checking every folder, every document. Searching for any clues as to where the missing money might be. I'm not sure what I'm looking for. The trip to Pat's didn't reveal much and that bloody clock is ticking. Six hours to snap, snap time. I pull all the files out, simply hoping something pops out at me. As I start on the second drawer I wonder how much space 1.3 million euros takes up. It's such an obvious question I had overlooked it. Am I looking for a warehouse of money, or a shoebox? I suppose it'll depend on what denomination notes the cash is made up of. If it's one-euro coins that will be one hell of a pile. Five hundred-euro notes would number two thousand six hundred. That sounds easy to hide.

In a file named Miscellaneous my finger brushes something hard at the bottom of the folder. I empty the contents on the desk. A small key is taped to the inside of the file. I think I've found the key to the cupboard where the tins live. I peel it free and look at it. I realise that I'm wrong. I know what this is. I have one in my pocket. A Safety Deposit + key. Now there's a place to hide cash. High-value notes, and I'd reckon you could squeeze 1.3 million in to one of the bigger boxes, and all right under the noses of the Twins. Cheeky. I smile at the thought of avoiding bone breaking time and pocket the key. I keep searching, but half an hour later I've come up blank. I recheck the office, the bar, front and back, and outside where the bins live but there is nothing of note. The only other place is back to my mum's flat. The room that's piled high with rubbish would be a great place to stash cash. If I find nothing there then I'm off to the Safety Deposit +.

Half an hour later and a quick walk up to the flat and I know there's no cash in the rubbish room. After removing the first rows of crap from there, everything else has thick layers of undisturbed dust. Nothing I can see has been moved in years and there is no money in the small amount of junk that's dust free. I spin once more around the house, now on the lookout for loose floorboards, panels and the like. I did this last time but with the number thirty-one on my mind I'm more thorough.

Zero.

I check my phone. It's gone one o'clock. Four hours to go. Four hours before bone breaking time. I drop to the car park and find my mum's Mini. It's unlocked and also a busted flush. It doesn't look like it's moved in months.

Safety Deposit + it is.

I almost walk into Skid as I leave the apartment entrance.

He's wearing a green and white striped version of the black and white shirt I saw him in last time. He's surprised to see me. He has to be the worst tail in history.

'How many something-and-white striped shirts do you own?'

He looks blank.

'Okay, let me ask you if you are following me, again,' I say.

'No.'

'You're such a bad liar. Why were you here, then?'

He stumbles and mumbles something about being out for a walk.

'A walk. So, Skid, that's not your car over there?'

An eighties Ford Escort XR3i, neon red with yellow racing stripes, is parked a few yards away.

'No,' he says.

'Really.'

I walk up to the car.

'Are there many people in this town called Skid Solo?' I say, pointing to the personalised sun strip on the windscreen, replete with his name picked out in red on dark blue.

'Maybe.'

'Jesus, Skid. Are you this dumb for fun?'

'Don't call me dumb.'

He tries to put some gravel into his voice.

'Then,' I reply, 'don't treat me like an idiot and make yourself useful. Give me a lift to the port. I'm on a tight schedule.'

He shrugs and opens the car doors.

I enter a world that has cliché so hard written into it that it's difficult to tell whether it's one giant piss-take or an homage to bad taste. The car lives in the eighties. Fur seat covers, front and back. Fur on the dashboard. Correct that—dirty fur on the dashboard. Eight track player in the console. A pool table eight-ball for a gear knob. A nodding dog on the back-parcel shelf. Midnight blue ceiling with pinprick lights above me. Badly applied shading on the windows. Red leather and aluminium steering wheel and, of course, two furry dice hanging from the rear-view mirror. Skid slips on fingerless driving gloves and a pair of what look like Ray-Ban Aviator sunglasses but are probably fakes. When he fires up the engine, Visage's 'Fade To Grey' bursts from the speakers. I hold my tongue, wanting him to get a move on.

He doesn't so much leave the parking space as fire us from it. Full wheel spin and hard lock, we mount the kerb and miss side-swiping a car by millimetres. He plants his foot to the floor and we drift over the cobbles, mounting the other kerb before fishtailing to a halt. He accelerates again, almost immediately slamming on the anchors as we approach the rear of a delivery truck. Rather than wait for the van to advance, Skid places two wheels on the pavement and tears by, to a rousing chorus of honking horns. He enters the main square and to my dismay cuts clean across the centre, a traffic free zone, weaving through a game of football.

'Skid, what the fuck?'

He ignores me and tries to power slide the car on to the next road but fails and spins the car. He stalls it. Refiring it, he plants his foot again. The man doesn't need an accelerator, he just requires an on/off switch. More by luck than skill he finds the road to the port. With no traffic in front he presses the on switch and leaves it on. The ancient engine still has some grunt and in a thirty-kilometre speed area we are soon triple that. A roundabout lies ahead. He hits the brakes too late to shed off enough speed and has to cross the centre line to avoid ploughing straight through the thing. We enter the port at warp speed and only God's own luck prevents us from paying a visit to the sea as he brakes and slews us to a halt in a disabled space.

He looks at me with a smile when we've stopped. 'Still got it.'

I shake my head. 'Got what, Skid? Got what? A fucking fifteen-year-old's first day out in a car. What the hell was that?'

His face falls. Genuinely disappointed at my reaction.

'You wanted here quickly,' he says.

'And alive. I don't know what racing school you went to, but you should ask for your money back if that's how they taught you to drive.'

'I'm good.'

'Skid, that wasn't good. That was just plain stupid. I'm sorry I asked for a lift.'

I open the door to Skid telling me, 'What do you know? I can still cut it with the best.'

I can't resist. 'The best? Pat was right: my mum was a better driver and I never saw her drive.'

He shouts after me, 'Pat Ratte said that?'

I walk away.

The key I found in the filing cabinet doesn't have a number on it. I need the Twins' help on this. They know what I'm looking for. So, if the money is in the box then my bargaining chip is gone—but I have no choice.

I enter the shop.

Sheryl is on her own.

'Hi, Sheryl.'

'Hi.'

'I found this in Mum's stuff,' I say, holding up the key. 'It looks like one of yours.'

'It is,' she says, taking it from me. 'Your mum kept a box here.'

'Can you open it?'

'I'm not supposed to. We need a lawyer's letter to access boxes of those that are deceased.'

'And what if the money is in there? Come on, just tell me what box it is and I'll open it. If she'd put the number on the key I'd have just come in and looked.'

'Give me a second.' She moves to the computer.

'No,' I say.

'What?' she says before she can touch the PC.

'I take it you are going to look up the box number on the computer.'

'I need to. I can't remember it.'

'Is that CCTV working?' I say, pointing to a camera on the wall.

'Not at the moment. Jordan was supposed to get it fixed but he hasn't got around to it.'

'So there's no way of anyone knowing what we are doing? Good. Don't use the computer. That will be traceable. You must have a rough idea of which box Mum used. We'll just do it the old-fashioned way.'

'Why?'

'Because if there is 1.3 million euros in the box you don't want a computer trail that ties you to looking up a dead person's box if, and when, the shit hits the proverbial.'

She thinks on this and says, 'Makes sense.'

'Just give me a rough location of the box and watch the front door.'

'It's one of the bigger ones, on the bottom, over there,' she says pointing.

'Right let me know if anyone approaches the shop.'

I start trialling each box with the key and, twelve boxes later, the key turns.

'Got it,' I say.

I open it and Sheryl leaves watch-duty to stare over my shoulder.

The box has a padded envelope in it and nothing else. I pull the envelope out. It doesn't look large enough to hold a million plus euros. I pull back the curtain of the privacy booth.

'I'm coming in with you,' Sheryl says.

'Feel free. It'll be cosy.'

We squeeze into the booth and I open the envelope. A passport falls out when I rip and tip the envelope. A small bundle of euros with it. The only other two things in the envelope are a small piece of paper with numbers written on it in my mum's scrawl and a cheap mobile phone. I flip the passport to the photo page. My mum's face stares at me. It looks like it was taken recently. Next to it is the name, Euphemia Ratte. The date of birth is wrong and makes her three years younger than she was. The issue date is four years back but the passport looks brand new. I flip through the document but there are no stamps in it. I count out the euros. Three hundred. I examine the piece of paper.

1-45-23-7-9-92

'Any idea what these numbers might be?' I say to Sheryl, holding up the piece of paper.

'No.'

'Ratte?' I say. 'Why would Mum have a passport in the name of Ratte?'

'I've no idea.'

'This is going to sound crazy,' I say. 'But is there any chance Mum and Pat married and no one knew?'

Sheryl picks up the passport. 'Anything is possible. Pat's wife died back in the UK a long time ago.'

'Someone would know though, right? I mean you'd struggle to keep that a secret around here.'

Sheryl looks at the passport and nods.

I take it from her. 'Maybe it's a forgery.'

'Looks real to me.'

'Mum can't be married to Pat,' I say to her. 'I mean wouldn't you tell your own daughter something like that?'

'You'd think,' says Sheryl. 'But if it's true, there goes your life in the sun.'

'Why?'

'Well, if your mum is married to Pat then he gets the pub and flat.'

'Christ, you're right.'

But that doesn't gel. Pat told me Mum and he had a deal. There would be no need for a deal if they were married—but I keep that to myself for the moment.

I reverse out of the booth, placing the passport and money back into the envelope. I keep the mobile phone and piece of paper. I close up the box and pocket the security box key. My head races at the implications of the passport and the name.

'How could we check if they were married?' I ask.

'Depends where they got married,' replies Sheryl. 'But if it was Spain then, on a Saturday, all the official offices will be shut. I don't know if you can check such things online but, if not, then you'll need to wait till Monday.'

'Sheryl, I need a coffee. Do you want to join me?'

'I can't leave the shop unattended.'

'Sure you can. The café in the square overlooks the front door of here. If someone comes along you can easily let them in.'

'Suppose.'

She locks the door as we leave and a minute later we have two *café con leches* and I add in a croissant with jam.

'Sheryl, someone in your group would know if Mum was married. Wouldn't they?'

'No one told me anything.'

'But Pat and her were close?'

'Yes. Although less so of late.'

A yacht is sailing out in the bay. Its sails momentarily lose cohesion and flap as the vessel tacks. I watch the sailor catch the turn and settle her back into a run, canvas now full and driving.

'If the money isn't in the box, then where is it?' asks Sheryl.

'I'm not sure. Is there anything else about the money I don't know?'

'We're sure that Effie moved it from a bank in Benidorm not that long ago. In cash and in multiple runs. But we've no idea where she moved it to.'

'And that's it?'

'Pretty much. She bribed one of the bank managers to help her but he knows nothing and neither does anyone else.'

I pull out Mum's phone. It's unlocked and still has some charge. I look up the phone's number. It's the one I have for her. I scroll through the call log. There are two numbers on it but one stands out as having been called a number of times in the last few weeks. It looks a little familiar. I show the number to Sheryl.

'Do you recognise this number?'

'Sure, ED Taxis.'

That's why it looked familiar. It's the taxi company that I have the card for.

'Did Effie use them a lot?'

'Mostly to get to the pub and home.'

'Was she in the pub every day?'

'No. She liked to take a couple of days off every week recently. Said the place was doing her head in.'

I check the call log. ED Taxis were called every day for the last three weeks, sometimes four times in a day.

'Sheryl, would ED Taxis tell me where Mum went?'

'Gabby Taylor would, if I asked her. She's the dispatcher and she's all mouth so she'd want to know why I'm asking.'

'Because my mum's dead and we are trying to trace her movements for the last few weeks.'

'She'll get suspicious. Is it important?'

'I think it might be.'

'Okay. I can ask.'

'Can you do it now?'

'Now?'

'I'm on a kind of tight schedule.'

Her answer is to take out her mobile and call.

'Here,' she says, handing me the phone after explaining what I wanted.

'Hi, Gabby, I'm Daniella Coulstoun.'

Gabby is true to her name, a real motormouth, and she is happy to tell me about every trip Mum made in the last few weeks. I pull a pencil from my pocket and signal to Sheryl to hand me some napkins. Scribbling down the trips I question a few and hang up with a promise to use Gabby's taxi company in the future. I look at the notes in front of me, a thought forming.

'How many other taxi companies are there in town?'

'Loads.'

There is only one other number on the call log of Mum's phone.

'Is this a taxi number?' I say, showing Sheryl the number.

'No. It's the pub number.'

'Could we find out if Mum used any other taxi companies? She might have called from the pub phone.'

'Or another mobile.'

'I doubt it. This mobile is the only number I have but then again she could have another—although it's not come to light.'

'Calling them all would take an age.'

'I'll buy lunch.'

Sheryl sighs and starts dialling. We order while she calls the companies and I chew as she talks.

Twenty minutes later and she has drawn a blank.

'What now,' Sheryl says as she nibbles at her *bocadillo*.

'Do you have the number of every taxi company in town on your phone?'

'That's it. There are no others.'

'So ED is it.'

'Seems so.'

'I need a little more time to work out a few things but could we get the Ex-Patriots together?'

'When?'

'Give me an hour and we can meet at Mum's house.'

'What if they can't come?'

'Tell them it's to do with the money.'

'You know where it is.'

I just smile.

MINESTERIO DEL INTERIOR
GUARDIA CIVIL
PUESTO DE EL DESCARO

DATE: Jueves 14 de Noviembre de 2019
Esta es una copia de la traducción al inglés de la entrevista con la persona o personas nombradas.
(The following is a copy of the English translation of the interview with the subject or subjects.)
PRESENT: Capitán Lozano, Teniente Perez and George Laidlaw

TRANSCRIPT AS FOLLOWS:

SPANISH POLICE OFFICER CAPITÁN LOZANO (CAPITÁN L): Señor Laidlaw, what is complicated about where you were just before you found Señora Coulstoun?

GL: It just is. Does it matter? I answered a shedload of questions in the pub and it was that bloody bodybuilder who was there when she died. Not me. Are you asking him all these questions?

CAPITÁN L: My colleagues asked many question at the pub but it would seem that our bodybuilder friend has gone on an unplanned vacation. No one seems to know where he is.

GL: Really?

CAPITÁN L: Really. Do you?

GL: Why would I know?

CAPITÁN L: Señor Laidlaw, you said that Señorita Coulstoun is the main beneficiary of Señora Coulstoun's will. So does that mean she inherits the pub?

GL: It's not that simple. Effie made some promises before she died that were never put into writing.

CAPITÁN L: Like selling Se Busca to Señor Ratte?

GL: So he says.

CAPITÁN L: Are you saying Señor Ratte is lying?

GL: I'm not saying that.

CAPITÁN L: And does Señorita Coulstoun know about this?

GL: She does now.

CAPITÁN L: And your fight with Señor Ratte? What was that about?

189

GL: Who said we fought?

CAPITÁN L: Señorita Coulstoun.

GL: It was nothing.

CAPITÁN L: And was this nothing the reason that Señorita Coulstoun broke into Señor Ratte's home? Or was that your idea?

GL: Who said anyone broke into Pat's house?

CAPITÁN L: I heard.

GL: From who?

CAPITÁN L: It's complicated.

20

Where's the Money?

Mum's front room is full of Ex-Patriots. Skid and Zia are sitting next to each other on one of the sofas and the Twins are in the chairs near the dining table. Saucy is resting on the arm of the other sofa and George has parked his backside on the dining table. I'm standing.

'So, did you find the money?' says George.

'No,' I say and the air of anticipation in the room evaporates like snow from a three-bar electric fire.

'So why are we here?' he moans. 'Why aren't you out looking for the cash?'

'I don't have it but I think I might know where it is,' I say.

That puts some buzz back in the room.

'Where?' George almost shouts.

'First things first,' I say, realising that I'm enjoying this. 'Let's look at this whole bag of washing with some degree of logic and dump all the emotional crap that's clouding everyone's vision.'

Everybody is now fixed on me.

'We know that my mum transferred money from the bank in Benidorm to El Descaro, I say. 'In cash. That much we know. What I now know, because I managed to access her mobile,' I hold it up, 'is that she used the same taxi company every time. Sheryl helped me check. Mum made eight trips to Benidorm in the last few weeks. The taxi took her straight to the bank and then straight back home. She didn't stop off on the way back so we need to assume that the money was, at one point, in this flat. But I've searched, as have some of you. It's not here now, of that I'm certain.'

Skid pipes up, 'She could have hidden it in a cubbyhole?'

'Skid, there is no cubbyhole, and, even if there was, she knew she risked getting caught by one of you. She would be scared you'd find it. This flat would be one of the first places you'd look. So, I don't think it stayed here long.'

'Where did she hide it then?' asks Sheryl.

'I'll get to that,' I reply. 'But before I do I think Mum had help in all this.'

That nails their attention to my mast.

'Who helped her?' says Zia.

'By all accounts, Mum wasn't mobile,' I point out. 'She took a taxi to Se Busca and back when she was working. Again, I checked. No deviation—pub and back. I asked the taxi company if she went anywhere else. They said she made only one other trip recently and that was to the Safety Deposit +.'

'She could have used another taxi company,' says Jordan.

'Sheryl checked. She rang fourteen other taxi companies and none of them picked up Mum recently. There's no other calls on the phone to any other numbers on the phone other than the pub. She has no landline in here and the pub landline seems to be dead. Unless she has another phone hidden, that's her movements for the last few weeks.'

'Effie cut off the line to the pub a while back,' says George. 'The internet is about to go down soon as well.'

'When did she go to the Safety Deposit +?' asks Jordan.

'It's the only trip that wasn't to Benidorm or Se Busca. Two weeks ago.'

'She has her Mini,' says Saucy.

'Have you seen it?' I ask them. 'It's in the underground garage beneath here. Three tyres are flat and the windshield is cracked. It hasn't moved in months. I'm telling you now, Mum has been to Benidorm, the pub, the Safety Deposit + and that's it in the last few weeks.'

'So, someone came here and took the money and hid it for her?' says Zia.

'If it's not here and it's not in the pub then that's my guess,' I reply. 'I can't see Mum hefting cash all over town. She wasn't one to walk. So someone else must have stepped in to help.'

I leave that hanging.

'Who?' George grunts.

I look at them all, one by one, deliberately staring at their eyes. I'm more of a voice person than a facial person. In my job I hear liars, I don't see them. But I'll still know if anyone in the room is part of this.

'It could be any one of you,' I point out. 'Maybe even a couple of you in on it with her. Who knows? She needed help. Of that I'm sure.'

'That makes no sense. She rolled us all. We all want the money back,' says George.

'Sure, and the guilty shout the loudest, George,' I say.

He bristles at that. 'What are you implying?'

'I'm not implying anything. I'm stating a fact. Mum had help. And anyone in here could have been in with her.'

Zia leans forward. 'And why would we still be here, if one of us had the money? Why wouldn't we run?'

'That is a good question, Zia,' I say. 'But maybe the timing of Mum's death fucked it all up for someone. Maybe the cash is somewhere it can't be reached. But I really don't think it was any of you. I don't think Mum would have trusted a single person in this room.'

'Screw you,' says Jordan. 'Who says we can't be trusted?'

'Jordan, all of you have been in on a scam that's ripping people off. Don't take the high ground, you don't deserve to be there. None of you can be trusted.'

George is on his feet. 'For fuck's sake, if you don't tell us who the hell has the money I'm going to start breaking some of those bones myself.'

I ignore his outburst but I'm also done tap dancing around this bloody subject.

'Sheryl,' I say, 'have you told everyone about Mum having a passport in Ratte's name?'

'Yes.'

'Well, that has to be a clue,' I state.

No one speaks and then Sheryl breaks the silence. 'Pat Ratte was helping Effie?'

'Isn't it obvious?' I say. 'They've seen a lot of each other. Pat has the connections to help get Mum out of here. We have a dodgy passport with his surname on it. What else could all that add up to? I can't think who else would have helped her.'

'And the cash?' says Saucy.

'Who knows?' I reply. 'If Pat was holding it then it could be anywhere.'

'I don't buy Pat as the helper,' says George. 'He doesn't need the money or the hassle.'

'George, tell me this, what did Pat say to you in the pub? What started that fight? Did he not tell you that my mum used you? Wasn't that what that stupid square-go thing was about?'

'He was talking about years ago. Him stepping in and me getting the bum's rush a long while back. It's an old story. I just got riled.'

'Are you sure, George? Maybe he was referring to the scam. Maybe he knew Mum was going to stiff you. Was he having a last dig at you? He was close to Mum. He might have a lot of cash but who could resist a share of 1.3 million if it came your way? If I was him I'd revel in rubbing your noses in it.'

George thinks on that and says, 'So what do we do? If Pat was helping he's hardly going to hand the money back.'

'True.' I root into my pocket and take out the paper with the numbers that I found in the security box Mum rented.

'Anyone know what this might be?' I say, offering the paper around.

The paper is passed from Ex-Patriot to Ex-Patriot with shakes of the head and muttered negatives until it reaches Saucy. He studies it and doesn't pass it on.

'Saucy, do you know what the numbers mean?' I ask.

'I'll tell you what they could be.'

'What?' says Zia.

He holds the paper up to the light. Rubbing his finger over the numbers.

'Well, I can't be certain,' he says, 'but it looks a lot like a code for an old-type safe. You know the ones that had tumblers. Pat was a safe cracker back in the day and a bloody good one. This could be the numbers for opening one of them.'

'And why would Mum have those numbers?' I ask.

'She had her own safe?' says George.

'Which you jimmied,' I point out.

Saucy shakes his head, 'No, her safe was a four-number job and the dial only went up to ten. This is much bigger, if the numbers are what I think they are. There are probably a hundred numbers on the dial of this bastard. There's a number 92 on this bit of paper.'

'So, there's a big safe? Somewhere? Where?' I say.

Saucy twirls the paper in his hand and says, 'Pat has a real old-time safe, with a real big dial, sitting in his house.'

'How do you know that?' George asks.

Saucy looks at the paper again. 'I did some accounts work for him for a while. He told me about the safe. Said it was a big swine of a thing. Very old-school, he said. He got it from some private bank in London when they moved into new premises. No bank would use one of those things any more. It's all electronics and gadgets for them nowadays—but Pat's old school and he liked the idea of owning the very type of safe he used to break into. Reminded him of the old days. He had it shipped out here and installed in his house while they were building it.'

'And,' Zia points out, 'if Pat was helping Effie, where better to store a million plus euros than in some bloody big safe?'

'But if it is there,' says George, 'as I said, Pat's hardly going to hand it over to us.'

'Daniella,' says Jordan, 'with that passport do you think your mum married Pat?'

'No. I thought hard on that and I'm not buying it,' I reply.

'Why?'

'Pat told me he had a verbal agreement with Mum for Se Busca. Why mention a deal? If he was married to Mum it's his by rights.'

'What does it say in her will?'

'The one I have doesn't mention Pat. But you know that,' I say looking at Skid. 'After all you have a copy.'

Skid looks away. He'd be a crap poker player.

'If Pat and Mum were married that changes it all,' I say. 'But I ask again, why? Why wouldn't Pat just show up with the marriage certificate and be done with it?'

'But if they're not married why does her passport have his surname on it?' says Zia.

'I have a thought on that,' I say. 'Going on the run with your own passport and 1.3 million euros would be hard. With you lot chasing her she wasn't going to be able to hole up in Spain. I think she was heading for the UK. She'd want far away once the investors found out about the scam—not to mention the police. Mum would need a new identity to get away with that.'

'But why use Pat's surname?' says George.

'I've no idea. I could be wrong on all this,' I say. 'But if I'm not and Pat does have the cash stashed in the safe, what next?'

'We could always steal it,' says Saucy.

'Steal from Pat Ratte,' squeals Skid.

Saucy passes the piece of paper back to me.

'Skid,' Saucy says, 'do you have a better idea? We have next to no time to get the cash and bug out and I think Daniella might be onto something here.'

George adds, 'Bloody right we need to move quickly. I've had two more of the investors get in touch. One that was very insistent. He's flying in from the UK tomorrow. I'm not sure we're going to be able to hold this back much longer.'

'And do we just wander up to Pat's house,' Zia says. 'And steal 1.3 million euros that may or may not be there?'

'I'm out of other ideas,' I say. 'My best guess is that Pat has the cash. Now you lot need to decide what to do. I'm out of this. You asked me to find the money. I've told you what I think. Over to you. And George, you can call off Jeep.'

George reacts. 'Not so fast, lassie. You're not walking away that easy.'

'*Easy?* George?' I say. 'What's bloody easy about this for me? Eh? I did what you asked and I did it under threat of violence. But what makes me laugh is that it wasn't that bloody hard to figure out. You didn't need me. Not really. You just all panicked. And that panic kept you looking at me. You were all so sure I knew more than I was saying. But, bloody hell, you are all so slow.'

'And you are a cheeky shit,' says Saucy.

'Give me a break. Look at the facts. Sheryl knew my Mum had a security box and she never thought to tell anyone. I mean, come on. Is that not just dumb?'

Sheryl stares at the table.

'Bloody hell,' I say. 'The cash could have been sitting there the whole time. How hard did you really all look? I'm thinking you were so used to my mum making decisions for all of you, that you've forgotten how to think for yourselves. Look at how easily she took the money from you.'

'She was clever with it,' says George.

'No, she wasn't. There were a hundred different ways she could have been caught. You let her run the whole cash side on her own. And none of you ever considered that she might abscond with the money,' I say. 'You never gave it a thought. Even when it was all coming up short and it wasn't enough, which you all knew, did any of you think she might take it all? Were you that blinded by her personality?'

'She was still recruiting investors,' says George on the defensive. 'Why do that if she was getting ready to run?'

I shake my head. 'Come on George, it's obvious. She was doing it for exactly that reason. To make it look like everything was still on track. But she knew it wasn't. There wasn't enough money for all of you. But there was enough for one of you maybe two at the most. Look, I've given you my best guess at where the cash is and I'm sure as hell not going to break into a gangster's home on the off-chance I'm right. For one thing I get fuck all out of it.'

George speaks. 'Thirty-one bones.'

I slap my hands together and he jumps.

'Give it a rest, George,' I say. 'How hard would it be for me to call Pat and tell him my suspicions? Tell him I found a note laying out that the cash is with him. Then you are all screwed. If he's got it he just shuts up shop. I don't need this and in one call I can make it a problem you can't solve. Don't bloody threaten me. Now, you can all chat it over and make whatever call you want but if I were any of you, I'd be getting out of town. I've been in Pat's house and the banks have nothing on his security. Even a professional would struggle to get in there. Maybe a full-frontal home invasion might work. If you've the balls for that. Maybe you can talk him out of the cash. Maybe he doesn't have it or he's already moved it or he's spent it. None of this makes me want to take this any further. So quit with the thirty-one bones thing, George, and get out of my fucking life.'

I walk to the window and finish by saying, 'And if I have one bit of advice for you all, it's this. If you're going to get out of this mess, start working together. Because from where I stand you're all so screwed you can't think straight, act straight or fucking walk straight.'

With this I leave.

21

Jumping Fences

It's my third time in three days in the café on the square. The waiter nods recognition as I sit down. There's another game of football going on. The kid with the Messi top is now clearly the worst player as his Ronaldo sidekick is missing. I've left the Ex-Patriots to talk. I'm done for the moment. My soul is sore from the last few days. Too much stress. Too much shit. Too much everything. Mum was down for the bar shift tonight. That means I need to step in and if I do, I'm on my own. I'm not asking for help.

I drain my coffee, pay the bill and decide to go for a walk. I've no particular destination in mind, I just feel I need to be moving. I enter a residential area with fewer high-rise apartment blocks and more villas and bungalows. Not as upmarket as those in Pat's rarefied playing field but still worth a few bucks. I lose myself in the maze of roads and let the sun and caffeine do their job. Chill and buzz.

I find myself next to a tiny park that contains a patch of scorched earth and a few benches. One of the benches is in the shade of a small tree. I plonk down on the bench and lay my head back, trying to close my mind off to events. I'm halfway to sleeping when a high-powered engine crashes my world. I open my eyes to find a jet-black, top-of-the-line Range Rover in front of me. The windows are blacked out. I stare at the vehicle, expecting the driver to kill the engine. Instead the driver treads gently on the accelerator sending wave after wave of soft roars into the afternoon sky. A thin blue cloud of smoke emerges from the exhaust each time the accelerator is depressed. I seem to remember that blue isn't a great colour to have coming from there.

The driver side window eventually powers down. Pat Ratte leans out. He's got a smile that suggests cold, not warmth.

'Get in,' he says.

'Why?' I reply.

'Because I said so.'

'Forgive me if I don't leap and do your bidding. I just paid you five grand. I expect a little bit of civility for that sort of cash.'

The rear door opens and Jeep gets out. I don't need to be a certified genius to know what might happen next.

'Do you know what, Pat?' I say.

'What?' he replies.

'You've got this protection thing all tit to arse. I'm paying you to stop any hassle, yet between paying you, having Jeep on my tail and now this—you are the one doing all the hassling.'

'Go figure, now get in.'

'I ask again, why?'

'Because I want to show you something.'

'In *your* car. Do we need to be in private to see whatever it is?'

Jeep moves in and I stand up. Pat signals for him to stop, my attempt at crude humour failing.

Pat points to the door. 'I told you Daniella, I don't do light hearted. Now get in.'

I round the purring monster and slide into the passenger seat. The smell of warm leather and saddle soap fills my nose. Jeep gets in the rear. Pat selects drive and pulls away. I slide my hand over the seat and feel the tiny cracks in the leather that come with age. The dashboard, despite the darkened windows, is badly sun-stained and the steering wheel in Pat's hands is sprouting tiny threads where the stitching is coming loose. The car has the air of wear and tear that the well-off either embrace or avoid.

We cruise towards the seafront in silence. I make a few attempts to kick-start a conversation but neither Jeep nor Pat responds. We roll onto the road that follows the shore, sea on one side, property on the other and, a few hundred yards along, Pat pulls the beast up, placing the two passenger side wheels on the pavement. He keeps the engine running and I can hear the faintest of misfires every few seconds. I'm looking out on a bare patch of land wedged between two large, seafront villas.

'Do you know what that is?' Pat says, reaching over me to point at the wasteland.

'Grass? Dirt?'

'That,' he says, 'is the scam that the Ex-Patriots are counting on for their pension.'

The land is a tiny sliver at the front, maybe wide enough for a one-lane road at best. Further back it widens out and wraps around and out of sight behind both villas.

'Now see the tiny piece of land right next to the pavement,' Pat says. 'They don't own that and there's no other way to get to the bit of land behind that they do own. Everything else around their land is built on and no one is for selling.'

I play a little dumb. 'And why are you telling me this?'

'Because you're trying to track down the cash they've been scamming.'

'Am I?'

'What do you know about the missing cash?'

'Nothing.'

Jeep smacks me from behind and my head snaps forward. I see a firework display as my vision blurs. I cry out and wrap my hands over my head.

'I don't believe you,' Pat says.

I rub at where Jeep struck.

'What do you know?' Pat asks.

I instinctively duck forward, expecting another blow from behind. Instead Pat cracks his elbow off my chin. I howl.

'What do you know?' Pat repeats.

'Nothing,' I shout.

I grab the car's door handle and pull, expecting it to be locked, but it isn't. I ram my shoulder into the window and push the door open, scrabbling to free my seat belt at the same time. Pat grabs at me. I strike out with my free arm and manage to stick a finger into his eye. He roars and lets me go. My seat buckle unclips and I tumble to the pavement. Scrabbling to stand up, I see the rear door swing open above me. Jeep lumbers out. I launch myself up to try to head butt him. A stupid idea and thankfully I miss. My momentum carries me past him. He turns and I break into a run, waving my hands in the air and shouting. The few people who are out for a walk, zone in on my voice. Jeep trudges after me but he's not built for speed. I can easily outrun him.

I hear the engine of the Range Rover scream and I know I can't outrun that. With the sea on my right and no roads leading inland for a few hundred yards I dive over a fence and into the garden of the villa next to the Ex-Patriots' land, just as the Range Rover screeches to a halt behind me. A couple are sitting on their veranda, drinks in hand. In front of them two paperbacks are open, face down on a small glass table. The couple are wearing sunglasses. They both lift them to get a better look at me as I skirt the swimming pool that burbles in front of me before I zip out of sight, along the side of the villa to the rear. I emerge on to a pristine strip of lawn that is being showered in water by pop-up sprinklers. I can't tell if Pat or Jeep are following me but I can't take the chance. I slide across the lawn and clamber up and over the wooden fence at the rear, dropping into a car park that services a block of second-line apartments. The exit for the car park to the road beyond is blocked by a large electric gate. I look for another way out. The property is wrapped in an eight feet high metal slated fence. I spot a small gate for pedestrians and run over to it. It takes a few seconds to find the release buzzer. I dash out on to the road, just as the Range Rover screams into view.

A block of flats lies opposite. I look for another place to run but the entire road is double edged with apartment blocks. All protected by fences or walls or both.

I start to move away from the car but I realise that I'm not going to outrun it. The next apartment block on the right has a small concrete wall topped off with a fence. As the Range Rover careers towards me I jump onto the wall and pull myself up and over the fence, catching my thigh on the sharp edge of one of the spikes that top it.

I fall to the ground on the other side and try to get up. An express train of pain runs up my leg and I see a small spray of blood arc from my leg as I try to stand.

'Get back here now,' screams Pat from the car.

Like that's going to happen. I hirple towards the apartment block to the sound of Pat shouting. I limp out of sight and once I reach the rear I'm faced with another swimming pool and more wall and fence. God but they love their protection around here. There is no above-ground car park to be seen but the driveway from the front gate dips under the rear of the building I'm behind. I spot a gate swinging open beneath me and a car exits from what must be the underground car park. I let the car roll past and hobble down the ramp, through the gate and into the half-light beyond. A few seconds later and the gate shuts automatically behind me. I move to a wall and rest on it, holding my breath, conscious that the exiting car will give Pat a chance to get into the compound if he wants.

Minutes pass and I hear the misfiring roar of the Range Rover as it drives away. I slump down the wall and examine my leg. My jeans are ripped from just beneath my crotch to my right knee. I prod at the rip and wince as my finger touches the cut on my leg. The light around me goes off and I'm left in the dark. I gently probe at the wound. Maybe three or four inches long. Enough to warrant stitches, I'm guessing. I have nothing to stem the blood loss other than by ripping something off my top. The blood flow isn't for stopping so I strip my top and tear an arm free, wrapping the fabric around my leg. I put the rest of the top back on. Not a great look but better than bleeding out.

I sit still, figuring my next move. I pull out my mobile and dial Zia. He answers on the first ring.

'Zia, I need help.'

'Where are you?'

I explain what has just happened.

'Christ,' he says. 'Pat came here, he wanted in. We wouldn't let him. He was screaming in anger.'

'Zia, I'm injured.'

'Tell me where you are.'

'I'm in the underground car park of a block of apartments near the front. One street back from the sea. Not far from the bit of land you all own.'

'Give me fifteen minutes. Don't move.'

'Can you bring some bandages? I'm bleeding quite badly.'

'I'll see what I can get. I'll call when I'm near and we can figure out exactly where you are.'

I lie against the wall and pray no one wants to park or leave. I'm sitting right next to the exit and will be in plain sight. Across from me there is a row of cars. I decide I'd be better hidden there. Less chance of being spotted, unless the owners of those cars turn up. I crawl over and slide between a dusty 4x4 and an even dustier soft top. I lay my head on the door of the soft top and stretch my legs under the 4x4.

I tighten up the cloth around my leg and wonder what in the hell had gotten into Pat. We had hardly been bosom buddies up in his place but things had changed and he'd clearly found out about the cash—and wanted to know where it was.

Ten minutes later my phone rings.

Zia's number.

'Daniella, where are you?'

DATE: Jueves 14 de Noviembre de 2019

Esta es una copia de la traducción al inglés de la entrevista con la persona o personas nombradas.

(The following is a copy of the English translation of the interview with the subject or subjects.)

PRESENT: Capitán Lozano, Teniente Perez and Zia MacFarlane

TRANSCRIPT AS FOLLOWS:

SPANISH POLICE OFFICER CAPITÁN LOZANO (CAPITÁN L): So what is so complicated about your relationship with Señor Solo?

ZM: I'm not in a relationship with Skid.

CAPITÁN L: Yet you live with him.

ZM: I told you I'm just sleeping on his sofa, although God alone knows why.

CAPITÁN L: You do not know why you are staying with Señor Solo?

ZM: He's a pain in the arse to live with. I've never seen anyone with so many lotions and potions. He has one bathroom and takes two hours in the morning to get ready. Two bloody hours. Who does that?

CAPITÁN L: Why did you take Señorita Coulstoun to the Centro De Salud?

ZM: She was injured.

CAPITÁN L: How did she get injured?

ZM: Ask her?

CAPITÁN L: I am asking you, Señor MacFarlane.

ZM: Her leg was badly cut.

CAPITÁN L: And how did Señorita Coulstoun obtain this cut?

ZM: On a fence.

CAPITÁN L: A fence?

ZM: That is what she said.

CAPITÁN L: You know nothing else?

ZM: Like what? She cut it on a fence. I helped by taking her to a doctor.

CAPITÁN L: Why was she climbing this fence?

ZM: How would I know? You would need to ask her.

CAPITÁN L: But you took care of Señorita Coulstoun? Why did she not take care of herself?

ZM: Because the cut was bad.

CAPITÁN L: Did this injury happen when you were around?

ZM: In what way?

CAPITÁN L: Did Señorita Coulstoun sustain this injury to her leg while you were present?

ZM: Not exactly.

CAPITÁN L: Where did it occur?

ZM: Near the seafront.

CAPITÁN L: And Señorita Coulstoun called you?

ZM: Yes.

CAPITÁN L: Why?

ZM: She was hurt.

CAPITÁN L: I know she was hurt. But why did she call you? Why not call an ambulance?

ZM: She doesn't speak Spanish and she didn't know the number to call.

CAPITÁN L: Ah. And this was the only reason you went to her aid?

ZM: Yes.

CAPITÁN L: And this so-called accident did not involve Señor Ratte?

ZM: I never saw Señor Ratte.

CAPITÁN L: That is not what I asked.

ZM: So you want me to comment on things that I never saw?

CAPITÁN L: Okay, okay. Am I right in saying that you are in a new relationship?

ZM: It is complicated.

CAPITÁN L: Señor MacFarlane, I hear that phrase more than any other. Are you now in a relationship with someone?

ZM: Yes.

CAPITÁN L: Who?

ZM: As I said, it is complicated.

CAPITÁN L: Who?

ZM: Daniella.

CAPITÁN L: Señorita Coulstoun?

ZM: Yes.

22

Kissing

Once the doctor had inserted a few stitches he'd prescribed some antibiotics and heavyweight painkillers. He wanted me to go the local hospital but Zia persuaded him otherwise. Zia had swung by my hotel to bring me a change of jeans and a fresh top and, with my leg bandaged and nipping like vinegar on a pulled fingernail, I'd limped out of the *Centro de Salud* and back into the sun with Zia's aid.

'Where is everyone?' I ask as we slip into Zia's car.

'Still at your mum's flat. Talking.'

'How did Pat know you were all there?'

'I don't know. It was maybe thirty minutes after you left that he turned up.'

I tell Zia what Pat and Jeep had done to me. Zia is a little shocked but not as much as I'd have expected. And that tells me what I already know. Violence lives just under the surface of the world according to Se Busca. Zia sees something in my eyes. The wariness. The *knowing*.

'Daniella,' he says, 'this town is not a bad place.'

'Tell me another one.'

'Daniella, you cannot look at Se Busca and see El Descaro or Spain or anywhere else. The people who live in El Descaro are wonderful, warm human beings—locals and expats alike. They live, work and play as well as any place I've ever been. Homes are at a premium because of how nice this town is. Se Busca is not this town. I've told you that already. It's a self-regulating mechanism. An autonomous realm with its own codes and values.'

'Why?'

'Sorry?'

'Why is that the case? Why is it like that? Why are the people who hang out in there predisposed to frequent such a place?'

Zia starts the car to ease a little aircon into our lives.

'They didn't used to hang out in there,' he says. 'It wasn't always the way it is. It was your mother that created it.'

'Created what?'

'She created Se Busca. The people were always around but they didn't have a place of their own. Their sort are always around. She just created a home for them.'

'Their sort? A home, Zia? A home for who?'

I rub my leg, feeling the roughness of the bandage, and want to pop one of the painkillers I have, but I was told two every two hours, no more.

'Everywhere has them, Daniella. Every town. Every city. The disenfranchised. Those who still feel like outsiders no matter how long they live in a place. Any place. The misfits. The outcasts. Those who don't blend in well.'

'You mean the criminals?'

'No. You don't get it. Yes, there are criminals in Se Busca but there are also criminals out there,' he says, waving his hand at the town. 'The people in Se Busca have found a way to belong for the first time. We don't belong in El Descaro. We belong *to* Se Busca. If your mum hadn't created the environment I'm sure someone else would have. Maybe not as intense a place. Maybe it would have been across a few bars and clubs scattered throughout the town. Your mum just saw the opportunity to provide a one-stop shop to do something for the town.'

'Which was what, exactly?'

'Save the town from itself.'

'Oh, come on Zia. What are you saying? That my mum is some sort of Florence Nightingale of the criminal classes?'

'I told you it's not about criminals.'

'You could have fooled me. I've yet to meet someone in Se Busca that isn't.'

'What about me?'

'You? You're part of a million-euro scam and you also, may I remind you, happily endorsed George's view that I had too many intact bones.'

'I didn't agree with that bit but I am desperate, Daniella. We all are. Every one of us needs the money. Every one of us is so low on cash we will soon have only one option. And,' he adds, 'if it counts for anything, I don't think that George will follow through with the threat from Jeep.'

'You don't *think*.'

'He was, or rather he is, desperate. He is trying to find leverage.'

'And will you stop him?'

'From hurting you? If I can.'

The words are soft, gentle, caring.

'You said you had one option,' I say. 'What's that?'

'Go home.'

'To the UK?'

'Yes.'

'So go.'

'I told you why I can't go before. I can't go as a failure. I came here for a reason,' he says. 'For a better life. Or maybe a different life. I came here with hopes and dreams. We all did. All seven of us, and many others besides, took the life in the sun option. The one that people dream of back home. The one that makes up day-time TV's schedule. All of us with a view of making a better fist of it than we had in the UK. But look at us. Me, a failed singer. Skid, a useless racing driver. George, struck off. Saucy, an alcoholic. The Twins, models no more. We all have to live with our past. All of us. I told you, none of us wants to go home with our tail between our legs.'

'Is that what Se Busca is *really* about? A place for those who think they've failed?'

'No, Daniella.' He pauses and stares into the middle distance. 'Not those who *think* they've failed. If we are honest it's about those who *know* they've failed.'

'And Mum made some sort of home for these people? And did she see herself as a failure?'

'No. She came out here and did well. Saw a gap in the market and filled it. Spotted the word *flop* written across our foreheads and gave us a place that we could call our own. We know it's a shithole. Windowless, horrible decoration, the works—but it's a place where that unspoken failure is never mentioned. Everyone can still be what they want. The future is still there for us to grab.'

'And the scam?'

'All part of the delusion. In fact, born of the delusion. If it had worked we would all have moved elsewhere. A bright new future possible. Of course we'd have had to hide. Carried on with the lie. Tried to find another Se Busca. But if I'd got my share of the cash I'd have been able to spin it out until I died.'

'Back home.'

'For me, yes. For the others, elsewhere.'

'But the money is far less than you need, maybe even gone.'

'It might be less but it's not gone. I can't believe that. Even a few hundred thousand would let me escape. I can still sing and still work. I can still happily lie to myself for a good few years yet.'

There is a gleam in his eye that suggests tears are not far away. He's pouring out a story that rips at his heart. I hardly know him and yet he's offloading like I'm his psychoanalyst.

Outside the car, two older women are chatting to each other. Lost in their own world. Oblivious to the one that Zia is describing to me.

'Zia, even if you do get some cash, you'll be on the run.'

'Daniella, we all know that. But we're on the run already. On the run from life and don't forget we'd all agreed to spread to the wind. Lose touch. Make it hard to track us down if some of the others were found. How much resource will they really put into finding us anyway? How many investors will step forward and admit to being conned?'

I let the cool air of the aircon play over my fingers.

'Most of them,' I say. 'I think I would. I might look stupid when the story breaks but I'd want my twenty thousand back. And as to the police, don't fool yourself. They'd find you, one way or the other.'

'Maybe, maybe not, but I can't go back to the UK without the cash. None of us can leave without it. That's why we need to get the money.'

'And how does Pat Ratte fit into the "failure" thing? He frequents the pub.'

'Pat's a lot of bluster. Saucy did some checking while you were gone. He called a few friends back home. Things are not right in Pat's world.'

'Like what?'

'Big money issues. And Saucy thinks they have got worse of late.'

'So maybe the 1.3 million is no small potatoes to him.'

'Maybe.'

'But he can't have it or why strong-arm me?'

'Because he wants to know what you know. That doesn't mean he doesn't have the cash.'

'Ah,' I say with realisation. 'And acting the way he did would be a great way to cover up the fact he has the cash. But how did he find out what we were up to? Who told him? He sure as hell didn't know when I went to see him or he'd have beaten the crap out of me in the privacy of his own home rather than in a car on a public road.'

Zia shrugs and signals to move us away from the pavement.

'Where are we going?' I ask. 'Back to the flat?'

'Not yet. I want to show you something.'

'I don't like that game. Pat said the same thing and then used me as a punchbag.'

'I promise I'm not intending violence.'

He says this with a smile.

I sit back, looking at him as he drives. He still has that something special that marked him out as a pop star. Not the voice. He probably has that but, for a singer, the vocal chords are not always the real currency of fame. Good singers can be found all over the planet and few are really successful. And then there's the bad singers that make it. Zia has a look about him. He's in his fifties, I'd guess, but could pass for ten years younger. His high cheekbones and dark-brown eyes give his face a radiance that glows when he smiles. Apart from Clyde, Se Busca's barman, he's been the only person who's helped me since I got here. Zia dug me out of a hole by helping at the bar and now he's here when I need him. And his confession about being a failure is well beyond that of a casual conversation. He wants something and I hope I know what it is.

The car climbs out of the town and into the hills beyond. After a while Zia's phone rings. George's name comes up on the screen but Zia ignores it. He turns off the road onto a dust track, curving deeper into the countryside. A mile of bumping later he stops the car and gets out. I follow.

There's a small track, more of a thought than a real path. Zia takes point and pushes through some scrub. We emerge onto the edge of a cliff, looking down on the sea. To our left is a ramshackle house. Roofless, windowless, doorless. The view it commands is spectacular but the house is past redemption.

'Where are we?' I ask.

'It's the next bay along from El Descaro,' he says, pointing to the view.

The panorama is wonderful. A large curving landscape of sea, sky and land. Uninterrupted. And, as far as I can see, with no other buildings nearby.

Zia points to the collapsing house. 'I own that.'

'A fixer-upper?'

He smiles. 'It is that, and more. A few years back I told you I picked up that gig with that Spanish band, La Mezcla de Pandilla.' We made a little money and this came up in an auction. A Brit who bought at the height of the market went bust. It didn't cost much but I had dreams of turning it into a recording studio.'

I could really see that working. Inspiration from the view and the isolation.

'And why are we here now?'

'This dream's gone for me now. Whatever happens, this is beyond me but I still have hope. But, Daniella, without you, there is no hope. For any of us.'

'Me?'

'You have your mother's blood in you and that counts for something.'

'Not as far as I've experienced.'

'We may not show it but look what you did back in the flat. You figured out where the cash might be. None of us had a clue. We were all circling before you came. Reeling from Effie's death. Rudderless.'

'And I could be completely wrong. So, in what way could I instil hope?'

'By taking up where your mum left off. Become the new Coulstoun of Se Busca. Help us get the cash back.'

'You don't need me. I told you as much in the flat. You're smart enough to figure this out. Or you can always run.'

He walks over to me.

'And there's something else.'

He leans in and what I hoped was about to happen happens. We kiss. Long. Deep. Slow.

23

Burglar Alarm

We lie in the sun, our feet a few yards from the cliff's edge, holding hands. The kiss had finished and we had lain down. Saying nothing. Neither of us moving things on. Just soaking rays. Thinking. Zia's actions are a mystery to me. I could ask if this is a game but I don't. I've had very few meaningful relationships in my life and that kiss was wonderful. I don't want to sour the moment. I know this is nuts. I don't know the man. He doesn't know me and the current situation is hardly conducive to the start of something. Although when is?

'So Mum was the saviour of El Descaro?' I say.

Zia rolls over to look at me. 'I think in a way she was. Not deliberately. As I said, she just saw an opportunity. A crowd who needed somewhere to be and she gave them it. I think, later, she began to realise what she had. She was respected and was able to mould the people to the place. Your mum had a lot of rules.'

'That square-go thing?'

'And others.'

'George told me that she built the place up on dodgy money. He threatened to tell the Office for Asset Recovery and Management or whatever it is called, about it. To strip me of it.'

'I'm certain the cash wasn't all clean. But so what?'

'And the police never got involved in Se Busca?'

'Effie had a good relationship with the local police and the Guardia Civil. She ran charity events for some of their causes. Helped out with drink at some of their events.'

'And that kept them out of Se Busca? Clyde told me that it was a bad idea to call them when I barred Saucy.'

'You don't want to do that. No trouble is the byword they like to associate with Se Busca. You need to keep to that if you are staying.'

'What keeps them out?'

'It's the way the place has kept, still keeps, some bad shit off the streets of El Descaro. They know that the people who frequent the pub are not the upstanding town dwellers they desire but then again, no town has all diamonds and no duds. From the authorities' end the people they'd like to keep an eye on are all in the one place and Se Busca, if nothing else, has a mean reputation for keeping the peace. As Effie used to say—what happens in Se Busca stays in Se Busca.'

'The police just turn a blind eye.'

'They do if there is nothing obvious to see.'

'But there must be plenty going on that they don't see.'

'There is, but it's all hidden away behind locked doors. If Effie caught anyone that was laying anything on the streets of El Descaro they were out the door. She wouldn't hear of it. And no one wants to be barred from Se Busca.'

'So as long as it doesn't impact El Descaro, then whatever is going on is deemed okay? But it must have impacted somewhere? The next town?'

'Exactly. Think on it. It's just like a burglar alarm on your house. At least that's what Effie used to say.'

'My mum said a lot, didn't she? But what does that mean?'

'A burglar alarm doesn't stop a hardened criminal if they want to get into your house. But it's not really for that. Is it? It's really there to make the burglar move on to the next house. Leave yours alone. Go for easier pickings.'

'And Se Busca is El Descaro's burglar alarm?'

'The analogy is flawed. But it kind of makes sense. For police, Guardia Civil and even the mayor's office, Se Busca keeps a lot of nonsense away from their desks.'

'And you want me to step into Mum's shoes?'

'Not for long. Just to sort us out.'

'Then what?'

'Whatever you want. Sell Se Busca. Sell the flat. Go home. Back to your job. Or stay here. Maybe you and I have a little me-time ahead.'

'You make it all sound so simple.'

He rolls over and kisses me on the cheek. 'It is. Whatever needs to happen, needs to happen quickly. We either fix this fast or it doesn't get fixed at all. And that means it needs to be simple.'

'So why wouldn't I just sit tight and pick up the pieces after this all crashes?'

He kisses me on the lips.

'Because, Daniella Coulstoun, George really will take the flat and the bar away.'

'I could live with that.'

'And he'll implicate you in the scam.'

'And you would back him up.'

'Me? No. The others. They might. If they see everything vanishing, then they have nothing to lose. They will lash out. And you will be their *piñata*. I can't stop that but there's another reason.'

'What?'

'I think you might be becoming one of us.'

'What?'

'An Ex-Patriot.'

'Me?'

'Is life back home a bed of roses, Daniella? Are you proud of what you have achieved back there? Does a life out here not have appeal?'

I don't answer.

'Tell me I'm wrong,' he says, resting his hand on my wrist.

I hesitate. He's on to something, of a kind. If I was to run the bar, live over here, I'd be able to do what he and the others can't—go home with my tail held high. Jealousy will flood the insurance claims floor when I tell them about the pub. And my friends—well, they would be out here in a shot for free holidays.

Zia's phone rings again.

It's George.

We sit for a few minutes after the phone stops ringing.

'What's your answer?' he eventually says.

'Mrs McLarty, the cleaner, said I wasn't family.'

'You weren't—but that's changing.'

A cold wind of reality blows across my shoulders. The sun, the kiss, the offer, the dream. Am I being played, again?

'Is it George pulling the strings here again?' I say. 'Setting you on me like this?'

It's the wrong thing to say. He yanks his hand away.

'Do you think I'm doing this to get you onside?' he says.

'I don't know.'

He stands up. 'Well, I'll tell you one thing, Daniella Coulstoun, I am not now, and never have been, that type of person. I sure as hell didn't kiss you because George Laidlaw told me to.'

He's angry and with good reason. I throw up my hand. 'I'm sorry. I'm just confused. My mother's death, the scam, Pat, his violence and now you and me. Forgive me. I spoke without thinking.'

'Let me tell you something, Daniella. I am not doing this for anyone but me. It hadn't even occurred to me that I had any feelings until I saw you sitting in that garage, blood running down your leg. You looked so vulnerable. I didn't mean for this to happen. And I'm not sure it's any more than a moment but I really am trying to help you. I'm trying to talk you into the only course of action that makes sense. You need to step up and take control.'

I sit up. *Control.*

He looks at the view. 'I'm just trying to sort my life out and maybe kissing you isn't the smartest thing I've done, but I wanted to.'

'And I wanted you to, don't get me wrong.'

And I did.

His phone rings again and he looks at me.

I lie back and try to order my thoughts. I'm being played but not in the way that places Zia as some gigolo. I'm being played by George's threat to take what's rightfully mine away and to hand me a cell in some Spanish prison for something I wasn't privy to a few days ago.

I stare at the sky. The contrail of a jet flows out behind a plane, high up. I think of all the people in the metal cigar tube who are unaware of my situation.

Zia's phone rings again and I roll on to one arm and hold out my hand.

'Can we just lie for a few minutes longer,' I say.

Zia sits down and takes my hand.

'I'm sorry,' I say.

'And your answer?'

Control.

'You know the answer. But will the other Ex-Patriots accept it?'

'There's only one way to find out.'

24

Keys

Back in the flat everyone else is where I left them. The smell of sweat, stale coffee and booze floats in the air. Saucy is nursing a half-pint tumbler of something golden and George has a baby version of the same. The Twins are on coffee and Skid is playing with a cheap plastic bottle of water. Zia leans on the wall next to me.

Everyone has aged a decade in my absence. The appearance of Pat and the reality of the situation is hitting them hard.

Zia stands up.

'Right,' he says. 'Here's where we are at. The lid is about to come off our pot roast and the recipe is rank. By tomorrow we may all have to bug out, cashless, homeless and any other less you can name. And I for one want to avoid that. As far as we know, Pat has the money and we need to get it from him. I propose that we install Daniella as the head of the Ex-Patriots until we get this sorted.'

Or we don't get it sorted, I think.

'Does she have an idea of how to get the cash?' says George as if I'm not here.

'No,' Zia replies.

'Then why give her the lead?'

'Because who else will do it?'

'No one elected you to appoint a leader,' George says. 'She doesn't know us.'

Screw this.

'George stop talking as if I was in the next town,' I say. 'You're the one that was asking me to sort this.'

'Effie ran the team. She earned the right over the years,' he says.

'And,' says Zia, 'if Daniella hadn't worked out where the cash might be we would all be screwed.'

'We're screwed anyway,' says Jordan.

'Screwed,' repeats Sheryl.

'We ain't getting the cash back from Pat,' slurs Saucy.

'They are all correct,' adds George.

'And we all give in, is that it? Just call it quits and run?' says Zia.

'Yes, we all run. Let's face it, we run,' says George.

'And me?' I ask. 'What about me?'

'You're as screwed as we are. If the money is in Pat's there's no way to get it,' says George, turning away from me.

Skid stands up, twirling his bottle, a nervous look on his face. I think he is going to the toilet but instead he makes a pronouncement that's far more interesting.

'I might know a way to get into Pat's place,' he says.

'Sure, Skid,' says Sheryl. 'It's called a door.'

'Yeah, Skid, a door,' says Jordan.

'No,' he says. 'I know you all think I'm dumb. But that doesn't mean you get to dismiss everything I say.'

'Okay, Skid,' Saucy says, too loud on the back of the drink. 'How do we get in to Pat's place, break his safe open, make our getaway and leave Pat none the wiser?'

Skid's eyes are flicking from person to person. He's like a school-kid giving their first-class presentation. All nerves and shits.

'I don't know all of that,' he stammers. 'But I know how to get in.'

'How?' I ask.

'Pat's place is built on an old castle, right?'

'Sure, that's going to help,' Saucy whispers.

'Saucy, give him a chance,' I say.

Skid lifts a foot and draws a small circle with his toes on the rug. Nervous or what?

'I've been to Pat's place a few times,' he says. 'He has some real cool F1 stuff up there.'

'I never knew you'd been,' says George.

I step in again. 'Can we just let him finish?'

Skid lifts his head and says, 'He has good security but he told me once that he had built an escape tunnel.'

George can't help himself. 'You mean an escape room?'

'No,' Skid replies. 'A *tunnel*. Well, he didn't exactly build it.'

'Jesus,' says Saucy, downing the last of his whisky and looking around for the bottle.

Skid explains: 'What I mean is that someone else built it.'

'No shit, Sherlock,' says Jordan. 'And here's me thinking Pat got out the shovel himself.'

I slam my hand off the wall, the noise cracking around the room.

'Look,' I say, 'let him finish and then all of you can have your say. Just stow it.'

Silence.

'Well,' says Skid, 'Pat told me that the castle was built a long time ago when the Christians and the Moors were fighting in Spain. He said that the guy who built the castle needed a way out because back then they were scared of . . .'

He can't think of the word.

'You know when they surround the place?' he says.

'Siege,' I offer.

'That's it. The guy that built the place was scared of a siege. He had a tunnel built that would let him escape.'

'And it's still there,' says Zia.

I glare at him but he blanks me.

'They found it when they were putting in the swimming pool,' Skid explains. 'Pat had them clean it out and make it stronger. He liked the idea that he could do a runner if things ever went bad.'

'Where does the tunnel go?' I ask.

'Pat says there's an old well at the top of the hill behind his house and that the tunnel runs from there to his swimming pool room.'

Jordan puts his hand in the air, as if back at school.

I nod at him.

'I know it,' he says. 'It's called the Well of Desires.'

'*El Pozo de los Deseos*,' says Zia. 'A wishing well. You're supposed to walk around it ten times and make a wish.'

'That's the place,' says Skid. 'There's a door at the bottom of the well.'

'An escape tunnel sounds a bit out there,' says George.

'Not for back then,' I say. 'Fairly essential in those days. Although if there is a tunnel I assume Pat will have it locked tight.'

'Pat keeps a key for the tunnel on him at all times,' says Skid.

'Even easier,' says Saucy. Having found a fresh bottle of whisky, he's pouring a large measure. 'So now we just have to pickpocket Pat, shimmy down a well, crawl through a tunnel, sneak in his house, break open a safe and make a run for it.'

'I'm trying to help,' snaps Skid.

'How do we get the keys off him?' Zia asks.

'Pat keeps another set in the car,' Skid says. Then he adds, 'He told me.'

'And this isn't a figment of your imagination?' George says.

'No,' Skid scowls. 'Pat showed me the door to it in the pool house. Opened it and sure enough there's an old tunnel.'

'Even if true we'd still need the keys,' I point out.

'Show me Pat's car and I can get them,' says Skid.

The insanity of what's being proposed spins around the room. There's a sudden babble of talking as George, Sheryl, Jordan and Saucy all speak at once. Some to each other, some to the room.

I let it run for a few seconds and slam my hand on the wall again.

'Okay,' I say. 'Skid has had one idea. I'm open to others.'

The fact they listen to me suggests that being my mum, albeit temporarily, is something that is happening to me. Half an hour later and there is nothing that approaches a better plan. We range through the whole gambit of options from midnight raids to kidnapping Pat. We all agree that even if we can get into the house the numbers from Mum's Safety Deposit + box might not be for Pat's safe. We also acknowledge that Pat's muscle will be on site and none of us are up to that. We even agree that the money might not be there.

As we run dry, the front door to the flat is battered and Pat's voice rings out. 'I know you're all in there. Open this fucking door.'

We all look to the sound.

'Will that door hold?' I ask.

'Effie had a security door installed. Even a battering ram would struggle,' says George.

Skid suddenly waves his hand. 'Daniella, come with me. The rest of you stay put.'

'What?'

'Please.'

Skid takes me to Mum's bedroom. He pushes open the doors to the small outside balcony. The street is beneath us, two floors down.

'We climb down,' he says.

'Are you kidding?'

'That's Pat's car there,' he says pointing to the Range Rover below. 'The keys to the tunnel are in there and Pat is at the flat door. If we're quick . . .'

'Skid, I'm not shinning down a drainpipe. My bloody leg hurts like a good 'un.'

'It might be our only chance to get the key.'

I look over the balcony. It looks possible but also dangerous.

'Daniella, while Pat's at the door. Please,' pleads Skid.

I dig out a couple of painkillers and swallow.

'Jeep could be in the car,' I say.

'No, he's not, look.'

Jeep is lighting a cigarette on the street corner. He hasn't seen us.

'Can you distract him?' says Skid. 'He can't see us from where he is once we start climbing down. He has his eyes on the front door.'

'Maybe,' I reply.

It's a plan. Of sorts.

I take a breath and step over the balcony, clinging to the rusting metal balustrade. My leg instantly screams at me but I drop to the next balcony and Skid follows. I teeter on the rail of the balcony below and drop on to the ledge next to it. By grabbing at some electric wiring, I swing out and land on the pavement. Skid follows suit. I'm breathing hard.

'I'll try to distract Jeep but with my leg I can't run fast,' I say. 'For God's sake be quick. When you get the key, go around to the café I met you at on the main square. I'll meet you at the rear, near the toilets.'

I jog on to the road and Jeep spots me. I flip him the middle finger and he yells. I turn one eighty as he gives chase. I have no intention of making this long or complicated. Even with my bad leg, Jeep is too slow to catch me. I just need him away from the car. I circle the back roads once, slowing down to make sure Jeep is keeping up. I arrive back at the corner Jeep was smoking on and see Skid vanish towards the square. He was bloody quick. I hirple after him and out of sight before Jeep arrives back.

When I reach the back of the café, Skid is standing there.

'Did you get the keys?' I ask.

He holds up a key ring with a Ferrari key fob. There is a large key and smaller one hanging on the ring.

'Are you sure they're the keys?'

'Yes. What now?'

'Have you got your mobile on you?'

'Yes.'

'Phone George and tell him we all need to meet up at the pub as soon as possible.'

'What about Pat?'

'If George is right about the door being secure, Pat'll move on. I hope.'

Skid makes the call.

'And now what?' he says after he hangs up.

'We go up to this well and try the key. It's all I have. If the key works then we make a call on what next.'

We give it five minutes and exit the café.

'My car is on the next street,' Skid says.

'I think I'll walk, if you don't mind.'

'Are we not in a hurry?'

'No one is in that much of a hurry that they need to share a car with you.'

'I'm a good driver.'

I ignore the statement and start to walk across the square, eyes out for Pat or Jeep. 'Skid, what's the best way to get to Se Busca from here without being seen?'

He points to a lane near the southwest corner of the square. 'If we walk down there, we can take a small back road almost all the way to the pub. It'll take us fifteen minutes max.'

'What if Pat uses that road?'

He shrugs.

I decide to take the risk and we slide into the alley. I pop another painkiller and, a few hundred yards in, the view around us opens up as the lane squirts out into the land between the back of the town and the hill that Pat's house sits on. Every time a car approaches we have to jump on to a wall to let it past. If Pat comes this way we are real dead meat.

'Skid,' I ask, 'are you sure about this tunnel thing?'

'Yes.'

'Roughly, Skid, how long is it?'

His head runs some calculations and I can see he's having trouble with that.

'Okay, Skid, how long would it take to walk from the well to the front door of Pat's house on the surface?'

'Oh, about five minutes.'

I do the arithmetic. 'That could be four or five hundred yards. Is the tunnel big?'

'I'm not sure.'

'Didn't you get a look at it?'

'It was just a glimpse.'

I spot the top of the pub in the distance. The flat roof is grimy black in the late afternoon sun.

Skid sees the roof as well. 'Your mum always said that the roof would make a good place to relax. She once said she was thinking of converting the attic into a flat and having the roof as her private sun terrace.'

'I never knew there was an attic in the pub.'

'It's empty. We cleaned it out of everything a year ago. I think your mum was considering what to do with it.'

We walk the rest of the way in silence. When we arrive at Se Busca, there are a few cars in the car park.

'Are any of those Ex-Patriot cars?' I ask Skid.

'No.'

At least they had the sense to keep any sign we are here off the parking lot.

We knock on the cellar door. Zia opens it. We enter and find everyone there. I take a peek at the bar. It's running about half full. Impressive for the time of day. Tara is on duty.

'Skid, how do you get to the attic?' I ask.

'There's a small door on the outside of the building, above the cellar door. You need a ladder. You can't get to it from in here.'

'Not from inside?'

'Only through a trapdoor above the pool table.'

'I think we should use it to talk,' I suggest. 'If I was Pat this would be the next place I would look once he's figured we have flown the coop.'

No one disagrees. The thought of meeting Pat and Jeep in this confined space doesn't appeal to anyone. Skid opens the cellar door and I check outside is clear. Skid grabs a ladder from behind the bin house and lays it up to a small square door painted in faded blue, that sits a few feet beneath the roof, floating in the pub wall. One by one we climb the ladder, me last. Saucy is in front of me and has acquired another bottle of whisky, George is ahead of him and has a plastic bag full of bottled water in his hands.

I slip through the door and find myself in a space the size of the pub with a roof high enough for an eight-foot-tall person to stand. Skid was right. The place is scraped clean.

'I told Tara to say nothing if Pat comes in,' says Zia.

I pull the ladder up behind me and close the door. It's already warm up here and won't get any cooler soon.

'I suggest we sit over there,' whispers Zia, pointing to a corner that looks very much like the other three.

He sees the confused looks on people's faces and explains, 'That's the corner that sits above the cellar. When Skid was helping Effie move stuff out last year I was in the bar and you could hear the conversation when they were above the public area.'

We all huddle in one corner, circling as if we are getting down and ready for a sing-song around the campfire.

'Did you get the keys?' asks Saucy, twisting off the top of the whisky bottle.

Skid holds them up.

'And they can really get us into Pat's house?' says Sheryl.

'Yes,' replies Skid.

George hands out the water and takes the keys from Skid and fiddles with the key ring. The big key is brass, about four inches long with a thin shank. At one end there is a simple bit and at the other is a ring bow. The other key looks like the sort that would fit a padlock.

'And for all the security that Pat has,' George states, 'this thing'— he holds the keys up between his forefinger and thumb as if they are infected—'will bypass his state-of-the-art systems?'

George's words have the desired effect on the group—disheartenment.

Skid chips in, 'I've seen the tunnel and this is the key. Trust me.'

'And all of this works how?' I ask. 'We are going to set off any alarms as soon as we get inside anyway.'

'And?' says Saucy, another swig down.

'And we get caught,' I point out.

'Not if Pat and Jeep aren't in the house,' says George. 'If they're out it'll take the police a while to check out the alarm. They're not the quickest. Too many false call-outs in the past. We'd be gone long before they turn up.'

'And how do we ensure they are not in?' I ask.

'I have an idea on that,' says George and the Twins both giggle. I look at them.

'Okay,' I say. 'Let's assume for one moment that this key can gain us access to Pat's gaffe. Who goes?'

The rush to volunteer almost overwhelms me. Kids in school being asked to stand in front of the class and explain nose picking would have had a better volunteer rate. Every head looks away.

'Okay, team, don't all rush at once,' I say.

Saucy puts his hand up. 'I could have a go.'

'Saucy,' I say, slugging water, 'with all due respect, your current state of inebriation hardly marks you out as a stealth-imbued cat burglar.'

He shrugs and swigs straight from the whisky bottle saying, 'Don't say I didn't offer.'

George pipes up, 'If the tunnel is low my back won't stand it.'

If I had a penny for every man I've met who claims to have a bad back I'd have been able to pay them all their share of the 1.3 million euros, years ago.

I look at the Twins. The Twins point at Skid. Skid smiles and puts his hand up. 'Okay, I'll go. I know where the safe is.'

'You two?' I say to the Twins.

Jordan replies, 'If you and Skid are going we won't be needed. Why put so many at risk?'

'*Me* and Skid,' I blurt. 'Not me. You two are best placed. You're the youngest.'

Sheryl kicks that one back. 'Skid knows where the safe is; we don't. You wanted to be leader so it makes sense that Skid and you take this one.'

'Zia,' I plead.

'It does makes sense, Daniella,' he says. 'You and Skid. In and out. You're both fit enough. No sense in putting more people in there than we need to risk. Anyway, it might all be for nothing. Let's take first things first and find out if there's a door at the well. Then we can see what's what?'

That brings out the nodding donkey in all of them, including Skid.

'There's no way I'm going,' I say. 'It's your money. Not mine. Send Skid in on his own.'

Zia throws his hands up. 'You think, Daniella? Send Skid on his *own*?'

If Skid finds this offensive he hides it well.

George intervenes. 'Daniella, you're the one who doesn't think any of us can be trusted. So here's why you should go. Because,' he pauses for some inane effect. 'Because if you send any of us without you, what's to say we won't screw the others over?'

'Sorry?' I say.

'What if whoever goes in finds the money and does a runner?'

'While we are at the other end of the tunnel, waiting on them?' I point out.

Skid grins. 'We could throw the money off the cliff at Pat's house for someone to collect later.'

I'd never even contemplated that.

'Exactly,' says George. He picks up the theme and runs with it. 'We could find the money, sling it and come back claiming we hadn't found it.'

'Or,' says Saucy, 'we could throw it over the wall on to the road.'

'Or,' adds Sheryl, 'we simply walk out the door with it.'

I put my hand up, realising what is going down. 'You lot have already had this chat. When I was away with Skid. In Mum's flat. You've been through all of this already.'

George, Sheryl, Jordan, Saucy and Zia don't do any denying.

'I was right. None of you can be trusted.' My voice is raised. 'Not bloody one of you.'

Then another thin light dawns through the thick curtain that is hanging in my head.

'And this all means that you really *don't* trust each other,' I say. 'There really is no combination of Ex-Patriots that you can figure out that can be put in Pat's house that works for you all. You know that come hell or high water you're all going to hit the road soon. Vanish. And it would be way better to leave with 1.3 million than a sixth of that. You've all been planning to hide. All got it worked out. And that's scared you. You can't afford to let someone go after the cash without insurance.'

A lot of water consumption goes on.

'And I'm the insurance,' I continue. 'If I go in and try to steal the cash from you, then my life is over. I'll have no pub, no flat and no way to return to the UK. A life on the run. Everyone here has already resigned themselves to that life. I haven't. Can't. Won't. You're bloody counting on me to go in. You bloody *need* me to go in. If there's even a slim chance that the cash is in Pat's place, I'm the only one you all trust to go in and bring it out.'

I'm such a bloody fool. I've handed myself to them on a gold plate. I can't trust a single sodding person in this town.

'So, are you good to go?' says George.

I'm at a loss.

Ten minutes later, we escape the stifling heat of the attic and George and Zia fetch their cars for the trip to the well. George takes me along with Jordan and Sheryl. Skid and Saucy go with Zia. As we drive I wonder what else they've cooked up for me. I'm scrambling for a way out of this and my best hope is that the whole well thing is a joke.

We climb up through the increasingly impressive houses and, as we pass Pat's house, I realise that there's no way of knowing if he's inside.

'George,' I say, 'you said you had an idea to ensure that Pat will not be at home? What?'

'An idea,' he repeats.

'And he'll just drop everything.'

Jordan nudges Sheryl and they both giggle. George throws them a look.

'He will for what I have in mind,' George says, turning off the road and driving up a dirt track. The Twins giggle again. I feel on the outside of something that I should be on the inside of. That sense of not belonging. Of not being, in any way, in *control* of this.

George stops his car near a small circle of stones.

'The well,' he says.

DATE: Jueves 14 de Noviembre de 2019

Esta es una copia de la traducción al inglés de la entrevista con la persona o personas nombradas.

(The following is a copy of the English translation of the interview with the subject or subjects.)

PRESENT: Capitán Lozano, Teniente Perez, Jordan Norman and Sheryl Norman

TRANSCRIPT AS FOLLOWS:

SPANISH POLICE OFFICER CAPITÁN LOZANO (CAPITÁN L): Why is it complicated to answer where you were when Señora Coulstoun died?

SN: Do we really have to answer?

CAPITÁN L: Yes.

JN: Do we?

CAPITÁN L: Yes.

SN: We were at George Laidlaw's home.

CAPITÁN L: Señor Laidlaw did not mention this.

JN: What did he tell you?

CAPITÁN L: What everyone says to me. It is complicated.

SN: It is.

CAPITÁN L: I'm tired of complications. Make it simple for me.

JN: We provide services for George.

CAPITÁN L: Services?

SN: Services.

CAPITÁN L: What kind of services?

JN: He likes to watch us dance.

CAPITÁN L: Dance?

SN: We are good dancers.

CAPITÁN L: And Señor Laidlaw likes to watch you dance?

SN: Yes.

CAPITÁN L: And you were dancing for Señor Laidlaw when Señora

Coulstoun died?

JN: We were.

CAPITÁN L: At his home?

SN: Yes.

CAPITÁN L: And was anyone else there?

JN: Do we have to say?

CAPITÁN L: You do.

SN: That could be bad for us.

CAPITÁN L: How so?

JN: One of the other people would not like us to say.

CAPITÁN L: Was the other person also a friend of Señora Coulstoun?

SN: Yes.

CAPITÁN L: Let me guess. Señor Ratte.

JN: Why would you say that?

CAPITÁN L: Because he was evasive about his location as well. Am I right: was Señor Ratte there as well?

JN: Eh?

CAPITÁN L: Well, was Señor Ratte there as well?

SN: Eh?

CAPITÁN L: Well?

BOTH: Yes.

CAPITÁN L: So both of you were dancing for Señor Laidlaw and Ratte? And another?

SN: Yes.

CAPITÁN L: Señor Heinz, by any chance?

JN: Yes.

CAPITÁN L: And this was all happening at ten o'clock in the morning?

JN: Yes.

CAPITÁN L: And Señors Heinz, Ratte and Laidlaw were there from when?

BOTH: Maybe eight o'clock.

CAPITÁN L: You dance for people at eight in the morning?

BOTH: Yes.

CAPITÁN L: Is that a usual thing?

SN: Sometimes.

CAPITÁN L: And this dancing. What kind of dancing is it?

JN: That is awkward.

CAPITÁN L: Indulge me.

SN: They pay us to dance naked.

JN: They like seeing us dance naked.

SN: And we like dancing naked.

JN: Naked.

25

The Tunnel

Jordan and Sheryl are still nudging each other as I push open the car door. Zia pulls his car in behind ours and everyone inside gets out.

The view of El Descaro and Pat's home is hidden by a small copse of trees. In the other direction, beyond the well, the land falls away in layered terraces of olive trees. Standing at the well you can see someone approaching from all but the tree side for a good mile away. The horizon is clear as we all walk.

The circle of stones around the well is about two feet high. Loose rocks lie scattered, suggesting it was once higher. The remaining well stones are cemented together and someone has spray-painted a red cross on one side. On the other side there's a blue heart with the initials CV scrawled in the centre. Strewn around the immediate area are empty beer cans and crisp packets. A condom wrapper lies next to one of the loose rocks. I lean over and look into the well. It's four feet in diameter and a large iron grate covers the hole. A padlock is looped through a ring on the grate and through another loop concreted into the base of the wall.

Skid reaches over and inserts the small key from the Ferrari key ring into the grate lock and it turns easily.

'Give me a hand,' he says.

George leans in and they pull the grating up. It's hinged at the opposite end to the padlock and swings up with a grinding noise.

With the grille open, we all look in. A black hole vanishes into the ground. The smell of damp rises to meet our noses. There's no obvious way down. I lean in a little further and take out my phone, flipping on the light. It allows me to see that there is a crude set of steps hacked out of the wall of the well. I reach the first one and explore it with my fingers. It's a six-inch-deep slot, a foot long and four inches high. Inside the slot a slit has been cut to allow climbers to stick their fingers in and gain some additional purchase. My hand comes out covered in dirt. No one has used this in a long time.

'Skid,' I say as I stand up, 'did Pat tell you when he last used the tunnel?'

'No.'

George gathers up the Twins. 'We are off to meet with Pat. We'll try to keep him occupied as long as we can but I can't promise how long. Get moving.'

'What are you going to do?' I ask.

'Don't worry about that, just go get our money,' he replies.

With that he leaves, the Twins trailing, giggling, behind him.

Zia says, 'Saucy and I will keep lookout. We might have to shut the grille if someone comes along. I've never seen it open. I'd hate for kids to fall in or someone to start chucking stuff down when you are in it. But we'll stay here if we have to shut it.'

I'm woefully unprepared for this, as is Skid. My Vans are hardly climbing gear, and neither are Skid's loafers. We should have a safety rope of some kind, a proper torch, headgear—the works. We have zip.

George drives away, and I wonder what he has up his sleeve to keep Pat occupied. Skid throws a leg over the wall and finds the first cut of the steps. 'Come on.'

He topples back and pinwheels his arms to stop himself falling in. I rush forward and grab him around the waist, pulling him to safety.

'Fuck's sake, Skid. Do you do everything at bloody breakneck speed?'

He looks a little shocked.

'Let's take it easy. Slowly. Okay?' I say to him.

He drops his foot down, feeling for the next hole and Zia switches on his phone light. Stronger than mine, it illuminates four slots. Zia kneels down and drapes his stomach over the wall, pushing his phone down as far as he can reach. Six slots are now lit. I have a top pocket in my top and I switch on my phone light and stuff the phone into the pocket. The torch lens pokes out above the material. Better than nothing. Skid has a button pocket in his shirt and I urge him to copy my lead and soon we both have light coming from our chests.

When Skid's head dips below the parapet I take a look around to see if anyone else has appeared, before stepping over the wall. Saucy is lying next to the well, whisky bottle in hand, close to comatose. Zia is still kneeling to help light our way and the horizon is empty. As soon as Skid's hands are clear of the first slot I start down.

'Skid,' I say. 'Stop every so often and shine your torch down. I'd like to know if we are about to drop into heaven knows what before we do.'

He pauses, extracts his phone and shines it down.

'Can't see the bottom yet.'

'Skid, stop a minute. Zia, grab a stone and drop it into the well.'

'Good idea,' Zia says.

He scrabbles at his feet and picks up one of the smaller stones. He drops it into the hole and a moment later there's a small splash.

'Again,' I say.

He repeats the process. I'd guess two seconds between release and splash, and if my school physics is still good I'd say it is probably close to sixty feet down.

Skid replaces his phone in his pocket and begins the descent again. I follow suit. The slots are evenly spaced and uniform but ragged. Suggesting that they were dug out by hand tools, not power. And that adds some weight to Skid's tale of an ancient escape tunnel, but only a little.

I look at Zia as I'm about to vanish. He smiles and I'm still wondering how much I'm being played. Or is he right? Is the life of an Ex-Patriot one for me? If I go down this well, am I really taking a step into another life? Partaking in this insane venture as a way of breaking my ties with back home? Why else would I be doing this? What is my life in the UK? Mum had worked hard to build up what she had here. Why *should* I not benefit from that? The chances of the cash being in Pat's are thin. I know this. They know this. But they all want to hope it's there. And I'm the one giving them that hope. But what if it is there? What happens then? Or if it's not, what then? The future is a strange place. But still I'm doing this stupid thing. Even with all the ifs and buts. Why? Because why the fuck not? This is probably the most exciting thing I've done in my entire life. I have a real buzz on and when Zia smiles in my face the buzz rises a notch.

With my thoughts in the clouds, my foot lands on Skid's hand and he yells. I pull back.

'Sorry, Skid,' I say.

He's stopped to try to see the bottom.

'Nothing,' he says.

We climb further down.

Two stops later and Skid shouts up, 'I think I see water.'

'What about a door?'

'I can see a hole, I need to go down a little more.'

The smell of damp is strong. The brickwork is thick with slime and even with the slot's design it would be easy to lose grip as the cuts are getting wetter and wetter as we descend. I look up and Zia is still looking down, the top half of his body picked out against the small circle of sky above him. He's switched off his phone light and is tracking our descent by our lights.

'Zia,' I shout.

'Yes.'

'Skid thinks he can see water. Are we still clear of people?'

His shadow vanishes and when it comes back he shouts, 'So far.'

Skid's voice comes up from below. 'There's a small tunnel here. Hang on let me get the angle right for my phone . . .'

There's a splash and, for a second, I see Skid's phone as it sinks into the water at the bottom of the well. Then the electrics short and the light goes out but it lasts long enough to tell me the water is deep.

'Shit, fucking shit,' shouts Skid. 'My phone.'

I carefully remove my own phone from my top pocket and shine it down, conscious that if I drop it the game's up. With no light this would be nuts.

'I'm going to jump in and get my phone,' Skid informs me.

'Stop,' I yell. 'Don't do that. It's a goner. The water looks deep and there's not enough room here for me to pull you out if you get into trouble.'

'But my phone.'

'Forget it. Can you crawl into the tunnel?'

'I can't see.'

'Hang on,' I say and climb down until my foot brushes his head again. I lean out and shine my phone into the hole. 'Can you see now?'

'A bit.'

'Can you crawl in?'

'I'll try.'

He moves and I hold my phone further out, maxing the angle. Skid vanishes.

'Is it deep?' I shout.

'There's a door here. I'll try the . . . Shit.'

'What?'

'Do you have the keys?'

'No. Do you not have them?'

'No.'

Fuck a duck.

'Zia,' I shout. 'Do you have the keys?'

'They're lying on the ground. Skid put them there after George and him opened the grate.'

Comedy Central has nothing on this.

'Zia, I'll come back up. Skid, stay put.'

I climb up. The ascent is a lot easier than the descent. I breach the top to find Zia standing there, waiting. Saucy is asleep, snoring like a trooper. Zia hands me the keys and I put them in my pocket. He leans over and kisses me on the head.

'Look,' I say.

A couple are coming up the hill.

239

'I need to shut the grille,' Zia says.

'Let me get to the bottom first.'

'Quick.'

I start down again but there is no quick to be had. One slip and I'll be going for a deep, dark swim in the well water. Before I'm back at the tunnel entrance, the light above goes out with a bang, as Zia shuts the grille. My foot reaches the tunnel floor and I swing my phone out to light it up. Skid is crammed in a space five feet long and three feet high. A round metal door blocks any further progress. I pass him the keys and shine my light on the door lock. Skid fiddles with the key and I'm amazed to hear a click as it turns. Skid pushes and the door swings in easily, noiselessly. I move the phone light to illuminate the space beyond. A brick-lined tube, akin to a Victoria sewer drain, stretches into the dark.

'It's really small,' says Skid.

'Are there any lights?' I ask.

'Not that I can see.'

'Let me take point,' I say and squeeze past Skid into the tunnel.

My wounded leg bitches as I squat down. Once on my hands and knees I quickly realise that gloves would have been a good idea. The brickwork is rough, tearing at flesh. I start crawling and hear Skid closing the door. He starts to scrape the key around, looking for the lock.

'Don't lock it,' I say.

'Why not?'

'Who in the hell is going to follow us, Skid? And what if we have to get out quickly? What then? If you've locked us in?'

'Oh, right.'

'For fuck's sake.'

Dumb is as dumb does.

The tunnel slopes up for the first ten yards, maybe at an angle of five degrees or so, then it crests and falls away. The rise is probably designed to prevent overflow from the well cascading into the rest of the tunnel if the well fills up. I've clamped my phone between my teeth as it will fall out of my pocket now I'm down on all fours.

Skid swears. 'Fuck, this floor is jaggy as hell and I keep hitting my head.'

There's nothing to be done but keep going.

The sheer lunacy of this is sinking home. This is no well thought-out plan. No carefully constructed process of retrieval. Who knows where this tunnel is going? Who knows what's at the other end? Who knows if there is any money? If it is, will it be in the safe? If the numbers are the combination, will they work? If, if, if. At times like this there are two choices in life. Blindly go forward and deal with the shit as it hits you or retreat. And today is a move on, do it, fuck it and keep fucking it. I catch the pinkie of my left hand on a protruding slice of brick, bending it back. I yell.

'Stop,' I say.

'What is it?' Skid asks.

'I just need a breather.'

We sit in silence. Neither sure what to say. I don't know Skid and he doesn't know me and small talk feels like the wrong thing to do in this situation. I mentally count up to sixty before moving again.

I curl my fingers into a fist to prevent them catching on the brickwork. It makes progress slower but a little less painful. I need to stop every so often to remove my phone from my mouth and wipe the saliva from both my lips and the casing of the phone. Skid follows behind me with a stream of invective that is growing in intensity as we travel. The tunnel takes on a steeper slope down and we both freeze when a loud rumble roars around the space.

'What the hell?' shouts Skid.

The roar fades.

'I think we are under the road outside Pat's place,' I say. 'That's probably a car driving overhead.'

We both look up. Wondering if the roof will hold.

'We can't be far from the house if that's the road,' I say.

The slope climbs back up. A metal door appears. A second roar, this time deeper and longer, fills our ears. A truck?

'Jesus,' says Skid. 'This wasn't in the fucking plan.'

'Pass me the keys,' I whisper when the noise has gone.

Skid shoves them in my hand.

'Don't speak,' I say as quietly as I can. 'I've no idea who is on the other side of this door.'

I gently place the key in the keyhole and turn it. It rotates with ease and the door opens an inch as the lock breaks its hold. I strain my ears to listen and hear the faint sound of water bubbling. The smell of chlorine fills my nose, a warm blast of wet air carrying it in. I push door a little further open, wrapping my finger around the edge to stop it flying free. Dim light filters into the tunnel and I reach up and kill my light, pushing the phone into the back pocket of my jeans.

I open the door a little more. There's a small drop to a tiled floor and I rotate myself and plant my feet on the ground. I'm in a small, fully tiled room. To my left is a wall and to my right is a shower head and drain. Beyond that a glass door is allowing the light in. I move to the door, trailing dirt-black footprints on the tiles. Skid slips out of the tunnel to join me.

'A shower?' he says. Too loud. He sounds surprised.

'Shhh,' I hush.

I open the shower door and look out. The space beyond holds two more shower cubicles and an archway through which flickering light is bobbing and weaving. I exit the shower cubicle, ears alive for any sound. Skid follows behind me and I peek through the archway and see the swimming pool. It's not as big as I'd thought it would be. More of a giant splash pool than one for doing serious strokes. It seems at odds with the expense and scale of the space around me. The lighting is low, mostly coming from underwater, giving the area an ethereal feel. The stone of the castle walls makes up two sides of the room, a third is white rendered concrete and the fourth is the glass wall looking on to the driveway with the lethal drop. The glass is heavily shaded, explaining why I couldn't see in when I'd visited before. A couple of sun loungers lie near us and, up against one of the castle walls, sits a glass table with two plastic chairs.

'Well, this doesn't work,' I say to Skid.

'Why?'

'Look,' I say, pointing at the driveway. 'We are inside the walls but outside the house.'

Skid pulls at my top. 'Over there.'

In the low light I stare and realise that the white rendered wall has a door in it, just next to the table and two chairs. I walk over and finger it. There's no handle but when I push at it, the door clicks and flicks open a little. I pull it wide to reveal a wooden panelled corridor leading into the dark. There's a light switch on the inside wall and I risk flicking it on. The light illuminates a corridor curving in the direction of the house, the arc of the bend hiding the end.

'In for a penny,' I say and enter.

The corridor is short and the next door opens into a study dominated by a large oak desk and high-backed leather swivel chair. There is no one in. An entire wall is given over to books and, at a first glance, most look like they have cars as their theme. Another Ferrari rug, similar to the one I'd seen in the living room on my earlier visit, covers most of the floor. The tail section of a racing car is mounted on one wall.

'Skid, where's the safe?'

'Eh, I'm not sure.'

'You said you knew.'

'No, I didn't.'

'You bloody did.'

I plant my face inches from his. He's still in the corridor.

'Okay,' I say, 'what in the hell is the deal here?'

For the first time I notice that there is some music playing somewhere.

'Back,' I say, pushing Skid back.

'Don't push me,' he snaps.

I close the door and step up to him again. 'What gives?'

'What are you talking about?'

'I'm going to spell this all out, and if you don't come up with some half decent answers I might just revoke my lifelong avoidance of violence.'

His face tells me I've hit a chord.

'How did you get the key so quickly from Pat's car?' I ask.

'What?'

243

'From Pat's car, how did you get the keys so quickly?'

'I knew where they were.'

'I don't know much about car breaking but I was out of sight for maybe two minutes and you'd got into the car, found the keys and were on your way to the square before I returned.'

'I'm good at breaking into cars.'

'So you say. Okay, let's skip that. Why were you surprised when we exited the tunnel into the shower cubicle back there?'

'I was?'

'Big time. I heard it in your voice.'

'It's an odd place to have a tunnel.'

'I agree, but according to you, Pat had already shown you it. You said he'd even opened it for you. So why would its location be a surprise?'

He says nothing.

'Unless you'd never seen it,' I say. 'And on top of that you're now telling me that you don't know where the safe is.'

'You should have asked Saucy.'

Something is so off kilter here. I can smell it. I just can't quite figure the deal.

'So, are you just going to stand here and talk?' he says.

'I'm not sure what's going on, Skid, but we still need to find that money, if it bloody exists.'

I open the door again.

Skid doesn't follow.

'Come on.'

'I'm not going any further.'

'Sorry?'

'This is as far as I go.'

'This isn't fucking optional.'

'You don't need me. As I said, I don't know where the safe is.'

'If we split up we can halve the time to find it.'

He shakes his head. 'You're on your own.'

'Are you serious?'

He backs away. The music has the four-on-the-floor beat of disco.

'Are you coming?' I ask.

'No.'

'You are up to something. So bloody up to something.'

Skid quickly pulls the door shut behind me. Then there's a click.

Like the door in the swimming pool, this door has no handle on this side, but it does have a small thumb latch with a four-digit code panel below it. I push the door, but it doesn't move. I stare at the code panel.

'Fuck's sake, Skid,' I whisper. 'Open up.'

As I push at the door, I think I hear Skid's retreating footsteps.

He has locked me in.

Bastard.

I stand in the study and figure that going forward is the only option.

The distant disco beat takes on a quicker tempo.

The study leads to the hallway that runs through to the top room with the spectacular view that I sat in when paying Pat. Across from me is the kitchen. Like the pool it's a little disappointing in size and grandeur. The only other room on this floor is a bedroom. A massive double bed dominates but the room holds no hiding space for a safe. I check the room with the view and come up blank. Back in the corridor there's a small, recessed area that reveals a spiral staircase, going down. It seems a little cramped for a house this spacious and descending it is not something for the thick of waist.

I go down, slowly, and emerge on to an unfinished floor. Bare concrete dominates. No sign of any furnishings or decoration. Four doorways, all without doors, range to my right. To my left there is another room with a spectacular view. Smaller than its cousin upstairs it's a bare shell and the single-paned window has a thick layer of dust dampening the view. The floor is unswept. A second staircase lies a few feet away. I check the four rooms but they are all barren shells. The last two are so dark that I need to use my phone light to see anything. Light switches are non-functioning.

The music is louder down here and is coming from below. I try to remember how many layers there are to the house. From the driveway the level I'm on looked like the middle one, with one more beneath, but there might be more. I grab the metal guard rail of the next staircase and creep down. At the bottom of the stairs the brutalist, unfinished theme continues, and now I need my phone light on all the time as there is no glassed wall view on this level. The room to the left has hardboard sheeting where glass should be. To my right there are two more doorless rooms but there *is* a door at the far end and that's where the music is coming from. After a quick look-see in the main room and doorless rooms, and with no more stairs to descend, the only place the safe could possibly be is in the room with the music.

I approach the music door. Everything inside me is screaming to back off. The music is loud and I swing away. Too risky. Just too risky. I'll hole up in one of the doorless rooms for a little while and see if anyone comes out. If I pick a spot just inside the entrance to the nearest room I'll be invisible unless someone walks in and looks for me.

The music door opens and light and music flood the hallway before I can hide.

'Took your time, Daniella,' says Pat. He's dressed in a large blue dressing gown. Behind him disco lights pulse and race.

'Come on in,' he says and steps back.

At the back of the room, on a raised platform, there are two people dancing. The Twins are both as naked as the day they popped out.

26

Rock and a Hard Place

Jordan sees me and waves. His dick is rock hard. I have no idea where to look. His sister is sliding down a pole and I decide to reject Pat's invitation and retreat. Pat follows me.

'Where are you going?' he asks.

'Away from here.'

I'm grateful that the door behind him swings partly closed, hiding the gyrating pair. In the remaining light Pat cuts a gnarled and wrinkled figure. He adjusts his dressing gown, tying it tight.

'The show is good,' he says. 'They might be crap as models but they can fairly lay it out on the dance floor when they want to.'

'Right.' It's all I can think to say. Now I know what George had in mind as a distraction for Pat.

I back another few steps down the hallway and Pat follows.

'Jeep's upstairs,' he says. 'I've told him you are not to leave. He's good at that sort of stuff.'

The music shifts to an even higher energy plane and the disco lights follow suit, throwing a crazed world of shifting rainbows around us.

'You're not surprised to see me?' I say.

'Why would I be? I've got you on camera. All the way from the study down to here. All in HD.'

He points to a corner of the hallway and I notice a small camera.

'Thirty of those little things are dotted all over the house,' he adds. 'Picking up your every movement. All with night vision.'

'And Skid's movements as well,' I add.

'Skid?' he says. 'Peter Solo. Are you saying he is with you?'

'You know damn well he is.'

'I didn't see him. I only saw you coming into the study from the pool door.'

Skid had hung back at that point.

'Are there no cameras in the pool house?'

'Funny thing but the pool house cameras are on the blink.'

'Of course they are,' I say. 'So the only person you have on camera is me?'

He smiles.

'And where does this go from here?' I enquire.

'Well, we could watch the Twins do their thing for a bit,' he says. 'They really are quite good. It's a rare treat to see them in action twice in such a short space of time. They usually ration their dancing to push the price up. But this was a cut-price, last-minute deal from George and he knows I can't resist them in full flow.'

'I'll pass.'

'Suit yourself. I'll just tell them to cool their heels for ten minutes.'

I turn my head while he goes back to talk to them, avoiding any more unnecessary glimpses.

'Upstairs,' he says as he arrives back.

'Not exactly the high end of the décor world around here,' I say as we rise.

'Had a few money problems with this place,' he replies. 'My architect turned out to be great on vision and a moron on practicalities. Converting the castle to a pool room was almost ruinous. The dickhead didn't have the first clue on the local laws about historic buildings. He got it so wrong that the costs piled up like shit on a stable floor. The pool is half the size it is supposed to be and I only just managed to get the top floor finished before the bank flew off the handle.'

I keep climbing, trying to figure out where this is going and figuring it isn't going anywhere that will benefit me but, at the moment, Pat seems happy to yak.

'And even then,' he continues, 'I've a bloody kitchen the size of a bathroom and the main window leaks when it rains.'

'It's a tough life,' I say as we reach the top floor.

'In there.' He points to the study with the door to the pool.

'And what next?'

He pushes me hard and I fall to the floor, gasping.

'Sorry about that,' he says. 'I just want to make sure that you don't think that this is some easy, I'll-be-going-soon moment. Because it's not. I know about Effie's little money vanishing trick and I'm looking to you to fetch it for me.'

I let my breathing catch up with me and kneel up. 'What the hell did you do that for?'

'Call it a down payment on what comes next unless you fetch me the money.'

'I don't know where the bloody money is. I thought it was here.'

'I know you did. Because you think that I've got it buried in my safe.'

'Yes.'

'And I'll happily tell you that's not the case.'

I stand up, holding up my hand. 'There's no need for violence.'

'That depends on how reasonable you are going to be. That money is mine by rights.'

'Who told you about the money?' I pause and think on that when he blanks me. A penny drops off a high shelf in my head. 'Of course, Skid told you. He set this all up. That's why he got the keys from your car so easily. Has he even been up here before?'

'A while back but only to see the F1 stuff. Amazing what a man will do if you promise to fulfil a lifelong ambition.'

'Like what?'

'He wants a shot in an F1 car.'

'And you told him you could make that happen?'

'I led him to believe that it might be possible.'

'And how did he get in touch with you? This wasn't planned that long ago. Otherwise you would have been on my case way before you picked me up in the car.'

He says nothing.

'Skid with his mobile phone,' I guess. 'In Mum's flat. He called you. Or texted you. After I'd thought I'd worked out where the money was. And then what? You promised to cut him in on the 1.3 million and to cut all the others out. Is that why he went along with the daft tunnel stuff?'

'Smart, aren't you?'

'No. I'm actually as dumb as they come. Tunnels, safes and Skid the lead. I thought his little burst of inspiration in my mum's flat to get the car keys was a bit out of character. All a bit too good to be true.'

'He follows instructions well. Even if I did have to text it all to him.'

'So there is no safe?' I say, pulling the piece of paper with the numbers out of my pocket.

He looks at it.

'Effie's copy,' he says. 'I have got a safe and that's the combination, but it currently holds two hundred euros and a gold watch worth half that. As I said, this house is the original money pit.'

'Do you mind if I sit down?'

'Yes, I do. That's my chair. Plank your backside on the desk if you want a rest.'

I take up the offer.

'Effie and I had an agreement,' he admits. 'In return for me helping her to vanish I was to get the pub.'

'Do you know I asked your mum to marry me? Not that long back, but she said no. Told me she was too old for that sort of thing and that what she really wanted was out of El Descaro, to spend the rest of her time somewhere quiet. She had an eye on a cottage north of Dundee. Somewhere she used to go when she was young.'

'I know it. In a village called Finavon. We used to holiday there. And what was she going to live off if you were getting the pub? You've just said you've no money because of this place.'

'I thought she had other money. Everybody thought she had other money. My job was to obtain her a new identity and, in return, I get the pub. She takes her money and lives out her days in the wilds of Scotland. That's what I thought.'

'Only she didn't have money.'

'Only she did. I just didn't know it was going to be 1.3 million

250

euros from a scam. That was her out. Simple really. Quite clever when you think on it. I never even got a whiff of the scam. And that's hard around here. But she figured out that when the investors and the police came knocking on doors they'd have six suspects bang to rights and she would have vanished. Sure, that lot would finger her but she'd be in the wind with a new name. And with six caught there would be a lot less pressure to find her. And, as I said, she managed to keep all of this from me. Smart woman, your mum.'

'She would never have gone to Finavon.'

'No. Why not?'

'Because she told you that's where she was going. Why would she tell you the truth?'

'Of course, you're right, she'd lie. The last thing she'd want is me rolling up sometime in the future.'

'Why did she ask you to get her a passport with your surname on it?'

'You saw that?' he smiles. 'You can't blame a man for trying. I thought it might show her I was serious about marriage. She could hardly throw the thing back at me. She needed it, and it's not easy to get a passport that'll fool the system. She wasn't too pleased at the name I chose but she couldn't do anything about it. I wasn't about to get her another.'

'So she leaves and you were going to run things here. Take over the pub. Be the kingpin of Se Busca.' I look around. 'And that would help pay off the debt you have amassed building this place. Am I close?'

He slumps, sighing. 'It would have helped a little.'

'But now I inherit the pub.'

'Effie and I had a deal.'

'True, but Mum's dead and I'm not.'

'That can be fixed,' he says with steel in his voice. 'Or better still you can hand me the 1.3 million.'

It's my turn to slump. 'Jesus, why does everyone think I know where the bloody money is?'

'Skid says you are it.'

'Skid wouldn't know *it* if *it* came up and *it* bit his dick on the end. I am not *it* and never have been *it*. And will never be *it*. I thought the money was here. That's how not *it* I am.'

'Well, here's how I see all this. I think you can still find it. So, you get me the money. All of it. In return I don't hand over the tape of you breaking into my house to the police. I'll give you until tomorrow morning to come up with the cash. Say ten o'clock.'

'Is that what the tunnel nonsense was about? To tape me and blackmail me?'

He stands up and walks up to me. 'It worked, didn't it?'

'Pat, I don't know where—'

Pat speaks, 'Money. Tomorrow morning. Ten o'clock. No later. Ten o'clock. Here. Is that crystal? Now I've a little more entertainment to enjoy. The front door is open. Leave when you're ready.'

A few minutes later I hear the disco music rise in volume, briefly, as Pat opens the door to the music room. Then we're back to a distant back beat and me wondering what in the hell I am supposed to do now.

MINESTERIO DEL INTERIOR
GUARDIA CIVIL
PUESTO DE EL DESCARO

DATE: Jueves 14 de Noviembre de 2019
Esta es una copia de la traducción al inglés de la entrevista con la
persona o personas nombradas.
*(The following is a copy of the English translation of the interview
with the subject or subjects.)*
PRESENT: Capitán Lozano, Teniente Perez and Jose Cholbi

TRANSCRIPT AS FOLLOWS:

SPANISH POLICE OFFICER CAPITÁN LORENZO (CAPITÁN L): You
say you are representing Señorita Coulstoun, Señor Cholbi? Is
that correct?

JC: Yes.

CAPITÁN L: In what capacity?

JC: I'm representing her interest in settling her mother's estate.

CAPITÁN L: Anything else?

JC: Like what?

CAPITÁN L: I am showing Señor Cholbi a page from the Internet
site: www.eldescarorocks.com.

JC: Ah.

CAPITÁN L: You know of this page?

JC: I do.

CAPITÁN L: Would you care to explain?

JC: You would need to talk to my client about that.

CAPITÁN L: And what will she say?

JC: That I helped her with the wording.

CAPITÁN L: And.

JC: It's ...

CAPITÁN L: *Sighs.*

27

Back to Bed

The walk down the hill is slow and painful. My leg hurts. But the bigger pain is the one in my head. The bursting headache from trying to figure out what to do next. The Ex-Patriots and Pat are both serious about the threats; I've no reason left to think otherwise. I can't win here. If the Ex-Patriots go down for the scam so do I. If I don't find the money Pat will hand over the tape and the Ex-Patriots will still implicate me in the scam. If, by some miracle, I find the money and give it to the Ex-Patriots, Pat will hand over the tape. If I find the money and give it to Pat I go down with the Ex-Patriots—I'm screwed every way up.

I keep my eyes open for either Zia or George's car while contemplating the only option open to me. Run. Get on a plane and head home. Except that isn't an option that will play out well. The police can easily stretch across Europe and bring me back here and I haven't enough cash to vanish. I could hide somewhere and try to arrange to sell the pub and apartment. Find a way to sneak the money home. How? No idea. Where would I even start on that one? And if George contacts the Office for Asset Recovery and Management, adios to the pub and flat.

How in the hell did I get here? Where in the hell is here?

I'm on shift tonight at the bar but I can't see that being a job worth doing. George and team will be looking for me. Expecting me to be carrying a bag full of money by five o'clock tonight. And if I avoid them I've got another deadline, until ten o'clock tomorrow morning to hand the cash to Pat.

I reach the port and wander aimlessly along the front. Around me people are chatting, walking, laughing, smiling—and I simply want to be one of them. Any one of them. I don't care which. I'd swap with any person here.

'Hi, Daniella.'

I turn around and Clyde the bar tender is standing there, smiling at me.

'Hi, Clyde,' I say. 'How was Valencia?'

'Okay. How was the bar? Aren't you on for the evening shift tonight?'

'I'm planning to shut up shop I think.'

'Tonight? Bad idea.'

'Why?'

'Big football game. El Classico. Barcelona v. Real Madrid. Se Busca is usually bursting at the seams for that one. You'll piss everyone off big time. Plans will have been made.'

'I can't help it. I don't suppose you fancy an extra shift. I'll pay double.'

'Double?'

'Double. Can you handle the night on your own?'

'Easy. On football nights all I have to do is switch on the lager tap and keep it running. The customers will even get the glasses for me to speed up service.'

'Deal. Thanks, Clyde. At least I've one person around here I can rely on.'

'Been a rough few days, has it?'

'And the rest. You don't fancy a coffee, do you?'

'A coffee would work.'

'Do you know a café where no one will bother us?'

'If you mean where the Ex-Patriots won't disturb us, that's easy. Just pick any bar other than Se Busca.'

'Lead on.'

Clyde buries us in the port and chooses a small café at the rear of a dead-end lane. The place is a step back in time. Simple décor, glass fronted tapas bar, brightly lit, lone beer tap, coffee machine on the go, single waiter. I order up a coffee for Clyde, a *vino blanco* for myself.

'Clyde, can I ask you a question?' I say.

'Sure.'

'Don't be so quick to agree. This is a question that comes with some complications.'

'Complications are the norm for those that frequent Se Busca. Nothing is as it seems. Nothing is as it should be. You learn to accept that, so just fire away.'

'I'm not even sure that I should talk to you about this but I'm at a loss as to what else to do.'

The coffee and wine arrive.

'Is it to do with the property scam?' Clyde asks.

'You know about that?'

'I should do. According to your mother it was ideal for a student.'

'But she didn't let you?'

'You mum steered me away from it.'

'And you knew it was a scam?'

'Not at first, but when Effie told me to back off I got the gig. She swore me to secrecy.'

'And that was that?'

'More or less.'

'Did she ever mention the money involved?'

'In what way?'

'In any way.'

'I asked once how it was all going. There had been a lot of people in the pub. Mainly when we were supposed to be shut. I'd often turn up for a shift and your mum would be chatting to some stranger. It happened a lot lately.'

'What did she say when you asked her about it?'

'That things were going well.'

A couple, man and woman, come into the café and sit at the bar. Irish by the sound of them.

'And did you ask about the money?' I ask.

He doesn't reply, preferring to let the question live in the air for a few moments. The couple at the bar are debating what to drink and the waiter is patiently standing by for their decision.

'Why are you asking?' he eventually says.

'I'm just trying to tie up the estate. My lawyer said I need to identify all of Mum's assets.'

Clyde picks up his coffee and licks some foam from the edge of the cup. 'Is there money missing or something?'

'Not that I know of,' I lie. 'But I need to check out anything that might be tied to Mum. No matter how out there it is.'

He sips the coffee. 'Daniella, your mum was a good person.'

'You probably know more about that than I do.'

'I just think in the end this place got to her.'

'Why do you say that?'

He looks into space, lost in the moment, before speaking.

'She wasn't too happy a while back. You could tell. She was always an on/off sort of person was your mum. High as a kite or silent as the grave. No in between, if you know what I mean. When she was quiet you knew something was eating her and she went very quiet for a long while. A long, long time. She had me worried. Then, a few weeks back, she seemed to perk up. I liked her that way. She was good to me. Always fair. Never talked down to me. Always saw me right.'

'It sounds like you were close.'

The couple have decided on half a dozen tapas dishes and a jug of sangria.

'It's really her I have to thank for getting through uni so far. Dad isn't great with money. He likes to gamble online. He has the estate agency and it does well but we never have enough cash. Your mum threw me all the shifts I could handle and I knew she paid me more per hour than the others. I don't think she knew I knew about that, but it was kind of obvious when you saw how much I could pull in for bar work. She even sorted out the accommodation up in Valencia when I need to stay over. I don't pay for it.'

I look at him. I see a younger me. Back in the day when life still held an open door to endless possibilities. I'm not old and I'm certainly not past it but until I arrived here my door was closing. Then it briefly opened with the thought of a bar and a home in the sun, only to slam shut with Pat and the Ex-Patriots on my case.

'Clyde, how long did you know my mum?'

He lets a small smile slip across his lips. 'She used to say she changed my nappies more often than my mum. The two were friends, until they fell out a few years back. But Effie never turned her back on me. She was just a fixture in my life.

'The offspring that I never was.'

'I didn't say that.'

'You didn't have to. I'm not offended. In fact it's quite nice to think that she had someone like you around. I had so little contact in the last twenty years.'

He wants to say more. His hands lift, his mouth opens.

'What is it?' I say.

'She used to talk about you. Sometimes.'

'What did she say?'

'She was sorry things had gone the way they had. She blamed herself.'

'She didn't try very hard to get in touch with me to say so.'

'Did you try to talk to her?'

'I did, but that's a fair question. I'm beginning to think I should have tried harder.'

'What will you do now?' he asks.

'I'm not sure.'

An understatement.

'Clyde, one last time: was there ever any talk about money? Large sums of money.'

This time he looks away, taking in the couple who are munching down on a plate of *patatas bravas* and sipping the sangria through straws. He's holding something back.

'Clyde, you know something about the money, don't you?'

He keeps observing the couple. Her raving about the sangria, him about the food. Both are lost to each other.

'Well, do you?' I say.

'It's a lot of money,' he sighs.

'You *do* know about it,' I whisper, almost gagging.

'Life-changing,' he says.

'Clyde, what the hell do you know?'

He turns his gaze from the couple. The woman is already discussing more sangria. Session time, I suspect.

'I've spent the days since your mum's death in a bit of a dream,' he says. 'Like I'm walking on the edge of some fantastical abyss, across which lies a world that I could never hope to visit. Up in Valencia I've been sitting in the lectures without listening, walking around without seeing. All I could do was think about what might be. What *could be*. Where my life is. What it would have been without Effie. And how different it could be. I mean how *very* different it *could* be.'

'With the money?'

My heart skips up a few notches. I'm still royally fucked even if he does know where the money is but I'd rather be 1.3 million euros fucked than fuck-all-fucked.

'Do you think the investors will come after it?' he asks. 'Want it back?'

'They're already here, Clyde, and more will come. And once word spreads more will become a lot more. 1.3 million is sixty-five people or more. Every one of them was promised riches. Every one of them is about to lose that dream and their twenty k. I'm amazed more haven't been here before now. But they will come. And even if some don't or won't, enough will. More than enough. And once they do the authorities will be right behind them—and they won't miss a trick. The Ex-Patriots, me, Pat Ratte, you—all of us will be taken in for questioning and that will be that.'

'Me?'

'Of course.'

'I haven't done anything! I wasn't involved,' he pleads.

'Sounds like you were. Sounds like you know where 1.3 million euros of stolen money might be. I don't know the technical term for what you're guilty of but I'd say you're guilty.'

'Do you know what I could do with that sort of money? How it would change my life?'

'I do, Clyde—but it's fool's gold. Take it and you'd be on the run for life and, trust me, 1.3 million might sound like a lot of money, but at your age it'll be gone before you know it. Unless you're planning to turn to a life of crime. Even then, one day you'll wake up, want to go home and when you do there will be a police van waiting on you. And all the time you are on the run it'll be hard to spend the cash. I know, I've thought about it. You can't put it in a bank, not all at once. It would be too suspicious and with a wanted poster over your head you'd need false ID to open an account. Do you know where to get that?'

The couple are starting to talk loudly, the booze kicking in. She's unhappy that he doesn't want her to order up another jug of sangria.

'It doesn't have to be that way,' Clyde says. 'I could just take a little bit out at a time, as I need it. No big fuss. A few thousand here, a few thousand there. Set up my own business. Wash the cash through it.'

He's been thinking hard about this.

'Sure,' I say, 'if no one catches on to the fact that you have so much cash. But you couldn't do that around here. Someone would notice, no matter how careful you were. You'd slip up somewhere along the line. Or you'd want to talk about it. Need to talk about it. It's eating you already. You didn't just stumble on me down at the front. Did you?'

He shakes his head.

'You were looking for me and in only a few minutes you've all but confessed to me, a stranger, that you know where the money is.'

'You're not really a stranger. You're Effie's daughter.'

'Clyde, you don't know me from Adam, regardless of what stories Mum might have let you in on. What makes you so sure I won't say anything about this conversation? And I'll let you in on another piece of really bad news. I'm right on the hook for the money as far as Pat and the Ex-Patriots are concerned. They're convinced I know where it is and they mean to hurt me if I don't find it. I could do myself a big favour and push them your way. Let them fight over you.'

'You wouldn't do that . . . would you?' he says.

'Why not?'

'Because your mum trusted me with it. You're her daughter. We could split it. She would have wanted that.'

'You don't get it, Clyde. It isn't enough money. Not for two of us. Not to hide forever and a day. Plus, I've a pub and an apartment here. I don't want to go on the run.'

The couple are now arguing. She's just ordered up another jug and he's just cancelled it.

'Clyde, tell me where the money is.'

Silence.

'Clyde, if you tell me I can sort this.'

'So much money.'

'Poisoned cash, Clyde. Badly poisoned.'

'So much money.'

'Clyde, I know, but it's not yours, it's not mine and no amount of scheming and dreaming will change that. You were looking for me. You've already decided you can't handle the cash. I can hear it in your voice.'

'What would you do with it?'

'That is a bloody good question, Clyde, and, to be frank, I've no idea. But, trust me, you don't want to be on the receiving end of whatever is coming.'

He sits back and listens to the couple who are now having a full on domestic. I let Clyde think. I don't know him. There are many, at his age, who would take the money and scarper. Work out the kinks later. I think, with a bit of luck and a devious mind, you could probably have a good life somewhere with that cash. Forty years at thirty odd thousand euros a year plus whatever you can do to earn a bit more. Pulling down another job. Bar work far from here. Seed the stolen money into your life as you need it. It could work. Except, all the while, you'd be looking over one shoulder. Wondering who would walk through the door. Clyde would need to quit university and that would raise eyebrows, point fingers at him, if he suddenly went walkabout. And there would be no contact with the family. That would be out. All in all, he would be better to hand me the cash and be done with it. Maybe scrape a few thousand off the top before I see it.

But it's 1.3 million euros and doing what's sensible isn't necessarily what most people would do.

'Clyde, please just tell where the money is.'

'I'll still be involved?'

'I'm not going to lie to you. You will. But you can always say my mum told you to tell me where it was. That she asked you to hide it for her.'

'So much money.'

'Clyde,' I say, exasperated, 'just tell me.'

The woman lashes out at her husband and he takes a slap to the cheek. I think the two of us have dragged a little of Se Busca in here. The place just breeds malevolence.

'In her house,' Clyde says.

'It's not. I looked.'

'It is. Try looking in the bed.'

'I did. There's nothing under there.'

'Not under it. *In* it.'

28

The Money

I stare at the collapsed bed. The headboard threadbare, the blankets moth-eaten, the dip in the middle severe. But the dip in the middle now has a new attraction. A reason to exist beyond that of my mother's ageing carcass weighing it down over the years. A very different reason. I place one knee on the mattress, uncomfortable at the thought of being on Mum's bed, and run my hand over the material. The lumps and bumps are numerous. I push and prod at them. I drop off the bed and look underneath, ramming my fingers into the dip that fills the space. More crevices and crannies to explore. I think on this in a more logical fashion and examine the edge of the mattress. Working my way round I reach the side hidden beneath the headboard and find a rip. It's a good foot long and a few inches wide. I lift the mattress clear of the bed frame and push my fingers into the tear. I feel the metal of springs but there's also plastic. I pull at the plastic and a packet rips free, spilling its contents on to the floor.

Euros lie everywhere.

I get to work, pulling the mattress free of the bed and, using a carving knife from the kitchen, slice open the top. Eight plastic bags are buried in the inner workings. All are packed tight with banded bundles of 500-euro notes. I lay the money on floor, thinking, too late, I should have used gloves to avoid fingerprints. On a simple count I make it 1.35 million euros. I leave the cash on the floor and make for the front door to ensure it's firmly locked. For a second, I'm certain that someone is out there. That they can smell the money and will, in a heartbeat, break in and steal it from me. Once I'm sure the door is secure I lift all the cash from the bedroom floor, move it to the front room and lay it on the table.

I stare at it.

My primary thought is one of relief. Relief that the cash exists. It may not save my skin but it'll delay the short-term alternatives that were hammering down my way. And it's a hell of a negotiating chip. I open the wine bottle I'd purchased on the way up to the apartment. I now need a plan of action and I need one before ten o'clock tomorrow morning.

I sit back on the sofa, pouring a glass and slugging liquid. I close my eyes. I let my head run free. No direction. No thought process. Just a random look at the variables. Laying them out in my head.

After twenty minutes I stand up and hunt out a pad of paper and a pen from a kitchen cupboard. I start scribbling.

Pat Ratte and the Ex-Patriots. Sounds like an old punk group. They want the cash. They will use violence. I will lose the pub. Lose the flat. I could go on the run? Hide? I have no friends out here— none. Strike that, maybe Clyde and I? Maybe Zia and I? But there's George and Jeep. Pat and Jeep. Pain waits. But Pat's skint. The Ex-Patriots are skint. Does that help? Maybe? Who else knows about the cash? Anyone else? The local bank manager? The bank manager in Benidorm? What about the taxi drivers? Would they know? Mum took parcels from bank? Or was the cash in a bag? Hidden. Not obvious. And there's my will. Rather, her will. Is there another will? Is there more than one? Does it matter? Other assets? Are there any? Does that matter? This is all Se Busca land v. El Descaro world. Square-go v. sunny retirement? And the investors? Who are they? When will they come? Some are already here. In summary, what don't I know? What do I know? What can I do? What should I do?

There's a knocking at the door. Loud. Hard. I sit bolt upright. I check the clock. It's nearly six o'clock. I hear George shouting at me. Wanting his money. The deadline past. I sit. Still. Eventually the knocking stops.

My phone starts to vibrate and I turn it off, glad I'd placed it on silent. George could hear it if he was still outside the door.

I check the windows and the balcony are secure. I'm thinking that if Skid and I could climb down then George could climb up. I haul the wardrobe over the bedroom balcony. It takes an age.

I collapse back to the sofa and pick up my scribblings.

I write and rewrite the list and, at some point, after my second glass of wine, I fall asleep.

When I wake up my head is a fuzz-ball and the clock tells me it's three thirty-five. The wee small hours. I pick up the last list I'd written before I'd fallen asleep. It makes things as clear as mud from a volcanic river. I go to the toilet to relieve myself. I check the front door again, more than glad Mum paid for an upgrade to the thing. I listen. For noises. For thieves. For the Ex-Patriots. For Pat. There's nothing.

I return to the living room and shuffle the money around. For no other reason than I've never touched this much cash.

I sit down, trying to work out my next steps and fall asleep again.

I rise slowly from dreamland. I scrub my eyes and check the time. It's a little after seven. Three hours till Pat's deadline. I risk switching on the mobile. It's alive with calls and texts from George. Each one an increasingly violent threat. Amongst them all is a text from Clyde. It's the list of names, numbers and everything in between for the pub he promised me, along with an addendum saying sorry that he forgot to send it earlier. He signs off by saying all was good at the pub last night and had I decided what to do next. I don't reply and switch the phone off again.

With only three hours to go to Pat's deadline, the wine and random thought process of last night now seems wasteful. My main bind is the dichotomy of who to give the money to. Give it to Pat, and the Ex-Patriots will sink me without trace. Give it to the Ex-Patriots, and Pat will hand in the tape and might even set Jeep on me. Run, and the world will run after me. I know I could use the money as a bargaining chip but in the real world Pat or George would just arrange to have the money's whereabouts beaten out of me.

I stand up and squeeze past the chest freezer, through to the living room's balcony windows, looking down on the street below.

Careful to keep out of sight. The sun is still below the horizon but the sky has some colour. A small truck zips by, clattering its wheels along the cobbles. The back is an open flat-bed, piled high with plastic bags. A sign on the truck is written in English and Spanish. The English reads: *The Giving-Back Crew.*

There are cartoon pictures of clothes dotted along the side of the vehicle; jumpers, T-shirts, trousers and so on—all with giant ticks overlaid. A clothing collection business. Probably a charitable one. Up with the lark and working on a Sunday suggests it's a busy concern.

I slump back on the sofa and the truck springs a thought into my head. I worry the thought. Work with it. Play with it. Work with it again and noodle it to death.

An hour later I take out my phone, switch it on and look up Señor Cholbi's number. I spend five minutes constructing a lengthy text. I apologise for the earliness of the hour and the inappropriateness of the day and ask for his forgiveness. Noting the irony on doing so on a Sunday. Surprisingly, he comes back quickly. *Give me an hour and I'll send what you need through.*

I jump on the internet and wish I had a better phone. I find the website that Clyde told me about when I first met him in Se Busca. The one that everyone uses, www.eldescarorocks.com, the local what's-on site. I find a registration page and sign up to the forum. I explain, to the administrator, that I'm Effie Coulstoun's daughter and again, swift for a Sunday, someone is up and approves me as a forum member.

Forty minutes later, following seven back and forth texts to Señor Cholbi, I have the copy I need. Señor Cholbi had made it clear his wife is none too happy with her Sunday morning being disturbed but once he got wind of the full facts, he was adamant that he wanted to help and get things sorted. I've no doubt I'll suffer when his bill comes in.

I craft the post for the El Descaro Rocks forum and check it half a dozen times. But before I post it, I text Señor Cholbi with another favour and when he agrees, I bundle all the cash into a black bin bag and hustle around to his offices, my eyes alive for Pat or the

Ex-Patriots, heart in my mouth the whole way. Señor Cholbi greets me dressed in a pair of jeans and a polo shirt and takes the bag from me, handing me a signed receipt.

I heave an enormous sigh of relief as he places the bag in his safe.

'You know that Pat or the Ex-Patriots will kill for that,' I say.

'Our front door is very secure, as is the safe and we have CCTV. Did you see anyone?'

I walk to the window and look down. There is no one around.

'I don't think so.'

'I have also asked a friend of mine to sit at reception,' he says. 'A *big* friend. He will be here soon. Just in case. I'll get the cash to the bank, first thing in the morning.'

I'm still nervous.

'You will also want to see this,' he says.

He hands me an envelope.

'Do I really want to?' I say.

'I would say that you do. It's for the owner of the piece of land that is causing you so much grief. I was told by the person who handed me this letter that I was required to give it to the correct people. You, Señorita Coulstoun, are the correct people, as your mother owned that land.'

'Along with the others.'

'No, she was sole owner.'

'What? Not the others, just her?'

'Just her. In her name only. I checked with the register late Friday. She owns all of it. I may be being premature with my judgment on the validity of your mother's will, just in case there is another, but if your will is valid, then you are the sole owner of that land and therefore the correct person for this letter.'

'And that would mean my post on the website is even more legitimate.'

'It is your land. I think the post is risky and some people will be unhappy but it is your call. Now if you don't mind, my wife and I are going to be late for church.'

With this we part, both of us checking the road thoroughly. I return to the apartment, wondering why no one told me the land was solely owned by Mum. I tidy up the mattress as best I can, read the post for the local website one more time and then, with a hell of a deep breath, I hit send. I see it appear on the website a few seconds later.

DATE: Jueves 14 de Noviembre de 2019
Esta es una copia de la traducción al inglés de la entrevista con la persona o personas nombradas.
(The following is a copy of the English translation of the interview with the subject or subjects.)
PRESENT: Capitán Lozano, Teniente Perez, Daniella Coulstoun and Señor Cholbi

TRANSCRIPT AS FOLLOWS:

SPANISH POLICE OFFICER CAPITÁN LOZANO (CAPITÁN L): Señorita Coulstoun, do you recognise this website? For the record I'm showing Señorita Coulstoun the eldescarorocks.com website.

DC: I do.

CAPITÁN L: And are you a member of the forum?

DC: I am. But only since last Sunday.

CAPITÁN L: And do you recognise this post?

DC: I do.

CAPITÁN L: And did you place this post on this site?

DC: I did.

CAPITÁN L: Did you write this post?

DC: I did.

CAPITÁN L: Why?

DC: Isn't it self-evident?

CAPITÁN L: And did you seek approval of others involved with this prior to posting on this site?

DC: I did not.

CAPITÁN L: Really? Why not?

DC: I didn't need to. I own the land mentioned.

CAPITÁN L: And all of this is legitimate and above board?

DC: So I am informed by Señor Cholbi.

CAPITÁN L: Señor Cholbi, is this correct?

JC: Yes.

CAPITÁN L: Are you both saying that the whole land and building scheme was, and is, above board?

DC: Do you have any evidence to say otherwise?

CAPITÁN L: No.

DC: Do you have any complaints about the scheme and the way the investors have been treated?

CAPITÁN L: There are murmurings of discontent.

DC: Murmurings?

CAPITÁN L: Many feel let down.

DC: But no one is officially complaining?

CAPITÁN L: No.

DC: Then why are we still talking?

CAPITÁN L: Because something smells bad here, Señorita Coulstoun. You arrive in Spain a matter of days ago—having, by your own admission, no prior contact with your mother or any of the others in this 'scheme'. Now you seem to be leading this merry little gang and helping to clean up what looks very much like a major criminal scam to me.

JC: Criminal? Scam? Those are serious accusations for my client. Have you proof of this?

CAPITÁN L: No.

DC: And what will happen next?

CAPITÁN L: I do not know.

DC: Why?

CAPITÁN L: It is complicated.

29

Kool-Aid

It is not yet ten o'clock on Monday morning and the assembled crew in Se Busca are not best pleased with me. Avoiding them all day Sunday and earlier this morning was no mean feat given the relentless manner in which they have told me that they sought to track me down. I'd finally fled to a small town eight miles away on Sunday evening, after a sneak visit to the pub office and Mum's computer. I'd escaped by walking the back paths and roads of the surrounding countryside, unwilling to call a taxi for fear of being traced. Luckily a small hotel in the nearby town had a room free and some of the euros from my mother's haul gave me board and food for the night. I'd switched my phone back on this morning and the message machine had gone into meltdown. Forty-one missed calls, fifteen messages, fifteen texts. I'd read and listened to none of them.

I'd called Clyde and told him to arrange this meeting. Everyone had sprinted to Se Busca to be here. A full house of Ex-Patriots. I'd told them to dump the cars and be as discreet as possible. I'm conscious that I have little time. I saw Jeep, at a distance, three times yesterday. Pat will be hunting me by now. I'm praying he hasn't staked this place out.

As I'd walked the backwaters of the town yesterday, I'd read and reread the letter that Señor Cholbi had given me and the weight on my shoulders had lightened further. There was a number to call on the letter and I'd texted Señor Cholbi to make contact first thing Monday morning. I told him to verify the contents of the letter, to pass on a message to the sender and to tell the sender I would call later today. I'd then asked him to draw up some paperwork.

The Ex-Patriots around me are fizzing mad. I would be, if I'd read the post on the local website from yesterday. I'd have probably gone hunting for me with a shotgun and a year's supply of ammo. I haven't answered a single question since they started arriving. Saucy is already on the pop. George has told me for the tenth time that Jeep has been informed what needs to be done. Zia kissed me when he arrived. Skid is doing his best to blend into the back wall. Given what Pat told me about Skid's complicity I hadn't expected to see him but in his world all things are acceptable. The Twins look sheepish and the image of them gyrating and shaking it all about in Pat's cellar is still fresh in my mind. Clyde looks lost and doesn't know why he's here or if here is even safe.

I'm with him on the safe thing.

I've no big reveal for them all. I don't need it. The post on the eldescarorocks website yesterday has done most of the job for me. They all know exactly why they are here. After Señor Cholbi called me this morning, following his chat with the letter writer, to say the paperwork was nearly ready, he had asked me if I would like him to attend the meeting. He is due in a little later. After I face the music.

'Anyone for a drink?' I ask.

The cold shoulders pointing in my direction is all the answer I need. I fetch Saucy a can of Coke. He doesn't see the funny side. George can't resist asking the same question he's asked before every bone-breaking threat this morning.

'Where is the fucking money? I'm not going to ask again, Daniella, I'm just going to—'

I walk up to him and grab his hand. His eyes flare. I use an old-school trick and bend his palm backwards. Grabbing his fingers and flexing them the wrong way. He flops backwards, trying to keep his digits from snapping. I push him back into his seat, release him and place my fingers to my lips. He rubs his hand and swears.

I step back into the centre of the pub and take it in turns to stare down each one of my audience until they look away. I'm a new alpha marking my territory. Whether that's how they see it doesn't matter for the moment. It's simply time that Effie's daughter took over *complete control* and that's what I'm doing.

'Clyde, could you make me a *café con leche*, please?' I ask.

Thankful to be doing something, Clyde scuttles behind the bar and gets to work.

'Why is he here?' says Saucy, pointing to Clyde.

I'm not ready to talk. I'm still of half a mind to simply walk out the door and let events unfold while I sun myself by a pool. The fact that that would implode in no time at all has a certain appeal. It gives me power in this room.

A minute ticks by and Clyde hands me the coffee.

I thank him.

Showtime.

'Okay, here's how this is going to work,' I say. 'We have very little time so I talk and you all listen. At the end you get to ask questions. Not before. Am I clear?'

'Fuck off,' says Saucy.

'Let me try this again,' I say, walking over to Saucy. 'We do it my way or I walk out. It really is that simple. Am I clear?'

'Fuck off,' he repeats.

'I tell you what,' I say. 'I'll take that as a yes for the moment.'

I sip the coffee and wait the few seconds it takes for the hot liquid to settle in my stomach. A caffeine buzz will help here.

'Do you know what the hardest thing about all this was?' I start. No one moves. No one says anything. 'The hardest bit was not seeing how dumb you all were from the outset.'

That lands like a plate of cold sick on a party table.

'That,' I say, waving my hand at them all, 'that, all of this—the scam, the money—all of it was about one thing and one thing only. Greed. And it was greed that blinded you all to the reality of what you were getting into. As my American boss used to say, each one of you drank the Kool-Aid.'

Blank looks all round.

'I didn't know what that meant either when he first said it,' I point out. 'It's not a nice reference. It's about the Jonestown

Massacre with Jim Jones back in 1978. He convinced his followers to commit suicide by drinking grape-flavoured Kool-Aid, which he'd laced with potassium cyanide. He sold them on the fact it was the best thing to do. Nine hundred and thirteen souls died that day. My boss used to use the phrase to warn us against buying into something with blind faith. And that's what you all did. You all drank the Kool-Aid. A whole damn glass each. And why? Why did you do that?'

I wait for any thoughts from the floor, even though I've just told them not to ask questions. Some things just need to be done in a certain way.

'Simple, really,' I go on. 'You didn't buy grape-flavoured Kool-Aid, you bought Effie-Coulstoun-flavoured Kool-Aid. In fact you'd been buying it so long that you were addicted to it. And that's how my mother blinded you to some real obvious truths.'

I wander to the dartboard and pull out a dart, placing it back in the bull's-eye.

'She had all of you, every one of you, by the short and curlies,' I say. 'Take Zia,' I stride up to him. 'You thought you had a friend. Strike that. You did have a friend who you could talk to about life's ills. A real feature in your life.'

I turn to the Twins. 'And Twins, you both had a modelling future, so my mum told you.'

I look at George. 'George, you were her lover and still had feelings for her. Maybe even hopes of getting back together.'

I point at Saucy. 'Saucy, free drink is the best I can come up with for you. But I suspect there is more.'

I nod at Skid. 'Skid, she introduced you to Pat and Pat was promising you a hell of a dream.'

Lastly, I look at Clyde. 'Clyde. Well, to Clyde she was a mum.'

I stroll back to the centre of the group.

'All of you had feelings for my mum,' I say. 'But more than that she gave you this place. Se Busca. This haven within a haven. A place that ran by rules that others don't understand. Can't understand. But you do. Effie's rules. Square-go and all. Inside here is, or rather was, the living, breathing Republic of Effie Coulstoun.

Somewhere that you all felt safe and secure. Even though, in my opinion, this place is about as safe as a prison on riot alert. You've all grown so inured to the undercurrent of spite in here you don't notice it. You bathe in it as if it's a warm pool and Mum used that. Day in day out she used that. Fear is a great controller. But overtly it wears thin. Loses its impact. People cower away. Covert fear is another matter altogether. She had you all scared and you didn't even know it. Scared that she would take this away and scared that she would pull the plug on what each of you had with her. Mum wrapped this drab concrete shell around your shoulders and you wore it with a perverse sense of pride. All the while scared of her and what she could do to your lives if she left. There was a hammer in here. Waiting to fall.'

They, to a person, are now hanging on my every word.

'Christ,' I say, 'she even got you to call yourself outsiders. Ex-Patriots. Tell me it wasn't her who came up with that name. That she didn't mould you into a group dependent on her.'

No one speaks.

'She managed to convince you to band together, as if, somehow, you'd ceded your citizenship of the UK in favour of becoming a citizen of Effie's world. I'm surprised you didn't have bloody passports printed.'

Skid sparks up, 'Effie talked about ID cards once.'

I laugh. 'Oh my God. Do you not see what this place had become?'

'Is this going somewhere?' says George.

'George, you must have seen it. Recognised it. This isn't a bloody bar. This isn't a place in the sun for retirees. This isn't a cosy home from home. This is a bloody prison. And you all know it. This place is a true shithole. Look at the décor. Appalling isn't close. But you all love it. Buy into it. And do you know what makes this even worse?'

Again nothing.

'This,' I tap the wall next to the dartboard, 'is a prison that was closing its doors on you for the last time. About to lock you all out and you didn't see it coming. And it wasn't closing to set you free. No. That would have been a mercy in some ways. This place was closing and lining you up for a real prison and my mum had planned it that way for a long time. Mum hated this place in the end and she wanted out. That much is obvious to me.'

'We all wanted out,' says Saucy.

'Saucy, I agree you all wanted free of here. And the only way that was happening was to make enough cash that you could run and keep running. But what you didn't see is that the stupid scam you came up with was only ever going to have one beneficiary—Effie Coulstoun. There was never going to be enough cash for all of you and she knew that right from the start. But you all trusted her so much that she convinced you to go along with it. Even towards the end, before she died, when investors were knocking on the door, demanding their money back, with too little cash in the bank for all of you—you still believed in her. Intimately trusted her.

'I called her a force of nature at the funeral. A fixer. And she was, but look at those posters on the far wall for a clue as to how long she'd been fixing this for herself. She stopped caring about this place nearly two years ago. George, she didn't cancel that bloody festival because it was unprofitable. She canned it, along with everything else, because she was planning to get the hell out of here and wanted to concentrate on nothing else. Hell, she's even cut off the phone. When I fell out with Mum at the airport the last time I was here I thought it was over some stupid top, but it wasn't. She was trying to tell me to go back home, that she was coming back soon and didn't want me here while she shafted you all. She knew the danger of what she was doing and wanted me out of the way. That's why she blanked me for the last two years.'

'She blanked you for a lot longer than that,' points out George.

'I know, but she had all of you mesmerised. Any right-thinking person would have seen the flaws in that damn scam. It was way too easy to check out. Way too easy to figure the flaws. But she had you by the throat and for two years she planned it. Then raised 1.3 million euros in how long?'

I stop. Nothing.

'Two weeks. She raised 1.3 million in two weeks. And you all helped. But why so quick? This was a big deal. Not one to be rushed. So why so fast?' I say. 'Obvious really. She knew she needed to move quickly for the scam to work. She knew it would go tits up at speed, that it was fatally flawed. She had arranged a new passport and had a brand-new car all fuelled and ready to go.'

Sheryl raises her hand. 'A car?'

'I found out about it when I managed to crack her computer last night when I sneaked back here. The car is parked in the underground car park near the council offices. Suitcases, knick-knacks and space in the boot for 1.3 million euros. She was ready to bug out fast, only her heart bugged out faster.'

'Fuck off,' says Saucy. 'This is shit.'

'You don't believe me, Saucy? I can show you the car and the passport—she even has a hotel reservation for near Toulouse. Her flat is up for sale with a local estate agent.'

I look at Clyde. 'Your dad took it on last week with instructions to wait until this week to put it up for sale. My lawyer found out. She'd also promised the pub to Pat in return for the passport. She was days away from dropping you all in the shit. And none of you saw it coming. She worked you all like a treat.'

I take a breath and let this all sink in.

'You expect us to take you at your word?' says George. 'You didn't know Effie. She wouldn't have just left me.'

'George, listen to yourself,' I say. 'You didn't say leave *us*. You said leave *me*. You all thought you had something special with her and maybe you did, but Mum was getting out of here and none of you were coming with her. That's the simple truth.'

'And the money? Where is the money? Why did you put that stupid post on that dumb El Descaro Rocks website?' says George.

'The money is in a bank and that stupid post is your get out of jail free card.'

'It wasn't your money,' he cries. 'Not your fucking money to hand back.'

'That's where you're wrong,' I say. 'It is as much mine as anyone in here. I inherited what Mum left behind and she had a share in that money. Wake up and smell the black stuff, all of you. None of you were getting squat. And that stupid post, as you call it, George, has kept you all out of jail. You don't think it occurred to me to just take the money and run? Do you? I have just handed 1.3 million euros away and didn't have to. I could have taken it. You lot would have been way too busy with the police, investors and lawyers to chase me down if I'd skipped out. I could have run, taken Mum's car, instructed the sale of the pub and flat from elsewhere and vanished. Instead, I put my neck on the line by signing my name to that post.'

Zia speaks, 'You handed the money back to the investors.'

'I did,' I say. 'That post told them to come and get it. It was the only way out of this. I simply posted that the deal was off and that all investors were to contact my lawyer for a full refund. I got the list of investors off Mum's computer; emails, the works. Every one of them has been contacted. The post on that website was to make it public and above board. To make it clear that you all had a development plan, that your plan hadn't worked out and you were now doing the honourable thing and handing the cash back. And that means no comebacks on any of you. No jail.'

'The police phoned this morning,' says Sheryl. 'A Capitán Lozano.'

As she speaks I send a pre-prepared text to Señor Cholbi.
Now.

'I'm sure we will all be taken in for questions,' I say. 'But what have they got on us? Nothing. We will soon have handed all the cash back. The police might want to know a few facts, try to trip us up. But just stick to this simple story. My mum was leading the investment. She misled you. She died, I stepped in and decided it was better to settle up.'

'And what do we do for money?' says Saucy.

There's a knock on the door and everyone freezes. My heart races, and I hope it's who I think it is and not Pat. I open the door and breathe deeply as Señor Cholbi walks in.

'Some of you may know Señor Cholbi,' I say as he nods at them. 'He is handling the return of the investors' money. As of this morning, how many investors have been in touch, Señor Cholbi?'

'All bar two,' he replies.

'There you go,' I say. 'That accounts for almost all of the money. It's now gone. Back where it belongs.'

There is a collective sigh in the room.

'I'm sunk,' says Skid. 'I owe money and I'd promised to pay soon.'

'You all have money problems,' I point out. 'But Señor Cholbi and I might be able to help with that.'

I hand the floor to Señor Cholbi.

'On Friday I received a letter,' he starts, hands on his hips, easy with talking to the crowd. 'This is most unusual. Most of my correspondence is electronic nowadays. This letter came from a lawyer based in Moscow. I know no lawyers in Russia. The letter had identified that I was working for Señorita Coulstoun and that, as Señora Coulstoun's next of kin, they wished to make her an offer.'

'Offer,' says George, 'for what?'

'For the parcel of land that Señora Coulstoun owned near the seafront. It is in Señora Coulstoun's name.'

'No,' George says. 'It's in all our names.'

'That is not true, Señor Laidlaw. It is only in Señora Coulstoun's name. I have checked.'

'I told you she was playing you,' I say. 'Go on, Señor Cholbi.'

'It transpires that an offer for the land is being made by the person who owns the small plot of land that would allow access to the seafront road for Señora Coulstoun's land.'

'The mysterious Russian,' I add.

'Only not so mysterious now,' says Señor Cholbi. 'He read on the internet, with great interest may I add, of the scheme to build apartments next to his land. He has been away for a few weeks and had only caught up with the details when he read that the owner of the land had died.'

'How did he know Effie owned it and not us?' says George.

'It is a matter of public record. Did you never check? As the owner of the access land the Russian had done his homework long ago.'

Silence.

'Kool-Aid,' I say to them all.

Señor Cholbi continues. 'This Russian is interested in acquiring that piece of land which now resides with Señorita Coulstoun. He is of the belief that together with his land the larger plot of land might be worth building on.'

'Of course it bloody is,' shouts George. 'How much is he offering?'

'None of your business,' I say. 'It was Mum's land. Now it's mine.'

'So, like mother like daughter, you're going to screw us,' says Saucy, half a bottle down.

'Why didn't you tell us about the land offer on Friday?' asks Jordan.

'Because I didn't know about it,' I say. 'Señor Cholbi?'

'The offer only came in late on Friday,' he explains. 'By the time I opened the letter, the Moscow offices that sent the letter were closed. I needed to wait until this morning to clarify a few points and ascertain the validity of the offer. I also had to check that the land was now truly owned by Señorita Coulstoun and that I was the right person to deal with the letter.'

'And this offer is all on the up?' says Sheryl.

'It is,' he replies.

'And you,' says George, pointing at me, 'are you going to walk away with the pub, the apartment, the money for the land and leave us for dead?'

'No, George, I'm not going to screw you all over. I could. I should after what you threatened to do to me. Given the way you have treated me who would blame me? Clyde, could you do me a second cup?'

'And while we are at it. Why *is* Clyde here?' asks Skid.

'He was the only person Mum trusted,' I say. 'I hate to tell you this but Mum didn't work out this scam and plan to cut you out because she wanted to shaft you. She *had* to cut you out because not one of you could be trusted not to screw her over. And she knew that. The fact you needed me to go on that stupid wild goose chase to Pat's house is proof enough. None of you trust each other. But Mum trusted Clyde. And she trusted him with the money.'

'Clyde knew where the money was?' say Sheryl and Jordan together.

Clyde hands me another coffee and says, 'She had it hidden here. Up in the attic.'

They all look up.

'But she was nervous,' he continues. 'She thought someone knew. She never said who. She asked me to take it to her flat the day before she died. I was to hide it.'

'I could fucking kill you,' spits George. 'You knew where the money was all the time and never said.'

Clyde visibly shrinks.

'Hold on, George,' I say. 'Clyde could have bugged out with the cash and left you all in the shit. He didn't. He only did what Mum told him to do. If you had been given the money by Mum, George, would you have told the others?'

He doesn't answer.

'Anyway, the one you should have a real go at is Skid,' I say. 'He's the one who ratted you out on the money in the first place. And ratted is a good term. He knew the money wasn't up at Pat's. That whole tunnel thing was dreamed up by Pat to catch me on camera. To threaten to hand me to the police if I didn't find *him* the cash. Pat didn't even know about the cash until Skid blabbed, by text, while you were all arguing the toss when I left Mum's flat after our chat. Even if you could have got the cash, Skid ensured that you would never have kept it.'

They all turn to look at Skid and he tries to meld with the wall.

'He told me he could get me a seat in an F1 car,' whines Skid. 'I couldn't turn that down.'

'So what now?' asks George.

'Señor Cholbi,' I say, 'can you do the honours?'

He reaches into his briefcase and pulls out a set of papers saying, 'Señorita Coulstoun has instructed me to draw up these papers. You each have to sign your individual copy and witness one other.'

'What are they?' asks Zia.

And this is the moment I become an Ex-Patriot. Put on the T-shirt and suntan lotion. Leave the UK and move to Se Busca.

Emigrate.

'Okay,' I say. 'I'm really not going to shaft you all. I could, and there is nothing you could do about it. Instead, I am giving you each fifty thousand euros from the sale of the land, *when and if* it goes through. I am also gifting you a share in Se Busca—but, again, only if the land sale goes through.'

This catches their attention.

'Why do this?' asks George.

'The fifty k is my way of making up for what my Mum was planning. It might be a lot less than you wanted but I've no doubt it will help.'

A few smiles tell me I'm right.

'The share in the pub is simple,' I say. 'Pat has already threatened to take the pub off me with menaces. And now, thanks to Skid, he smells blood. I don't think he *can* take the pub from me but I need you all to back me. To stop him doing anything stupid. And to stop you doing anything stupid. I'm planning to stay in El Descaro, for a while at least, and I want you all on board. And I want you where I can watch you. If I give you all a share you have a vested interest in making this place work, protecting it, and that makes it a lot more difficult for Pat to roll me over if he has a mind to. He'd need to take all of you down as well. You each get two and a half per cent of the pub and two and a half per cent of the profits. That means you own, between you, seventeen and a half per cent of Se Busca. But . . .'

Clyde hands me a fresh coffee.

'. . . but the shares cannot be sold on to anyone but me. Señor Cholbi here will act as an independent referee to determine the value should that happen. That way you each get fifty grand and a share in the pub. But in return you need to help out around here. There will be no free drinks because you part own the place. And that goes double for you, Saucy. You all start paying from now on. The shares have no other rights. If any of you don't want your shares then I keep them and you do not get your fifty grand.'

'Bloody hell,' says Jordan, 'I was expecting a lot more.'

'Jordan, this is a good deal,' I say. 'Señor Cholbi tried to advise me against this. As I said, I could just keep it all. I'd say fifty grand, a share in a pub and no jail time is a bloody good deal.'

'Wait. Why seventeen and a half per cent?' says Saucy. 'There are six of us. That's fifteen per cent.'

'Clyde,' I say. 'He also gets cash and a share.'

His face explodes with a smile.

'This is dumb,' says George.

'You know what they say, George,' I say with a grin. 'Keep your friends close and your enemies closer. And that's exactly why this is the right idea.'

'And what about Pat?' says Zia.

'Leave that to me. Now I'll give you ten minutes to make your minds up and then the offer is off the table. Pat will be on his way.'

Five minutes later, every document has been signed and witnessed.

'And that goes double for you, Skid. I so wanted to let you fly in the wind on this, but Pat will be a handful, and I don't need him working with any more sidekicks than necessary—so I decided to give you a share as well.'

Skid looks at his feet and shuffles.

30

Downsizing

I'm back in Pat's house. We are in the front room, the view as good as ever. Pat is in his dressing gown but at least there is no disco music going on in the distance. Pat is standing above me, hand held high.

I hold my hand up. 'Jesus, let me talk first.'

'You just fucking handed 1.3 million euros away. I read that fucking post. You just gave it all back.'

'I did, and there's nothing you can do about it now. All but two of the investors have been in touch. Paperwork is flowing. So you can hit me from here to kingdom come and I won't be able to change that.'

'Do you know how much I owe?' he shouts.

'No, but I have an idea it is a lot. But hitting me won't solve your problem.'

'What in the hell will?'

'This,' I say, pointing to the floor.

'What?'

'The house.'

'It's mortgaged to the hilt; do you think I've not thought about that?'

'It's worth 3.2 million.'

He stops moving.

'Where did you get that figure?'

'Clyde, the student who does the bar at Se Busca; his dad is an estate agent. I asked him. Even unfinished he reckons that's conservative. The market has gone nuts in the last year.'

'3.2? I'd been told 2.5, tops.'

'Would 3.2 get you out of your hole?'

'None of your business.'

I take that as a yes.

'I can't get the other money back,' I say. 'And if you try to take Se Busca I've ensured the business walks out of the door. You'll own a shell and some shit furniture. Worth nothing.'

'I could kill you right now.'

'You could, if it wasn't for the fact everyone knows I'm up here.'

'So the answer is to sell this place?'

'Tell me you love it?'

'What?'

'Tell me you love this house?'

'I don't. I hate the fucking place. Nothing but problems. A shit pool, too small kitchen, no cash to do it up. I hate it.'

'Sell. Find somewhere smaller for a while and I'm sure you'll find the money to upgrade again in the future.'

'You really just handed all that money back?' he says.

'It hurt. But you and the Ex-Patriots put me in a hole. Whichever way I turned I was fucked. Handing the money back was the only solution. It's gone.'

'And the others, they have no money?'

'They have their freedom.'

I'm sure he'll find out about the cash they are getting from the land but I'll deal with that later.

'I just sell up?' he says. 'Is that it?'

'Clyde's dad indicated he might even have a buyer. A Russian who owns some land and wants to build some flats around here. He likes what he can see of the house.'

'And where do I move to?'

'There are no end of rentals around here, but I know a nice apartment in the centre of town that, with a lick of paint, could be an ideal place for a man like you.'

He turns to the view. 'I will miss the hell out of this view.'

'So would anyone, but if I read things around here I see a bubble in the housing market. You might want to get your skates on before prices fall.'

He tightens his dressing gown. 'You really handed 1.3 million euros away?'

'I know. I'm a fucking idiot. But let me make this crystal-clear, Pat. If you try to roll me, I'll go to the police and tell them you hit me in the car on the sea front. I'm sure a few of the walkers out that day will remember the incident. And I'll also make it my business to fuck you over any other way I can. You're getting out of jail free here, and I expect some slack.'

MINESTERIO DEL INTERIOR
GUARDIA CIVIL
PUESTO DE EL DESCARO

DATE: Jueves 14 de Noviembre de 2019
Esta es una copia de la traducción al inglés de la entrevista con la persona o personas nombradas.
(The following is a copy of the English translation of the interview with the subject or subjects.)
PRESENT: Capitán Lozano, Teniente Perez, Daniella Coulstoun and Jose Cholbi

TRANSCRIPT AS FOLLOWS:

DANIELLA COULSTON: Are we finished here?

SPANISH POLICE OFFICER CAPITÁN LOZANO (CAPITÁN L): Señorita Coulstoun, you were free to go whenever you wanted.

DC: I want to leave now.

CAPITÁN L: I may have some more questions.

DC: About what?

CAPITÁN L: Señorita Coulstoun, there are many things that I do not understand.

DC: That makes two of us.

CAPITÁN L: I believe you are now planning to stay and run Se Busca.

DC: In the short term, yes. To see if it works out.

CAPITÁN L: And you now have new partners in the pub?

DC: Yes.

CAPITÁN L: Partners that you know virtually nothing about.

DC: True.

CAPITÁN L: And Señor Ratte is to become a a tenant in your mother's old apartment.

DC: His house sale came through very quickly. I'm happy to help him.

CAPITÁN L: And where are you staying in the meantime?

DC: I couldn't stay at my mum's old place. It just felt wrong.

CAPITÁN L: So where are you living?

DC: In a rental near the front.

CAPITÁN L: On your own?

DC: No.

CAPITÁN L: With Señor MacFarlane.

DC: Yes.

CAPITÁN L: I would say, Señorita Coulstoun, that a great many things have changed in your life in a very short period of time.

DC: That they have.

CAPITÁN L: And given your new circle of friends, you will forgive me if I keep a watchful eye on how you settle in.

DC: Will that be easy?

CAPITÁN L: It will not be complicated.

31

Murder

The sun is bouncing off the water like a million silver fish at play. The front is heavily peppered with people. This is the festive period and space is at a premium in the outlets that are open. Zia is using the bathroom and I'm hogging the spare seat at our table with my hand. In this crowd it would vanish to a new bum in a heartbeat. I don't expect the service to be quick so I lean back, hand still on the other chair, looking out to sea, staring at nothing in particular.

It's been a month since my chat with the Ex-Patriots and Pat. Pat put his house up for sale the day after our chat and the Russian dived in. Clyde said he overpaid. Pat is happy. He's staying in my mum's old apartment. I used some of the excess cash from Mum's stash to pay a firm to empty it, someone to decorate it and a friend of Zia's to furnish it, part to Pat's taste. The wing and tail of the F1 cars are far too large for the space but he likes them on the wall. Skid goes by every so often to stroke them and in the ridiculous hope that the lie he was told by Pat about a seat in a F1 car might still turn out to be true.

Señor Cholbi has been a star. Without a hitch, he's transferred all the cash back to the investors apart from two who have never responded. Señor Cholbi thinks they may have been trying to wash dirty money clean and didn't want to come back to it. That's good for me; it goes in my bank account.

The Russian's land offer was a little more generous than I let on. Despite the required clean-up of Mum's land and other costs, the profit projected is high. He made me a decent offer and I pocketed

600,000 euros, after I'd given away the fifty grand slugs to the Ex-Patriots and Clyde. I'll owe tax on the whole thing. Saucy had offered to fix it but I'd rather keep my finances out of the local paper. Señor Cholbi came up trumps with a wonderful local accountant who managed to save me from unnecessary tax by restructuring the share deal with the others and allowing me to write off the gift to them at a far more generous rate than I'd have received cold calling the Spanish tax authorities.

Se Busca is unchanged, save the profits are up now that Saucy is actually paying for booze. With Zia in charge of the roster I'm not on duty much. Clyde is a happy bunny as Zia's number two and, with them receiving a bonus of two and a half per cent of the net profit, first payment in two weeks' time, I'm as popular as my mother ever was, at least on the surface.

I'd expected more push-back from Pat but it transpires his money problems, although not out of control, were of the seriously urgent type. Beating me up wouldn't have got him a cent closer to safety. The surprise valuation on his house was his saviour. He's not as cocky at the moment, my mum's old apartment is a step down for him, but George says Pat's already meddling in a few things that could pay off. I'll expect him to give me notice at some point.

The conversion above the pub is going well. Zia was horrified at the thought of living there. I'm not. From the roof you can see the sea and there are no other buildings around for hundreds of yards. Plus, the land nearby has a restriction on it for future building. That may change, but for the moment it means I can open up the rear as a beer garden for the punters and have a private patio for me up top with unspoilt views. I've sprung for industrial soundproofing all around the flat and air conditioning that would cool a supernova. A new set of stairs leads to a new front door above the back of the pub, with a private path up from the road. In other words—no punters allowed.

The press picked up on the land deal falling through and speculated on it being a scam but once the Russian puts in proper planning permission for his development that will vanish. People will assume he got it right and we screwed it up. I hear the land clear-up bill is also lower than he thought it was going to be—but I'm happy with my money.

Zia returns and has magicked up a waiter who, world weary, is still glad to take our order.

Zia plonks down next to me. 'Are you on tonight?'

'I promised Clyde I'd spell him tonight. He has exams this week and needs the time to study.'

A kid on a skateboard is using the pedestrians as cones, zipping in between them with a devil-may-care look in his eye. He clips a woman's handbag and she grunts after him.

'So is Se Busca the future for you, Daniella?'

Zia has asked this question before. It's code for the future of our relationship.

'I'll wait until the flat above the pub is ready,' I reply. 'I'll live there and give it a little time. Then make a call.'

His face gives away the disappointment in that answer.

'And us?' he's forced to ask.

'Us,' I say. 'I like us. Us is good. The only question is does Se Busca like us? That's what really matters.'

He doesn't smile. He doesn't frown. He just looks to the sea and nods.

A small man in a heavy, woollen overcoat approaches us and I look up.

'Capitán Lozano,' I say. 'What a pleasant surprise.'

'Señorita Coulstoun, it is good to see you again.'

'Is this a coincidence, or are you looking for me?'

'I am actually looking for Señor MacFarlane.'

'Why do you want to see me?' Zia asks.

'We have received a recording, Señor MacFarlane. One that you feature in. One that talks about a property scam. Made the week before I interviewed you last time.'

'Really,' he says.

'I have already interviewed the others and as a result I have one more piece of news.'

'What?'

He looks at me. 'I'm sorry to say this, Señorita Coulstoun, but we have arrested and charged Señor Ratte with the death of your mother, Señora Coulstoun.'

My mouth drops open. 'Pat murdered Mum?'

'I did not say that,' he replies, sitting down next to me. 'We do not know if it is murder but we have applied to have your mother's body exhumed. I will need your help on this matter.'

'But Mum died of a heart attack.'

'That is true, but it was brought on by taking an excessive dose of Ecstasy.'

'Ecstasy?'

'Given to her by Señor Ratte the morning she died.'

'Mum took E?'

'Señor Ratte has admitted giving her half a dozen pills that morning, and since we found none at the scene we have to assume she took them all in a very short period. We have gone back and checked the blood taken from your mother at the autopsy and it is loaded with the drug. We did not check for any drugs originally as your mother was clearly overweight and her arteries were clogged. It was assumed to be a death by natural causes. That's why we need to exhume her. To double check.'

'And Pat meant to kill my mum?'

'That is up to a judge to decide. Señor Ratte denies it. He says he only gave her the pills as a pick-me-up. We will need to interview you again, Señorita Coulstoun. We will need to reopen the case.'

I sit back, trying to ingest the news. 'So your telling me that Pat was there that morning when Mum died.'

'It was not a surprise to me. To be honest, Señorita Coulstoun, there were many things about the original interviews after your mother's death that gave me cause for concern. Many people were evasive about where they were when your mother died.'

'Including Pat?'

'Especially Señor Ratte. Señor Norman and Señorita Norman claimed that he was with them that morning—something to do with dancing—but when I re-interviewed them about the recording of the property scam we received they changed their story. That Señor Ratte. had threatened them and told them to say that he was with them all morning. We then got a search warrant and found a quantity of the drug in your flat along with Señor Ratte.'

'And giving those pills to Mum killed her?'

'In her condition taking half a dozen of those pills would have been fatal.'

'And Pat would have known that?'

'Again, that is for the judge to determine. But would you know of any reason why he might want to kill your mother?'

I sit, staring at the sea thinking back on the conversation with Pat in his house and his relationship with my Mum and how he knew she was leaving him for good. Then there was the cockeyed fight with George when Pat had goaded him. If all the others were addicted to Effie's Kool-Aid, I wonder if maybe Pat had drunk deeper than anyone and the thought of her leaving was too much. If he couldn't have her—then no one could. Was that it? Or was he just helping an old lady get by?

'Well, Señorita Coulstoun?'

'Effie's Kool-Aid,' I mumble.

'Sorry, Señorita Coulstoun,' he says, 'what did you say? Do you know of any reason for Señor Ratte to have killed your mother?'

'Maybe.'

'Really,' he says. 'And why would that be?'

'It's complicated,' I say.

ACKNOWLEDGEMENTS

There are a number of people to thank for helping me get this book into some sort of fit shape. To Denzil Meyrick for having belief in me and giving me a helping hand just when I needed it—a good man. To Alison Rae and the team at Polygon for their support and encouragement. To Alison Irvine, my editor for wrestling with my jottings. To Helen White, out in Javea, who made sure that the Spanish in the book is as good as it could be. To Pere Cervantes, a great author and a serving Spanish police officer, who kept me on the straight and narrow on police procedure. To my agent Kevin Pocklington for taking me under his wing. And to Lesley for putting up with my typing at all times of the day and night—and for, with endless patience, listening to me as I freewheel idea after idea after idea.

ABOUT THE AUTHOR

Gordon Brown was born in Glasgow, and lived in London, Toronto and a small village called Tutbury before returning home. His day job, for many years, was as a marketing strategy specialist, and he helped found Scotland's International Crime Writing Festival Bloody Scotland. He's a DJ on local radio, has delivered pizzas in Toronto, sold non-alcoholic beer in the Middle East, floated a high-tech company on the London Stock Exchange, compered the main stage at a two-day music festival and was once booed by 49,000 people while on the pitch at a major football Cup Final. He has also written several short stories including one in the Anthony Award-winning *Blood on the Bayou*.

He is married with two children and *Thirty-One Bones* is his eighth novel (his first writing under the name of Morgan Cry).